PITCH DARK

COURTNEY ALAMEDA

FEIWEL AND FRIENDS
NEW YORK

To all the girls who write their own histories,
Who resist men telling them to "stop,"
And save themselves in the end,
This one's for you.

A FEIWEL AND FRIENDS BOOK

An imprint of Macmillan Publishing Group, LLC
175 Fifth Avenue, New York, NY 10010

PITCH DARK. Copyright © 2018 by Courtney Alameda. All rights reserved.
Printed in the United States of America.

Our books may be purchased in bulk for promotional, educational, or business use.
Please contact your local bookseller or the Macmillan Corporate and Premium Sales
Department at (800) 221-7945 ext. 5442 or by e-mail at
MacmillanSpecialMarkets@macmillan.com.

Library of Congress Cataloging-in-Publication Data is available.

ISBN 978-1-250-08589-4 (hardcover) / ISBN 978-1-250-08588-7 (ebook)

Feiwel and Friends logo designed by Filomena Tuosto

First edition, 2018

1   3   5   7   9   10   8   6   4   2

fiercereads.com

"Fortune and glory, kid. Fortune and glory."

—INDIANA JONES,

INDIANA JONES AND THE TEMPLE OF DOOM

"You can do this, Lara. After all, you're a Croft."

—CONRAD ROTH, *TOMB RAIDER*

"Oh *crap!*"

—NATHAN DRAKE MORGAN, *UNCHARTED*

TUCK

The wake-up shock hits like a sledgehammer to the chest.

I jerk awake, blind, cold, and wet. My muscles twitch. Bones creak. Joints pop. Air tubes are stuck down my throat and up my nostrils. The plastic clings to my spongy insides like cellophane. A mechanized puff of air forces my lungs to expand. The feeling tickles. I cough. Bad idea—the air tube's not ribbed for my pleasure.

It's a hell of a way to wake up.

Where am I?

Besides shivering like a little kid in the dark, I mean.

I reach out, my knuckles stumbling across a flat surface in front of me. My bones make small knocking noises on metal: *Tock-tock, tock-tock-tock.* The darkness moves, creaking open, letting in a dash of light.

It's a door.

No, a lid.

I'm in a box? . . . No, not a *box*. It's a windowless stasis pod, which is cozy.

As a vertical *coffin*.

No wonder I've got a jackhammer of a headache and am deep-throating an air tube. *How long have I been in this thing?* My neoprene circulation suit used to strain across my arms and chest. Now it sags loose, my muscles atrophied. My balls feel hard and shriveled as walnuts, and my bony shoulders no longer brush against the pod's sides. My head's restrained with a strap, my torso's harnessed to a webbed nylon gurney, and my legs are belted separately. Vitawater ripples around my feet. The skin on my fingertips sticks up like stiff fins.

When I try to move, bile shoves a fist up my esophagus. I swallow it down. Last time I threw up in an air tube, I was ten and on my first spacewalk. The stuff got into my air supply tank, and . . . you know what? Not a story you need to hear.

Gravity licks water off my fingers and nose. My arms are free to move. At least I'm upright, and at least there's gravity. It's the little things in life that make it worth living. You know, like *air*.

As I shake off exhaustion, my last memories surface: Me. Lying on a gurney while arctic-cold vitawater bubbled around my body, initiating hypothermia. Gasping. Stasis chems put my brain and nervous system on ice. Mom had leaned over my stasis pod. *Sleep tight, Tuck. Don't let the bedbugs bite.*

Mom's sense of humor was never on point. She thought she was being funny, but her voice cracked with the stress of our situation. I guess it was her way of saying *good night* without having to say good-*bye*. For now. Maybe forever, if our ship wasn't found or rescued. It feels like centuries ago. Could've been, for all I know.

My eyes adjust too slowly. *C'mon, shake it off, bruh.* Blue light leaks in from outside, highlighting the other stasis pods but nothing else. I don't need Mom's literal rocket science to know something's wrong. Where are the people in white lab coats barking orders, wrapping up the freshies in heated blankets, injecting their bones with thermal marrow, and rubbing their wasted muscles? I've woken up from stasis before. I know how this is supposed to go down, and this isn't it.

We were supposed to wake up saved, or not wake up at all. That was the deal we made with fate.

But it looks like karma crapped out on us again.

This time, it feels personal.

"Hey," I say "aloud" on the coglink network. Before we launched, every member of the USS *John Muir*'s crew had a coglink chip implanted in their prefrontal cortex. The coglinks connected the crew's bionics with the ship's AI for monitoring and regulation, but they also allowed the crew to communicate with one another and the ship. Mom called it *silent spatialized communication.* The rest of us called it telepathy.

I never "heard" my crewmates' undirected thoughts, per se; but their presence, their *awareness*, always created a subtle static in my head.

There's no hum now. Only silence.

"Anyone out there? Mom? . . . Hello?"

I wait for three full seconds, mentally checking the coglink network for a signal. No response. No blip of human or artificial cognitive activity.

"Bueller . . . Bueller?" I ask, knowing Mom and her boyfriend, Aren, are the only ones aboard who would get the joke. They love retro movies and old pop culture just as much as I do.

"Hello? Dejah?" Dejah's the ship's main AI. While Mom put the AI into hibernation when we went into stasis, it should've roused with us, too. *"Mom?"*

Why isn't anyone answering me on the coglinks?

My stomach churns.

Maybe it's because there isn't an *us* anymore.

I've got to get out of here. No way could I be the only one awake. Reaching up, I work the breathing mask off my face, dragging the tubes from my throat and nose. They rake my insides, tracking bloody chunks on my tongue. I cough, spit. Pressure from coughing pounds on the insides of my eyes—they feel ripe, like they might burst from their sockets. Warm blood flecks my lips. My lungs shudder as I take an unassisted breath of air. It tastes metallic, tinged with the blood on my tongue.

"Shite," I whisper without any real voice. My vocal cords are stiff, dry. Static crackles in my ears. Tinnitus. My favorite after-effect of stasis, next to nausea.

Over the static in my head, a groan rises and tumbles through a few different octaves. The sound's one part dying whale, another part nails-on-chalkboard. Pain spikes under my right temple, right where my coglink chip's implanted in my frontal lobe.

The hell? I think, tugging my legs out of their restraints. The voice sounds alien. But *figuratively* alien and *literally* alien are different things. We never found alien life, but I guess it could've found us out here. In reality, it's probably some poor bastard with a voice as raw as mine. That, or my eardrums are more like earmuffs, and it's someone screaming at the top of their lungs.

Let's hope for option one.

Think positive, Tuck, Aren would say. My mom's boyfriend is the patron saint of persistent optimism. Even after we ended up on the far side of the universe with dead engines, a busted communications array, and zero hope of rescue, he still said, *Hey, at least we're alive.*

Sorry, Aren. Being alive isn't the same thing as living.

I pull the release tabs on my head brace, thrilled to see I'm as toned as a corpse. And not a fresh one, either. My head falls forward, my neck muscles too weak to hold up my skull. It takes three tries for my fingers to grasp the loose straps around my chest. Another five to work them free. When I manage to get them off, I tumble into the bottom of the pod in a heap. The water at the bottom of the pod's dead cold. My blood creeps through my veins like mud. I've got no feeling in my feet or calves yet.

Shivering, I push myself into a sitting position, fall into one of the pod doors, and tumble my sorry ass onto the walkway outside.

I'm alone. Some of the other pods hang open. Empty. Black. Others are sealed up tight. Mom's pod and Aren's pod had been on my . . . *What, dammit?* Left, or right? Had they been across from me? I can't remember. A few of the pods look fresh-cracked, their lids gleaming wet in the low, bruised light. The ones on my right hang open. The ones to the left are sealed.

"Hello?" My voice rasps one note above a whisper. No answer. Fear makes a fist in my guts.

I'm sure everyone else is just stella, because I'm going to be all optimistic and stuff.

Yeah, maybe stella *dead*.

I manage to half crawl, half slide across the walkway, then prop myself up against a closed pod. The digital interfaces on the pods' lids show their inhabitants' stats: brain activity, height, weight, the temperature inside pod, *et cetera, et cetera, et cetera*, as Mom would say, quoting an old musical I couldn't stand.

Mom liked everything to come in threes: her spouses (my dad was number one, he left; we don't talk about number two, who's aptly named; Aren was supposed to be her "third time's the charm"). She always had three coffees in the morning, and three was the number of times she showered every day. The woman was hell on our water tanks out here.

The numbers on the digital interfaces flicker, changing order and position, creating weird patterns across the screens. Only one set of numbers remains constant across every pod:

    02 07 2433

The hell? I crush the heels of my palms into my eyes and rub.

    02 07 2433

It looks like a date.

Nah. Uh-uh. No, no, no-no-no. Not possible.

We went into stasis in 2087. While my thoughts are a little too tangled to do the math, I know there's a big jump between 2087 and 2433.

    02 07 2433

No way nobody ever found us.

    02 07 2433

It's a glitch.

    02 07 2433

A giant-ass glitch.

Scrubbing my face with my palms, I take stock of myself. My circ-suit's falling apart, left sleeve ripping off, zipper broken almost to my crotch. My hair's as long as a girl's. Not sexy, though. Neither are my nails, which twist like spikes off the tips of my fingers. I can count my own ribs. My skin's fragile as rice paper, but my blood runs so thick, it beads from the rips in my skin in silicone-like bubbles.

What if Mom woke up before me? What if she's already dead and gone? What if everyone's gone? I'd be alone. Lost in space on this godforsaken—

Something moves on my left. I turn my head, groaning as a rocket of pain launches itself up my spine. I wince.

A man stands about six meters away. In the darkness, he's a shadow. His head's down, and it rattles and twitches back and forth, like he's having a super-localized seizure.

"Hey," I huff, finding myself breathless. My voice scrapes out, gritty. "You . . . okay?"

A dark mark skids down the front of his circ-suit, staining it from collar to navel. His bony hands and forearms are covered with an oily, dark substance. It drips off the ends of his fingers and patters on the metal floor. *Drip. Drip. Drip.*

He takes a shaky step forward, wheezing.

Stasis has a lot of nasty side effects. Seizures aren't supposed to be one of them. I try to get up, but my legs won't respond. I can feel my hips and thighs, but not my knees or calves. Fragging stasis paralysis. Fear reaches past my ribs, pinching the soft things inside my chest.

"Hey, bruh," I say. "How long have you been—"

His head spasms, lolling back on his shoulders.

"—awake . . ."

Even in the dimness, the unnatural swell of his throat's visible. His cheeks are torn open, jaw unhinged like a snake's. Tentacles reach from between his bloated lips to suckle his torn flesh and chin.

Holy mother of—

He groans, and the weight of his voice hits my temple, physical as a fist. Pain explodes from the crown of my head to my cheekbone. My nose cracks. Blood faucets from my left nostril, splattering over my mouth and chin.

Ah crap, ah hell. Literal alien shite going down. I scramble backward, half kicking, half dragging my useless legs. Fear's got me by the balls, and they're doing all the thinking. Not something I'd recommend.

The man takes two shambling steps toward me. He wheezes again, head convulsing. His breath hitches several times in a row, like someone about to sneeze. I look around for a weapon, for a place to hide. There's nothing but stasis pods for meters around, most of which hang open. I could pull myself back into a pod, but I'm too weak to keep the door closed against this bastard. And I can't outrun him with bum legs.

With a growl, he shambles forward.

My next heartbeat hits like a spike through the chest.

We're going to go mano a mano with me stranded here on my ass.

The guy trips, tumbling atop me. He smells of bile. His jaws snap twice, centimeters away from my nose. I jam my palm against his mouth, holding his face shut. His tentacles wrap around my wrist. Needle-like teeth bite into my palm. I grunt. No way will

I be able to fight him off. Half my body isn't responding to my brain's cries of *fight or fragging flight, you dumbass!*

A mechanical whirr explodes behind him. White light bursts over the pods. The bright blade of an ion saw bisects his forehead. I jerk my hand away. The beam splits his head in two and pops the balloon of his throat. Blood strikes me in the face and chest. He gurgles, and I shove him to the floor beside me. It's only then I notice his eyes are blackened and swollen shut. *He couldn't even see me . . . what the hell?*

"Tuck?"

I look up, panting. Aren stands in front of me, an ionized chainsaw guttering in his hands. Red blood sloughs off its glowing teeth. He wields it like a sword, trembling. "You're alive."

His face crumples as if he's about to cry. All I can do is nod. If he cries, *I'm* going to cry. And I don't need to puss out any more than I already have today, thanks.

Aren looks like hell, soaking wet and so bony, his circ-suit hangs off his body like a drape. He used to be a big guy. Mom liked them muscular, but not necessarily dumb. Now he's a pole. His hair clings to his face in wet, black spirals. His eyes are sunken like deep wells, more skull than face. He's weak, and it takes him four tries to shut the ion chainsaw off.

I'm so damn glad to see another human being, I don't care that it's my mom's much younger boyfriend. And I can't imagine I look any less piss-scared than Aren does at the moment. "Where's Mom?" I gasp, throat burning.

He swallows hard and looks down, but not at the corpse on the ground.

"Dead?" I ask.

"Let's hope not." He steps over the man, almost tripping. "Your mom's the only one who can save this ship."

"What happened to him?" I say, gesturing at the corpse.

"We don't know yet."

"*We?*" As in, other survivors?

"We," he affirms, offering me a hand up. I grab his bony forearm. He pulls me to my feet. We limp forward in the slowest three-legged race ever run.

"You're skinny enough to be a crutch," I huff.

"Yeah? And you're just a regular Rambo," he retorts. Told you he loves retro movies. "Glad to see a near-death experience hasn't affected your sense of humor."

"Just trying to lighten the—"

Another scream echoes through the darkness, cutting me off. Aren shudders. "Been awake an hour. The pods are opening on their own. The ship's AI is nonfunctional"—he takes a deep breath before continuing—"so we can't work with Dejah to rescue the people inside. Not sure we'd want to, since they're half-mad ninety percent of the time anyway."

"And Mom's pod? Open or closed?"

Aren exhales through his nose, making his nostrils flare. "Open," he says. "But dry. She's gone. We woke up in this nightmare without her."

"Come on, Aren, bubby," I say. My feet are still light and handy as bricks. "You're supposed to be the optimistic one on this mission."

"Huh, a *Die Hard* reference, nice," he says as we stumble down the aisle, both trying to stay vertical. "Well, yippie-ki-yay, kid, that is optimism. Otherwise, I'd say we woke up in hell."

PART ONE

THE CRASH

As a student of Exodus-era history, I am often asked, "If the
ecoterrorist cells of Pitch Dark still exist, why haven't we
heard from them in decades?"

In almost four centuries of operation, Pitch Dark ha
managed to deprive humanity of her past and undermine he
future, leaving us in a tenuous present. During the Exodus o
2087, the Pitch Dark organization jettisoned almost one-third
of Earth's surviving population into deep space. Since then
they have bombed our places of government, blighted ou
soil, poisoned our water, and assassinated beloved leaders
With our torus colonies now far beyond peak efficiency and
on the brink of collapse, it seems that the organization's goa
of destroying humanity may be within reach. If Panamerica
fails to terraform Mars within the next fifty years—or make
significant advancements in cloning the bacteria Pitch Dark
has stripped from our soil—our colonies will fail.

The organization has heralded the twilight of humanity
Now its adherents wait for full dark to come.

FROM *THE NATURE OF DARKNESS: THE IMPACT OF PRE-EXODU*
  IDEALS ON A POSTCOLONIAL WORLD
  LAURA MARÍA SALVATIERRA CRUZ
  PRESENTED TO THE PANAMERICAN HERITAGE ORGANIZATION
  SEPTIEMBRE 2433

SS PANAM-12715 *CONQUISTADOR*
H II REGION, IC 4703, 7,000 LIGHT-YEARS
FROM THE COLONIES
SHIP'S NARROWS
12 ABRIL 2435
0123 BELLS

<u>LAURA</u>

Tonight, my future hangs by the tips of my fingers. Never in my life did I want to break any of Mami's rules—but here I am, climbing the ship's massive silocomputers during the late bells. Breaking rules.

But this may be my only chance to escape.

As I reach for a new handhold, a translucent ioScreen dialog box opens over my wrist, displaying a ping message from my friend Alex: *You on your way, chiquita?* Its notification buzz tremors through my arm bones. My fingers slip. *Wedge it,* I curse in my head, nearly losing my grip. I halt my climb, wrapping my left thumb around the tops of my nails, anchoring myself to a black-body radiation meter. *That was close.*

Jutting fifteen centimeters off the silocomputer's facade,

the radiation meter makes a decent grip. But I can't rest here long. Radiation meters were designed to measure the potency of the electromagnetic waves in deep space, not to support the weight of a fifty-kilogram girl.

A second ping follows the first, this one from Faye: *Where are you, Laura?* The dialog boxes hover over the bioware node embedded in the back of my left wrist, shimmering, demanding my attention. No pasa nada if I'm hanging sixty meters above the floor, right? Strung up by a rope and barefoot? In a place I'm not supposed to be at *any* hour of the day, but especially not now? It's almost two bells past midnight. My little detour's taking longer than I imagined it would.

No mames, Faye adds in disbelief, *this is the most important party of your* life. *If you miss it, I'll never forgive you.*

Liar. She always forgives me. But if I don't make an appearance at Faye's soon, someone will realize I'm not at my family's party or my friends' party, or at *any* party, for that matter. If that someone is not as forgiving as Alex and Faye, they could ruin my plans for tonight.

Mami allows for few holiday permits once the ship's past the Interstellar Guard's—or ISG's—dead zone, but it's not every day one's archeologist parents stumble across what *appears* to be a fully operational, yet potentially abandoned, terrarium-class starship. If the ship contains even a remnant of the extinct bacteria and enzymes humanity needs to finish terraforming Mars, my parents will be national heroes. Tomorrow they might save the world; so tonight everyone's celebrating. Naturally.

Everyone but me.

Securing my rope, I sit back in my ancient climbing harness, wiping the sweat off my forehead with the back of my hand. I snuck out of the family party early, after Mami and Dad made their ship-wide public speeches, then their private, family-only ones. I waited till Lena slipped away with her boyfriend, then ran to my room, changed into my climbing gear, and headed out the back door. Nobody noticed me missing. Till now.

A third ping arrives, again from Alex: *We're missing you, cari.* Still braced by my climbing harness, I open the image he attached. In the foreground, Faye waves at the camera. She looks radiant, her long brown hair falling in barrel rolls around her shoulders, big topaz eyes warm as Nueva Baja's solarshine.

Behind Faye and out of focus, my ex-boyfriend, Sebastian Smithson, holds court, surrounded by a gaggle of milk-pale, leggy girls. Emphasis on *gag.* Looking at Sebastian causes the muscles in my throat to constrict.

That pendejo. Why isn't he celebrating with his bruja of a mother? My stomach curls up into the fetal position when I realize he's probably waiting for me. After all, he's the heir to the Smithsonian Institution's legacy, and my parents just made the greatest find of the twenty-fifth century. No doubt he's planning to make my life even more of a living hell.

I swallow hard. The small piece of tech hidden in the hollow of my throat grates against my windpipe. I have to escape it, I have to finish my work here. *I must.*

Holding my left arm parallel to my chest, I select *Reply All* and type: *Give me 30, but tell my mamá I was with you all night.*

The replies ping back in nanoseconds.

Alex: *People are noticing you're not around, Lalita. Your cousins are here.*

Me: *Mierda, which ones?*

Alex: *Marta and Lena. Thought I saw Esteban, too.*

I blow out a breath. Marta and Lena won't tattle. Esteban might, since he makes it his business to "take care" of me. The fool. I'm the daughter of Elena Cruz. I take care of myself.

Faye shoulders her way back into the conversation: *Why do you hate fun, Laura?*

I don't hate fun, I type. My harness creaks as I sway back and forth on the rope. If I could be at Faye's party now, I would. But tonight provided too perfect an alibi, and I knew the ship's silo-computers wouldn't be monitored for a few hours. Maintenance workers are at gatherings all over the ship, everyone taking advantage of the captain's holiday permit. The ship's guards presented a minor concern, so I hacked their secure-cams and inserted a few protocols to blind them to my bioware signature. Then I spoofed Mami's geopersonnel locator. If she checks her GPL tonight, it will show my biomarker in the Peréz-Spiegels' apartment, not in the ship's Narrows . . . where I am *definitely* not supposed to be.

My bioware pings. It's Faye again: *I swear, Laura Cruz, if you're studying some nerd history of Uzbekistan in the twenty-first century during* my *party . . .*

Pachanguera, I type back, clicking my tongue. *Party girl.* It wouldn't hurt her to do a little more studying, seeing as how she's just putting in her uni applications *now.* I'll finish college in another year, maybe two. *Don't be so dramatic, I am* not *studying.* Though I almost wish I were doing something so plebe.

I'm an artist, drama's what I do, Faye replies. **He *keeps asking me when you're going to get here, y'know.***

Who? I ping back.

You know who, Faye says.

She's right, I do.

The güero, Alex answers.

I don't know what you saw in him, Faye writes. *Seb's like cotija cheese—pale, but twice as bland. But I guess you both like to study?*

I almost type *Don't let Dr. Smithson hear you two throwing the* G *word at her son,* but don't. Had it not been for Sebastian, his mother, and their gringo attitudes, I wouldn't be here now, climbing the Narrows during a ship-wide celebration, lying to everyone I love and breaking all of Mami's rules. I won't defend Sebastian's actions, nor those of his mother.

Be there soon, I type as that familiar, yet artificial, lump rises in my throat. **Don't *let Sebastian out of your sight.*** He's the square root of trouble.

Obvi, she writes back, eye roll implied. *Hurry, k?*

I will.

Shaking my wrist to shut off my bioware's ioScreen, I consider the route up the rest of the silocomputer's face. Mami and Dad nicknamed the computers Lucita and Etel. I'm currently halfway up Lucita's portside face.

Lucita and Etel stand parallel to each other, two towering, hundred-meter-tall defenses between the *Conquistador,* her crew, and space's utter desolation. White lights wink like tiny stars across their surfaces. Heat radiates off the silos' absorption shields, bringing the temperature up to almost ninety degrees.

Hot enough to make me sweat while climbing. The computers hum and beep. Except for the whir of cooled air through the HVAC systems and the blinking of machines, the Narrows lie quiet at this time of night.

I love the *Conquistador*'s silos more than any other part of the ship; Lucita and Etel represent almost five hundred years of evolution. Their ancestors were born in garages and labs on a defunct Earth. Now these masterworks of engineering soar into the deepest regions of space.

"¡Ay!" I say, sparks nipping at my fingers when I grip the wrong end of a transfer tube. I shake out my hand. On either side of me, the ship's crysteel flanks let the Eagle Nebula's light inside. There's a murder of stars out there, lurking past the *Conquistador*'s hull. Despite the danger, I'd rather cling to the edge of the universe by a fingertip, riding the edge of disaster, than stand on the Colonies' bioengineered but dead soil, safe and sound.

So it seems like I climb through space itself, cradled in a mountain-climbing harness I'm not supposed to have. Anchored by a rope I stole during the Alpha Centauri archeological dig. Hacking a computer I'm not supposed to touch. As captain and lead archeologist on this mission, Mami decides on all my *supposed to*'s, none of which include having access to the ship's main systems.

Mami's nicknamed the Lioness of Baja for good reason—her honor, keen intelligence, persistence, and temper are all as legendary in Nueva Baja as the extinct beasts themselves. I'd never betray her trust if I weren't so desperate to escape the Smithsons' invisible shackles.

If my hands tremble as I climb, it's because this is the closest I've been to true freedom in three months.

After another seventeen meters, I reach Lucita's upper partition gates. Clipping myself to one of maintenance's U-bars, I pause, patting the silo's forepanel affectionately, like one might a cat.

"Come on, Lucita bonita, let's end this now." I take a deep breath to steady the drums beating in my chest. My lungs rattle as I breathe. *You can do this, Laura.* I repeat the words Mami always says to me. *You're a Cruz.*

"Fortuna y gloria," I whisper to myself.

Go.

I pop the silo's forepanel, then shut down a meter-high section of the absorption shield. The blue haze surrounding the partition gates automagically snaps off. So does the static hum. Shaking my left wrist, I rouse one of my bioware units again. Bioware consists of a pair of millimeter-thick crysteel diodes set into the user's wrists and wired to the nervous system, one that acts as a personal computer, a communication device, a GPL tracker, health monitor, games server . . . and more, if the user's clever. When activated, a touch-sensitive ioScreen shoots out of the diode. The screen can be resized and repositioned at will, though I generally keep it set to float above my forearm.

Using my fingers like virtual suction cups, I move my ioScreen beside Lucita's interface. Within seconds, I've initiated an upload for a new partition onto Lucita's slag drives, which will keep her from alerting the bridge while I work. I don't need to announce my presence to the night crew.

I spent a week writing the partition code in secret: in the

bathroom between classes, while monitoring the ship's gravidar for Dad, or late at night, after everyone went to bed.

Once the partition loads and installs, I breathe a bit easier. Luci won't be telling on me now. I order her to shift all her Sector 41.08 responsibilities to her sister, Etel, for the next twenty minutes.

Now I'm a ghost in the machine.

I initiate a brute-force attack on the captain's chair, watching thousands of lines of code spill over my ioScreen. The text moves so quickly, it almost looks like water cascading down the ioScreen's translucent facade. Ten billion lines of code stand between me and freedom. My ioScreen can't possibly display those lines fast enough.

Since the mission's Launch Day, my body hasn't been my own. For three months, I've carried a secret, silent spy, one forced upon me by two-faced enemies who masquerade as allies of my family's. The device, known as a subjugator, is illegal in all twenty-six Panamerican torus colonies. It allows an external user to program commands into a victim's bioware, thus allowing the user a modicum of control over the victim's behaviors. A *modicum*, of course, is not synonymous with *complete*; however, the subjugator's mere presence is an insult. A terror. A danger.

I press two fingers against the strange, alien lump residing in the hollow place between my collarbones. The subjugator's shaped like a spider—one metal knot in the middle, with eight fibrous legs anchoring it in my tissue. When the Smithsons held me down and dropped the thing in my mouth, it crawled down my tongue, its little feet pricking my skin like needles. I retched as the device entered my throat, then screamed myself hoarse as it burrowed into my flesh.

Throughout the implantation procedure, Sebastian watched. He stood by as I writhed in pain. He said nothing while his mother scolded me for coughing bright blossoms of blood on their white marble floors. He looked away when she wiped my face with the cloth she'd just used on the floor, tutting at me.

The Smithsons programmed my subjugator with three main protocols:

One, I could never tell anyone about the device, on pain of death;

Two, I was barred from attempting to harm or injure a member of the Smithson family in any way: physically, emotionally, or otherwise;

And three, I was never to speak the secrets I overheard Dr. Smithson utter on Launch Day, or tell my parents of the Smithsons' plans to undermine and discredit the Cruz family and seize the artifacts in our collection. Dr. Smithson is keen on obtaining one piece in particular—the former United States of America's Declaration of Independence. My parents have refused to part with the document on the grounds that it belongs to all of Panamerica, and not solely the Smithsonian Institution.

So I'm breaking all the Smithsons' rules and smashing through their protocols. I'm exacting retribution for the last three months of shame, torment, and horror I've endured at their hands. I will hack into the captain's chair on the *Conquistador*'s bridge and use it to shut my bioware down. Then I will run straight to Mami and tell her everything I know. All the secrets. A world of lies. I will save my family's fortunes, the terrarium of our future, and myself.

My bioware rumbles, the lines of code on the ioScreen slamming to a stop. Two long numbers blink at the end of all those lines of text—the passcodes to the captain's chair.

Excellent! I smile when I recognize the numbers. The first passcode's made up of my immediate family's birthdays in chronological order: Dad's, then Mami's; my older brother Gael's, my mother's so-called Golden Lion; mine, the middle child and the one to whom all the work falls, not that I mind; and my babied younger sister, Sofía. The next number—Mami's personal bioware marker—is the longitudinal number for our home on Nueva Baja. That's Mami. No matter how far she flies, family and home are never far from her heart.

Moving quietly, I wipe all traces of my presence, physical and digital, from the silocomputer. I replace Lucita's forepanel and reignite her absorption shield. If everything goes according to plan, nobody will ever know I've been here.

As I rappel down, a shadow moves along the floor below. I land on my toes between the hindrance oscillators sticking off the wall, quiet as a cat and certain I've been caught. Tucking myself between the enormous, wing-shaped machines, I hold my breath. I expect someone to shine a light up the silocomputer's flank. To call my name and say I'm under arrest for breaking twelve Panamerican laws by hacking a silo while in-flight.

Who could have figured out my location? Besides the Smithsons, of course—my subjugator features a tracking function. But if it were Sebastian or his mother, they would have entered the room in the most dramatic way possible, with a contingent of their own guards, turning on the Narrows' great floodlights and ordering me down from the silo's face.

None of that happens. Instead, one of the floor-level interfaces boots up. A rectangular floatscreen throws the intruder into an EVA-suited silhouette. From this distance, the bulk of the EVA and the wearer's helmet make it impossible to ascertain anything about the figure below—age, gender, ethnicity, none of it. One thing I do know: the *Conquistador*'s standard-issue EVAs aren't nearly so bulky.

If it's not a Smithson below me, it means I have more than one enemy aboard this ship.

Fury swells within me, coloring my world red. Nobody gets to hack the *Conquistador*'s silocomputers but *me*. This ship belongs to *my family*. While I would never jeopardize the ship's mission or the safety of her crew, I can't say the same for everyone aboard. The ship carries almost four hundred people. While I'd like to trust all of them, I've already been betrayed by the boy I thought I loved. Now I know better than to trust the hearts of anyone who isn't family.

I shift my weight, bracing myself against an oscillator. My rope creaks. The intruder's accessing the ship's gravidar servers—I know, because I've memorized the silos' every nanoboard and microframe. After life support, gravidar's our most mission-critical tech. It measures the Big Gs, or gravitational constants, of objects in deep space, helping us find the ships an earlier age of humanity scattered all over the galaxy. It's the tech Dad uses to track Panamerica's lost ships, one that also helps us to avoid colliding with objects while in-flight.

Now someone's hacking into the gravidar, on the night my

parents located a terrarium. Everyone's on holiday. It can't be a coincidence.

It has to be an attack.

Wedge me. I grit my teeth, wishing I had a pair of Specs to cut down the darkness and distance. If the intruder on the ground's any sort of hacker, they might have noticed how I spoofed the secure-cams, too. We won't be able to identify them on the security footage. Once I tell Mami about my subjugator and she's dealt with the Smithsons, I might be able to pick up the intruder's trail and reverse engineer their work—but if they're good, they won't leave much of a trace. It would be better to catch them here and now, if I can.

Quietly, I crawl down Lucita's face. I put my toes to the horseshoe-shaped electromagnetic accelerometers. Then one hand to the boxy capacitance sensor, which whirs at my touch. My harness clanks and I freeze, flattening myself to Lucita as much as possible. Below me, the intruder pauses, looking around. Of course, they don't think to look *up*, because the silos' six lifts are grounded on the floor. Why should anyone be above them, in the dark?

The figure hurries now, shaking their wrist to power up their bioware's ioScreen, then hitting a few keys to upload something into the gravidar's interface. I narrow my eyes, but it's no use. I'm too high and at the wrong angle to read either of the screens.

The interface winks out. The figure ducks into the shadows. I wait until a door slams, and then I move, rappelling down Lucita's surface in enormous leaps. My stomach flips each time I launch myself into the shadows. I reach the floor in twenty seconds. Less.

Touching down, I untie the knots in my rope, kick it under a nearby cart, and sprint after the intruder.

At this time of night, the *Conquistador*'s rounded tunnels are lit to 20 percent. Blue-white light leaks from the seed lighting along the ceiling. Shadows pool in the crannies between the auto-riveted plates, gears, and valves set in the walls. Long, multicolored pipes vein the ceiling in vibrant reds, oranges, teals, and greens. The grates underfoot punch into my bare feet as I run down the hall, climbing gear clanking as I go.

I pause at the first major intersection, catching myself on a wall. Panting. Nobody's dead ahead. The right tunnel stands clear. Down the left, I catch sight of an EVA-clad form, moving some thirty-five meters uptunnel. I could try to cut them off at the Colorado bulkhead, but I don't want to let the pendejo out of my sight.

Resisting the urge to shout *Stop!,* I launch myself off a wall, sprinting past a sign reading No CORRA/No RUNNING. The man in the EVA—he's built like a man, at least, tall and broad in the shoulders—pauses and glances back, startling, as if the sight of me has electrocuted him. In better light, I realize he's wearing one of the *Conquistador*'s old EVAs, one with the identifying markings rubbed out. We got rid of those suits when I was ten.

A long-term crew member? Someone we trust? No, it's got to be a trick.

We stare each other down for two seconds; then he scrambles into a run. I give chase. Down two tunnels and through the

Solar Quads, which lie deserted at this time of night. The intruder's quick, and not exhausted from a fifty-meter ascent up a silocomputer's face.

Adrenaline surges through my body. I pump my arms. My feet slap against the tunnel floors. I don't dare call out for the ship's guards. They'll ask questions about my climbing gear. My bare feet. The spark burns on my left hand.

I'm gaining—four seconds behind and closing—when the intruder turns a right corner. I plunge down the hall to follow him, then stop cold when I find myself staring down a dead end.

He's disappeared. Without a sound. Without a trace. Almost like he's ghosted into the ship's walls. I put my hands on my hips, lungs burning, breath exploding. Dios mío, even my insides feel like they are sweating.

"Where did you go, pendejo?" I say in a choked cough. This close to the ship's medical wings, there aren't any hidden tunnels or hatches. Having done most of my growing up on this ship, I'd play escondidas with my siblings and the other children in the ship's halls. The best places to hide were near the loading docks or mech bays, places riddled with hatches, loose grates, and big pipes. But here, near the living quarters, the walls are smooth and featureless. There's nowhere to run, and nowhere to hide.

How did you escape? Where did you go?

There's another hacker on this ship, one who may be a black hat looking to somehow undermine us and this new find. After all, we needed the gravidar to locate the USS *John Muir*, as well as keep our own ship within range. A malicious attack on the gravidar is an attack on the terrarium inside the *John Muir*, which is an attack on humanity's future.

Historically, there's only one organization that wants to watch humanity burn.

"Dammit!" I say, wishing I had something or someone to punch. I hate being bested.

My bioware pings with another message from Alex. I ignore it. I need to get to the bridge, access Mami's captain's chair, and shut down the bioware. That's my first priority. After the Smithsons are locked up in the brig, I can work with my parents to find and—

"Laura?" a male voice asks.

I startle. My heart stumbles in my chest. I turn, shock sparking in my fingers and toes.

Sebastian Smithson stands behind me, pinning me with his gaze. As one of the few people authorized to bring non-mission-critical clothing aboard, he's not dressed in a flight suit like me, but in a chest-hugging V-neck and matching black pants. He's all sugar-white skin, black hair, and eyes so green, even jealousy would envy them. I spend a full second wondering if he was the hacker in the Narrows, but no. Sebastian's taller than the man I saw in the hallway. And unless he's got a way to spoof his height and weight, it wasn't him.

Even now, I feel a sort of magnetic pull toward Sebastian, as if he could use the subjugator to command my heart. But I know the symptoms of Stockholm syndrome, too. Maybe my most primal instincts respond to his square-cut jaw, muscular shoulders, and full lips, but my head knows he can't be trusted.

He's a bastard. A pendejo. A betrayer. A liar. He thinks he's el mero mero, but to me, he's *scum*.

"It's *Lao*-ra. Accented *au* sound," I snap. "Not your white-bread *Law*-ra, you know that." Ever since we broke up, Sebastian stopped pronouncing my name with the proper Spanish accent—the subjugator only seems to respond to the mispronunciation of my name. It's a weapon the Smithsons use to crush my confidence. To belittle me. Each time Sebastian says *Laura* wrong, it's a slap in the face. Another way to try to take away who I am, and to try to separate me from the people and culture that gave me my name.

"Would you like to explain why your GPL locator shows you at the Spiegels' apartment?" Sebastian doesn't even acknowledge that Faye's a *Peréz* first. "But strangely enough, your little . . . *device* pegged you in the Narrows?"

Sebastian doesn't say the word *subjugator* aloud. Even *he* refuses to name the ways in which he oppresses me, as if using a euphemism somehow absolves him of guilt. It makes me sad and sick and furious, all at the same time.

"I went to that bloody party to find you," he says, spreading his arms wide. "But lo and behold, you weren't there."

I don't have to reach far to find a plausible lie: "I caught a hacker in the Narrows—some jerk messing with the ship's gravidar systems. Thanks to your interruption, he's escaped." Lifting my head, I turn my back on Sebastian, heading downtunnel, trying to go somewhere, *anywhere* else. After what happened on Launch Day, I've made it a point to never be alone in a room with him. His ability to command my subjugator is in check when we're in a crowd, but alone? I'm vulnerable. My body knows it, too, every muscle screaming at me to run. "I need to check the ship's logs to ensure he hasn't cokebottled anything—"

"Laura," Sebastian says. "Stop."

The subjugator responds, issuing orders to the nanobots in my bloodstream. Every muscle in my body locks up. Even my lungs struggle against the command.

Ten, nine . . . , I count aloud in my head, not even able to move my eyes while he's locked me down. Subjugator voice commands last ten seconds. Every ten seconds, he has to reinitiate the voice commands or else they lapse.

Sebastian's footsteps echo behind me. Sweat flushes against the small of my back. My heart quivers, but still beats. I tell myself I'm not afraid of him, knowing it's a lie.

Eight, seven . . .

Having been raised by an archeologist mother and a historian father, I know a few things about pre-Exodus human history. Like about Manifest Destiny, and the so-called Divine Right of Kings, and the rise of the Nazi Third Reich, all these ideas white men propagated to secure power and turn it against people who didn't look, think, or believe like them. I'd like to say that in the last few centuries, humanity's grown past those compulsions in a moral sense, that we've become better. Nobler. Wiser.

But we haven't.

Sebastian's power over me is terrifying on so many levels. When I tried to tell Mami about what happened with the Smithsons on Launch Day, the subjugator closed my throat up. The sensation was like going into anaphylactic shock, as if I was allergic to the words I was about to speak. When I started to ping Faye and Alex about the device, it forced my fingers to delete the message. I've attempted to reverse engineer the subjugator's code; ventured to tip off the ship's doctors; even considered breaking my own wrists to deactivate my bioware, if only to keep the subjugator from controlling me.

After three months of racking my brain, trying to find a solution, I gave up and made plans to break my parents' rules and hack the captain's chair. Unless I escape Sebastian now, he'll foil that plan, too.

"Now, look at me," Sebastian says, lifting my face to his with a finger. Grinning, he leans close and kisses me on the lips.

Three, two, one . . . My stomach clenches. I feel like the ground might be shaking under my feet. When his hold on me breaks, I shove him back. "I'd punch you if I could," I say.

"That's against the rules, now, isn't it?" he says, his gaze dropping to my lips. "You still have the softest lips of any girl I've kissed. Have I told you that?"

I'm trapped, alone, with my ex-boyfriend. My abuser. My captor.

And nobody knows.

22 MONTHS AFTER WAKING
USS *JOHN MUIR* NPS-3500
SHIP'S DEEPS, TIER TWO, SECTOR 15
DEEPDOWN TRAM TUNNELS
DATE: APRIL 12, 2435
TIME: 1:35:02 A.M.

TUCK

We are the forgotten, the fearless, and the totally fragged. Nobody knows we're out here, so nobody cares.

The dim light flickers across gristle and bone. The ship's air smells meaty. Warm. Four bodies lay broken on the tram tracks. Shredded muscle and tendon stretch between their torsos and dismembered limbs. Blood puddles in the tracks' ladder-like rungs. It looks like crude oil in the near darkness. One body's decapitated, head missing. The torsos are hollowed out like retro Halloween pumpkins. Broken ribs stick up at right angles, tenting the flesh.

One man's strung up by his own entrails. He hangs from a train platform beam, swaying gently, throwing shadows.

Fan-*frickin*-tastic.

Blood's splattered across the crumbling procrete platform. Gobs of gore cover one of the platform signs, which reads:

PLATFORM 21

E-CLASS QUARTERS

DOMESTIC WATER PUMPS

SANITATION ENGINES

Twin tram tunnels arch overhead, riddled with rust and decay. My memory's not what it used to be, but I remember what this place looked like before it went through time's guts and got shat out the other side. Every surface used to gleam. Now the metal's weak with age. Kick one of these tracks too hard and it crumbles. The *John Muir* wasn't built to last a human lifetime, much less four hundred years. Yet here we are, struggling to keep this shite heap running for another day. Another hour. Another breath.

Sometimes I wonder why we even bother.

That's a lie.

I wonder why we bother *all the time*.

I halt on the train tracks, huffing. My temporary partner, Holly, stops beside me. We've run five klicks of the tram tunnel in the last twenty minutes. We have another five before we reach our destination.

"*Oh god*," Holly says through the coglinks, looking at the bodies. The chips implanted in our frontal lobes are useful to a group of people who rely on silence for their survival. Even a whispered word can be a death warrant out here.

Holly turns away from the bodies. Her stiflecloth cape swirls around her feet. Pulling her ebony hair away from her face, she bends over and vomits. Yellow, chalky chunks of reconstituted egg slime the tracks.

"*Keep it down, newb.*" I crouch down by the bodies. Unlucky bastards, these guys. Least they've escaped this hellhole. Not sure how much pain I'd be willing to suffer to get off this ship, but the amount gets a little higher by the day. "*We don't know if whatever did this is still running these tunnels.*"

"*I'm not a newb, but I've never seen, um . . . what the bodies look like, after?*" Holly spits and wipes her mouth with the back of her hand. "*W-what happened here?*"

"*Looks like a griefer's work.*" I touch the blood and rub it between my fingers and thumb. It's cold and tacky. The victims have been dead an hour or more. I flick the stuff off my fingers. "*You see those circular wounds in their torsos? Those were created by a specific harmonic resonance a griefer uses to turn your organs into bombs. If it were mourners, there'd be nothing but scraps. And none of them would be tall enough to do that—*" I gesture at the man hanging from the entrails noose.

Or mean enough.

Holly shudders. So I don't mention how the victims are surrounded by bullet shells, but there aren't any guns in sight. It's too weird. Or how one of the victims has an ouroboros tattoo on his jugular. You know, the snake eating its own tail? I narrow my eyes, telling my rigid heads-up display lens, or HUD, to zoom in on the guy's neck. The snake's looped around the Earth. I've seen the logo before. It hides in deep, dark places within the

John Muir, painted on pipes or walls, sectors other curators fear to go. My memories aren't great, but I think it's a logo I saw back on Earth a few times.

Never seen it on a person, though.

"They're not dressed like our curators." Holly pulls her balaclava over her mouth and nose to block the stench. She turns back to the scene.

"That's because they aren't ours," I say, pulling my knife from my belt.

"How is that possible? Nobody could survive in the deepdowns," she says.

"Someone obviously is."

"But how could anyone live outside the park, down here . . ." Holly pauses. *"Tuck, what are you doing?"*

I skin the side of the man's neck with my knife, taking a ragged piece of tattooed flesh from him. I pull a sample kit from my slimpack and plaster the skin to a glass slide.

"Tuck!" Holly cries.

"What?" I ask, sticking the sample kit back into my bag. *"He doesn't need it."*

"That's . . . that's so . . . ugh."

"Survival's a barbaric thing, sweetheart."

"You're going to carry a piece of him around with you?"

"That's the idea."

"No wonder no one wants to run tunnels with you—"

The floor trembles. A moan crawls out of the tunnel's bowels. Holly whirls around to look behind her, checking our six. There are two directions in a tram tunnel, but the metal walls and ribs bend sound. I can't tell if the groan's coming from the fore or the aft part of the tunnel. It rises in pitch before dropping into a lower, grittier register.

"Mourners," Holly says.

"No shit, Sherlock." I rise, scanning the flickering darkness ahead of us. Nothing moves.

She glares at me, gripping the knife at her hip. *"Sherlock? What's that mean?"* At least Holly gets that I'm mocking her, even if she's not well read enough to get the reference. Plenty of curators aren't. Or worse, they lost their sense of humor when they found themselves on the wrong side of the universe with no viable engines and zero hope of rescue.

My mom used to say hate and hope are hard to kill. She was wrong about hope, but hey, I'm doing okay living on piss and vinegar.

"It means pay attention to our six, not my handsome face," I say.

She smirks, but still looks a greener shade of pale. *"Becca's right, you are a jerk."*

"'Jerk' is just people's default reaction to my special brand of humor, bruh." Or any humor out here, for that matter. *You never take anything seriously!* they say. *This isn't funny!* they say. But here's the thing *they* don't understand: When you've given up on life, everything seems like a joke.

"'Bruh'? Is that another one of your old-timey words?" she asks.

"Well, I'm not here for your comedy show, bruh.*"*

"That's a damn shame. I'm funny in the deepdowns."

"I'm pretty sure humanity stopped thinking that being an asshole was funny in 2016."

I swallow my laugh, 'cause I can't make a sound out here. Why'd it take a catastrophe to have a conversation with Holly?

The girl's got grit. Maybe it's because she's a few years younger than me. And she's right about one thing—I'm not anyone's first or last pick of partners for tunnel runs, either. The other curators think I'm cursed.

So I run solo.

It keeps me from breathing the bouquet of someone else's vomit.

Aren wouldn't let me run this job alone, though. Thirty minutes ago, our ship's maglev hub went offline. Aren asked for two curators to run the tram tunnels to the aft deck to reboot the system. We curators are jacks-of-all-trades, mechanics, engineers, and duct-tape slingers. We're the ship's last line of defense, shaken awake from stasis when she started to fall apart from the inside out. Of the original ten thousand members of the *Muir*'s crew, only about a hundred and fifty of us woke up on the human side of the stasis pod. Of that number, only a few have the skills to run tunnels and make repairs to our dying ship.

Without the maglev hub, our trains won't work. Without the trains, the curators can't reach the ship's primary and auxiliary systems. Without the ship's systems, everyone's as good as dead—ship, park, and the remnants of our crew, yada, yada, yada.

But nobody runs these tram tunnels anymore. There's no need, not when the trams do all the running for us. Stretching some twenty-five kilometers across the *Muir*'s outer crescent, the tram tunnels offer no cover, no protection. No places to hide. Here, the silence owns a soul-crushing gravity. The metal ceiling sheds rusty patches of skin. Aging LE-1 lights flicker.

Shadows scatter off the dead maglev rails under our bare feet. Even the smallest sound will bury us.

But the track's the fastest way to the maglev station.

I volunteered for this mission, surprising nobody. The whole crew knows I've been chasing death for months in the deep-down tunnels, triple-dog-daring the ship to gank me. I've traversed almost every centimeter of this place, with the exception of the bridge and some of the outboard stations. I've paddled across the deepdown sea. I've jumped into a defunct biomaterials processor. I've crawled through kilometers and kilometers of ducts and pipes and tunnels, just to see where they led. I've fought mourners on top of moving trams, infiltrated Sector Seven to shut down the malfunctioning chlorophyll generators, and nearly been electrocuted by a griefer in the power rooms.

Nobody knows this ship better than me. Not Aren. Not the other curators.

Maybe not even Mom.

Aren says risk taking's my way of dealing with grief. If that's true, my five stages of grief weren't so much stages but sewers. I've slogged through them all and made peace with my Maker. When the end comes, I'll be ready.

When I get to the pearly gates, I'm going to punch that angel right in his shiny face.

Even the gods have abandoned us out here.

The other curators drew straws for the second spot for this trip. Nobody wants to tunnel run with the guy with the half-baked death wish. Everyone blames Mom for getting us deep-sixed, for not stopping the hacker who jettisoned us. I know better. Of all the things I remember from before—not much, to be honest—I remember my mother's work ethic best. And all she ever wanted was to save the world.

All I ever wanted to do, though, was *live* in it. Make some movies about it, maybe. See, heroism on the silver screen's a different sort of thing than it is in real life. When you're watching a movie, someone else is dragging their partner's corpse to a safe room, hoping the monsters don't find them first. When you're watching a movie, someone else gets hit in the face with the arterial spray of the curator who didn't duck behind the tunnel rib quick enough. When you're watching a movie, you're not the one wresting the bloody knife out of the hand of the girl who just flayed her own leg, confused from listening to too much mourner-song.

In fact, being a hero is a shite job, which is why I stopped running the tunnels with other people.

Then Holly Ayakawa pulled the short straw.

Aren made me promise I wouldn't do anything stupid on this run. Translation? Not to do anything that'll get Holly killed. Let's get one thing straight: I might have a death wish, but I'm not taking anyone with me. Especially not Holly. She's fifteen. A violinist, I think? Or maybe she plays guitar, I don't know. Something with strings. Plus, she's the only curator left on the ship who speaks fluent Japanese. A lot of the engineers left their logs in Japanese hiragana. I don't trust Dejah to translate them.

And postscript? I'm not an asshole.

Edit that: Not a *complete* asshole, at least.

Not all the time.

A red light blinks on my HUD in the upper-right periphery of my vision. *"Here we go,"* I say. That tiny light blinks whenever our coglink chips pick up the mourners' subsonic calls. It's a mod I engineered to keep our curators safer in the tunnels.

"*Dejah?*" Holly asks, checking in with the ship's AI. "*You there?*"

"*Changing channels to the t-Two floor now,*" Dejah says. Her voice pitches and falls in all the right places, but not even Mom could make Dejah's AI sound fully human. "*How can I help you, Holly?*"

"*Do you have a visual on any mourners near our position?*" Holly asks.

"*I'll scan the tunnels. One moment, please,*" Dejah says. We wait for ten seconds. Twenty. Why does anyone say *one moment* when they really mean *shush*? Then: "*There's a large mourner pod half a kilometer aft of your position, moving steadily toward you.*"

Dejah uploads her live video feed onto my HUD. The mourners stalk through the tunnel. Blind, except for their echolocation. Once human, their locomotion has now evolved to support their top-heavy rib cages. They walk on their knuckles like apes, their clothing in tatters, skin bleached pale. In the vidfeed's low resolution, I can't tell how many of them are out there. The tunnel walls look like they're made of writhing white flesh.

"*Have they heard us?*" Holly whips back, facing my side of the tunnel. She pulls her hood over her head. It shadows her face. Her skin's pale as bone. I could reach out and trace the blue veins in her cheeks, if I didn't have a strict no-touching-people policy. Touching makes you care. Touching fills up the emptiness. And that empty air in my chest is all I have left to burn.

"*I am 95.75 percent sure they have,*" Dejah replies. "*The pod is in the process of changing direction.*"

"*Thanks for the warning,*" I snap.

"*I detect a tone of sarcasm,*" Dejah says. "*You know Dr. Morgan did not program me—*"

"To read and respond to sarcasm," I finish for her. "*Blah, blah, blah. I know, Dejah.*" I tug my balaclava mask over my mouth and nose. Our garments are made of black anechoic platelets—stiflecloth. Our clothing deflects the mourners' searching trills, but not their killing blows. The trills function like echo-location, drawing our shapes for their blind eyes. The best defenses against them are stillness, silence, luck . . .

And in a pinch, a well-aimed knife.

A howl unfurls, a shredded, tortured sort of song. The crew calls them *mourners* because their shrieks sound like someone sobbing at a funeral. Even at this distance, their cries grate against my exposed forehead like sandpaper.

"*Guess that's an affirmative,*" I say to the girls. "*Let's move.*"

"*There's a tram station less than a kilometer ahead of you,*" Dejah says, her calm, nonchalant tone jarring against my rising panic. "*I have a visual on a weeper. Get out of the tunnel.*"

"*Ooh, a weeper,*" I say to them. "*Things are getting interesting.*"

"*Shut up, Tuck!*" Holly snaps.

We leave the dead bodies for the mourners and sprint for the station.

Curators run barefoot to keep our footsteps whisper quiet. We've been trained to underpronate each step, so the fleshy outsides of our feet hit the ground first. Over time, the impact will shred the cartilage in our knees and ankles. I've got huge calluses on the soles of my feet. But rough skin, bum knees, and bad hips are better than being flayed alive.

Holly's stiflecloth cape streaks out behind her as she runs. The girl's good, fast, and silent. I'm not as quick. For one, I'm bigger. Two, I tore my right ACL playing center halfback on Earth. That's soccer, for the uninformed. I remember scraps of playing sports, of getting injured. My leg's never been the same since. Anytime I run, there's always a twinge of pain under the kneecap.

The injury feels like it happened hundreds of years ago. Four hundred-ish, to be more or less exact. And when the *Muir* got deep-sixed and shoved in a random corner of space, the whole crew chose hyperstasis. We woke up centuries later for no apparent reason. One percent of us exited stasis with raging headaches—most of the kids, teens, and younger adults. The other ninety-nine percent came out sounding like a bunch of whales gargling glass.

Stasis stole something from everyone:

It burned the memories from our heads.

It stole our stories, our humanity.

Our families, too.

In most cases, it ended our lives.

We don't know how it happened—none of the stasis engineers survived. You know, the people who could tell us what went wrong with the pods? On top of that shite heap, nobody's been able to breach the mourner nest infesting the bridge, which means we don't have access to the ship's logs, either.

Some of the curators believe that an alien substance contaminated our stasis tubes, creating the mourners. Others think it was an act of God. Aren, however, once told me it wasn't aliens or God or any paranormal shit like that.

It was *us*.

Long story short, when humanity tried to restore Earth's failing atmosphere, the plans backfired. *Royally.* We poisoned the planet's air, thus accelerating the rapid deterioration of the ozone layer. People lived under big domes while scientists like Mom scrambled to find a way to save our stupid-ass species, but the domes took time to build. People breathed that poisoned air for months, sucking it straight into their blood and bones and brains. They died by the hundreds of millions.

One evening—after Aren and I had returned from a repair job on the *Muir* that almost killed us both—we sat on the lodge's deck and watched the ship's solar rings set. He handed me one of his home-brewed beers, his knuckles all scraped to hell, a cut still scabbing over one eye, and said, *There's something you should know about them.*

About who? I asked.

The mourners. Aren glanced over his shoulder, making sure no one else was in earshot. *Dr. Knowles . . . told me something today. Said she'd connected the mourners' mutated DNA back to the contaminants in the Earth's atmosphere. They're not aliens or zombies, just our own mistake.*

Well, that was one hell of a mistake.

Then again, human beings did find a way to kill an entire *planet.*

Halfway to the tram station, Holly stumbles. Screams. The pure, crisp note echoes through the tunnels, along with a metal *crack!*

Ah crap—

Holly crumples to the ground, clutching her right foot. A

rusted spike impales her flesh, broken off the track. The blackened sole of her foot dimples around the metal. The puncture's clean through.

One.

"Omigod . . . omigod . . . ," she sobs aloud.

Two.

On instinct, I fall over her and cover us both with my cape. I clap a hand over her mouth. *"Shut up, shut up, shut up! It's okay, you're okay, I've got you. Breathe."*

Three.

A tornado of shrieking rips up the tunnel. I swear I feel my eardrums flex against the sound. FYI, that doesn't feel good.

Holly bites down on my hand, screaming into the flesh. The pain's sharp. Blood gushes from my skin. Sweat scales my forehead. *We're screwed now.*

I keep us pressed against the ground. At this distance, the stiflecloth blocks us from taking additional damage. The procrete tunnel floor's chilly and rough. We're lying on a bed of junk, on broken glass and rusted bolts and screws. *Where'd all this crap come from? Why haven't the cleaning bots swept it away?*

"The pod is a kilometer away," Dejah says in my head. *"Leave the girl."*

"What?" I snap. *"When did Holly become 'the girl'?"*

"You know protocol, Tuck," Dejah says. In my head, the words *A lame curator is a dead curator* echo in Aren's voice.

"No, no, no," Holly says. "P-p-please no, don't leave me, I'll be good. I don't want to end up like those dead people back there. I'll be quiet—"

"C'mon, Holly. I might be a jerk, but I'm not *that* much of a jerk."

I toss the cape off my head and tap the corner of my HUD eye twice. It switches the viewing mode over to infrared. The dim tunnel light disappears. In the distance, small red-and-green shapes lope toward us. Some of the mourners run up the walls, using tiny suckers on their palms to attach themselves to vertical spaces. Farther back, green infrared light rings the whole tunnel.

Damn, the whole place's lousy with the bastards.

"It's the alpha pod," I think. The big one, made up of some two thousand individuals. In a pod that large, mourners aren't our only problem. Do the math—for every hundred mourners there's a weeper. For every five hundred, a griefer. These bastards take advantage of the *Muir's* extra-dense air and weaponize it via their shrieks and screams.

You see—and I'm not going to get too scientific here, because in case you haven't noticed, I'm about to die—sound moves through all matter in waves. Mourners pitch their voices to sharpen those sound waves, which turns the air around you into a weapon, so that when the waves hit the human body, they cut. They flay. They blast out your organs, or make your eyeballs explode like zits under pressure. Mourners can use their voices to cause blunt-force trauma. Some have voices that travel through walls and make people hallucinate and harm themselves.

Lovely, right?

Mourners make up the bulk of every pod. They're quadrupeds and awkward as hell, running about half as quickly as your average curator. Imagine a hairless, skinny-ass gorilla with the ballooning throat of a frog, and you've got the right idea.

Remnants of their humanity cling to their bodies—tattered flight suits, jewelry sometimes. Their voices have a max trajectory of around twenty meters, depending on the individual.

Weepers are their bigger, badder cousins, ones with ropy muscle, a fifty-meter scream radius, and claws. Neither is very smart. I've seen both types disembowel grown men, lop off heads, and tear organs from still-living bodies.

Then there's the griefers.

Griefers are invulnerable, powerful, and smart. Bipedal, too, making them as fast as most curators. Armored with thick, fingernail-like platelets all over their bodies, they can't be harmed by blunt weapons. Our ion saws require close combat. Those are out. Nobody wants to be in arm's—or tentacle's—reach of those bastards. Griefers use a full spectrum of vocalizations, capable of cutting off a limb or bursting an organ in your gut. Humans are their toys. They live to hear us scream.

Even healthy, I wouldn't try to outrun a pod this large.

Well, maybe if I was alone, dammit.

What a rush.

I switch my HUD's function to a ship schematic by tapping my tear duct instead of the outer corner of my eye. The HUD edges every element of the tunnel in green. Machinery and ductwork hidden in the walls appear in blue. Malfunctioning equipment is highlighted in red, making the maglev tracks look like the crimson highway to hell. The electric wiring looks spotty, too, which explains the flickering lights. Our HUD lenses are hooked up to the AI and allow curators to identify problems with the ship in real time. We lifted this tech from the ship's original maintenance crew.

Desperation rising, I scan the nearby tunnel until I spot something: a derailed, unarmored tram. The massive carriage lies in the black shadows, smashed against one of the walls. *Well, that's where all the garbage on the ground came from.* The dead guys uptunnel must've been using it to get around, because the tram's not one of our armored ones.

"*The pod is now a quarter kilometer away,*" Dejah says. "*Leave the girl, or die with her.*"

I throw my stiflecloth cape off Holly. Scooping her into my arms, I rise. "*I'm not leaving her behind, Dejah.*"

"*I think that means you are a fool,*" Dejah says.

"*Better a fool than a puss-out,*" I say. "*Someone left me behind when I was little. Swore I'd never do the same.*" I ease past a field of shattered glass. The tracks shake underfoot, the mourners' calls growing closer. Holly presses her face into my neck, her eyes hot with tears. Least she's quiet, least she's light. One more whimper could end us. So could one shard of glass.

In the deepdowns, our lives depend on such small things.

I approach the derailed tram, inching around its shattered windshield. Most of the windows are intact. If we can make it inside, we might be able to huddle under the seats, wrapped in our cloaks. Maybe the mourners will pass us by.

I'm not afraid to die, but with my track record, I'm afraid Holly *will.* Maybe that's why I'm nervous. Or why my hands are so slick with sweat.

"*Fifty meters,*" Dejah says. The monsters' feet and fists pound the ground. The shattered glass tinkles, dancing across the floor. In seconds, the mourners will be close enough to sense our heartbeats. Close enough to kill.

We need to hide.

The light weakens near the tram. One lone bulb hangs loose from the ceiling about ten meters away, sparking. Dying. Holly's breathing ratchets tighter. She touches the outer corner of her eye twice, watching over my shoulder. *"Vanguard's here,"* she says.

"Get inside and wrap up in your cloak," I say. *"Keep it quiet."*

I place a bioluminescent flare inside the tram's windshield, then duck past the toothy, busted-out glass. Inside, I ease Holly into the aisle. She crawls into the tram, favoring her impaled foot. I follow her, helping her hide behind the last seat.

"Don't move," I say, draping her cloak over her head. *"Do your chi breathing exercises to handle the pain, got it?"*

"Okay."

I can tell she's trying hard not to cry. Wish I could get her out of here.

Glass crunches behind me. I freeze, balanced against the side of a seat. My heart slams up against my ribs. Fear curdles between my teeth.

Carefully, I turn my head.

If my bones creak, that's it. Player One down.

A mourner stands in the broken glass outside. My flare casts its white skin in sick green light. Pale flesh bubbles over its eye sockets, blinding it. Ropy, powerful muscle rustles under its dry, flaky shoulders. A black, fleshy sac sags against its throat.

Relief burns through me. It's not Mom. Every mourner I see, I have this moment of panic in which I expect to see my mother's face on a monster. But this time, it's not her. One day it might be, but not here. Not now.

The mourner's throat swells up like a frog's, its mouth cracking open, ready to scream.

One.

"Nice try, Tuck," Dejah says. *"I suppose now you die."*

Two.

But Holly won't survive without me.

To my own surprise, I reply, *"Not today."*

Three.

The creature screams.

LAURA

My fingers twitch, my brain screaming at the nanomechs in my blood. *Every second I spend with this stupid pendejo nukes my chances of reaching the bridge—*

"Imagine finding you here, all alone." Sebastian takes my arm, yanking me down the hall.

I glare at him, stumbling when he tugs at me. "Yeah, I can't *imagine* how you managed to find me." It's not like he can't track my subjugator, after all.

"Drop the sarcasm. We need to talk."

"I have nothing to say to you—"

He jerks me to a halt. Shoves me against the wall. The metal is so cold it feels like pressing my back against a block of ice. When I fight, Sebastian says, "Stop, Laura." The words stun my muscles and bones. My breath bursts out, merging with a sob of pain. My heart beats on my rib bones like a fist on cage bars.

Stop, Laura.

I hate what those words do to me. I hate what *he* does to me.

While the hijacking lasts only a few seconds, my emotional response is violent and lasting. It leaves me with the sensation of maggots chewing through my abdomen and spilling out on the floor, as if something inside me's gone rotten.

Nothing I've experienced replicates the feeling of losing my independence—no shame quite like being treated as a commodity, a puppet, a *thing* to be used up and discarded.

I can't even glare at him. My right eyelid twitches when I try.

The Smithsons will pay for what they've done to me. I will make them wish they never stripped me of my will, my voice. They forget they're dealing with a hacker, a girl who lives to find loopholes in systems. They've written off my talents because I'm young. Pretty. They think hacking's a cute pastime for me, and not a tool I can use to bring them to their knees.

As Dad always says, *Quisieron enterrarnos, no sabían que éramos semillas.* Or, *They tried to bury us, but they didn't know we were seeds.* It's an old saying, one espoused by twentieth-century Mexican rebels. Dad has a soft spot for insurgents, protesters, and rebellions of all kinds—maybe that's why he's downloaded illegal files on hacking for me behind Mami's back.

Dad has no idea how hacking's going to save the Cruz family's work. Our legacy, too. Maybe even our lives; if the Smithsons were willing to implant a subjugator in me to gain control of the Declaration, who knows what lengths they would go to in order to possess the *John Muir*, too?

"Now listen," Sebastian says, pressing his body against mine. He turns my face toward his with a finger, lips hovering centimeters away. Everything in me recoils. If anyone happened upon us, they might think we'd made up in the wake of the *John Muir* find and were stealing kisses in the halls to celebrate. Sebastian knows how to manipulate a situation and people's biases to tell a story. "Before we located the *John Muir*'s terrarium, all this"—he gestures at the subjugator in my neck—"was just to buy your silence while my mother and I worked to undermine your mother's credibility with her crew. Had your family merely agreed to sell the Declaration of Independence to the Smithsonian Institution when we kindly asked—"

Kindly? Something inside me boils. "Your offer didn't even cover the costs of the initial expedition that retrieved the artifact," I say through gritted teeth. "That entire expedition was funded by *my* family—why do you think you should profit so soundly from our sweat and blood?"

"Laura, I know you are upset, but your tone isn't as civilized as it should be—"

"Don't you lecture me about being *civilized*," I say, pointing to the hollow of my throat before the subjugator can lock the action up. "Not when you think it's acceptable to undermine my . . . my . . ." But the subjugator's swelling in my throat, cutting off my words. I wanted to say, *Not when you think it's acceptable to undermine everything my family's achieved.*

Sebastian smiles, his gaze touching on my throat. "So if we can't buy the document from you, we'll take it by subversion. It's just that your crew's ungodly loyal to you, so it's been difficult to disparage the Cruz name in front of them. You're almost like . . . like a *family.*"

The Smithsons don't care to understand how the crew aboard the *Conquistador* thinks. We *are* family. Sometimes we are bound by blood, or time, or space, but we are just as concerned about our collective well-being as we are about the individual good. Sometimes, more so.

Still, it's frightening to think that the Smithsons have been laboring to discredit my family in front of others, especially the crew. "You say 'family' like it's a bad thing," I say.

"It is when your people forget who's paying them," Sebastian says.

"Money can't buy loyalty," I spit back.

"Can't it?" he asks, stroking the hollow of my throat. "Money bought a collar for a little lioness."

"I think *you've* forgotten lion cubs have claws," I snap, smacking his hand away.

He lifts one of my hands, pressing the tips of my fingers into his lips. "Oh, but my cariño, can't you see I've clipped them off?"

"Don't you call me cariño." My lip curls. "Not when you don't have the cojones to stand up to your mother—"

Sebastian smashes me against the wall. My head bounces off the metal, rattling my brain inside my skull. Galaxies dance through my vision. I groan. If it weren't for the way he's got me pinned, I might slide to the floor.

"You think you're so clever, don't you?" he says in my ear, the heat of his breath bristling against my skin. His hands slide down the sides of my waist. I shudder. He digs his fingers into my flesh. It's hard to believe I ever liked his touch. "But here's the thing, you *clever* girl"—he pulls a few centimeters away—"tonight, you made my job of discrediting your family easier. What will the crew think, once they hear the Lioness's little cub snuck into the Narrows and hacked the silocomputers?"

My eyes widen. I hadn't considered also being blamed for a

black-hat hacker's work, not even by Sebastian. I fight to swallow down the panic crawling from my heart through my throat, not wanting it to show on my face. I'd prepared for this very situation. I do nothing without a solid, achievable plan, along with backups and safeties to make sure I succeed.

While I might not be able to prove I wasn't the hacker in the Narrows, I *can* prove Sebastian's a liar and a blackmailer.

I must do a terrible job at feigning nonchalance, because Sebastian continues, "Ah, now the little cub understands the trouble she's in." He smiles as if he's just made a game-winning play in pulseball. He clucks his tongue. "Hacking a civilian-class starship is a major federal offense, Laura."

"So is assaulting a fellow crew member aboard a starship," I say, nodding toward the secure-cam, whose eye targets us with dynamic precision. "Tell me, do you think they'll be able to read your lips on camera? Perhaps notice what happened to me when you said the word 'stop'?"

Sebastian pushes off me without a word, gaze locked on the cam. The color bleeds from his face. His lip lifts in a small snarl. "All the ship's sentinels are drunk tonight. I checked."

"Why should that matter?" I say, quietly pressing the attack. "After what happened on Launch Day, I used the ship's GPL systems and facial-recognition tech to document any and all of our encounters. That data gets bitloaded into one of three hundred fifty random off-colony, dark web accounts. I press the right button, and this very moment will be seen by people all over Panamerica."

He crushes his lips into a thin, bloodless line. I watch fury coil in his eyes, two great green snakes constricting around his pupils till they turn to pinpricks. This is Sebastian Smithson, plotting his next move, looking for an opening, still trying to win. We are alike in some ways, but mostly in the way we both hate to lose.

"Which people?" he asks.

I shrug, which I hope hides the terror creeping into my gut. "I had a hacker friend set it up for me, just as an additional layer of protection. They didn't know why I needed it, and I don't know where anything's stored, nor where it would go, should it be released."

"You must be lying. Your sub . . ." He pauses, glancing up at the secure-cam and turning his back on its lens. "Your little *friend* is programmed to keep you from doing anything that could harm my family." He says these words through his teeth.

"Ay, that's true," I say. "I don't know who built your AI, but it's not that smart. I've spent the last three months testing its limits, and let me tell you, it's got loopholes."

"*Loopholes?*"

I allow myself a little grin. "What did I always tell you? Hacking isn't magic, it's *logic*. I find loopholes in systems and exploit them. Did you really think your system would be superior to my skills? That I wouldn't find *some* way to exploit its code?"

Sebastian points a finger in my face. I wish I could bite the tip of it off. "Mother always told me you were too proud."

"And Mami always told me you were a racista."

The word's off my tongue before I even think it through. There's a pause, a single moment where the word sinks into him, irretrievable. Sebastian lifts his hand as if to strike me, thinks twice, and steps back, breathing so hard his shoulders heave. We glare at each other.

Sometimes anger drags harsh truths off your lips. Though the Smithsons would deny it to their dying breath, what I said was true. Panamerica's a mezcla of the former North, Central, and South Americas, plus Japan through an alliance with the United States. Pale skin's uncommon, often curated by white families as carefully as a museum collection.

When Sebastian and I first started dating, Mami warned me his skin was too pale, and that it might mean something about his family. I didn't listen, believing that if I loved him enough, I could change him.

After all, Sebastian's intelligent. Driven. Kind when he wants to be, and not lacking in empathy. Qualities I could work with.

Then Launch Day came. I learned all my love couldn't change seventeen years of social conditioning. It couldn't shift thousand-year-old thinking, no matter how erroneous that thinking might be. No matter how accomplished I was, or how many historical papers I'd written for my uni classes and presented at major forums, or awards I'd received for my work, it didn't matter. Not to Dr. Smithson. Not to her son.

"Laura." This time he says my name right, and there's heartbreak packed into his voice. I can't tell if he's acting. "How could you even imply . . . much less say . . ."

"History isn't something you colonize, Sebastian," I say, my words firm but quiet. "Its stories don't belong to you because of your family name. My family's crew doesn't belong to you because you pay them. I don't belong to you just because you used to be my boyfriend."

His eyes narrow, almost to slits. As he opens his mouth to respond, someone calls out:

"Laura? You there?" The voice is a deep bass, maybe Alex's.

"Over here!" I shout before Sebastian can command me to be silent.

Alex strides into view, some fifteen meters uptunnel. When he turns his head, his gaze checks me from head to toe, then zeroes in on Sebastian.

"There you are," Alex says, the lightness of his tone belying the wariness in his features. Relief floods my body, releasing the tension in my muscles and slowing my heart.

When Alex moves, he's all grace, lithe muscles, and sharp intellect. His locs are gathered off his face in a loose ponytail at the back of his neck, the brown of his hair a few shades darker than his umber skin. His parents are historians—old uni friends of my father's—but Alex is in flight school and already training to fly ships in the *Conquistador*'s class. His parents are very vocal about his brilliant mathematical mind, knifelike reflexes, and captain-material charisma . . . and only a little less so about his casual disinterest in their life's work.

"You okay, flaca?" Alex asks, his gaze shifting from Sebastian to me. When I move to him, he wraps an arm around my shoulders.

I nod, swallowing hard. My subjugator pricks my muscles. "I was just on my way to the party," I say, trying on a smile. It doesn't fit right with my mood, and I've never been an emotional chameleon like my older brother, or Faye. Mami says I wear my heart on my sleeve, and it's usually true.

"Looks like you got held up," Alex says.

"Nothing I couldn't handle," I say, glancing at the secure-cam. Sebastian follows my gaze, and I make a show of straightening my shirt and rolling back my shoulders. Sebastian and I have reached a point of mutually assured interpersonal destruction, with our families' futures hanging on each move we make. One thing I know for certain: he and his mother won't try to harm me unless they can be assured of a neat, incontrovertible victory. If the footage of Sebastian commanding me to *stop* were ever seen by the right pair of eyes, well, the Smithsons could count out the rest of their days behind bars. Sebastian knows so much; but his mother, with a much larger legacy to lose, will feel that threat more keenly. Good.

A muted call warbles through the tunnels.

"She's over here, Faye!" Alex shouts, a riff of anger in his voice.

Faye shouts something several tunnels away. The distance erodes the meaning off her words. The horsey *clip-clop* of her high heels bounces downtunnel.

"Is she really running around the ship in heels?" I ask Alex.

He shrugs. "It's Faye."

"I know, but she's going to wedge her ankle—"

"Laurita!" Faye shouts. I turn, smiling despite the ache in my head and the panic in my heart. Faye has to walk on her toes here or else her heels will sink through the grates. She wobbles, her A-line, midmodern skirt swinging like a red bell. Earlier today, she used her bioware's canvases to paint an entire mural about the terrarium find, and then used her illusory shifters to apply it temporarily to her skirt. The effect doesn't last long, though—after a few hours, the painting's dimming, the regular fabric showing through.

I squint at her skirt and wonder: *Could that effect be applied to a spacesuit?*

"Are you okay?" Faye's arms go around my neck, breaking through my thoughts. Part of me wants to shatter into a million little pieces, but if I did, Faye would catch them as they fell. There will be time enough to fall apart later, when I can tell her the whole story. Right now, I need to focus, get to the bridge, and get my personal bioware offline. My family's future depends on it, as does the fate of one of humanity's greatest finds.

I pull back from Faye's embrace. "I'm sorry about the party, cari—"

"Laura, *what* are you *wearing*?" she asks, her perfectly stenciled brows arching, lips pouting. She tugs on one of my carabiners. "And what is this thing? Never mind, you can borrow something of mine. Ven conmigo, back to the party. I'll make you a margarita." Her voice lilts on the last note as she slips her arm through mine.

"I can't," I say, digging my feet into the ground as she tries to tug me back toward the ship's residential areas. "I need to get to the bridge."

"What, why?" Alex and Faye ask, almost in tandem.

"I saw a hacker in the Narrows," I say. "The pendejo messed with the ship's gravidar and—"

"You should *go to the party*, Laura," Sebastian says, stressing the command so the subjugator takes hold of my body. I halt in the hallway, one eyelid twitching at the mispronunciation of my name. In order for the subjugator to read the command, Sebastian has to say my name with that exact pronunciation and intonation.

"It's *Laora*," Faye snaps, oblivious. "Say her name right, or don't say it at all, chico."

The subjugator works best on simple, one-word voice commands. The more complex the command, the easier it is to ignore. *Just a few more seconds . . . five . . . four . . .*

"Laura?" Alex asks behind me. He rests a hand on my shoulder. "What's wrong?"

"You know Laura," Sebastian says, his voice easy, tone mocking, a poor attempt to hide a tinge of anxiety. "She hates being told what to do."

"I think she just hates *you*," Faye says, snapping her fingers at Sebastian.

Three . . . screw you too . . . one. By the end, I'm breathing hard. I doubt Sebastian will attempt something like that again, risky as it was to issue such a complicated command right in front of the two people who know me best, and on camera. *Why is he acting so foolishly?* I shake it off, wishing I could slap the smug grin from Sebastian's face.

He's getting bolder. That doesn't bode well.

As Faye and Sebastian exchange barbs, Alex leans down. "What's this gringo doing to you?" he asks me under his breath, as if I could chalk my reactions to Sebastian up to something like, say, trauma. Alex may be the most observant of my friends, but for most people, subjugators aren't part of ordinary life. They're the stuff of thriller fiction and sordid news stories, not everyday reality.

He glances at Sebastian and Faye. "This probably isn't the time for this conversation, is it?"

I shake my head. "I'm not sure I can explain it, Alex," I say softly. "Even to you."

"You know you can tell me anything, right?"

"There's a big difference between *wanting to* and *being able to*, sometimes."

His eyes search mine. When I don't say anything more, he squeezes my shoulder and kisses my temple. It's not a romantic gesture; we've always been close. Sebastian couldn't stand the casual warmth in my relationship with Alex—it's fraternal, really, but it's not something Sebastian's touch-phobic family understands. I've never seen Dr. Smithson so much as hug Sebastian in public. Their relationship seems almost . . . *clinical*, at least in public. Though I admit, it's not much better in private, either.

"Help me on the bridge?" I ask Alex. "I promise, it's important."

"Órale," he says. "Did you really think you had to ask?"

As we turn and walk away, Faye cries out, "Ay, where are you two going?"

"To your party." I meet Sebastian's gaze before adding, "By way of the bridge."

"What?!" Faye runs after us, her heels clacking against the floor.

"I hope you know what you're doing," Alex says under his breath. "We don't have clearance to be on the ship's bridge during the late bells." There's an unspoken *And we definitely don't have clearance to be on the Alfa Bridge ever* in those words, too.

"Oh, I do," I say.

When it comes to the ship's computers, I always do.

A few minutes later, we enter the Hall of Artifacts, a gallery of the finds my parents and their teams are currently studying.

It takes all my nerve to keep from sprinting straight to the bridge. I tell myself I've spent weeks preparing for this, and I know my plans both backward and forward. Still, I walk faster. I've worked toward escaping Sebastian's subjugator for months now, and it's all I've wanted. My hands shake, because I know my freedom's twined up with failure, and that my future now rests on a knife's edge.

Situated at the top of the manta ray–shaped *Conquistador*, the long, arched Hall of Artifacts runs down the ship's spine. Stars glitter overhead, visible through arches of crysteel supported by metal vertebrae. The artifacts stand in floatglass cases anchored to the walls. We pass a terra-cotta soldier from Emperor Qin's army—Dad's almost finished studying the molecular makeup of the clay, and then it will be returned to the Chinese. A huge stone Mayan calendar wheel graces the wall on my right, beside Neil Armstrong's 1969 moon-landing EVA suit. It's hard to believe midmodern people wore such bulky, yet fragile suits in space. It seems like a micrometeorite could tear straight through that suit, causing havoc on a massive scale.

A golden sarcophagus stands mag-gravved onto a pedestal to my left. The figure carved on it glares at me with slitted, golden eyes. A little farther down, the Winged Victory of Samothrace occupies a prime hollow, along with murals from Diego Rivera; a gorgeous, golden Moche idol depicting the octopus god, Ai Apaec; and a Gutenberg Bible.

Behind us, the tunnel splits. Two large walkways spiral around Michelangelo's *David* statue, which stands four and a half meters tall, even without his head. The age-old marble glows blue in the louver lights, a faint radiance tumbling off the edges of the floatglass walkways. Mami accidentally decapitated the

David in a dig, when a rival shipraider group, the Cortés family, crashed our site and fought us for the haul. During a Wild West–style shootout, Mami figuratively lost her head.

Unfortunately for *David*, his loss was more literal.

One of the centerpieces of my parents' collection, though, remains their original copy of the former United States of America's Declaration of Independence. It sits in the middle of the hall in a freestanding, multi-layered crysteel vault, and is protected by UV radiation blockers, and interior vacu-chambers. After so many hundreds of years, the ink's paled. My parents have restored it, but I've never been able to make out the ancient, spidery handwriting and strange spellings. Nobody's written anything by hand for hundreds of years. Except locos like Dad, who enjoy making pen nubs and crushing their own ink to study the art of handwriting. Dad's a purist.

I press my hand to the case as we pass the Declaration, the document's irony not lost on me. It talks about freedom and liberty as being "self-evident," and yet *this* was the artifact the Smithsons subjugated me to gain. The Smithsons' subjugator keeps me from telling my parents about the Smithsons' plans; though now that the *John Muir* terrarium's been found, no doubt they will redouble their efforts to steal my family's legacy.

"That jerk's still following us," Faye says, glancing over her shoulder at Sebastian.

"Ignore him," I say, loud enough for Sebastian to hear. "He won't try anything, not if he's smart."

"What's that supposed to mean?" Faye asks.

I don't answer her, but shoot a look at Sebastian before

pushing off the Declaration's case and heading toward the bridge.

The Rio Grande bulkhead arches as high as El Arco did in Labná—it's a giant gateway made of metal and glass, one that connects or partitions two separate areas of the ship as needed. This particular bulkhead opens into the largest continuous room onboard: the lower bridge rotunda.

I pause beneath the high point of the bulkhead's arch. The rotunda beyond is massive, giving a 180-degree, uninterrupted view of the ship's surroundings. Crysteel windows stretch from floor to ceiling. From here, the nebula's colors are glorious, vast tapestries set against the unending darkness of space. As the largest room aboard the ship, the lower bridge houses much of the ship's control tech beneath a glowing crysteel floor. If the Narrows is the *Conquistador*'s nervous system, the lower bridge is its brain.

The evening's celebrations started here, under the glow of the nebula . . . and my parents' latest find, an Exodus-era spacecraft known as the USS *John Muir*, NPS-3500. Right now, the crysteel floor remains closed and covered in celebratory debris—trampled holo-confetti and clustered bubble balloons. The Alfa Bridge—my destination—floats over the lower bridge like a giant lily pad, the twin stalks of its antigrav elevators reaching down to the floor.

Freedom is finally within reach. And with any luck, the Colonies' salvation, too: the lower bridge's large windows frame the terrarium ship perfectly. The *John Muir*'s almost as big as a Panamerican torus colony, and round as a soap bubble. From this distance, it looks too delicate to stand up to the dangers of deep-space travel. A large crescent-shaped ship hugs the sphere on the left side, mirroring the gravitational rings making slow rotations around the craft. The landscape inside the sphere isn't visible against the brilliant backdrop of stars, but there's some kind of craggy, mountainous terra firma in there. The rock stands out in stark, black profile. Clouds puff around the mountaintops.

After being lost for almost four hundred years, the ships we find are no better than tombs. Ancient, creaking, and filled with the bones of the dead. But miraculously, the *John Muir*'s lights still twinkle. Clouds in the aerodome indicate the ship's atmosphere has enough power, air, and heat to function. If there's water and air, there's life. And if there's life in the *soil*, my family might be able to save our people, our country.

Four hundred years ago, Pitch Dark ecoterrorists tried to end humanity by jettisoning our Exodus starcraft into the farthest reaches of space. They succeeded in divesting us of one-third of the surviving human population, our landmarks, our history. A hundred years later, the healthy bacteria in the Colonies' soil broke down and died. The soil in the colonies of both China and the EuroUnion deteriorated, too, until it could no longer support life. Hydroponic farming became policy, but hydroponics can't finish terraforming a planet.

But the soil inside the *John Muir* might.

On the far side of the room, members of the night crew kick back in their chairs, heels on their desks, their backs to us. The nebula's light glows through several empty bottles of beer. The booming laughter from the crew echoes through the entire bridge. *Bueno.* If they're drunk and we're quiet, they may not notice us sneaking up to the Alfa Bridge.

Glancing back at Faye, I point at her shoes. She gives me this look that almost screams, *Really?* and I nod. She slips them off. I stride onto the bridge.

Overhead, the Panamerican flag glimmers on several screens—Earth surrounded by a laurel wreath, the tip of former South America pointing to the heavens, with North America below. Thirty-five stars—one for each of the former American countries—encircle the planet. Most of those countries are still represented by modern-day Panamerica, in some form or another.

A small shower of sparks erupts from one of the screens, before the flag flips upside down, displaying Earth in the ancient Eurocentric style. It looks foreign to my eyes. *Wrong*, somehow. The light rattles, dies; and when the flag appears again, it's normal. I make a mental note to tell Mami the radiant filaments need to be checked. No part of a starship can ever be allowed to deteriorate, not if one wants to survive in deep space.

I approach the Alfa Bridge's elevators. *This is it,* I tell myself. With a glance at the night crew—*they're still oblivious*—I scan my bioware at the lift. The words *Buenas noches, Capitana Cruz* pulse across the transparent doors. Faye and Alex follow me into the antigrav elevator. As Sebastian moves to join us, Alex presses a hand against one of the floatglass doors, blocking him.

"If you don't let me on," Sebastian whispers, glancing at the night crew, "I will bring every mercenary on this ship straight to you."

Alex glances back at me. I shrug a shoulder. What was that

old phrase Dad used to say? *Keep your enemies close, but your friends closer?* Or was it the other way around?

"Fine," Alex says, moving his arm aside to let Sebastian onboard. The doors close behind him.

"Since when do you have your mother's access codes?" Faye asks softly, stopping beside me with a little whirl. Her dress hem orbits her knees like planetary rings, the edges smacking my dusty, frayed khakis.

"Since twenty-six minutes ago," I reply.

Sebastian scowls, but says nothing.

Faye tuts. "Laura, I swear, if you've been up to some illegal stuff again—"

"Remember, I'm a white hat?" I say, tapping the up button, grinning internally at her use of the word *again*. Early on, I got caught hacking. Quite a lot, actually, but it taught me how to cover my tracks. "I'm one of the good ones, Faye. I'm not out to set the world on fire."

"Yeah, I'm sure that's what *all* the evil geniuses say," she replies.

"Ay, I thought you were supposed to be my best friend," I say.

"I am." She elbows me with a teasing grin. "Don't be so self-*conchas*."

Alex groans. "You said you were done with the puns, flaca."

Faye flutters her lashes at Alex. "I know it's cheesy—"

"Don't." Alex chuckles.

"—But I feel *grate* about that last one," she says.

"Unbelievable," Sebastian says as the lift glides to a stop.

Faye clucks her tongue. "I think you meant *pun*-believable, chico—"

"Faye!" Alex and I chorus together, mostly laughing our protest. Faye finds loopholes in language the way I find them in code. Perhaps that's why we've become so close over the years— we see the world the same way, even if we're looking through slightly different lenses.

Before Faye can fire another pun at us, the lift doors slide open.

We fall silent.

Nothing moves on the Alfa Bridge, not even the shadows. The stars glitter through a domed crysteel ceiling. The Alfa Bridge seats the ship's twenty main officers, their workstations built into two concentric arcs facing the front of the room. Mami's chair sits on a raised platform, giving her a bird's-eye view of the deck. Giant floatglass screens curve around the workstations, their displays hovering several meters off the ground, humming quietly. The *Conquistador*'s core stats look good. My parents run a tight ship.

"You're sure about this, Laura?" It's Sebastian who asks this time, a subtle warning hidden under the simplicity of his question, like a knife punched into my chest through a pillow. I pause and glance at him over my shoulder. He stands inside the lift, the light shadowing his features and casting the rest of him in two-dimensional silhouette. Alex and Faye pause, looking to me for direction.

There's no reason to engage him now, not when I'm so close to winning.

Without another word, I turn on my heel. Sebastian sighs as I climb the steps to the captain's platform. Sweat dampens my palms as I sink into Mami's chair and hold my wrists over the armrests, letting my bioware sync with the ship's systems. Her chair's comfortable, made from pliable, heirloom calfskin and old-world wood.

But I feel anything but relaxed as I engage the chair's clear, hard-shelled screens, which envelop me in an egg-shaped space. With the hard-shells up, Sebastian won't be able to interrupt my work. I've waited so long for this chance—now all I need to do is follow my plan. *Fortuna y gloria.*

"Should I even ask?" Alex says, joining me on the platform. The floatscreens come online, making it difficult to see Faye and Sebastian down below, but I can definitely hear them arguing.

"It's important, I promise," I say, running the silocomputers' diagnostic to check for malware in the gravidar. "Keep Sebastian away from me, ay? I don't want him to interfere."

Alex chuckles, putting his hands on his hips. "Faye's got him contained." He shrugs. "For now."

The ship's diagnostic tool starts scanning the mission-critical tech, looking for the black-hat hacker's intrusion. While I wait, I pull up the captain's personnel menu and select **BIOWARE**. It's not difficult to find my name—families are grouped together, and Mami's and Dad's names are at the top of the crew lists—*Laura María Salvatierra Cruz*, bioware number 1044-A-6876.

I move to select my name. My finger freezes a millimeter from the screen.

No.

I try to double-tap my name once, twice, then switch to another finger. My subjugator lets me highlight my mother's name, *Elena Concepción Cruz San Roman*, or my father's name, *Jaime*

Luis Salvatierra Fuentes. My siblings' names—*Gael Antonio Salvatierra Cruz* and *Sofía Librada Salvatierra Cruz*—are also clickable. But my subjugator won't let me touch my own.

"No manches," I whisper under my breath. Panic rising, I consider shutting down the bioware system ship-wide for several minutes. Even a few seconds would be enough to allow me to grab Alex, point to my throat, and whisper, *subjugator.* A few seconds shouldn't harm anyone aboard—though turning it off too long could get someone killed. Bioware regulates our immune systems and medications, corrects hormonal imbalances, and generally tracks the crew's overall health while in space. My cousin, for example, relies on her bioware to manage her insulin levels.

As I scroll back to the personnel menu, a new chat client opens up beneath my fingers. Its interface blocks me from accessing the **BIOWARE** menu.

Hello, Laura, the message says.

A soulless, empty-eyed icon stares at me from beside the message, depicting a bone-white face set atop a black background. At first I think it's a Guy Fawkes mask—perhaps in homage to early twenty-first-century hacker collectives—but no, it's missing the signature mustache. Then my memory is triggered: it's a Japanese Noh theater mask, one with an oval-shaped face and thick, high-set eyebrows. The mask's thousand-yard stare seems to look everywhere and nowhere at once. Something about its aspect makes the tiny hairs on my body rise. I glance over my shoulder, forgetting for a moment that I'm in Mami's chair with the hard-shells on. No one can touch me.

Except, perhaps, another hacker.

A second line of text appears: *Who thought a hacker of your skill would struggle with such a simple task?*

The words irk me. I know better than to ask who they are—no hacker would reveal that sort of information. *The captain's chair isn't accessible remotely. How are you doing this?*

Their reply? *Magic.*

A chill pricks the base of my spine, not unlike the sensation of cold needles being stuck between my vertebrae. I'd said the words *hacking isn't magic, it's logic* to Sebastian not more than fifteen minutes ago. Coincidence? No, it couldn't be. If there's no honor among thieves, there are no coincidences among hackers.

I'm being monitored. The question is *by whom?* Sebastian and his mother seem like obvious answers, but not the right ones.

Outside the captain's chair, Alex shouts, "Hey, vato! Don't you touch her!" and leaps off the platform. Voices snap and snarl, but it's difficult to focus on two crises at once.

Let's dispense with the pleasantries, then, pendejo, I type back. *Were you the hacker in the Narrows tonight?*

They reply, *There was only one hacker in the Narrows to-night.*

You know that's not true.

Do I? The other hacker sends me a shadowy image, one showing me hidden between the hindrance oscillators. Panic makes my skin burn too hot and my heart beat too hard.

Someone has hard evidence that I hacked the Narrows. If they're good enough to hack Mami's chair remotely, it's possible they know about my subjugator, too. The hacker can't be Dr. Smithson—she's currently preparing for an international press conference with Mami—which means I have an anonymous enemy onboard the *Conquistador*.

A hacker who thinks they're better and smarter than me.

"Alex, don't you get all machista, too!" Faye shouts. The sounds of a scuffle reach me—the resonant, meaty drum of a fist striking flesh, grunts and groans. Concerned for Alex, I hit the button to dissipate the chair's hard-shells.

Nothing happens. I tap the button again. The chair doesn't respond.

I'm trapped.

I'm sorry, did you want to get up? the other hacker replies. *I'm afraid that's not possible. I need you to sit there and look pretty for another, oh, 36.8 seconds.*

What? I type back. *Why?*

The other hacker sends a smiley face as a reply.

Sweat beads on my brow, my head swimming as claustrophobia born of panic fills me. I jam my fingers into the hard-shell release button, hitting it so fast it chatters like teeth. Failing that, I pound on the shell with the side of my fist. "Hey!" I shout at the others. "Help me!"

Down below, chairs screech as the boys tumble into them, barely in view. They ignore me. "Stop it!" Faye shrieks, fisting her hands as she follows them. Her bioware's ioScreen clings to one wrist, maybe to record the fight to prove Alex's innocence later. "The night crew will hear you!"

Seconds later, all the Alfa Bridge's floatscreens surge back online, washing everything in cool blue light. The boys pause, look at the screens, then back at me. Faye turns to me with wide-eyed confusion.

"What did you just do, Laura?" Sebastian asks, pushing Alex away. Blood gushes from one of his nostrils, marking a bright crimson path to his chin.

"Nothing!" I say, putting my hands in the air. "Someone is remotely hijacking Mami's chair!"

"Bullshit," Sebastian replies. "What did you *do*?"

Just think, the other hacker writes. *Someday, some other shipraider will find your bones. And when they do, they'll blame you for the crash.*

"Crash?" I whisper, my brows knotting together. I sink back into the chair to type, *What kind of crash are you talking about?* when the ship lurches. A tinny whine starts up under my feet, the faraway sound of the scramengines screaming as they start pushing the ship forward.

"What's happening, Laura?" Alex shouts. The ship kicks forward, racing toward the *John Muir*. Faye trips, spilling into Alex's arms.

You have 180 seconds to try and stop the crash, Laura, the other hacker writes. The *John Muir* swells in the windows, growing larger as we speed toward her outer rim. Crimson warnings flash over the floatscreens, casting the bridge in a hellish light.

Not even luck can save you now.

TUCK

Luck saves my life. I escape death by dropping between two seats, but I don't move my hand quick enough—a bit of shriek echo skims off the tips of my fingers. They're sore and bloody before I ease to the floor, but hell, I'm alive. *"See, Dejah?"* I ask the AI as I sink into a puddle of stiflecloth. *"I'm not dead yet."*

"Your tone implies you are not taking this situation seriously," she replies.

"'Tis but a flesh wound."

"Pardon?" Dejah asks.

I roll my eyes. The bulk of the inside jokes I shared with my mother were built on Monty Pythonesque humor. Mom could recite every movie by heart. The thought makes my chest ache, as if it somehow lanced an abscess of grief in there. I shove the feeling away. Missing Mom does jack shite for me now. It won't bring her, my old life, or our busted planet back.

A low growl resonates through the car. Glass cracks as the mourner shuffles inside. The bastard's so close, I don't think

Holly or I can move without alerting him. It's probably stupid even to breathe. A footrest digs into my back, putting pressure on a kidney. Or what I guess is probably a kidney. Good thing I only need one of them, right? My leg got twisted under me at a bad angle, which means my bum knee's complaining while the feeling drains from my foot.

Despite it all, I don't dare move. Gritty vibrations work their way through the floor, dragging themselves toward us. Outside, the pod overwhelms the tunnel. The tram shudders as their hands pound the tracks. Their calls ricochet off the car's metal sides, punching holes straight through the metal. Some of the intact windows shatter. Glass rains to the floor. In the chaos, my ears lose track of where our big bastard's lurking.

Until he puts a hand on my head.

I snort my breath back in and freeze.

Ah, crap.

The mourner slides his fingers down my face. Broken fingernails catch and drag the fabric across my skin. They cross the crests of my brows. I try not to imagine him shoving his thumbs into my eye sockets. Or the way the jelly of my eyes would burst under pressure from his cracked nails, or how I'd have to swallow a scream as he dug around in my skull. Just to keep Holly safe—hell, at this point, everything I do will be to keep her alive. Without me, she's dead.

The mourner gurgles, incoherent. My lungs start to burn from holding my breath. The bastard puts a hand down on my bum knee. My hip bone pops in its socket. He growls at the sound, pawing at my side, sending bright shocks of pain up my spine and to my brain.

It takes a lot of nerve to sit here quietly. All I want to do is grab the bastard by the throat and punch him till his face caves in. While there might be enough noise pollution in the tunnel to keep the other mourners from hearing me kill *this* one, it's not a risk I can take.

Not with Holly sitting nearby.

"Tuck?" Holly asks. *"Are you okay?"*

"Still not dead." I grind my teeth to cope with the pain. Two rows down, Holly prays in her head to a god we left back on Earth. When the mourner can't find meat in the twisted layers of stiflecloth, it growls and leaps up on the seat beside me, then out the window.

I don't know if Holly's god heard her or not, but the mourners don't find us.

An hour later, I almost wish they had.

My gut churns. Saliva rises like a hot tide in my mouth. For the third time in twenty minutes, I press my fist against my mouth and swallow bile back. It burns all the way down.

When the mourner pod couldn't find us, they camped around the cold corpses a few hundred meters back. The pod stretches for a good klick once bedded down, much to my endless annoyance. As they sleep, they hum. The sound crawls into the tram. It eats its way through my ears and into my brain, where it scrambles my equilibrium and makes the floor seem like it's rolling beneath me.

We curators don't know why mourners hum in their sleep. We *do* know they create infrasound harmonics when they hum, which can cause everything from nausea and dizziness to paranoia in humans. I'd get into the science of it all if I didn't feel so damn *sick*. For now, just blame it on the infrasound.

"*You okay out there, kid?*" Aren asks for the umpteenth time.

"*That depends on how you define 'okay,'*" I reply, hanging my head between my knees, like Mom always told me to do. For the record, it doesn't help. My mouth still tastes like I've eaten out an armpit.

"*Glad to see your attitude's still alive and kicking,*" Aren says. "*How's Holly?*"

"*Quiet,*" I reply.

"*Her vitals aren't looking good, and she's not responding to the med team anymore,*" Aren says. "*We're coming to help get you kids out.*"

I almost laugh. "*What happened to not risking lives to save lives?*"

"*What happened to 'a lame curator is a dead curator'?*" he asks.

"*Touché.*"

"*Exactly. Holly's the last person aboard the ship who reads Japanese fluently. We can't afford to lose her—*"

"*Thanks, I really feel loved and appreciated.*"

"*Shut up, there's not much time. I'm going to take Layla and Marco and create a distraction on Plat 17, three klicks aft of your position. A med team will meet you at Plat 22, but it'll be up to you to get Holly there. Capisce?*"

"*What kind of distraction are we talking here?*"

"*A loud one.*" He doesn't elaborate, which means it's probably something stupid and dangerous and he doesn't want me to call precedent on it the next time I do something stupid and dangerous. To be honest, Aren and I never got along back on Earth. But out here, in space? He's become my de facto parent. We work hard to make each other's lives infinitely more craptastic.

"Once the pod's moved, get Holly out of there, kid," Aren says. *"Focus on that one job, got it? We'll give you a heads-up once we're in position."*

I nod, squeezing the bridge of my nose with my fingers, then realize he can't see me. *"Okay, I'm gonna check on Holly. Don't get ganked by a mourner out there."*

"Be careful. Run silent, run hard."

"Yeah, yeah, may the force be with you, never give up, never surrender, and live long and prosper, old man." I roll onto the balls of my feet, inching toward the tram's aisle. My stomach bucks. I rest my forehead on the seat back in front of me till the dizziness passes. The journey of a half meter starts with a single scoot. I inch around the tram seat.

Blood stains the aisle. It's cold and tacky between my toes and looks black in the low light. I sink down beside Holly, saying, *"Holly? Hey, you awake?"* before gently tugging the hood off her head.

She's unconscious, but breathing.

At least she's not suffering.

Bracing myself against the seat, I rise, gritting my teeth against the nausea's twist and roll. Outside the tram, a sole LE-1 bulb flickers about ten meters away. Shadows rest over the mourners' backs like blankets. It's hard to tell where one monster ends and the other begins. They sleep in small, disorganized piles. Feet spoon with faces, limbs get triangled and tangled, and nothing lies still. The mourners move in their sleep, twitching, writhing, moaning.

They sure don't sleep peaceful or quiet. Sometimes I wonder if they ever remember their human lives, even if only in their dreams.

Plat 17 is a few klicks on the right. Aren's distraction will come from that direction. Once the pod's cleared out, I'll take Holly and run left, fast as I can.

For now, all I can do is wait.

L A U R A

When the ship-wide alarm sounds, there's no time to hesitate or wait. Emergency lights wash across the deck as an impact timer appears on the Alfa Bridge's main floatglass screens:

00:02:26

Two minutes, twenty-six seconds. And counting.

The hard-shells around the captain's chair snap off, the bridge's cooler air rushing in. I scramble onto the captain's platform, bracing myself against the railing. Below me, all the bridge's workstations burn bright with warnings, two crescents of bloodred light. "Alex!" I shout. "I need your help. That loco hacker's trying to crash the *Conquistador*!"

"What?!" everyone below me cries.

I hurry down the steps. "Faye, Sebastian, get to the crash pods. Alex, please—"

"Cari, I'm *not* going to leave you," Faye says, grabbing my hand.

Sebastian sneers. "If I'm going, you're coming with me," he says, taking my other wrist. I pull myself away from them both.

"Please, just go," I shout at them, pushing Faye toward the crash pods at the back of the bridge. "I'll be right behind you, I promise. *Go.*" With the clock winding down, I turn on my heel and run toward the workstations. The main navigational systems—including the gravidar controls—are situated in the middle of the first ring. Alex follows me to them.

"What did you do, Laura?" he asks under his breath, dropping into the chair.

"Nothing," I say. "The other hacker hijacked Mami's chair remotely and started the scramengines."

"The gravidar shouldn't allow the *Conquistador* to collide with anything," he says. "That's what it was originally engineered for—"

"They *compromised* our gravidar, Alex."

"*They?*"

"They."

He's silent for a moment, searching my gaze with his. The fact that he doesn't trust me, even for a second, slips between my ribs and pricks my heart. "Alex," I say, grabbing him by the shoulders. I shake him. "You *know* I would never do anything to jeopardize this crew. We're *family.*"

He looks back at the navigational screens, blowing out a breath.

Time continues to slide toward zero:

00:01:58

He claps one hand over my own. "I trust you, Laurita. Okay?"

"Okay." I squeeze his shoulder as he connects his bioware to the station. I use Mami's codes to gain access to the system, then use my fingers to move the ioScreen in front of him. He clicks through the menus, initiating the navigational aeroboard and its joystick controls. An entire frame of translucent buttons and switches appears over his chair.

"I only know what half of these things do . . . ," he mutters, taking both joysticks in hand.

The minute he grips the controls, the aeroboard disappears. All the floatscreens shut off in a puff of air—*poof!* Alex lifts his hands in the air, scooting back from the machine. The rest of the workstations' screens darken, falling like tiles in an ancient domino game, one after the other.

Alex and I stand at the center of their dark gravity.

"What the hell was that?" Alex whispers.

My mouth goes dry. "I—I don't know—"

All the screens blast on again, their light blinding. Brilliant. I squint at the screens, shielding my face with my hand. An image sears itself into my retinas, branding a black mark on my vision, no matter if my eyes are open or shut. It's a circular image of a snake eating its own tail. A symbol that's haunted my dreams since I was young, and an icon that's appeared in ancient cultures worldwide, symbolizing the death of the world.

It's the symbol members of Pitch Dark have rallied around since the Exodus.

The other hacker isn't just a black hat.

He's a *terrorist*.

"We need to get out of here," Alex says, taking me by the arm. The ship announces, *"Sixty seconds until impact. Please report to your nearest safety pod and complete bracing procedure immediately,"* in a voice that sounds so calm, it mocks us. Alex hustles me away from the screens, from Mami's chair, toward the safety pods at the back of the Alfa Bridge. As we move toward the pods, three members of the night crew stumble out of the antigrav elevators, cursing drunkenly at one another. Someone points at the countdown clock on the floatscreens, his eyes wide, mouth agape. Two men hurry for the safety pods; one sprints for the navigational systems at the front of the deck.

"Don't!" Alex shouts after him, but the man's already out of earshot. "Keep going," he says to me. "Nobody needs to be a hero today."

"But he'll die—"

"*Go!*"

As we run for the pods, worst-case scenarios fill my mind: from the crash killing my family and friends, to being bodily jettisoned into space without an EVA suit, to one of our artifacts being destroyed. . . .

The artifacts!

I shove my heels into the ground, tugging my arm out of Alex's grip. "The artifacts," I say, thinking of the Hall of Artifacts downstairs, my heart pounding so hard I wonder if it will beat itself to death on my ribs. "S-s-someone has to fill their floatcases with closed-cell foam manually." Fear makes my voice tremble. After one of our officers initiated the so-called "Foamacalpyse" during an emergency drill, Mami removed remote access to the artifacts' security board. Nowadays, it has to be done inside the safety pod adjacent to the bridge.

If I run, I can make it to the Hall of Artifacts in time.

"*Fifty seconds to impact,*" the *Conquistador*'s system says.

I don't deliberate. Alex shouts, "Laura, no!" as I turn on my heel and run for the antigrav elevators. I race inside, the doors sliding closed behind me. Alex runs into the translucent barrier, pushing his palms against the crysteel, his eyes wide and wild.

"Get to a safety pod!" I shout at him, pressing my palms against his before the lift drops. "¡Ten cuidado, Alex!"

"Laura!" he shouts again. My stomach feels weightless as the lift plunges down, his voice echoing through the lift chamber.

"Forty seconds to impact."

I pound on the lift doors till they open, then sprint across the lower bridge and through the ship's Rio Grande bulkhead.

"Thirty seconds to impact."

I slide into the Hall of Artifacts, almost tripping over my own feet. On my right, the hall stretches out, the emergency pod lights casting everything in a nightmarish glow. Along the middle far wall, the lower-level crash pod sign blinks like a bright red eye.

"Twenty seconds to impact—"

The ship jolts underfoot, knocking me to my knees. A metallic scream, louder than any sound I've ever heard before, slices through the air. The lights flicker overhead like fireworks, cutting to black before flaring bright again. A rapid-fire succession of explosions rock the ship: *Boom! Boom! Boom-boom-boom!*

The *Conquistador* lurches sideways, throwing me against the wall. The scramengines begin to whine over the din. Their squeals stab into my ears like needles. Overhead, the emergency lights turn from white to orange, signaling a fault in one of the ship's mission-critical systems. The floor trembles, chugs like a carnival ride, then drops out from under me.

For a full second, I float.

Then the ship's gravity seizes me, slamming me into the

metal floor. I feel the impact in my spine first, like all my vertebrae are a strand of pearls being yanked taut and pulverized under an anvil. Something crunches in my body. My head hits next, the world blinking black and spotty. No, it's not my vision—the lights are strobing, flickering on and off as the ship shakes and screams and shivers.

On the next great *boom*, I slam up against one of the tunnel walls. The Winged Victory rocks on her pedestal, her great stone wings clawing a huge hole into the wall. She tips in slow motion, as if falling through zero gravity. A floatglass case crashes to the ground in front of me. The lights die.

Darkness rushes into me on my next breath, and everything goes silent.

TUCK

For the last few minutes, the coglinks have been quiet. Dark. You know that old saying from John Wayne's *The Lucky Texan*, "It's quiet . . . too quiet"?

Well, it's too damn quiet right now.

I keep expecting—well, maybe hoping—to hear coglink buzz from the other curators. Something to let me know they're not bleeding out somewhere in the deepdowns. Dejah hasn't said a word to me. The mourners' hum has dampened. Even the *Muir* itself seems to be holding her breath, her systems buzzing low. The silence puts my teeth on edge. In any movie, this would be the part when the griefer stabbed Wolverine-like claws into the tram's side, the tips of its talons just centimeters from my face. But that doesn't happen, because griefers don't have claws like Wolverine's.

The weepers do, though.

I sink down beside Holly, drawing her inside my cloak and under one arm. Ready, whenever Aren gives the signal, to run.

Metallic shrieks echo up the tunnel. Holly stirs. The sounds aren't organic, almost like God's taking a can opener to the ship to rend open the hull. *"Aren?"* I ask. *"Sure sounds like you're hitting the ship with a wrecking ball."*

I can't make sense of Aren's answer: *"Tuck"*—static—*"g-g-et girl"*—static—*"tunnels . . ."*

"Hey, what was that? You're breaking up, old man," I say.

"What's happening?" Holly asks, yawning as she wakes. The pain must hit her then, because she bites down on her lower lip and sinks her fingers into my shirt. *"Why's the ground shaking?"*

"Aren's supposed to be making a distraction, but—"

The tram tunnel shudders. Panicked mourner calls spiral through the darkness. Holly clings to me, making a small noise at the back of her throat. I grab the seats to keep us steady. In the distance, a *crack-pow-bam!* echoes up the tunnels.

"Dejah?" I ask the AI. *"What's going on?"*

"One moment, please," Dejah says. Frag me, are there any words in the English language more infuriating than *one moment, please*?

The tram lurches hard. Adrenaline bursts through my fingers and toes. Letting go of Holly, I get to my feet, wincing at the stiffness in my knee. Outside the tram, the mourners stampede past, sometimes trampling one another. Up the tunnel, in the direction of Plat 17, the lights wink out one by one. Metallic shrieks race toward me, chasing the mourner pod away.

"Aren!" I shout through the coglinks. *"What the hell did you do?"*

The floor slopes underneath me. I tumble backward until I slam into the back of one of the seats. *"Dejah!"* I say through a breathless daze. *"What's going on?"*

All she can say is, *"One moment, please."*

"What do I do?" Holly screams. *"We're falling, oh my God, the tunnel's falling—"*

"Buckle yourself into a seat!" I shout at her, all caution gone. My voice feels like sandpaper grinding against my throat.

"Are you crazy?" she shrieks.

"Do it!" Pain radiates up my back and rattles in my skull. Crawling around in the dark, I fumble my way into a seat. My hands find the four-point harness. I slam the buckle into the latch between my legs and brace myself.

The tunnel shakes and drops several meters, tilting at a freakish, roller-coastering angle. Debris whistles past me. Below, fire blooms toward me like the crown of a mushroom cloud. Mourners tumble into the fire, screaming. The flames show me exposed magstructs and wilting metal. The ship burns faster than I had imagined anything could.

"Dejah?" I ask in one final, desperate call. *"Dejah, are you there?"*

"One moment, please."

Holly screams, high and loud.

The tunnel falls.

L A U R A

I wake on the Hall of Artifacts' crysteel ceiling, stars beneath my head, the world inverted. Fallen.

My vision's blurry, but there's no mistaking the fire crackling a meter away. It pops and hisses as it licks up oxygen. A thin layer of smoke bubbles along the roof. The alarms, now silent, have been replaced by two terrifying sounds—the fire's growl and the raspy whistle of escaping air.

What happened? I barely remember the crash: the terrarium, looming impossibly large in the *Conquistador*'s windows, Alex screaming my name, and the ouroboros symbols burning bright on the Alfa Bridge's workstations.

How long have I been out?

Groaning, I roll onto my back. *Ay, ay, ay, everything hurts.* My bioware nodes gleam like glassy fish eyes set in my wrists. I tap one node with a fingernail. It doesn't respond. No surprises there—if the ship's on fire and leaking air, her silos have been damaged and no longer support bioware functionality. My sub-jugator lies dead, too.

I'd call it a silver lining if the crash weren't total and complete mierda. Maybe I'm free from Smithson influence, but for all I know, I won't be alive long enough to enjoy my freedom. The ISG calls the regions beyond the Kuiper Belt the "dead zone" for a reason—if a ship gets into trouble so far from home, the ISG won't come to the rescue.

We're on our own.

The pressure's too low in the room. I draw deep, dizzying breaths to get enough oxygen. We must be leaking air and cabin pressure, and fast. The grav systems are active, but if I'm on the ceiling, the crash must have scrambled the grav's drag angles. Everything smells chemical. My head throbs, the pain stabbing through my left eye and out the back of my skull. It's frigid, so cold I can't feel the tips of my fingers, nose, or ears.

Floatglass glints amber in the oscillating emergency lights. A few artifact cases remain in place, hanging like the old images of cave stalactites I've seen. The rest lie on the floor, broken and busted, their artifacts destroyed. Thousands of years of history, gone in an instant because I failed to stop a terrorist. The Noh Mask hacker bested me, and now everything I love lies in ruins.

Now I can only hope my family and friends have survived, too.

I squeeze my eyes shut, saying a quick prayer to whatever god might be listening. *Let my family have survived the crash,* I think as loudly as I can. *Let us find a way to get out of this mess.*

But when I open my eyes, I know no savior's coming.

Shivering, I sit up, wincing as the vertebrae in my spine

separate, crack, and adjust themselves back into place. A world map of bruises purples my skin. My clothing's shredded in places. Small cuts hatch my exposed flesh. Pain bites down on my leg and I moan, finding a bloody piece of shrapnel buried in my thigh.

Wedge me, seriously? The metal's five centimeters long and about a centimeter thick, stuck into what I *hope* isn't an artery. Blood gums up the edges and stains my pants. When I tug on the shard, pain socks me behind the eyes and bile burns the back of my throat. The agony shoves me back to the ground.

"Okay, okay, está bien," I say, blowing out a breath and looking back at the wound. I'm not going anywhere with shrapnel in my leg, but without functioning bioware, I can't ping for help.

"Hello?" I call out, my voice raspy. "Mami? Dad?"

Nobody answers.

"Ay! Help!"

Nothing, nada, zip. I clench my teeth and breathe evenly, like Mami taught me to do when I broke my arm out at a dig site. I don't know if anyone else survived the crash. Listening to the air leakage, I *do* know I can't stay here long. My teeth are already chattering. I need to find my family, and then see if there's a way to save the *Conquistador* from total burnout.

But first, I have to save myself.

Pinching the shard between my fingers and thumb, I try to tug it from my flesh. The pain rolls over me in a wave, pounding my brain and better senses. Cursing, I roll on my side and clutch my thigh.

If I rip the shard out fast, I won't have time to think about the pain . . . at least not till after.

It takes a few seconds to get my courage together.

Now.

I tear the shard out. The pain hits hard, shooting through my body and bursting out of me on a scream. I chuck the shrapnel away and it patters off somewhere in the darkness. For several long moments, my whole world's made up of nothing but my pounding heartbeat and an overdose of agony. I curl into the fetal position, tears leaking from my eyes. Blood seeps through my fingers as I grip my injured leg, trying to put pressure on the wound. Part of me wishes I'd just black out, that my brain could be so merciful.

Am I bleeding too much? My head feels light, like it's going to float away. I press down harder on my wound, fumbling around for something to stanch the blood with. *I think I'm losing too much blood—*

A long, low wail slices through the haze in my head.

I pause. *What was that?*

Blinking, I prop myself up on my elbows, listening. Thirty seconds pass and I think my pain-stricken brain may have been imagining things, until I hear the wail a second time. It's closer now, echoing down the Hall of Artifacts and bouncing off the wreckage.

My heart jags. It sounds like the cries of La Llorona, the weeping woman, whose wails bode ill for those who hear them, or so the legend goes.

I rest my head back down, hidden behind a collapsed artifact case, its glass spiderwebbed and opaque. The glass on my side shattered in the crash. A suit of fifteenth-century European armor lies jumbled inside.

If not for the nearby pedestal the case fell into, the float-glass case would've crushed me into the wall during the crash. I'm lucky. *I think.* Nothing moves on the other side of the case, but I'm not alone. In the maze of broken artifacts, something pads and rasps along the floor. Like footsteps, but not quite.

Wincing, I sit up again, stamping the ground with my blood-ied handprints. I roll into a crouch, using the floatglass case to brace myself and gritting my teeth against the pain. The glass cracks under my touch. Several large pieces shatter on the ground. I freeze.

The scraping sounds stop. A voice titters, making a giggly, breathy sort of noise. I can't discern any intelligible language. It doesn't sound like someone dragging themselves toward the medbay, crying for help. I don't dare call out to whoever—or *whatever*—is out there. I'm scared, but I'm not stupid.

The scraping sounds resume and grow closer, accompanied by a chittering, batlike squeak. *Humans can't make sounds like that, can they?* Panic seizes me, squeezing my chest between the tectonic plates of stress and helplessness. Desperate, I examine the shards of the floatglass case to see if one would make a serviceable dagger, but the pieces are too small or too broken.

Then I spot the bow.

An ancient recurve bow lies at the bottom of the case, among the glitter of shattered glass. Several other old British weapons had been on display with this particular suit of armor—one of three medieval suits Dad christened Larry, Curly, and Moe—including a mace and a broadsword. I know I won't be able to lift a mace or a sword, but I'm a decent shot with a bow.

I silently thank my dad, who insisted that before his kids

entered uni, we learn an instrument (guitar, for me), a dead language (Latin), an ancient weapon and school of martial arts (archery and a little aikido), a Latin dance (flamenco), and a recipe (tamales). Dad's loco about keeping dead traditions alive. For the first time in my life, I'm grateful.

Peering over the top of the case, I don't see anything moving in the darkness except the flames. It's getting colder, and my breath bursts from me in big, cumulonimbus-sized puffs. My flight suit's not meant to deal with subzero temperatures, and it can't adjust to colder temps without my bioware's input. I need to move, before I either suffocate or freeze to death, and there might only be a few minutes to find shelter or an EVA suit. I grit my teeth to keep them from chattering.

Another burst of giggles resonates down the hall. Closer now.

I rise, the injured muscles in my thigh burning and dripping blood. Swallowing a whimper, I push broken glass away and kneel beside the case, still stupidly barefoot from climbing the Narrows.

As I move to retrieve the bow, carefully avoiding the glass's serrated edges, a shriek rends the air. I clap my hands over my ears. The big cracks in the glass deepen, their veins branching through the glass. My blood patters on the ground, regular as a leaky tap.

What is that thing?

Reaching into the case, I collect the bow off the ground and test its string with my thumb. It's weak, but the restoration hemp string will do for the moment. The bow's made of yew wood the color of yellow peppers, smooth to the touch. The quiver's top-grain leather, stitched and waxed, and holds some twenty-five goose-feather arrows. I pull an arrow out to make sure it's not a blank, relieved to see a reproduction iron arrowhead at the end of the shaft. Iron isn't cheap these days, either. No Earth resource can be mined easily; while we can still send people in EVA suits to the planet's surface to recover materials, the operations are expensive.

Thank you, Mami, for your insistence on historical accuracy.

Thank you, Dad, for teaching me how to shoot a bow.

Light ripples on the other side of the cracked glass. A pale being stalks by on all fours, dragging its knuckles along the ground. Small hiccuping noises burst from its throat. My hands shake as I nock the arrow and rest the bow on the tops of my thighs, one hand keeping the arrow in place, the other ready on the string. Every heartbeat feels like a tiny explosion in my chest. My adrenaline spikes.

What the hell is that thing?

Did we find extraterrestrial life?

. . . Or did it find us?

The creature's starved angles and ropy, inhuman muscle refract in the broken glass. It pauses on the other side of the floatglass case, cocking its bald head, its back to me. Big, bony spikes stick out of its vertebrae.

Move along, you ugly chupacabra . . . está bien . . . just walk away . . .

Then it screams. The sound barrels over the ground, a shock wave that's got mass, shape, and sharp edges. The floatglass case implodes in front of me, glass blasting in my direction. My hands jump from my bow to my face, shielding my eyes from the barrage. The shards clip my hands, my arms, and cut tiny red lines into my skin. I fall backward onto my tailbone with a grunt.

The creature whirls on me, growling. The sound has heft, slicing off a section of my hair. I take in too many details at once: the creature's white, flaky skin covered in pus-filled boils; its teeth jutting from its jaw like jagged shale fragments; its eyes crusted shut, nose flattened and half-gone. When its throat balloons, the flesh turns yellow and translucent.

But the most frightening thing about the monster? Its . . . no, *his* golden wedding band glinting on his left hand.

No way he was human. No. Way.

I grab my bow. He coils back like a compressed spring, chest swelling, getting ready to shriek at me. My hand tightens on the bow's grip, but when I try to lift it, one corner gets stuck on the floatglass case. With no room to draw and no time to aim, I jam my foot against the bow's limb and push forward, releasing the string when it bites into my fingers. I fire.

The arrow catches the creature in the roof of the mouth and slams out the back of his skull, dark matter and bone clinging to the arrowhead.

He collapses to the floor.

I spend about 0.23 seconds gasping, then scramble away from the floatglass case, bow in hand, and toss the quiver's strap over one shoulder. With a quick scan of the hall, I limp toward the bridge, picking my way through the worst of the devastation.

What the hell?

What. The. Actual. Hell?

He was human!

What happened to him?

Stumbling forward, I keep watch for sharp objects along the floor, skirting broken cases and knocking away chunks of floatglass with my toes. As I approach the bulkhead, I walk under the shattered vault that used to house the Declaration of Independence. The top of the case broke off in the crash. Long spikes of broken glass reach for me as I pass, fragments falling on my shoulders.

When I look back, the Declaration's case hangs by a fistful of cables through a hole in the case's side. It turns, glinting in the low light.

All my parents' hard work, destroyed in an instant. We may be able to salvage some of this, but not all. Not even most.

With a sob, I limp as fast as I can for the bridge.

As I move past the bulkhead, I hear my mother's voice echoing through the bridge: ". . . Find us."

"Mami?" I call out, my spirits lifting. I hurry past the bulkhead. My hopes shatter like little sugar skulls when I see a projection of my mother shooting out of a portaScreen node placed on the floor, and not the woman in the flesh.

Mami's image stands about as tall as she does in life, a compact 165 centimeters. I still remember the day I grew taller than her, and she grumbled about me taking after my father. Her bright aureole of bleached-blond curls glows like a saint's halo in the portaScreen's light. Mami looks bloodied, but the fierce cast of her eyes hasn't changed a bit.

She survived the crash. Tears press against my eyes and I don't bother to blink them away.

Beyond her, darkness looms. The *Conquistador* is wrenched

open like an old tin can. The bridge is busted, entire shears of metal are bent up like teeth in a prehistoric shark's mouth, or rolled up in crazy spirals like snail shells. The *Conquistador* hit the *John Muir* so hard, the ships have merged together.

"Attention all crew and staff," Mami's projection says, straightening a bit. "For reasons we're currently still investigating, the *Conquistador* has crashed and is presumed to be unsalvageable. Due to the failure of our bioware systems, those of you who didn't make it into an emergency pod remain unaccounted for—"

Mami's voice wobbles. She presses the back of her hand against her mouth, composing herself. I've never seen her even teeter on the brink of losing her composure, not once in my life.

"No, Mami," I say to her image, taking a step toward her. It takes all my courage to suppress the fear rising through my chest. "Don't tell me you left me here, alone."

After a long moment, she composes herself. "I've taken the sixty-odd survivors into the *John Muir*, as the ship appears to have viable life support. Follow us. We'll be marking our path every five meters with phosphorescent paint. We've left some supplies, including flashlights and shortwave radios." Her image gestures to a now-empty box, which means I wasn't the only crew member to be left behind. It was probably full of things Dad kept "on hand" because old-world tech could be useful in emergencies. But people like us—prepared, professional, and practiced—aren't *supposed* to have emergencies.

My lip quivers.

I couldn't be *left behind*, my family doesn't *leave* people behind.

No.

I'm alone against the darkness, to cross dangerous terrain without bioware support, an EVA suit, medical supplies, or even a proper weapon. I hug myself tight. In all my life, I have *never* been alone. Not like this. I look down at my feet. My toes are blackened with dirt and soot, and crusted with blood. I don't even have the proper *shoes* for adventuring, but don't dare try to get back to my quarters. Not with the *Conquistador* failing by the second.

"And Laura?" Mami's image says.

I lift my head.

"We looked for you," she says, her face crumpling. She swallows a sob. "In every accessible part of the ship. In my heart of hearts, I don't want to believe you're gone, corazón."

I want to scream at her, *I was behind a floatglass case in the Hall of Artifacts! Fifty meters from where you recorded this message! I. Was. Right. Here!*

All I can muster is a whisper: "But you still left me."

"If you're alive and watching this, follow the markers," Mami says, wiping her eyes. "They will lead you to your father and me."

"How?" I ask. "You could be hours ahead of me, lost in a ship as large as a torus colony." There's no one to consult with, no maps of the *John Muir*'s tunnels, no way to prepare myself for whatever's out there.

As if Mami anticipated this response, she says, "You can do this, Laura. Never forget, you're a Cruz. Our ancestors tamed the stars. Find us. Find *me*."

Her message winks out.

"Dammit!" I say, pressing the heels of my hands against my

face. My tears gush and burn. I whip my hands down, flinging them off my skin.

All my life, I've had my family around me. Supporting me. Guiding me. Protecting me. Never have I faced any sort of real danger alone—I've always had Mami's hand on my shoulder, or Dad at my back; one of the tíos on the communicator; or my older brother, Gael, holding a rope out to me in the darkness. I've always had Tía Rosa to tell my secrets to; or my abuela to wrap me in a blanket after a difficult raid. And now I'm left to wonder how many of them survived the crash, only to follow their ghosts into the darkness of a strange ship.

On one level, I understand why Mami had to leave—she's the captain, after all. People look to her for leadership, and it's not like she could risk the lives of the remaining crew to look for her missing daughter. On the other hand, she's my *mother*, the woman who's protected me my whole life long. But to think not even my brother, or Alex, or even Faye stayed behind, to be left for dead by everyone I love . . . it aches, as if I'm using my own fingernails to tear through my flesh and rip my heart out, piece by piece.

Of course, it's possible none of those people survived the crash, and that thought aches twice as much. If I ever want to see my family or friends again, I will have to venture into the *John Muir*.

Alone.

And to think I ever wished for adventure.

"You can do this, Laura," my mother's voice echoes through the bridge's empty chaos as the message plays again. "Never forget, you're a Cruz."

Fortuna, gloria, y familia.

You're a Cruz. My ancestors were among the first to leave the Colonies, searching for the history we'd lost to the stars. They were explorers and adventurers, masters of physics, and great storytellers of history. While not every Cruz has fallen in love with shipraiding, it still *feels* like a family tradition. So much so that, when the day came for me to enroll at the uni, I chose to enroll under my *mother's* surname, Cruz, and not my father's name, which would have been a more traditional choice. I suppose the move was political, too, knowing my mother will choose one of her children to succeed her someday, and that Gael has no interest in running the Cruz outfit.

I do.

You can do this.

Using an arrowhead to cut the top half of my flight suit away, I make bandages from the extra fabric. I tie several wide bands around the hole in my thigh. When I stand again, the pain's less intense. With only a tank top and bra underneath, I shudder in the cold.

There's one other thing my mother left behind, something I can't bear to leave.

I trudge back through the Rio Grande bulkhead, my eyes on the Declaration's case. Of all the artifacts on display, it's the only one small enough to take with me into the *John Muir*, and the only thing I might be able to save.

Nocking an arrow, I take aim and fire straight into the cables. They hold. I fire a second arrow, then a third, till the cables rip and the case falls. When it hits the floor, the floatglass shatters.

The sound's dampened by the lack of air pressure in the tunnel, but still makes my shoulders rack up around my ears. I glance over my shoulder.

Nothing moves.

Taking a knee, I remove the remaining floatglass shards from the Declaration. It's a large artifact—almost a meter in length—but light. If my father caught me touching it bare-handed, he'd probably murder me on the spot. I don't know how long it took Dad to restore this document. Days. Weeks. I doubt he even breathed on it while he worked.

And here I am, cradling the fragile parchment in my bare, dirty hands. I don't dare fold the thing. Carrying it in my hands seems foolhardy. I need some sort of transporter tube or case. We have lots of tubes in the stockroom . . . which lies on the other side of the ship. I won't have time to reach them, not when the air pressure has dipped so low it's hard to breathe.

I cast around for something, anything I can use to protect the artifact. My elbow hits the side of my quiver, and an idea forms half a second after. Setting the Declaration aside, I swing the quiver off my shoulder and remove the arrows inside.

The quiver stands taller than the Declaration is wide. It's not an ideal transportation method for a six-hundred-year-old document, but it'll have to do.

Holding my breath, I roll the Declaration into a tube, then slide it into my quiver. To keep the document safe, I tuck some of the artifact's mounting materials inside, too: a piece of bio-engineered vellum that will hydrate the parchment and keep it from drying out and cracking; a flexible sheet of clear titanium, one that will keep my arrowheads from scratching or damaging the document; and a hunk of gauze at the bottom to keep everything in place.

With the artifact stowed safely away—or at least safely *enough*—I sling the quiver over my shoulder and rise. Stringing my bow over my chest, I trudge back through the bulkhead, past Mami's message, and toward the wreckage of the *John Muir*. Unprepared. Unready. But not unafraid.

Heading toward the unknown.

TUCK

I wake up slowly.

In the dark unknown.

A cold breeze curls inside my hood.

Metal creaks in the darkness.

Dripping water echoes in the hollow space around me. Each *plop* sends ripples of pain through my skull. I can feel every centimeter of the harness that keeps me bolted to my seat. The side of my head aches. My flesh is gashed open. Tender. When I reach up to touch it, I find my hair thatched over the wound.

What . . . the . . . hell happened?

I wipe condensation off my face with one hand. I remember fire. And falling. Holly, screaming.

"*Holly?*" I ask, wringing a few words from my groggy brain. "*You there?*"

Silence.

"*Hey . . . answer me!*"

Nothing.

"Dejah, hello?"

No answer, no luck. No stir, no hum in my head. The ebb and flow of images, thoughts, and emotions fed to me via the coglinks lies silent. I haven't been this alone in ages.

Frag me.

With a shaking hand, I reach for one of the flares sewn onto my slimpack. I bend its plastic body, snapping its insides like bone. Light bleeds out, casting a green glow on everything within a five-meter radius.

I'm in the tram car, which seems to be perched at a sharp angle on a chunk of tunnel procrete. Water simmers below, black as crude oil. It looks like the deepdown sea—a massive water well that spans the outer deck of the *Muir*'s deepdown ring. If the deepdown sea is visible, I've fallen through not one, but *two* of the ship's decks.

That was one helluva distraction, Aren. Whatever his plan had been, this couldn't have been the outcome he'd been hoping for—situation normal: all fragged up.

The sights sucker punch me. Shattered chunks of the *Muir*'s tunnels thrust out of the darkness like eldritch teeth. Apocalyptic. Busted tram tracks roller-coaster in the air. Cavernous moans reverberate through the space. This time, *this busted time* should've been the end. Nobody deserves this kind of luck, to wake up in time to watch the last star of hope explode. Who knows what systems went down with the tunnels? We might've lost mission-critical stuff. Life support. Air pressure. Heating coils. From where I hang, the *Muir* doesn't look salvageable.

No way she'll survive a fallout this bad.

If the ship doesn't survive, neither will we.

The coglinks aren't functional, so the ship's power grid must be down. Neither the ship nor the park will last long without power. Six hours, tops. The air reclaimers stagnate without an energy supply, so the park will suffocate from an excess of carbon dioxide. Without heat, everything will freeze. Without the tram systems, the other curators won't be able to reach the main power hives for hours—assuming the power hives aren't also damaged. Depending on my location, I'll need to get either the main or auxiliary power hives back online. Or else *hasta la vista, baby.* We'll all die.

The good news? Our gravitational rings haven't failed . . . or else I wouldn't be hanging here like a little glitch. Good on you, Mom, for making those rings store solar power. My solar *plexus* is thanking you right now.

Since no one's coming to save the ship's damsel-in-distressed ass—or mine, for that matter—I should probably get to work. And quick.

Holding my flare high, I glance around me. "Holly?" I whisper.

The seats behind me are empty. *Dammit, where is she? Did she wake up first? Nah, I don't think she'd leave me here.* As much as I don't want Holly to be dead, the *Muir* desperately depends on her being alive. Two people need to turn the keys in the power hives to bring the ship back online after a crash. I can't save the *Muir* without another set of hands, and I have a feeling the mourners won't oblige.

"Holly?" I hiss, a little louder this time. No answer.

I put a hand on my harness's release. My lungs and guts tighten, shallowing up my breathing. I fight to take a deep breath. Yank the release tab.

The harness dumps me onto the seats in front of me.

I lie still for a few seconds. Blood's on my tongue. My chest's bruised so deep, I feel like the harness's straps still dig into my skin.

The tram groans, a tired, low creak that aches in my teeth. It wobbles on an unsteady fulcrum of procrete. Even a small shift in its center of gravity could send it plummeting into the deepdown sea. But I've already been on that ride, and spoiler alert, it *sucked*.

I scoot toward the aisle, slow and steady, then climb the sides of the seats like a ladder. The tram senses every shift in my weight and complains.

When I don't find Holly curled atop the seats, I curse under my breath and check the seats across the aisle. The girl's gone without a trace. She left no blood, no swatch of fabric, no proof of life. I've got to find her. Best-case scenario, she woke up before me, maybe thought I was dead, and moved on. Worst case, she was thrown from the tram in the fall. She could've ended up anywhere in the wreckage.

I drop my flare, counting the number of seconds it takes to hit the water. *One. Two.* I make a quick calculation in my head, figuring I'm fifteen meters above the surface. If I make a mistake free-climbing the tram, the water's surface tension won't feel like hitting procrete at that height. Unless the water's real shallow or hiding metal spikes under its surface, it's a survivable fall.

Striking a second flare, I crawl out of the tram's window. I wish the power grid hadn't gone down with the tunnels. Wish I could call Holly's name aloud out here, too, but if I endured the fall, so did the mourners.

Ignoring how the metal squeals, I pull myself onto the tram's roof. The back half of the tram's caught between two slabs of procrete. I climb the crag with clumsy, cold fingers. The grade isn't steep. The edges drop off into nothingness, though. Blackness, a sort of darkness we didn't have on Earth.

A perfect pitch dark. A complete absence of light. Void-like. Terrible.

I spend the better part of an hour searching for Holly among the ruins. There's no evidence anyone's been here, no curators, no mourners. She's disappeared, and with every minute that passes, my panic and frustration only ferment in my gut.

Where are you, Holly?

Eventually, I pull myself up onto the t-One tunnel's outer flank and find a large crack. I drop into the main pipeline, landing on the balls of my feet. My knee twinges.

Though I know the *Muir* better than anyone else, her ruins feel foreign. The tunnel's structural ribs—spaced ten meters apart—place hurdles in my path. Mourners croak somewhere in the darkness, making small, froglike sounds. They're searching for one another. Others make death rattles in the darkness. Their bodies clang against the tunnels ribs or whistle past me in the air as they fall.

Holding the flare high, I work my way up the tunnel. I freeze whenever a croak sounds close. The grade grows steeper with each rib. Soon I'm climbing again, wedging my hands and feet into cracks, resting on the ribs jutting out from the walls. I realize the tunnel must rejoin the aft deck at some point, but it's nowhere in sight.

As I pull myself up onto another ledge, something moves at

the edge of the flare's light. My hand goes to my knife. When I lift my flare higher, I realize it's not a mourner.

It's Holly.

She lies on a slab of procrete, half-crushed under a large boulder. Her dark hair spreads like an oil slick under her head. Wait, that's not her hair.

My lips open in an unspoken *no.*

No, no, no—not another one.

I scramble across the rib toward the blood-blackened procrete ridge she's on. Her breathing whistles, wet. The burst vessels in the whites of her eyes make them look diseased. Blood speckles her lips.

Christ, God, dammit, take me instead. She's just an innocent kid. Haven't enough people died on my watch?

Holly's eyes burn in the flare's light, fearful. I kneel beside her. My toes squelch in her blood. I lay a hand on her forehead. Her skin burns hot enough to blister. She trembles under my touch. A sheen of sweat clings to her brow. Her hair soaks up her blood. She looks so fragile, like the bones in her face are a cheap plastic shell.

With the ship's systems down, we can't communicate via our coglinks.

Holly squints at me, trying to see past the flare's brilliance. "*Tuck . . . ?*" she signs one-handed, forced to spell everything out letter by letter. Her other arm lies useless, broken in a compound fracture. The shattered bone thrusts from her skin, glistening. "*Don't . . . stay . . . mourners . . . close.*"

She's dying, and she's thinking about *my* welfare? I put my flare down.

"*I not leave you.*" My sign language isn't great, but I can read it okay. Aren made all curators learn it, just in case we needed to communicate in the deepdowns during a power failure. At the time, I blew the classes off.

I am the biggest asshole in the whole universe.

At this point, I'm not even certain that's much of an exaggeration.

"*Save . . . the . . . ship . . . ,*" Holly signs. "*The park . . . it's important . . .*"

"*I will. Ship survive.*"

"*Go . . . I . . . am . . . dead . . . already . . .*"

My hands hang in the empty space between us.

"*Survival . . . is . . . a . . . barbaric . . . thing,*" she says.

Why do the stupid things I say always come back to bite me in the ass?

Holly coughs. The sound echoes up the tunnel like an explosion. Blood splatters my arm. I cast my cloak around her body to shield her from the monsters. She uses the back of her good hand to wipe at her mouth.

Croaks and chirps tumble down the tunnel.

"*Go,*" she signs to me. "*But . . . before . . .*" Holly presses her dekapen into my hand. Most curators carry them—a single shot of barbiturates, paralytics, and potassium. But it's not the *nice,* yellow kind of potassium you used to find in bananas. It's part of a deadly cocktail, an escape hatch, a last resort.

Mercy on a stick.

My eyes widen. "*No.*" I shake my head. "*No.*" That's one word in sign language I know for sure.

"Please . . . can't . . . do . . . this . . . myself . . ."

"No," I sign as violently as I can. "No, not that."

Holly folds the pen in my fist, lifts it, and positions the tip over her jugular. Her fingers leave bloodstains on my skin. "Easy . . . ," she mouths, but her fingers tremble. "We . . . can . . . together . . ."

Tear tracks cut through the blood on her face. Her breath begins to wheeze. It's the very edge of a sob, held back. The sound's trapped in her throat.

"Please . . . ," she mouths.

The croaks of the mourners crawl closer. My fingers curl tight around the dekapen.

I can't take her life.

I won't leave her alone.

But I've got to get the power back on.

Clock's ticking. Tick. Tock.

I can't look in her eyes and do this, I can't, even if killing her looks like mercy and will get me out of this damned tunnel with my honor intact and with enough time to save the ship and everyone on it, so maybe I don't lose the rest of them tonight, too.

We're all so lost out here.

Forgotten.

Alone.

I lean down and press my mouth to Holly's, tasting her blood, her sweat, her saliva, and the last few seconds of her life. It's the only way to articulate any kind of human affection and warmth in this dark place.

She deepens the kiss, mouth opening to meet mine. Her

chest expands as she takes one last breath. My hand shakes and sweats. She slips her good hand into my hair, down my neck, and finally, grasps my hand that holds the dekapen.

Her fingers squeeze mine.

Don't miss, I tell myself. *For the love of God, don't miss.*

L A U R A

After the crash, the *Conquistador*'s smarthull melded itself to the terrarium ship, creating a tight seam . . . or so I hope. The closer I get to the big ship, the stronger the gravity becomes. The first phosphorescent arrow painted on the floor glows near the maw of the *John Muir*, left behind by Mami's crew. The path tilts down at a twenty-degree angle, the arrow pointing into the ship's throaty, unbroken shadows.

I creep toward the tunnel, careful of my bare feet and the crash debris, nocking an arrow. With each step, pain stabs into the wound on my thigh. A breeze whooshes by me, eager to escape into the *Conquistador* and beyond that, space. It's so cold, the air plucks my skin and leaves gooseflesh in its wake. It smells peppery, like carbon and blood. The scent wakens some primal knowledge in me, one telling me to *run*. Leave this place. But I can't. As Dad would say, quoting some old poet, *the only way out is through*.

The light strangles where the ships meet, the fascia of one

of the *John Muir*'s tunnels ripped away. Inside, the floor drops about two meters. The big ship's viscera hang from the ceiling, ducts and tubes and cords, now barely contained by an arched support beam. The metal walls wear rust, but otherwise stand bare. Shipbuilders didn't start using the sensitive nanoparticle paint until about two hundred years ago, so it's what I expected from an Exodus-era craft.

At the bottom, three human-shaped lumps lie in ponds of blood. Guts blister out of abdomens. Chunks of bone lay scattered about like jagged, broken glass. One man's been decapitated, his head resting on its ear a meter away. Their flight suits, while shredded, bear both the rearing Cruz lion and the Panamerican flag. Their faces are too ravaged to recognize, especially since they lie deep in the darkness.

Nothing moves. My breath snags on a skipped heartbeat.

Blinking back tears, I lift some tubing aside and ease down into the tunnel below. My bow's bottom edge rattles against the shorn metal lip of the ship. I land inside the *John Muir* with a *whump*, then creep around the bodies and gore on the floor.

"What did this to you?" I ask them.

I spot my answer in another step: a fourth corpse rests down here, one with sagging pale skin and tattered clothing. A trail of black blood leaks out of the plasma bolt hole in the monster's skull. Its rib cage looks too big, the skin no thicker than a papery membrane over the bones. In the fleshier places, the lower back and buttocks, the creature's pores resemble Dad's Great Barrier Reef coral fossils, the surfaces bleached pale. A few holes yawn so wide, I could almost stick my pinkie finger inside.

The corpse looks like the chupacabra I saw back on the *Conquistador*, the one who broke floatglass with a weapon no more potent than a scream.

I glance at the corpses behind me.

Now I know what happens when the full extent of those screams hit flesh.

Rusty footprints lead into the tunnel, some of the tracks no more than smears. Everything beyond the corpses lies dark, except for the hand-drawn arrow floating about ten meters up ahead.

I reach out to touch the tunnel wall. My hand shakes. The metal surface feels like sandpaper. Rust sloughs off under my fingertips. Maybe Mami believes in me, but my confidence comes up short when walking into the darkness, alone. Mami has a lion's heart and the survival experience to handle a situation like this. As for me, my heart beats like a rabbit's.

A thousand bad things could hide in that darkness: monsters who kill with a scream. Crash debris that could bite into my bare feet. I could wander forever and never find my parents. Or I might stumble over their corpses. I suppose the crew will have to come back to the *Conquistador* at some point, but standing still will probably get me killed. Even if the monsters don't find me first, the plunging temperature and thinning air supply will. Survival means moving forward.

"Okay," I whisper to myself. *Fortune and glory, Laura.* "Just take a single step"—and I do—"there, that wasn't hard. Now another, está bien."

I talk myself into the darkness. My voice gets quieter as the shadows draw me in, wrapping themselves around me, shutting out all visual stimuli. They silence me. The light at the tunnel opening fades into a small bruise on the darkness. I reach Mami's second arrow and keep walking, my hand striking a tunnel support strut every ten meters or so. For every two or three struts I pass, I'm rewarded with another arrow in the darkness.

Reaching out, I run my fingers over the paint. It turns to dust under my fingers, long dry.

Está bien, it's okay. I'm okay, I'm okay, I tell myself.

My footsteps whisper off the walls. The ship groans as if it aches, and far away, a scream cuts through the tunnels. I freeze, but I can't know if the sound's organic, human, or otherwise. Taps and knocks echo from inside the walls and underfoot. Every few seconds, the floor shudders. The temperature climbs the farther I descend into the ship.

Without warning, the wall stops. My hand shoots into empty space and I freeze. Gasp. A weak cross breeze tumbles over my exposed skin, tugging at the loose hairs at the nape of my neck. I'm in an intersection between tunnels, I think. I scramble back a step, heart pounding until my hand finds the wall again, my lifeline.

If I get lost in this darkness, I'll never find my parents. I'll never get out. I'll die here.

I slide one hand over the wall till I find its edge, then place my second hand on the corner to anchor myself. I peer down the corridors. None of Mami's arrows glow on my right. Straight ahead, nada. To the left, there's a smudge of phosphorlight in the distance. With no whistle of air here, I can only hope I'm walking away from the crash damage, and not toward more.

It's not that far away. I step away from the wall, keeping my gaze focused on the bright spot in front of me, unable to gauge the distance between me and safety. *You can do this.*

I'm deep across the intersection, moving unguided through empty space, when something croaks. I halt, my muscles locking up with fear.

That sounded close. I swallow down my heart as it tries to beat its way up my trachea. One of those pale monsters stalks into my imagination, the front of its throat swelling up like a toad's. Cold sweat condenses on my palms, and I wrap my arms around my stomach, not daring to move.

The second croak comes from my right. The ship's rounded tunnel walls make it difficult to judge the distance between the creatures and me. I press the side of my hand into my mouth, biting down to suppress a gasp. I don't know much about these monsters, but they're not deaf. Over the years, they must've gotten used to hunting in darkness.

Bueno, but hunting what? I ask myself, easing forward with both hands out in front of me. *Or whom? Has anyone survived out here, or do they just eat each other?*

My hands stumble into another wall. I feel my way along until I reach another large support strut, slip behind it, and press my back to the chilly metal. My bow makes a quiet *click*. I curse myself for forgetting I'm wearing it on my back.

The monsters' footsteps drag along the floor. Their giggles bloom in the darkness like spots of sonic mold. I pull an arrow from my quiver, trying not to make a sound. The arrows' fletchings rasp against one another. When one's free, I finger the arrowhead, not minding when it cuts a shallow line into my thumb.

I squeeze my eyes closed—it makes no difference if they're open anyway—and wait. My heart beats hard. My knees tremble. At any second, I expect to hear a scream. I expect darkness to slice through my skin and seep into my consciousness.

One wanders close, its snuffles and short croaks no more than three paces back. I grip the arrow in my fist, thinking of how quick that pale flesh rips, and how easily their blood spills . . . and how impossible it will be to hit a mortal spot in the dark.

The monster knocks on the other side of my strut, letting out a half cry: *"Grraaak."* The sound reverberates through the metal, making my teeth vibrate. Its fingers make sucking noises against the metal strut.

This isn't happening, this isn't happening, I tell myself. *Don't move, don't move, don't move. . . .*

My stomach squelches and groans, angry and empty. *¡Cállate!* I snap at myself. *Shut up!* The traitorous sound rumbles through the tunnel.

Two or three curious calls bound off the walls in response. The monster's fingers brush my shoulder. My next heartbeat spikes through every extremity in my body. I will myself not to move, not to gasp, not to cry.

As jagged nails prick my exposed skin, a shout echoes through the tunnel.

The voice sounds baritone range. Masculine.

Human.

And it's coming from the opposite direction of Mami's bread-crumb arrows.

With a cry, the monster launches itself off the strut, running toward the sound. Its companion croaks, hands and feet beating the metal floor like drums in pursuit. I wait for several seconds, giving them the lead; but if that shout came from a human being, he must be one of the *Conquistador*'s crew members. And if he's one of ours, he's as good as family.

What kind of Cruz would I be, were I to stand aside and let him die?

Another scream rips through the air. Keeping one hand on the wall, I take off at a half jog, half limp, following the screams.

TUCK

When I reach the main deepdown tunnels, I let a scream rip and rage. For Holly. For me. For every poor bastard who died on this ship. For the hopeful and the hopeless.

I don't care if they hear.

And they do.

A mourner stumbles into the flare's pod of light. It's twitchier than most, head shaking so bad its neck bones crack. It shambles sideways on its knuckles and feet. Clicking. Trilling. It gobbles up air in little giggles, rib cage expanding until its flesh turns translucent. Black lungs inflate between its bones.

I scream at it first, preempting the beast. It halts, confused. Chucking my flare on the ground, I backhand the monster's face, slamming it into the tunnel wall. Its head bounces back from the procrete, body swiveling like a punching bag. I grab it by the head and twist. Violent. Fragile neck bones crack under the force of the blow.

I let go. The mourner's body *whumps* against the floor, an empty sack of meat. *Screw you and screw this ship. I'm done.*

Another mourner—this asshole's faster, more lithe—comes charging into the light. It growls at me. The sound cuts my forearm in three places and shreds my cloak's edge. Yanking my knife from its shoulder sheath, I throw it. The blade catches the mourner in its swelling throat sac.

I breathe heavily for a few seconds. The creature gasps around the steel lodged in its trachea. It stumbles to the ground, thick blood splattering over the metal floor. It's just as red as the stuff dripping off my fingertips. Thirty-seven degrees, too, as it spreads around my toes. Warm as mine.

Our doctors proved it's still 99 percent human. A few tiny tweaks to the genome turn people into terrors. These creatures aren't alien.

They're *us*.

Us, with the stories ripped from our skulls.

Us, with the empathy drained from our hearts.

Us, with the spark of curiosity and logic and pursuit of knowledge, gone.

People stripped of everything that makes us human, made animal, primal. *Alive.*

Falling to my knees, I yank my knife from the corpse. Scraping noises emerge from the darkness, knuckles knocking across the floor. I lift my head, wishing I could feel anything but cold fury. Loneliness. Or hate.

Another mourner crawls into the light, chittering. It's smaller than most of the others, younger maybe, with strands of yellow hair clinging to its chalky scalp. Cocking its head, it looks at me with a mourner's eyeless, direct gaze.

"I thought there would be some relief in it," I tell her, because her longish hair makes me think she was female once. "In killing, in taking something back."

With a click, her jaw dislocates. She growls, her lips retracting back over her gray, craggy teeth. Her chest swells, her throat ballooning. She's so close, I can see the black mandibles in her throat rubbing against each other. One click from those guns and I'm dead at point-blank range.

"Spoiler alert," I say to her, chuckling. "I still feel like shit."

The mourner's spine arches like a cat's. I close my eyes. At least I get to choose, here and now. If I can't tempt fate, I'll force her hand.

As the mourner steps forward to release the scream, there's a sharp whistle. A crack. I open my eyes. The mourner collapses backward, an arrow shaft sticking out of her eye socket. The creature gurgles, her pale fingers flexing, before she goes still.

"Good *hell*, are you serious?" I rise and whirl, and the sight strikes me dumb:

A girl stands at the edge of my flare's light, her bowstring quivering.

I've never seen her before.

So that's not weird; the *Muir* had ten thousand people aboard at liftoff. I knew maybe fifty of them. But nobody I know would be stupid enough to run the ship's deepdowns wearing anything but stiflecloth. And here she is, dressed in khaki cargo pants and a white tank. Her skin's blackened with soot. A dirty, blood-soaked bandage is tied around one of her thighs.

This girl wasn't on the *Muir* at takeoff.

She didn't survive hundreds of years in a stasis pod.

She's an *outsider*.

The rage drains out of my body. My mouth drops open. I take a step back. Wonder if she's a hallucination made of grief and fury and a desperate wish, or a need to hope for something better than death. She lowers her bow, her eyes so wide I can see their whites.

Someone found us.

Someone.

Found.

Us.

PART TWO

THE

DEEPDOWNS

Almost nothing is known of Pitch Dark's modus operandi, but evidence points to a grassroots organization with little to no hierarchal structure. This form of "leaderless resistance"—with cells that operate without a centralized authority to direct their activities—has proven difficult for law enforcement to infiltrate or terminate. It's thought that Pitch Dark cells have recaptured the lost art of handwriting, or have taken the bulk of their activities offline. In this case, archaic human technology is trumping modern advances, which is an ironic if not unforeseen twist of fate.

Our lack of knowledge about how the organization operates, combined with members' almost fanatical devotion to their beliefs, is why the organization continues to dominate the landscape of Panamerican fear well into this century.

FROM *ON FEAR AND FANATICISM: HOW PITCH DARK MAINTAINS
ITS RELEVANCE IN THE TWENTY-FIFTH CENTURY*
LAURA MARÍA SALVATIERRA CRUZ
SENIOR CAPSTONE THESIS, ABRIL 2432

LAURA

No manches, it's not possible.

A boy stands before me. A *human* boy . . . or at least he looks human.

Not. Possible.

His flare throws spitting, erratic light from the floor, casting his eyes in shadow. He must be about eighteen—maybe just a year or two older than me—but his gaze looks ancient. Tired. He stands almost as tall as Sebastian, but with a more muscular chest and broader shoulders, and his skin looks as white as scar tissue. He's barefoot, his chest heaving, blood splattered across his forehead and coating his fists. The crimson-black stuff drips off his knife's point.

The boy reaches up and tugs the balaclava mask off his face. His hood falls back, revealing short, thick brown hair. Jaw slack and eyes wide, he doesn't try to disguise his shock and awe. The emotions seem so human, so plain. He's so pale I'm guessing his skin hasn't had a good dose of melanin in maybe ever. He almost looks . . . *bleached*. Ghostly, even in the flare's eerie light.

My mind whirls: *How did humans survive four centuries lost to deep space? On the far fringes of the universe, orbiting no star, with no planet to support their resources? What about disease? Does he harbor germs or parasites we've eradicated? My bioware's nonfunctional, which means my boosted immunity's down—what if he makes me sick?*

And the most important question: *Is he one of* them? One of the knuckle-dragging monsters that break floatglass and rend flesh with sound?

The thought galvanizes me. I yank an arrow from my quiver and nock it, the muscle memory coming back smoothly now that I've had a little practice. The boy's gaze drops to the arrowhead, but he doesn't look frightened of the weapon, no matter what he just saw me do. He lifts his hands in the air. Cool. Calm.

The action's so human, I'm almost convinced to point my bow at the ground, rather than at him. When threatened, it's easy to kill a monster, a creature with no discernible humanity. Harder to kill something—no, someone—who looks and acts like a living, breathing human being.

"Wh-who are you?" I whisper, my voice barely louder than my bowstring's creak. "Did you see people passing by here? Please, I'm following—"

He slices a finger across his throat, points at the corpses bleeding out on the ground, then taps his ear. Lifting his hands, he makes a few clumsy hand gestures, maybe trying to speak sign language to me, I'm not sure.

I shake my head. Nobody's spoken sign language in hundreds

of years, not since Panamerican doctors discovered how to regrow human organs in labs. My own little sister, Sofía, had her vocal cords regrown three years ago after an accident on an archeological dig.

A wail echoes down the tunnel, coming from the direction my parents went. The boy turns, moving like liquid, with no seams or sound. The ripples in the fabric of his cloak fall still around his feet with unnatural speed. He listens for three seconds, cocking his head, and then scoops his flare off the floor.

He makes a motion that, no matter what language you speak, means *follow me*. Holding his flare aloft, he disappears down a corridor I hadn't noticed before.

As the light fades away—and the monsters' calls grow closer—I'm forced to make a split-second decision: *Follow a stranger, or try to find my mother's trail?* I glance over my shoulder, barely able to see the light from one of Mami's arrows. If I die here and now, I *know* I will never see my family again. Seeing them in the future means surviving *now*.

I turn to follow the boy in the cape.

TUCK

The girl follows me to the closest panic room.

Damn my luck. I lose one girl, only to find another in the tunnels. Really, I'm thrilled to see another human being. Just delighted. It means I'll have someone to turn the power hives' keys with. But it also means I'm going to have to find a way to get a newb through the deepdown tunnels without her getting us both killed.

We're pretty much screwed.

. . . But I would like to know where the *hell* she came from.

The curators' panic room is a half klick away. The panic rooms are soundproofed, with walls covered with large bricks of anechoic foam. They're stocked with medical supplies, food, and water, as well as cots and bathroom facilities. We'll be safe enough inside, able to communicate, even. Assuming she speaks more than a little English. For all I know, she's from the future.

No, not *from* the future. I'm from her past.

Or something.

Dammit.

With the ship's power offline, I have to open the door by hand. Handing the flare to the new girl, I take an analog crank out of my pack and insert it between the door's iris panels. Then I pump till the crank expands, pushing those door panels back into the wall. It takes a lot of effort to move them at all.

The flare's light fades as the new girl holds it higher, turning in a circle. Almost as if she's . . . *examining* the place. She mouths words, reading an emergency evacuation procedure off a plaque on the wall. Exploring, maybe?

Hey, girl. I snap my fingers at her without a sound, pointing at the open door.

She gives me *the* finger.

I grin. Glad to see some things never change. *"Ladies first,"* I mouth at her.

Glaring at me, the new girl ducks under the crank's legs and into the panic room. I follow her.

Two steps after the door clicks closed, she drops the flare and whirls on me. Bow up, arrow loaded. Or nocked or whatever. The flare's light ices the arrowhead's edges in green.

"Well, nice to meet you too, sweetheart," I say, eyeing the bow.

Her arrowhead drops a centimeter. "You speak English?"

Thank God people in the future still do. "Sorry, did you expect Martian?" I snipe back, walking toward her. She pulls her bowstring taut. The bow's wood creaks, and the thing must be a thousand years old if it's a day.

"Nobody speaks Martian," she replies. "We haven't managed to terraform the planet yet."

"It was a joke," I say, checking my impulse to roll my eyes. "And would you put that down, please? I'm not going to hurt you, and you're not going to shoot me."

"Says who?" Her accent's different, softer, and more melodious than English used to be. It sounds as if some of the consonants in American English have merged with Romance-language equivalents, probably Spanish and Portuguese. English sounds prettier rolling off her tongue than it does mine.

I reach out, putting my finger on the arrowhead. It nips my skin as I push it down, taking the bow with it. "Says the guy who just saved your ass from a pack of mourners."

She tsks. "Last time I checked, *I* saved *yours*. What are those things?"

"I'll get to the mourners in a second," I say, tugging my balaclava down. I'm spitballing here, but only a crash would've caused the shite heap of trouble we're now in. "Because let me tell you, my partner's dead because of you and your rogue ship."

Hey, that's only sort of a lie.

The girl's eyes widen. "The crash wasn't my fault," she says, voice shaking. "This ship's *priceless*, I would never have done anything to harm it—"

"So it *was* a crash?" I ask.

She nods.

"What happened?"

"A hacker seized control of my parents' ship and drove it into yours." Her gaze flicks away, just for an instant, making me wonder if she's lying. "I would never do anything to threaten your ship, I swear."

"Yeah, okay. Relax." I let go of the arrowhead, trying to shake the impression that she's pretty. No, more than *pretty*: The sun itself seems to radiate from her, glowing from every centimeter of her brown skin. There a keen intelligence in her eyes, and the muscles in her arms and back betray the toughness beneath her exterior. But what gets me? Her hair's black as obsidian at the crown but melts into a rich brown at the tips. It looks soft as feathers, especially the long curls cascading from her ponytail.

I haven't seen long hair on a girl in *ages*. The women on the *Muir* keep their hair short for water conservation.

No doubt I make her nervous. Hell, if I were her, *I'd* make me nervous. I must have ten centimeters and at least thirty kilograms on her. Not to mention her *great-great*-double-dog-dare-you-*great*-*grandparents* are younger than me. Unless humanity's figured out immortality, her greats are very, *very* dead.

"What's your name?" I ask.

She looks me up and down, easing a step backward. Those big brown eyes of hers narrow a few millimeters.

"Okay, sorry, I'll go first. Been a while since I've met anyone new," I say, putting my palms up, trying to look as nonthreatening as possible. "The name's Tuck. I'm a member of the *John Muir*'s original crew. Four hundred years ago, our ship was hijacked and jettisoned into deep space. We woke up from stasis twenty-two months ago. Well, *some* of us did. . . ."

Her bow lowers a little bit with each word, along with her jaw. Her lips make a perfect little O shape.

"What?" I ask.

"You were born on Earth?" she whispers. "Not here, on the ship?"

"If I say yes, will you put the bow down?"

"Well, I wouldn't be much of an archeologist if I shot and killed a human *relic*, now would I?" she says, replacing the arrow in its quiver and stringing the bow around her chest. She pulls her hair away from the bow, letting the ends rest on her left shoulder.

"Human *relic*?" I ask, rubbing the back of my neck with one hand. "Next thing, you're going to be telling me I belong in a museum."

"Most ancient history does," she says, arching a brow and putting her hands on her hips.

"Oh, so I'm ancient now?" I ask. A grin tugs one corner of her mouth. "I promise I'll be much more interesting *outside* a museum, Dr. Jones."

"We'll see about that," she says, extending her hand. "Laura Cruz. My family runs a raiding outfit that searches for the lost Exodus ships—"

"*Ships?* As in plural?" I ask, only half-distracted by how good the name *Laura* sounds when pronounced with a Spanish accent. *Focus, man, and not just on those lips of hers.* "There were more ships lost than the *Muir*?"

She nods.

Nobody's ever knocked the wind out of me with a nod. I sink down on one of the panic room's cots.

I didn't know other ships were jettisoned.

I didn't ever think there *could've* been others.

"The *John Muir* is the first Exodus-era ship we've found

with survivors," Laura adds. "After so many years lost to deep space . . . you're a statistical *impossibility*. I can't believe I'm here, looking at you."

I know that much is true: before the ship's crew went into stasis, Mom calculated our chances of ever waking back up again. I'm not much of a numbers guy, but a lot of zeroes after a decimal point meant we were fragged. I had no idea other people ended up like us. Stranded. Lost. Without hope. And to know they didn't make it, when *we* did . . .

Well, *some* of us, anyway.

"How many of your crew survived the stint in stasis?" Laura asks.

I shake my head. Shock slurs her words together so bad, they almost don't make sense. I try to focus on something in the room. Anything that will ground me, anything to keep me from sparking. Or exploding. The Exodus ships were Mom's greatest achievement. We thought the jettison of the *John Muir* was a personal vendetta, a singular attack on the scientist who saved humanity and its great treasures.

To know that other ships suffered our fate . . . and that help came too late . . . it's . . . it's . . .

It's *shit*.

"Are you okay?" Laura asks.

I pinch my nose between my thumb and forefinger. The small ridges in the bone—the place where I took a rogue soccer ball to the face—grind under the pressure. I don't know how to express the fury knotting in my chest. There aren't words for it, dammit. And I'm not talking about it with a stranger. "I'm just glad my mom's not around to hear this."

Laura's quiet for a moment. Then the cot creaks as she sits down next to me. She sets her bow on the floor. "Why? Was your mother the captain, or a navigator or engineer aboard the ship? Maybe . . . a politician who helped fund the project?"

I wish. Things would've been simpler if the woman had been less ambitious. I chuckle, but it sounds hollow even to my ears. "Not exactly." But I don't *exactly* want to talk about Mom, either.

Mom and I had a difficult relationship back at home; she, the brilliant polymath trying to save the world, and me, the son still trying to *grow up* in it. The kid who preferred doing things with his hands rather than looking at equations. The theories Mom scrawled on retro chalkboards—*Einstein-style,* she called it while dusting the white stuff off her fingertips—eventually went from castles in those chalky clouds to ships in the stars.

Sob story aside, there's a real good reason I don't talk about Mom anymore. If I mention the name *Katherine Morgan* on the coglinks, or so much as say the word *Mom* in the park, her whispers start up. I'll be deep in the ship. Running tunnels. Fixing old wiring or repairing a duct. And then, *Tuck, listen . . .*

Can you hear me . . .

You . . . to the bridge . . .

The rest of Mom's words would fade in static, unintelligible. One thing's for sure—my mom's dead. Beyond the echoes in my head, the ones nobody else seems to hear, she's gone. We don't know if she woke up before us. We don't know if she never went into stasis in the *first* place. We've never found a body, or any remains we could identify as hers.

I don't think Mom's left me a message—I think my brain

refuses to accept she's gone, most days. I just hope she's not one of *them*.

Rising, I cross the room for the hand-crank generator on the wall, pumping till the room's lights come up. Laura shields her eyes. I turn toward the lockers along the other wall. They're rusted old things, the metal gritty against my fingertips. The first one creaks when I open it, setting my teeth on edge. We've stocked panic rooms all over the ship with basic survival supplies—everything from flashlights to energy bars and first aid kits. I shudder as my hand brushes against a dekapen.

Holly, I'm so sorry.

"Tuck?" Laura asks, tilting her chin down as she eyes me. I know what she's asking of me—she doesn't have to say it in so many words—but I'm not talking about Mom with a complete stranger. Nope. Nuh-uh. Not even a girl as cute as Laura Cruz. Not even with the power out and the coglinks down. For all I know, Mom's ghost haunts this ship *Ringu*-style and I'll find her crawling out of one of the ship's sludge wells, one of these days.

Assuming we have more days left.

"I can only imagine what it must be like," Laura continues, trying to draw conversation out of me, "making contact with humanity after all this time in deep space."

That's not a conversation I'm about to have, either.

"You hungry?" I ask, tossing her an energy bar from inside the locker. She catches it easy, turning the package over in her hands. "I heard your stomach growling a second ago."

"This had an expiration date of . . . *four hundred years ago*?" she says, eyeing me.

I unwrap half a bar and shove the end in my mouth, grinning.

"They're still good, or at least good*ish*, like Twinkies. Never go bad," I say around the bar. Kneeling, I rifle through the bottom of the second locker, looking for a spare stiflecloth cloak. The energy bars taste like reconstituted powdered rocks with some tree bark mixed in. But trust me, the flavor's better than getting ganked by a mourner.

"What's a Twinkie?" she asks, tugging at the bar's wrapper.

"And you call yourself an archeologist."

"I don't have my PhD yet," Laura says absently, examining the chalky bar. "I'm still a uni student."

The educational system of the future must be amazing, because there's no way Laura Cruz is any older than sixteen. "And what's a Twinkie? Good hell, Laura. *Ghostbusters*? *Zombieland*? *Die Hard*? Twinkies are in *all* those movies. Don't you people watch the classics?"

"It's *Lao*-ra," she says. "Not *Law*-ra."

I chuckle. "My apologies, *Lao*-ra. It's been a while since I've taken any Spanish." Or eaten a Twinkie, for that matter. Or seen *Ghostbusters*. For whatever reason, Mom didn't upload that one into the *Muir*'s entertainment systems.

"And I *am* an archeologist," she says, managing to break into the energy bar's packaging. "Or at least, I will be in a few years. I know a lot about your world and culture, as the pre-Exodus rise of Pitch Dark has been the topic of a lot of my theses in high school and college."

Theses? Frag that, my *mom* used to write theses for fun.

"Pitch Dark?" I ask, but it's a miracle the words sound like anything more than the lumps of "food" in my mouth. The bars are even worse than I'd remembered, ugh. "What's that?"

"The terrorist organization responsible for jettisoning your ship," she says softly.

I freeze, swallowing hard. My hand slips on a pile of small boxes and spills some of the locker's contents. A box of flares falls out, the sticks bursting free and rolling across the floor.

For years, the bastards who did this to us have been nameless. Faceless. The people who destroyed my mother's work and killed thousands—I refuse to believe the mourners are still *alive*, really—have a name.

Pitch Dark.

What a *stupid* name for a terrorist organization.

If you're going to run around destroying my life, at least do it with a little panache, good hell.

I want to know "Why?" and the word bubbles out of me like a croak.

Laura stretches her legs out in front of her, crossing her arms over her chest. "Because they don't believe humanity should get another chance. For four centuries, Pitch Dark has blocked our attempts to terraform Mars, bombed strategic Panamerican colony locations, killed influential leaders, and poisoned our soil. I'm certain there were terrorist sympathizers involved in crashing my parents' ship, the *Conquistador*, into the *John Muir*."

I crouch down, starting to collect the flares off the floor. "Why would they do that?"

"Because if the soil on the *John Muir* is still viable, even a single sample could allow my country to terraform a new planet." She pushes off the cot, crossing the room to crouch next to me. "The Panamerican torus colonies were never meant to survive four hundred years—"

"I could've told you that," I say, chucking my wrapper to the ground. "The guy who designed them? Real douche bag. Mom hated . . . I mean, I saw him on the news a few times. He was a know-it-all blowhard who stole other people's work and passed it off as his own."

Shitty save there, man.

Laura looks at me a little funny. I've lived my whole life around hyperintelligent people, so I'm good at spotting their cogs turning. Little signs that indicate they're thinking. Mom had a thousand-mile-long stare. Aren walks around snapping his fingers. Laura's nostrils flare a little bit, as if she's scenting something. The skin at the corners of her eyes tightens as she examines my face. She doesn't believe me.

She's too *smart* to believe me.

But for some reason I don't understand, she doesn't call me out for burying the truth, either. She reaches forward, gripping my shoulder. The action paralyzes me. I want to jerk away, to tell her not to touch me. But it's hard not to get drawn in to the intensity of her grip. The earnestness of her voice.

"We've got to find a way to save this ship or whatever portion of Earth it contains," she says.

"Yosemite National Park," I say.

"What?" She blinks at me as if I've just said something in actual Martian.

"The terrarium. It contains Yosemite National Park," I repeat.

L A U R A

The words *Yosemite National Park* conjure up a few dim memories from my twelfth year, when my father and I examined some of the Americas' more important natural landmarks: Iguazu Falls of Argentina and Brazil; the Galapagos Islands; the geysers and pools of Yellowstone; the Torres del Paine of Chile; and Half Dome of Yosemite National Park.

I remember how Half Dome stretched so impossibly high off the valley floor, its sheer, straight cliff plunging at a ninety-degree angle toward the ground. To think humanity found a way to wrap such a massive natural wonder inside a starship and *transport it off-planet* . . . it's still so remarkable, it feels like magic. Impossible, but we did it anyway.

"Is the park's soil still viable?" I ask.

"If by *viable*, you mean do plants and shite grow out of it?" Tuck asks, taking an extra rucksack from the locker and tossing it on the ground beside me. "Yeah, it's viable."

"No manches." I release his shoulder, letting my forearm

rest on my knee. But soon I'm shaking, trembling with the thrill of knowing I am *living* history, with what the ship means to my country. If Tuck isn't lying to me, the *John Muir* could change everything for Panamerica. We could win back our future. We could blast the creeping twilight back and watch the sun rise over a new era of human development.

We could *survive* the present we've been dealt. We could move *forward*.

My whole body palpitates as if I've had too much caffeine to drink. I rise and begin to pace, trying to shake off my jitters. My head's light, as if it's been pumped full of air, and I can't tell if it's the thrill or the strange shift in pressure caused by the anechoic foam on the walls.

"We have to find a way to get your ship back to the Colonies," I tell Tuck. "We have to find a way to get her *home*."

"What, so you can be a hero and have a parade?" he asks.

"I'd be a heroine, and *no*," I say, with an emphatic shake of my head. "This isn't about me, but about all the people hoping and praying for a miracle back at home—"

"And why's it my responsibility to save them?" he asks. "My world's been gone for a helluva long time, Laura. I'm not sure it's worth fighting for a new one."

"Don't you understand?" I say, stepping forward and grabbing him by the shirtfront. His eyes widen. "This isn't about what you want, or what I want. It's about what millions of people need to *survive*. They don't deserve death just because you and I are afraid of what's out *there*—" I gesture toward the panic room door. "The *John Muir* might be my people's last chance. *Our* people's last chance."

I find myself breathless, heaving, and surprised by the passion in my words.

"You are human, aren't you?" I ask.

"Sometimes, I'm not sure anymore," he says. Silence shoulders its way between us, awkward. Thick. Tuck shifts his weight, examining me for several tense seconds. "And I'm not afraid of what's in the deepdowns," he says finally. Too quickly.

"Is that so?"

"Death doesn't scare me." He holds my gaze for a long, uncomfortable moment, and it's only then I realize I'm still gripping his shirt. "But caring about other people? Yeah, that scares me a lot. And I don't want to care about what's in *here*."

I draw back from him, as if his words burned my fingertips. *What does that mean?* When I try to form a response, I stammer until he rolls his eyes and says: "Fine. Just come with me to get the ship's power back on, okay?"

"Deal," I say.

He tosses a folded black square of cloth at me. I catch it in both hands. It's a packet of nubby fabric, one identical to the one Tuck wears on his back. It billows from my hands as I unfold it, the hem hitting the floor without a sound.

"Put that on," he says. "It's a stiflecloth cloak and hood."

Stiflecloth? "Where did this come from?" I ask, finding the neck and tugging it on, losing myself in yards and yards of stiff, unfamiliar fabric. It smells a little musty, probably from sitting in a storage locker for too long. "The fabric, I mean. I've never seen anything like it before."

"We had to get creative out here." Tuck crosses the room,

helping me settle the thing over my shoulders and loop the balaclava around my neck.

I almost pull away, but his gestures are so gentle for someone with so many scars hatched across his hands. He seems like he should be so rough, so . . . *barbaric*, almost. He's from a time rife with overconsumption, one that burned through our planet's resources and left humanity out in space's cold void. After hundreds of years in deep space, who knows how much of his humanity he's managed to retain? There's so little light in the depths of his eyes.

"This cloak will save your life out there," Tuck says, tugging the fabric into place. He picks up a hank of it, running his thumb over the cloth's nubs. "These foam studs absorb sound, making you invisible to the mourners' echolocation. Keep quiet while wearing this, and they can't see you. Just remember, it's a cloak, not a shield. It won't stop them from killing you."

I draw the hood over my head. It dulls some of the sound around me, as if I've stepped into a bubble of white noise. "Mourners," I say, looking up at him from under my hood's edge. "I assume you mean those nasty monsters in the halls? What are they?"

"The part of the *Muir*'s crew that didn't wake up right," Tuck says, stepping back from me. Turning away, he loads additional supplies into his own bag. Flares. A few more of those disgusting "energy bars," which make me miss my tías' enchiladas so much, grief pangs through my gut almost as loud as the hunger.

I know Mami survived the crash, but as for the rest of my family? I have no guarantees they still live, or if Faye or Alex survived. Or the Smithsons. Or anyone, really, even the black-hat

Noh Mask hacker. I touch the subjugator hibernating in my throat. With the *Conquistador*'s silocomputers nonfunctional, my bioware's offline, taking my subjugator down, too. It's the first time I've thought about the damned thing since the crash; and it's the *only* positive I've netted thus far. As soon as I see Mami again, I'll be able to tell her all the secrets I know, and all the lies.

So I will follow this strange boy into the depths of the *John Muir*. Outwitting my enemies and saving myself starts by salvaging this ship.

"Laura, you listening?" Tuck asks, startling me out of my thoughts.

"Lo siento, yes," I say.

"Uh-huh," he says. "I know that look. My mom used to . . ." But he trails off, his words disappearing into a quick chuckle and a grin. He rubs the back of his neck with one palm, and then says, "Aw, never mind."

"Your mom used to what?" I ask.

Tuck doesn't answer straightaway. He seems to roll a few statements around in his head, debating his answer. "My mom was a thinker, like you," Tuck finally says. "But right now, if we're not *doers*, the *Muir*'s not going to make it." He hoists his backpack on one shoulder. "The ship needs power. The auxiliary power hive is nearby, about three klicks up the t-Two tunnel. Since I don't know if anyone from my crew survived, it's us, or it's no one."

Dread worms into my heart, sending its sugary poison into my veins. A shudder runs its stubby fingers over my skin. All the courage I knew before deserts me. It's one thing to *talk* about saving humanity; it's quite another to go out there and actually do the work.

"Listen." Tuck reaches out and places a knuckle under my chin, turning my face up. I step back, glaring at him.

To his credit, he glares right back at me.

Something in his gaze transports me past the splatter of old gore on his face, the bruises on his cheekbone and neck. The fear in him resonates with the fear in me. It vibrates between us on some unseen wavelength, this terror of being alone in the hostile darkness, with the vast odds ready to topple and crush us beneath their weight. It's *human*. We are different, yet the same; two kids shivering in the shadows, scared of the monsters in the halls and death at the door. The vacuum of hopelessness can't have sucked away all his humanity, because when I look at him, I see it staring me straight in the face.

For all we know, we're the last two people alive on this ship, the only beating hearts on the far side of the universe. We might be the last two stars standing between humanity and an endless night.

The thought makes a sob roll up from the center of my chest, but I swallow it down. I don't want him to think I'm upset because I'm afraid of the monsters.

I'm upset because I'm afraid of what those monsters have done to my *family*.

"If we're going to do this, you've got to be all-in," Tuck says. "Once all three auxiliary core rooms are functional, we'll both need to turn keys at the same time to bring the ship back online. I can't do it alone."

I close my eyes and take a deep, centering breath. *Do this for your family, Laura*, I tell myself. *Do it for your future. For all humanity's future. Fortuna, gloria, y familia.*

"How much is a klick?" I ask, surprised at how calm my voice sounds despite the frantic fluttering of my heart. I drag my fingertips across my lower eyelids, just to make sure there aren't any tears hiding in my lashes.

"About a kilometer," he says. "You a good runner?"

"Good enough to run a few kilometers."

"*Without* huffing and puffing? We run silent, or we don't run at all."

I roll my eyes. "I just free-climbed a hundred-meter-tall computer a few hours ago, survived a major ship crash, and fought off a few of your *mourners*. I think I can handle running a few kilometers."

"Good. Keep it up with the piss-off attitude," he says, shaking his head at me. "You're going to need it out there."

Ancient history or no, maybe I *should* have shot him when I had the chance.

TUCK

I lied. So shoot me.

Laura will need more than attitude to survive in the deep-downs. The other curators I've run with? All tough, like Laura. All smart, like Laura. All quick, like Laura. But most of them wound up dead anyway. I've already lost Holly today. If I were to lose Laura, too, I'd be done with this.

For her sake—and my own—I need to get her through this. *Alive.*

So I teach her to underpronate her steps. Rather than putting the weight of a step on the bony heel, curators place the fleshy outside of the foot down first and roll toward the middle. The knees absorb most of the shock. And trust me, my busted knee feels it *every* night.

Never thought about how retro this strategy must look to an outsider, though.

I walk across the room, demonstrating the steps. "Silence is your friend in the deepdowns," I say, pivoting to face her. "Most mourners use echolocation to track their prey. Don't give them anything to work with, even if you're hurt. Understand?"

"What if there's noise pollution in the ship?" Laura asks, falling into step beside me. She holds out her hands to keep from wobbling with each step. "Once we reestablish the ship's power grid, won't its systems make a lot of noise?"

"They might. Don't count on it, especially in the deepdown tunnels," I reply, halting by the lockers. She looks like a duckling, waddling back and forth across the room. "Okay, good"—*she's so not good*—"do that now, but faster. I'm going to watch your form."

Laura jogs a few steps away from me. Tripping, she catches herself on one of the foam-covered walls. The foam pyramids depress under her weight, sucking up the sound from our voices and steps.

"*Mierda*, it's going to take a miracle not to roll my ankle out there," she says with a wince.

"Let's wrap your ankles for support, *Stumble-lina*."

"This isn't a joke," she snaps.

"Laura, my whole *life's* a bad joke." I pull some stiff bandages from the lockers. I show her how to wrap her ankle the way we used to on the soccer field, with the bandage crisscrossing the ankle and looping under the heel.

Should I tell her the communications arrays are busted? I wonder as she secures a bandage to her left ankle, then the right. *That even if we manage to get the power hives online, the ship probably won't survive?*

If I don't tell her these things, have I lied to her?

And why, with this girl, does it feel like being honest matters so much?

Laura practices running with the bandages—back and forth, back and forth. After a few attempts, her footsteps whisper against the floor. She moves quicker, with more confidence, and she's got decent form for long-distance running. And I admit, I could watch that ponytail of hers swing across her back all damn day.

If she can hold it together in the tunnels—and that's a big *if*—we might make it to the auxiliary power hives. *If* we get the ship's power back on, we'll have Dejah on our side. The AI will seal off the crash site, as well as scan the ship's tunnels for additional survivors. Once I can talk to Aren again, he'll put the other curators to work.

With a little luck—God knows I've got that in spades—we might survive this crash.

I've got to make that happen.

For Mom, as crazy as she used to make me.

For Laura, the girl who dreams of history.

For me, and whatever the future brings my way.

And I guess for humanity—despite the lot of good they've done, burning down our fragging planet. Mom believed in them, though. Laura does, too.

Right now, that's enough.

"Good, that's good," I tell Laura when her footsteps grow so quiet, they almost melt into the floor. "Now try it with all your gear." Her quiver clacks like a set of old dentures. When I reach for it, she snatches it back and clutches it against her chest, cheeks flushed.

"*O*-kay," I say, lifting a brow, looking her up and down.

"Sorry," she says with a small shake of her head, as if

chastising herself. "It's . . . well, it's the only artifact I was able to save from my parents' ship."

"An old-ass arrow bag is *that* important to you?"

"It's a *quiver*," she says, and I grin because that's *exactly* what I expected her to say. "It might be the only part of my parents' collection that survived the crash."

"You really are a history nerd, aren't you?"

"Shut up. And yes." Laura settles her bow and quiver over her stiflecloth cape, which I hope won't be a problem.

"Well, stuff some stiflecloth inside your *quiver*, Dr. Jones." I chuckle, sliding a slimpack on. "And let's go save this goddamned ship."

LAURA

Who knew it could be difficult to convince someone to save their own starship?

Tuck takes the lead, holding a flare over his head as we step into the deepdown tunnels. It's colder than the *Conquistador*'s walk-in freezer here, the chill stiffening my joints. I draw the cloak around me, surprised at how well the fabric traps my body heat; and perhaps even more dumbfounded by the *John Muir* crew's ingenuity for creating a garment like this, a fusion of ancient design and smart tech.

They're survivors in every sense of the word.

Tuck moves like a puff of air, his footfalls deft. His exhalations look like clouds of toxic smoke, illuminated by his flare's green light. If he's bothered by the cold, he shows no sign. His flare highlights the tunnel's rounded ribs, which appear every ten meters or so. The metal floors feel like ice, numbing my feet. Behind me, the darkness feels as solid as a wall. The ship lies silent, save for the occasional metallic groan rising from its depths.

My heart thuds in my chest, dosing my system with adrenaline. The last time I walked through these tunnels, I'd been alone. Abandoned. I had no light to guide me, nor any idea of what lurked in the ship's bowels. Now I have Tuck. Together, we have a fighting chance to save this ship. In the meantime, I can only hope Mami and the rest of my family can manage to survive on their own.

Tuck pops me on the arm, and with a grin, takes off running. I follow him, focusing on each step till I ease into a rhythm. Every so often, I misstep onto my heel, or my cloak snaps in the wind. Tuck recoils a little each time but doesn't stop running. *Whatever you do, don't stay in one place. Keep moving,* he told me as he prepared to open the panic room door.

In the darkness, it's hard to tell how far we've run. I count the tunnel's ribs as we pass them. *Eighty-five, eighty-six . . .* Every hundred should make a kilometer, or a *klick*, as Tuck says. My bowstring presses into my collarbone as I go, chafing the skin through my clothing and cloak. While it's uncomfortable, and I have to brace the bow with one hand to keep it from sliding, I wouldn't have left it behind for anything. Not so long as the quiver holds one of the most important artifacts of the eighteenth century.

My body starts to feel the distance in my lungs first— they burn with each breath. I breathe in through my nose, and out through my mouth, keeping each one as quiet as I can. Up ahead, Tuck moves like a machine. He's mastered this technique, wholly committed to the business of survival in a hostile environment.

After almost two full kilometers, Tuck puts up one hand, warning me to slow down. I halt beside him.

He lifts up the flare, throwing light over a meaty mass. It spreads across the floor and up the walls. Tentacles burst from vents and seethe over the ceiling. Pulsating and dripping, everything smells of bile, of feces and rotting flesh, the stench burning the back of my throat and my tear ducts. I cover my nose and mouth with the balaclava. When I point out the shelflike fungi growing up the wall, Tuck mouths something like *"the fester"* at me and slices a finger across his throat.

No pasa nada, right? Just avoid the alien mold growing all over the ship and it'll all be *fine.*

What's going on in this place? I wonder, following Tuck as he skirts the red, spongy outer rim of the stuff. I know the *John Muir's* crew woke up as mourners, but this stuff looks like a biohazard. Alien, almost. *Did people get infected? How did they metamorphose into monsters while in stasis, anyway?*

The fester fills the tunnels in all directions. It gurgles, pustules bursting on the surface, emitting gas from its depths. We hug the wall for several meters, moving slowly, keeping our feet out of the stuff. I walk on the balls of my feet, gritting my teeth when something spongy and wet bursts between my toes.

Needing no directions or map, Tuck turns left. He cranks open another door, stepping past the half-opened panels before waving me through.

I enter a room of towering, silent machines. The flare's nauseating green light slicks tall turbines, all of which are built from a smoky metal, maybe a steel alloy. A thick layer of dust covers the floor. We're in the ship's mechanical sectors, most likely the support bays for the scramengines. I haven't studied pre-Exodus ship craft like my brother Gael has, but I know I saw a huge line of engines on the deepdowns' outermost rim. Which accounts for the cold. The heat would leach from the ship's outermost areas first.

Faded numbers and letters mark the walls and machinery, most of their codes now unrecognizable. I've never seen such a well-preserved ship from this era. I want to know how Tuck's people managed to keep the *John Muir* shipshape for so long, especially while the crew was in stasis. *It's remarkable,* I think, taking a moment to absorb the ship's details.

Tuck leads me between two towering machines. The walkway is so narrow, I feel like a cave spelunker from pre-Exodus times. The machinery's smooth to the touch but lacks the buoyant, static-safe layer of electrons my people use to protect our tech in deep space. I'm accustomed to touching tech on the *Conquistador* and feeling an airy resistance, even when the machines are off.

Tuck pauses on the other side of the silent machines, so suddenly that I almost crash into him. He holds up a hand as I glare at the back of his head.

The clash and clang of metal echoes in the distance. I almost ask *What was that?* but bite my tongue. Tuck motions at me to hunch down behind a large, boxy machine. As we do, he snuffs his flare, drawing the darkness down around us. He sits close enough to let our knees touch, keeping us connected as we hide in the shadows.

My heart thumps. Questions itch under my skin: *Why did we stop? What's so horrible that it's better to hide from it than run?*

Or worse, what if he doesn't even know *what's following us?*

Tuck and I hide for a few minutes in the dark, unmoving. The silence lies thick in the room, the chill creeping into my bones. My pounding heart begins to slow its pace. Tuck shifts beside me. Our knees break apart. In a blind panic, I reach out for him, missing his knee and accidentally grabbing his thigh. He snatches my hand away, taking my palm in his rough, callused one.

He holds on a second longer than he should.

Cheeks burning, I pull my hand from his grasp. We sit in awkward silence—then I see a light glittering in the distance, one moving slowly between the large machines in the room.

The light stutters. It flares again, then winks out. As the glimmer draws closer, I realize it's a man dressed in a white EVA suit, passing behind a row of machines on the other side of the room. His lantern's brightness slicks his rounded EVA helmet.

Tuck draws a sharp breath. I suppose the man's no ally of Tuck's, or else we wouldn't remain hidden here in the shadows. The man in the suit passes out of sight, but Tuck doesn't release the breath he was holding until another metal clank resounds in the room.

Who was that? I want to ask. *Where were they going? And if he wasn't one of your allies, is this entire ship just full of locos?*

Tuck strikes a new flare and stands. Inclining his head left, he scoots past a series of grates protecting huge switchboards, and down a short flight of steps sheltered by an awning. I follow him through another set of massive machines, the spaces between them so tight I have to squeeze the breath from my lungs to fit. Then it's through another door, back into the tunnels.

We run again, moving as quietly as stolen whispers.

The next time Tuck halts, it's beside a set of doors wearing an orange stripe down their middles. The words AUXILIARY POWER ROOMS are painted in large letters on their faces.

We're here.

TUCK

Part of me can't believe we made it here. We had a clean run from the crash site to the auxiliary power hive. No mourners, but the guy in the EVA suit couldn't be anything but trouble.

Laura did okay out there—no tripping, no talking. A few stumbles, but nothing that took her down shrieking. Maybe fate's finally tossing me a little slack.

. . . Or maybe it just knows I'm desperate enough to fall for the long con. I shouldn't have touched Laura, dammit. Even holding her hand, lost in the dark, has made me want to slide my hand into hers and twine our fingers together.

It's *stupid*.

I can't afford to care about anyone these days.

Not if I want them to live.

Despite the cold, I'm sweating by the time I pry the auxiliary power hive's ocular panels apart. Without power, all the ship's touchlocks are down, forcing me to open the doors manually.

Taking the flare from Laura, I step into the Hive's antechamber first. These rooms haven't been used for centuries. My toes sink into the dust on the floor. I wriggle them around. Nothing better than the feeling of dead skin, spores, and space rock between the toes, am I right?

Laura follows me inside, making a face at the grime on the floor. Once the door panels lock behind her, I say, "We're okay to talk here. The Hive's hermetically sealed off from the rest of the ship—"

"Who was that man we saw?" she asks, interrupting me.

"Santa Claus, for all I know," I reply.

She steps closer. "You mean there are unaccounted for persons aboard the *John Muir?* People who may or may not support your crew's mission?"

"Yeah, I'd say so. My crew hasn't had access to a functioning EVA suit since stasisbreak. Whoever he is, he's not one of ours."

Her brows knit and her mouth opens in an O shape, but before she can say anything smart-assed, I take her by the wrist and lead her over to an aged map of the place, one that hangs on the wall by the door. *Dammit, touched her again.*

The map shows a top-down view of the auxiliary power hives, a grid of twenty-one hexagon-shaped chambers, positioned in three groups of seven.

"You see why we call the power rooms the Hive?" I ask, pointing to the honeycombed rooms. "Six power reactors are attached to each of the three auxiliary core rooms. We need twelve cores total to power the ship, though we'd be more comfortable at eighteen." To be honest, the cores look less like beehives and more like flowers—six reactor rooms surround each of the core rooms like petals. Hallways connect the three core rooms, making it possible to move between them.

Laura considers the map. "Basically, our existence depends on this one sector of the ship."

"Pretty much," I say.

"Is there any way to defend them?"

"Maybe? What do you mean?"

"*If* the hacker survived the crash, he will no doubt try to sabotage the *John Muir*," she says, tapping the core rooms with a knuckle. "Is there a way to secure them from attack? Can we use one of the ship's systems to lock their doors, or build a protocol that will keep unauthorized persons from accessing the cores?"

I consider her for a moment: the long nautilus curl of her eyelashes, the determined set of her jaw.

This is the part where, in movies, the guy says something really charming to impress the girl. "You really are a nerd," I say.

I'm not very good at being charming, am I?

"*¿Y que?*" She laughs. "You think you're *el muy muy*? I don't think you have the right to call anyone a *nerd*, Tuck. Mr. I've Seen Every Pre-Exodus Movie Ever Made."

"Fair point," I say, and think, *Is she flirting with me?*
Nah.

But now I wish I'd paid a little more attention in high school Spanish.

We cross the auxiliary antechamber. The three doors to the core rooms stand closed. My flare's light bounces off the doors' dusty, stainless-steel surfaces. A single horizontal break point bifurcates the doors through their middles. Faded two-meter-tall letters—*A*, *B*, and *C*, respectively—mark each door.

Blast doors.

"Dammit," I say, rubbing my chin with my hand. My crank's useless on doors like these. "I forgot these doors don't open easy. We'll have to crawl through the maintenance ducts."

"Maintenance ducts?" Laura asks, but I'm already moving past the door for core room C. To the left of the core room doors, there sits a rebar ladder. Three meters up that ladder, there's a small door that leads to a smaller duct. The door's heavy, made of fifteen-centimeter-thick steel, and meant to protect the ship from radiation leakage in case of a reactor failure.

Like from a *crash*.

What I haven't told Laura? I'm not certain the reactors will be stable. In order to reach the core rooms, we'll have to travel through about fifteen meters of tunnel, which could potentially be exposed to radiation. Since my Geiger counter was built into my HUD—which depends on the ship having, y'know, *power*—I'm not going to know if we're being exposed to something nasty.

But without her, I won't be able to get the cores online. Two people have to turn the keys in each of the core rooms, at the same time, in order to reroute the power systems.

I won't make that decision for her.

I don't want to be that kind of asshole.

As she joins me at the ladder, I pause. Turn. "You should know . . . if the reactors are busted, we might be exposed to some radiation."

"I'd say more than some, *ay*?" Laura says, looking up at the meter-wide maintenance duct. She pulls her hood a few centimeters closer around her face, as if to shield herself. "Eighteen nuclear reactors will create more than *some* radiation."

"It wouldn't be a pretty way to go," I say.

"Neither would suffocation in the dark," she replies, putting her hands on her hips. "Come on, *vato*, I'm starting to think you're scared."

Hell yeah, I'm afraid.

I'm scared my stupidity's going to get you killed.

"*Pfft*," I say, more to myself than to Laura. "I've got nothing to be scared of in there." Gripping the ladder's rungs, I climb up to the duct door and unlock the manual clamps securing it to the wall. The hinges groan as they move for the first time in centuries. Dust explodes in my face. I sneeze. "Hope you don't mind a little dust."

"I'm an archeologist-in-training," she says, coming up the ladder below me. "Dust is *kind* of my thing."

"And you think *I'm* the nerd," I say, using both hands to propel myself into the duct. I remind myself to breathe, only to snort dust like cocaine. "Grab the door, will you?"

Behind me, Laura sneezes as she reaches up to close the duct door behind us.

"I thought you liked dust," I say, crawling forward a couple of meters.

"Not up my nose, I don't," she replies.

"Lightweight."

"Pardon?"

"Nothing."

She snorts. "That's what I thought."

It takes a few minutes to crawl through the ducts. Laura coughs and hacks behind me. Perhaps I should've let the lady go first, but you know what they say about hindsight.

When I find the first core room door—marked with a big red C—I pop it open, then slide out feetfirst, ignoring the ladder. I land in a crouch. Dust plumes around my toes. Laura climbs down the ladder, civilized and neat. She comes to my side, smacking the grime from her clothing.

"It's like a tomb in here," she says, examining the room as I hold up a flare. Dust covers everything. It slides off instruments and coats the soles of my feet. Laura's flare strikes several dingy glass screens. Each one of the room's six walls has a large rectangular window set inside it, to allow technicians to monitor the cores while they are in use.

Right now, nothing's visible through the cloudy glass. All light passes through the panes and withers on the other side. We can't see *in*. Thanks to my flare, something could definitely see *out*.

"Oh my *god!*" Laura almost squeals, holding her flare over the computer. "Is that a *keyboard*?"

"Uh . . . yes?" I say lamely.

She sets her flare down on the desk, using a single finger to punch the arthritic keys. They *click* to the touch. "I've only heard about these. You really needed physical buttons to input information into your computers?" She lifts up the keyboard, looking underneath. "Had you moved on from Bluetooth by this point, or was that still popular? I've always been unclear on midmodern methods of wireless transmission."

Anxiety fists in my chest. I tell myself to shake it off, but I realize if we get out of here—*if we make it off this ship*—I won't understand a thing about her world. To her, my tech's no more impressive than, say, an abacus would be to me.

I'm a relic, just like everything in this room.

Everyone I loved on Earth has been dead for centuries.

I've known this for a long time, of course. There's a big difference between knowing something and *feeling* it.

"Wow," Laura says, setting the keyboard down. "I heard the Nero group tracked one of these things down recently, but I haven't seen it yet. I've seen the desk-mounted variety—"

"You realize you're creeping me out, right?"

She looks up at me. Blinks. "What do you mean?"

I open my mouth to explain but realize I don't have the words. Explaining things to people takes too much energy and time, two things I don't currently have. "Just . . . never mind. Keep an eye on those screens while I cycle the breakers?"

"Cycle the breakers?" she asks.

"Reboot the power."

"Ah, alternating power systems must've been *such* a pain. Sure thing." Laura drops into a chair, dust swirling around her hips. She wipes the screens in front of her with the corner of her cape, humming a song I don't know.

I turn toward the reactor control panels. The buttons, knobs, and switches are hidden under a century's worth of dust. Most of the labels are for different areas of the ship. Current redirects and such. A big red button is marked EMERGENCY SHUTDOWN. The breakers dot the far side of the control panel. They're old and crackle to the touch. One switch snaps off when I try to cycle it, and I curse. I doubt anyone's touched these switches since the crew went into stasis—after all, we've never needed anything more than the main power hive.

"How weird is it," Laura says softly, looking into the control panel's blank screens, "to know the world has moved on without you?"

"Let's just say I have a little more empathy for Marty McFly these days," I say, frowning when I can't manage to get the control board to respond. *Damn.* Did we need to turn the reboot box keys before we tried to cycle the breakers, or after? *Or is the ship fragged beyond repair?*

Laura looks up at me from the chair, lips pursed. I study the switches, trying to let on that I *would like to skip this conversation* without having to be an asshole. If I don't look at her, maybe she'll take the hint and abandon her questions.

"Tuck?" she asks. I pretend to ignore her. I want to go back to the light banter, which never means much of anything. Banter doesn't ache, it doesn't hurt, and it never takes itself too seriously.

"I'm sorry," she says, clearing her throat. "I can see how it would hurt to be left behind. Maybe not forgotten, but *left*."

Sadness sneaks into her voice. I'm not sure she notices, but I do.

"Hey," I say, reaching out to touch her shoulder. I stop myself. My hand hangs in the air, all awkward. She eyes me like I'm crazy, but I shouldn't get too close. Touching her will only create more problems for me down the line. I drop my hand. "Let's just save the heavy stuff for after we get the ship back online, okay?"

"Okay." She cocks her head a little, spinning in the chair. "You and me, off to save ourselves and the whole human race."

"Damn skippy," I say, kneeling down by the desk and prying an old drawer open. I rifle through its contents, looking for the keys to the room's reboot box. "I'm here to kick ass and chew gum, and, girl, I'm *all* out of gum."

She looks at me funny, a half smile, half frown on her face, until I say, "It's a movie quote. From *They Live*? The *Muir* ran out of gum about six months ago."

"You like old movies, don't you?"

"Anything retro and lame, yeah. I watch them at night—not much else to do around here. You guys still have movies, wherever it is you're from?"

"*Panamerica*. And 'movies' are a little different now . . . more like immersive versions of your old video games. Very few films are made for a flat screen."

"Then cancel what I said before. I don't want to go back."

Laura laughs. Reaching into her pocket, she pulls out half a pack of mint gum. Taking a piece, she hands the rest to me.

It's the nicest thing anyone's done for me in centuries. I can say that literally, you know.

Maybe I'll want a life on the other side of the universe after all.

L A U R A

"There are two reboot boxes in each core room." Tuck points to the rusty, dingy beige panels on either side of the room, positioned between reactor observation windows. Each panel has a silver eye, one with a vertical black pupil that bisects its cornea.

No, not an *eye*. I search for the word in my head—it's an analog lock. People used to put them on doors, vehicles, and such to keep valuables safe. We have passcodes and facial recognition tech in Panamerica, so no one has used analog locks in centuries.

Tuck continues, "If we want to reboot the systems, we need to turn our keys at the same time in every room. I think."

"You *think*?" I ask. "You're not sure?"

"We need to find the keys for those reboot boxes," he says, ignoring my question as he walks toward the door. "Keep looking in here, I'll check core room B . . ."

Tuck pauses, glancing back at me.

". . . You do know what a key looks like, right?" he asks.

"Of course I do," I say, rolling my eyes as I rise from my chair. Dad keeps an entire glass jar full of useless old keys at home. Coins, too.

Tuck grins, and I realize he was teasing me. "Be right back."

As he cranks open the door and steps into the hallway beyond, I take a knee in front of a small filing cabinet under the control panel. Rust covers the drawers' facades. One of the drawer pulls breaks off in my hand when I touch it, forcing me to pry the drawer open with my fingernails. Nothing inside looks helpful—I find rusty pens, old calculators, and brittle notepads; a mug with a crackle of dry coffee at the bottom; and a few strange coins. I search through the cabinet, in the closets, even in the trash cans, hoping to find something. *Anything.*

I see plenty of junk, but no keys. Frustrated, I peer at the control panel, scraping dust off it with my fingertips, looking for clues. The panel buttons, though rimed with dust and age, glitter like raw gems. Despite the danger and desperation of our situation, there's something awe-inspiring about it, too. How many archeologists have seen a *functioning* Exodus-era ship? As far as I know, my family and crew are the first.

If we make it back to the Colonies, we'll have the most amazing story to tell.

Something thumps behind me. "Bueno, that was quick," I say, turning. "Did you find them—"

Tuck isn't standing behind me.

In fact, the door Tuck left through isn't even open.

The maintenance duct bangs closed as a man in a full EVA suit—bulkier than anything we have on the *Conquistador*—rises to his feet. I drop my flare on the ground, shocked.

Tuck's words echo in my head: *Whoever he is, he's not one of ours.*

The man's ancient EVA creaks as he steps forward. I watch myself stumble backward in the reflection of the helmet, catching myself on the control panel. He's got some sort of long wrench, one thick as my wrist and covered in old blood. A long time ago, that EVA suit must have been white; now it's gray with age and covered in rusty stains. Someone's drawn an ouroboros insignia under the old US flag on his arm.

I pull my bow off my back and reach for an arrow.

The man in the EVA's too quick. He lunges at me before I can nock, swinging the wrench in an arc. I duck under his swing. The air whistles over my head. Grunting, I kick a trash can into his legs. He turns into the attack, going down hard on one hip and tumbling into the chair behind me. The wrench bounces free of his hand, clattering on the floor.

I scramble for an arrow as he untangles his limbs from the chair. Just as I yank a shaft from my quiver, he pushes me into the ground, crushing the air out of my lungs. I drive my elbow into his rib cage. The EVA suit protects him from some of the damage, but I still feel a bone crack under the pressure. Agony shudders through his frame. My own elbow buzzes with pain. He grabs my head, smacking it against the floor, but not hard enough to daze me. His EVA suit impairs his speed, but also makes him invulnerable to pressure point attacks.

"¡Hijo de puta!" I snap. My fingers curl around the wrench as he shoves my head into the ground again. I use physics against him, relying on my lower center of gravity to twist, unseat him, and dump him on the ground next to me. Scrambling away, I get to my feet. I throw the wrench out of reach, grab my bow off the floor, and whirl on him.

My hands shake as I nock the arrow. The man in the EVA rises, hands up.

"Hey, Laura, I found these in the . . ." Tuck says as he walks back into the room. He spots the man in the EVA, eyes widening. He glances at me, appraising my condition with a glance, then back at the guy in the EVA. "Who the hell are you?"

"He attacked me after you left the room," I say, keeping an arrow trained on the man. "Do you think he's the one we saw in—"

The man collapses. When his head hits the floor, his helmet bounces off and rolls toward me. I stop it beneath one foot, like a soccer ball, and lower my bow, pointing the arrowhead at the ground.

The man seizes for a few seconds, his bald head exposing a network of blackened veins along his cranium and face. The same dark veins thread across his sallow, scarred skin. Frothy saliva bubbles over his mouth as if he's gone rabid. A white film covers his eyes.

"Is he dead?" I whisper.

Tuck takes a knee beside the man, pressing two fingers into his throat. "Dead and gone. See these veins?" Tuck asks, pointing to the spidery network inching under the man's skin. "Looks like he poisoned himself. Not a pretty way to go."

"Do you know him?"

Tuck shakes his head. "But this isn't the first time I've seen this symbol," he says, tapping the ouroboros snake with his index finger.

"It's the insignia for Pitch Dark," I say. "Well, more accurately, one they appropriated from ancient civilizations."

"You're shitting me?" Tuck looks up at me, gauging my face to see if I'm toying with him. When he sees my stony expression, he swears. Hard. "I just took some skin off a guy tattooed with this insignia earlier. I've seen it all over the *Muir*."

"Which means your ship's been harboring terrorists from the beginning," I say, putting my arrow back in its quiver.

"We know *someone* else survived—we just don't know who. Supplies go missing. Trams crash mysteriously. Hell, let's blame the gum shortage on them, too." He kicks the guy in the arm as he stands up. "Thanks a lot, asshole."

"You should know this same insignia appeared on the *Conquistador*'s screens, right before we crashed," I say, omitting the greater part of the story, at least for now. "I told you a hacker compromised our navigational systems with the intention to destroy the *John Muir*."

"Well, I guess there's one less bastard to worry about now," Tuck says after a moment. "Hasta la vista, baby."

He rises, jangling a set of rust-splattered keys at me. "Forget him, let's get the power back on and get out of here."

With once last glance back at my attacker, I follow Tuck into core room A. The six hexagonal-shaped, core-monitoring windows spread throughout the room, their faces opaque. Dark.

"Once the ship's power grid comes back online, I'll be able to communicate with the other curators," he says, handing me one of the keys. The small piece of metal—browned and dulled with age—seems too small and light to be of any significance. "They need to know about the crash, and someone needs to find the rest of your people."

"How do you plan to do that?" I ask.

He taps his right temple. "Everyone onboard had a coglink chip implanted in their brains before takeoff. We use them to chat telepathically."

"You have a computer chip in your *brain*?" I ask, jaw dropping. "Weren't your people afraid someone would hack into these coglinks?"

"Yeah, like who, E.T.? There aren't any hackers out here."

A hacker was responsible for jettisoning your ship, I think. *And for crashing mine.*

Tuck motions me over to one of the reboot boxes in the room. As I cross to him, I catch my reflection in the blackened observation windows. Cast in the flare's green light, I look like a ghost. As the glare rolls over the glass, small white worms shrink away on the other side, disappearing into the shadows. Squinting my eyes, I approach the window, realizing a festering growth covers the opposite side of the glass.

"We need to hurry," Tuck says, standing beside the reboot box and holding his flare high. In the windows on either side of him, oily masses throb behind the glass. A heavy thud resounds through one of the windows, and Tuck steps back, swearing under his breath.

"Tuck?" I ask, my voice quavering.

"Take the other box," he says, pointing to an identical reboot panel about five meters away. With another glance at the windows, I cross the room, slide my key into the lock, and glance at him over my shoulder.

"Ready?" he asks.

I nod.

"Three, two, one." His lock clicks.

My key won't budge. Its metal edges bite into my fingers as I struggle to rotate it in the lock. "I think it's stuck," I say. "Rusted, maybe." We switch places. Tuck tries turning my key with his hand. Failing that, he fetches the wrench from the other room. I admit it's a little validating to watch him fail, too.

"Not now," he says to the lock, glancing over his shoulder. I follow his line of sight, examining the windows in turn. Perhaps I'm still haunted from the surprise attack, but some old instinct tells me we're being watched.

Tuck steps back from the panel, wiping his forehead with the back of his hand. "If I'm not careful, I'm going to snap the key in half."

"So what do we do?" I ask, thinking, *This is why analog keys fell out of use.*

He kneels, rifling through his bag. "We need some WD-40 in there," he says. "Some lubricant to, uh, reduce friction . . ."

As he talks, the fester convulses in the window above the room's control panel, shuddering like a rotted version of the tías' multicolored gelatins. The sight makes my stomach feel as if it's been turned upside down. If I'd eaten anything more than a chalky energy bar today, I might have vomited.

"Where is it . . . ?" Tuck asks, still digging through his bag, his reflection visible in the glass. "Dammit, I could've sworn I had some—"

Something thuds behind the window. "Tuck?" I whisper.

"Hang on," he says, not bothering to look up.

Pinpricks of light appear in the fester. I step closer, cocking my head. Then something cleaves through the muck, its claws screeching against the glass.

Tuck leaps to his feet, the big vein in his throat throbbing, jaw clenching. "No time for lube, we gotta go," he says, taking hold of the wrench.

"What is that thing?" I ask, backing across the room.

"There's more than one kind of mourner," Tuck says. "And the worst ones grow out of the fester—"

A growl crawls into the room, making the windows around us shiver. I remember how the mourner on the *Conquistador* turned a floatglass case into a veritable dirty bomb.

I don't want to be in the room when this monster screams.

"We've got to get out of here," I say.

"Thank you, Captain Obvious."

"That's *Capitana Obvious* to you!" I race to the reboot panel, gripping Tuck's key. Adrenaline slicks my hands with sweat and makes my heart beat hard.

"Turn the keys in sync. One, two, three—" Tuck grunts as he tries to get the key to budge. The metal inside the panel groans as the key moves a few degrees, and I turn mine to the same angle.

"C'mon, c'mon," he says to the stuck key, glancing over his shoulder as another growl rolls through the room. "Ah, crap."

"Shut up and turn your key!" I half shriek, my pulse pounding in my fingertips.

He swears as he puts his back into turning the wrench, winning another fifteen degrees or so, putting our keys at the halfway mark. "Almost there," he says, switching up his grip on the wrench handle.

The monster slams its forehead into the glass, startling me. Long, silvery cracks spread out like wings, glittering in the light. It cocks its head and growls again. The glass tremors, the cracks spreading to the window's edges.

"*Now!*" Tuck puts all his weight on the wrench, forcing the key to turn farther.

I copy his angle until our keys click home. Tuck races to the control board, flips two switches, and the six cores around us rumble like scramengines, their whine drowning out all other sound. The HVAC coughs a mouthful of dust into the room. The lights flicker, die, and then burst into full brilliance as the floor bucks and quakes.

"Let's go!" I shout, sprinting to the threshold of the room before I realize Tuck isn't following me. I catch myself on the door, looking back.

I almost wish I hadn't.

Behind me, only the silhouette of some massive beast is visible through the fester-covered glass: the creature stands on two legs, but that's where its similarities to a human being end. As the monster steps up to the window, something slithers away from its back—a hundred long, thick tentacles unfurl like diabolical wings, writhing as if they each have a mind of their own.

Tuck kneels on the ground by the control board, holding his head.

Mouth open in a silent scream.

TUCK

In another breath, I'm under siege. Voices scream through my head. My HUD flashes back on. Glitching up. A thousand distorted shapes flare across my lens, stabbing laser lights straight into my cornea.

"Tuck! Do you read? Are you okay?" Aren shouts through the coglinks.

A chorus of twenty curators calls my name. Their questions hit my brain like bullets:

"What's going on?"

"Where's Holly?!"

"I don't sense any consciousnesses out there but yours, Tuck!"

"How did you get the power back on?"

"What did you do to the girl?"

Everything hits like a jackhammer. The physical agony, the guilt. I cradle my forehead in my palms, hunching over. Individual coglinks weren't built to handle this much traffic. A thin line of blood drips out of my left nostril. I tap the outside of my right eye with a thumb. Frantic. My HUD won't shut down.

"*Shut up, all of you!*" Aren shouts over the noise. "*You're overloading his circuits!*"

The voices in my head snap off. The ship, on the other hand, screams, pops, and quakes. Though it sounds like the world's about to end, I think we just saved the day.

A hand alights on my shoulder. Laura kneels next to me. A strange blue light erupts from the crystal-like objects in the backs of her wrists. "Tuck?" she whispers, taking hold of my biceps and looking up at the glass window.

That's right. Griefer. Focus, man.

Don't let her end up like Holly.

Not again.

Never again.

"What's wrong?" Laura whispers.

"Coglinks," I gasp. "Too much, too . . ."

"*Ándale*, get up. We need to go."

I lift my head. The griefer slams itself against the glass again, the motion disjointed. Inhuman. In all my time on the *John Muir*, I've never managed to gank one of these assholes. Got close, once. Let's just say it involved rocket propulsion, an old stuffed teddy bear, and zero gravity. I'll let your imagination take care of the rest.

Laura's nails dig into my arm. The griefer's chest expands, the tips of its rib bones poking out through its flesh like teeth. Taking in air to power a scream.

"*I will answer your questions,*" Dejah says to the rest of the crew. "*Tuck is currently code yellow and cannot assist any of you.*"

"*That's the understatement of the year!*" I grab Laura by the arm and sprint for the core room door, tapping the touchlock and shoving her through the door when its panels slide open. We both scramble out of the room, tripping over each other and landing in a tangle in the hallway. I prop myself over her, shielding her with my back.

The griefer screams. World-cracking. Glass-shattering. Eardrum-breaking. Laura claps her hands over her ears. Echoes hit the ground in front of us, denting the metal floor like ricochets in an old shoot-'em-up movie.

The griefer leaps into the core room, thumping on the floor and sliding into view. It vaults toward the doorjamb, tentacles wrapping around the edges.

Launching myself off the floor, I slam the edge of my fist against the touchlock. The door's ocular panels slam shut. Meaty bits of tentacle thud on the floor near my feet. I kick one away, then tear open the touchlock's control panel. Sparks explode and glitter around my hand as I rip out a handful of wires.

On a scale of one to ball shriveling, griefers are a puss-out.

You don't fight them.

You *run*.

The bastard slams himself against the door. The ocular panels part a few centimeters, but hold.

"Screw this, six cores will be enough. *Hasta la vista*, baby," I say, putting a hand on Laura's back and shoving her toward the deepdown tunnels.

As we run down the octagonal path between core rooms, the ceiling thumps. A crack appears overhead, spreading like a slow-motion lightning bolt. Dust tumbles down. *Wonderful, he's found a way into the maintenance ducts.* One lone tentacle slides out, curling, suckers undulating. Laura ducks beneath it, eyeing it as if she expects it to grab her by the neck. When she looks back at me, I put a finger to my lips. So long as we keep it quiet, we might be able to slip away from the bastard before he finds his way out of the ducts.

"*First,*" Dejah says, "*the starship* Conquistador *crashed into the USS* John Muir *at approximately 0230 hours this morning—*"

Another burst of excited voices slams into my temple. "*Shut. Up!*" I snap at them all, massaging one of my temples as we reach the antechamber's blast door. I tap the touchlock.

The doors slide open.

A small pod of mourners turns toward us, hissing as they gulp down air.

How did they get in here?! And then I see the crank left in the tunnel-side door panels.

Our little EVA-suited terrorist friend forgot to lock up behind himself. *Damn him!*

Laura catches her gasp behind her hand, stepping back from the door. Behind us, the griefer roars from inside one of the other core rooms. A *whump* rocks the floor underfoot.

We both glance back.

Trapped.

In one fluid motion, Laura takes her bow off her back. Nocking an arrow, she fires at the far wall. The arrow shatters with a loud *crack!* The pieces rattle on the floor. All the mourners turn toward the sound with a growl. Laura sidesteps across the antechamber, heading for the door, firing arrow after arrow. Distracting the mourners.

Okay, I have to admit—the girl's fragging *brilliant* at this.

I follow her across the room and tap the touchlock, knowing the noise from the door will draw their attention. And it does. As the panels slide open, the terrorist's door crank clatters to the ground. Mourners spin with a snarl, their lips pulling away from their teeth.

Pushing Laura through the door, I smash my fist against the touchlock again, hard enough to break the dial and trap the mourners inside. Sparks pop. Crackle. My teeth buzz from the shock. The door panels begin to close. I leap through the narrow gap in the panels and roll, landing on the ground next to Laura. The broken lock will force the griefer to ram through the door. I hope.

I've bought us minutes. The doors to the Hive aren't flimsy like the ones sealing off the core rooms—it'll take the bastard longer to break through.

"*Run!*" I whisper to Laura. She strings her bow back over her chest. Launching myself off the floor, I sprint down the hall, and I hear her take off after me.

The maglev station's about three klicks aft. The ship's lights sputter overhead now, which means we have no need for flares. Just speed. The griefer will outpace both of us, once it's through those doors.

We run. Fast and hard, until the floor turns cold as ice underfoot. Laura breathes too loudly but keeps up. Every passing second winds me tighter. My HUD's back up, too, red numbers dancing across my vision. Blinking, I center the HUD lens back over my right eye. It shows the pressure in the tunnel (too low); the oxygen quality (deteriorating); the temperature (dropping).

In short, we're screwed.

"There are human survivors from the crew of the Conquistador *now aboard the John Muir,"* Dejah continues. *"I am in the process of downloading their ship's logs and examining them. At first glance, the crew's mission seems to be of an exploratory or archeological endeavor."*

"Can confirm," I say as I run. *"I ran into one of their crew members after the crash."*

"He with you?" Aren asks.

"She," I say. *"And yes. We're heading toward the trams now. Dejah, can you seal off the bulkheads around the worst of the damage? We're losing too much pressure."*

"Initiating bulkhead closure now," Dejah says. *"I have a position for the* Conquistador's *crew in the deepdowns—Aren, they are within two klicks of your current location."*

"Roger that." I count the tunnel's ribs. We've passed ten intersections. One klick isn't enough space between us and a death punch.

"Tuck," Aren says. *"What happened to Holly?"*

No way to run away from that question. I'm not sure how to answer it, either, or how honest I'm required to be. I don't think I'll tell anyone what happened after the crash.

Ever.

After I pass a few more ribs, Aren asks, *"Tuck?"*

"I'm sorry," I say, and I really am. *"She didn't survive the crash. The tunnels collapsed, and . . ."* I don't dare upload the vidfeed of her last few moments before the crash to everyone's coglinks. Nobody else needs to see that girl suffering.

"Everyone, observe a full minute of silence on the coglinks in her memory," Aren says. *"That includes you, Dejah. Holly was beloved of our crew and will be much missed by all."*

No argument here.

A few minutes pass. Talk resumes on the coglinks. I tune it out, the memories of Holly's death chasing me down the tunnel. I can't focus on anything but putting one foot in front of the other.

It's not long before the tunnel straightens out. The tram station's bulkhead drops into view. I'm relieved.

No doubt that'll be short-lived.

The *Muir*'s aft tram station is massive, stretching across five platforms with a variety of vehicles capable of traveling by rail. The interior's raw gray metal. Round train tubes open their giant maws, their propellant rings bleating with blue and green light. The tracks lie dead. Silent. So quiet, I can hear the air throb with a faraway roar. Mourner calls, too.

Ironically, the aft tram station was my original destination with Holly. Standing here now, without her, feels like a cruel cosmic joke.

Laura glances over her shoulder. *"What now?"* she mouths to me.

Our big problem? I don't see any of the curators' armored trams docked here. We'll have to call one from elsewhere in the ship. The trams aren't quick, so after I reboot the station's systems, we'll have to wait for an armored tram to arrive.

We don't have time to wait, but we can't take a regular tram car, either.

Laura and I enter the maglev traffic control room—an enclosed, pressurized section of the station. I shut the door behind us, sealing in any sounds we might make.

The entire space isn't more than fifteen meters by five.

Huge, cloudy windows look out over the darkened rail lines. Four-hundred-year-old dust frosts everything in here. It slides off the instruments. Two large, dingy glass screens hover over the control panel. Ice crystals form on the glass edges. The aged buttons on the control panel stick so badly, I have to smash them with my fist to depress them.

It takes me a few seconds, but I manage to get the system rebooted. Outside, the rails snap and hum with electricity. The trams clank, their G-shaped runners lifting off the tracks.

A rail map glimmers up on the glass screens in front of me, showing the three tiers of rail lines running through the deepdowns. The lines stack up like layers of a cake. I use the side of my fist to clean a circle on the screen.

Toward the aft section of the map, the t-One and t-Two tracks burn red around the crash site. It looks like Jaws took a giant, bleeding bite out of the ship. The damaged tracks and tunnels are offline. Gone. Crashed into the ship's deepdown sea. The t-Two tracks—our floor—aren't fully glitched, and tracks four and five may still be operational. Stella. One point for Team Human.

"There's not a tram close," I say, bracing myself against the control panel. "We'll have company before we've got a ride back to the park."

Laura hugs herself and looks around the room, shivering from fear or cold or both. Not that I blame her—our big bastard's going to be here in minutes.

The closest tram's parked at the R-3 station, fourth track. I tap the screen to call the tram. My pulse thuds in my ears. ETA? "Six minutes, thirty seconds till the tram arrives." My brain scrambles for a plan.

Thing is, I've never been very good at plans.

"*No manches,*" Laura says.

Moving fast, I lock down the tram's commands so nobody will interfere with our trip once we're onboard. Until we reach the park's ingress door some fifteen klicks away, the only command the tram car will listen to is *GO*. "You'll need to hide," I tell Laura, pointing to a bunch of gutted, multi-car trains sitting on the far edge of the tracks. "Our tram will be big, spiky. The minute I give the signal, make a run for it."

"I don't think we should split up," she says, shifting her weight and crossing her arms over her chest.

"Look, splitting up might get people killed in B horror flicks," I say, straightening. "But you'll have a better chance of survival if you're close to the tram when it gets here."

"And what will you do?"

"Stay in the station and release a bunch of dummy trams into the tunnels. Hopefully, that will draw the attention of most of the mourners—"

"*Hopefully?*" she says, but startles when a loud shriek echoes through the halls. "I'm not just going to leave you behind. That's not what my people do, and it's a stupid plan."

"Please, Laura," I say, not sure how to help her understand that I can't watch another person die on me. Holly's death is still so fresh it burns. Rusty crescent moons of her blood still rise over the pink skies of my nails.

It should've been me under that rock, not her. *Never* her.

"Do I have to beg?" I ask Laura. "Because I will."

"Don't patronize me. Let me help you."

"I'll concentrate better if I know you're safe." Or at least safe-*ish*.

"Don't feel like you have to protect me," she says. "I don't need a white knight."

Blinking hard, I squeeze the bridge of my nose between my thumb and forefinger. *I wish you could see, Laura, that I've already lost one good person today.* But I can't say those words out loud. They embody the kind of sentiment that shows too much of what's inside on the outside, and I've never been good at that sort of thing.

"Don't fight me on this," I say, adding a quick "Please" to soften the request.

"*Don't* think I can't take care of myself, *vato*," she snaps, placing her fists on her hips and lifting her chin. I've only known her for a few hours, but that reaction is just *so. Laura. Cruz.*

"You want to help?" I take a step toward her, my frustration racing neck and neck with my fear. "Take a position inside the trams on the far right side and fire arrows at the walls to distract the griefer. Keep your ass out of sight. I don't want to have to come rescue you."

But I will if I need to.

"Don't worry," she says, "you won't have to."

L A U R A

I don't need rescuing, but I *do* need Tuck on my side, especially since by some miracle, my bioware's operational again.

I jog up to the last row of train cars with an arrow nocked, cursing myself for being so stubborn. I'm not certain how restoring power to the *John Muir* affected the *Conquistador*, or why my bioware's working again. Both bioware nodes powered on a few moments after the *John Muir* came online, though I haven't had a moment's breath to run a diagnostic check on either of them. On the positive side, I'll be able to contact my family as soon as I'm safe. But active bioware means an active subjugator—if any of the Smithsons survived, I'll be running from the clutches of one monster into the claws of another.

¡Estúpida! I tell myself. *You need Tuck to vouch for you if the Smithsons try to blame you for the crash!* My stomach bucks at the thought. The Smithsons could be behind all this, somehow; they've concocted a perfect trap for me, one that will wrest the most important find of the twenty-fifth century—even the

John Muir and Yosemite National Park—out of my family's hands.

But even I have to admit, crashing the *Conquistador* under Pitch Dark's banner is too extreme for them.

A loud shriek shreds the silence behind me, the distance between us diluting the sound. My abdominal muscles cramp. I pivot, scanning the bulkhead area. The tram platforms are an ugly, utilitarian part of the ship. Black-and-gray metal braces the floor, the tracks racing into the tunnels' maws on the far side of the station. Giant procrete buffer-stops stand at the end of each track, meant to halt runaway trains. Paint flakes off the tubes overhead like diseased skin. Lights wink at me from the walls and ceiling.

Nothing moves. Keeping my bow pointed at the ground, I move sideways until I slide behind a large train car. Slipping inside, I find myself inside a midmodern-styled car with lots of passenger seating. Much of the maroon upholstery's rotted away, leaving behind moldy mounds of stuffing. Rust maps the metal ceiling, drawing strange continents in the metal. I hold back a sneeze, pinching my nostrils tight, to keep the dust from swirling up my nose. The pressure throbs through my head.

Outside, the tracks click as Tuck tests the trams. The whistle of depressurizing hydraulics and the screech of rusted metal echo through the cavernous station.

The windows don't open automagically, but I manage to figure out the analog latch. The glass hisses as I prop it open, dust flowing over the edge. The particles glitter in the station's low lights. Taking cover behind the wide sill, I brace my bow against the window, waiting. From this vantage point, I've got a good view of the station's bulkhead and control room.

I'm exhausted, aching, and famished. My hands tremble, nerves shot with an overdose of adrenaline combined with a nearly empty stomach. So much depends on the next few minutes.

You can do this, Laura, I hear my mother's words echo in my heart. *You're a Cruz.*

Something moves on the station's threshold. A lone mourner crawls into view, backlit by the tunnel's light. Long spikes jut off his back. He sniffs the floor, then arches and howls like all the lonely things in the world.

In seconds, he's overtaken by a mob that moves like a plague of maggots. Their calls thump through the tunnel, bouncing off the sides of trams and boxing my ears. These pitches are different from the shrieks I heard before—these are rounder, fuller in their harmonic range. Rather than a targeted blow, these cries spread out, filling the entire station with wave after wave of pummeling sound.

They're looking for us. If I step out into that maelstrom, every one of those monsters will see me. I sink deeper into my cloak. With my shoulder pressed to the train car's wall, I wait, watching the station.

In the control room, Tuck drops out of sight as a mourner crawls across the room's large windows, gecko-like. A mass of writhing, shrieking white bodies froths between us. Some convulse so much—their heads shaking like old bobbleheads—they wheel about drunkenly, banging their heads on the train rails and stumbling off the platform ledges.

A roar shakes the tram station, the sound powerful enough to make my train car shudder, even at a distance. In the control room, Tuck reaches up and hits a few keys. The tram cars stowed on the first and third tracks clank. The first tram rolls forward. Half the mourners leap after it, some landing too close and getting hit by the tram and crushed. Others lope alongside as it disappears into the tunnel.

On a second roar, the griefer stalks through the station bulkhead, moving with murderous grace. My mind fills in the blanks left by the darkness: The towering physique. The mandibles. The spikes along the spine and shoulders.

The tentacles.

Still shrouded in the bulkhead's shadows, the griefer pauses to scent the air. Panic flares in my fingertips as it starts toward the control room. I scan the station, looking for something— *anything*—to buy Tuck a few extra seconds. Bracing my knee on an old seat, I take aim at one of the big, egg-shaped chandeliers hanging over the platform closest to the station, then fire.

My arrow slams into the light fixture. Sparks explode like fireworks. Glass glitters down to the ground, and the mourners wheel toward the sound as I shoot out a second light, then a third.

Tuck launches the tram off the third track while the griefer turns toward the shattered, sparking lights. The monster leaps off the platform, eyes narrowed, following the loose tram down the tracks.

That's it, I say, my stomach in such knots I think I'm going to vomit. *That's right. You just follow that tram right down into the tunnel, you big, stupid chupacabra. . . .*

As the griefer goes to grab the tram's side ladder, my bio-ware pings. The bright *ding!* of a new notification resounds like cannon fire in the train station.

The griefer halts on the tracks. He releases the tram ladder, turning his head toward my position. Not his body, just the head. It turns too far for a human head, bones shifting and adjusting in the spine to allow the creature to look almost 180 degrees behind him. Straight at the train car I'm hiding in.

For a horrible moment, I feel stripped naked, as if the train's metal walls have withered away.

A ping message screen inflates from my wrist: *Hi, Laura,* the Noh Mask hacker writes. *So glad to see you survived the crash. This mission would've been dull without you.*

Stomach plummeting, I scramble through my ioScreen's menus, trying to turn the sound for my notifications off. Another *ping!* echoes through the station, a message appearing in the upper right-hand corner of my screen: *You'll be glad to know I just figured out how to link the crew's bioware to the* John Muir's *systems. I'm uploading all your missed pings to your system now. Enjoy!*

He adds a smiley face to the end of the message. My heart feels like it's been shoved off the top of a building, and now plunges through my chest.

Ping! from Mami: *Where are you, m'ija?! Gracias a dios, you're alive! Are you okay?*

Ping! from Dad: *Laura, where are you?*

Ping! from Faye: *Omigod are you okay? Laura! What's happened to you?*

Ping! from Alex: ***Chiquita, for real, everyone can see you're online. Where are you?***

Ping! from my brother Gael: ***Flaca, you'd better answer us . . .***

Pings! from the tías.

Pings! from my friends.

Ping!

Ping!

Ping!

Shut up, shut up, shut up! I beg my bioware, but my hands shake so much, I can't shut the notification off. As my wrist shakes, my ioScreen bobs and weaves, and I resort to punching it with a thumb until the pinging stops.

The silence settles around me.

A chill threads my spine as the mourners outside begin to keen, long and low. The sound crawls into the train and rattles around. At that moment, all the mourners' heads lift together in a strange, awful synchronicity, turning to look at my hiding place.

The griefer starts for my train, punting the other mourners out of his way. He stomps on their necks, snapping the bones or breaking rib cages. All the creatures around him growl and arch, ready to scream.

I drop to one knee as the screeching hits the train's flank, blowing out the train's windows and rocking it on its rails. I cover my head with my hands as glass glitters around me. A mourner bursts through the train car at the back, its neck sac swelling. I roll on my back and skewer its throat with an arrow. My chest constricts with fear.

Pushing to my feet, I scramble through the train cars,

looking for somewhere, *anywhere*, to hide on this train. The cars are empty, with no restrooms, no trapdoors, and no places to hide.

As the mourners pile into the train, it breaks open at a sagging accordion connector. The doors between two cars yawn wide open. I leap from one car to the next, crossing the breach and landing with a *clunk*. The toes of my right foot jam into a fallen seat. I hear the *crack* of bone with my body, not my ears. Pain stabs from my soles to the crown of my head, electrifying my bones. I clap a hand over my mouth to muffle any noise, launching myself forward. My biggest toe bones feel like they're grinding together with each step. Hot tears leak from my eyes.

I stumble into the last car, bracing myself against one of the seats. It looks utilitarian, with corrugated metal floors and gear racks running over the tops of the seats. I'm boxed in. Mourners spill onto train cars behind me, coming through the windows. Chasing me. Out on the tracks, the monsters seethe like maggots on a corpse, their flesh yellowed and thin. They will overtake this train car in seconds.

With nowhere to run, I hoist myself up onto one of the gear racks and hunker down among giant, overstuffed duffel bags, cracked crates spilling dusty electrical equipment, and rolls of insulation. Wrapping myself up in my cloak, I press as much of my body behind a massive, dusty roll of insulation as I can and squeeze my eyes closed.

The griefer roars. The train shudders and keens on its rails. I don't move, taking slow, shallow breaths, just enough air to keep myself conscious, but not enough to make any sound. The monster pounds its body against the car. Once, twice, three times. Violent fast. As if trying to frighten me from my hiding place. Metal screeches as one of the cars behind me crashes to the ground.

I wonder if the monsters can hear the bang and pound of my heart. Tuck never mentioned anything about that, but my heart slams so hard in my ears, it sounds like a drum.

With a snort, the griefer steps onto the train at least one car back. The aged floors groan, shuddering under his weight. While I can't see the monster from my hiding spot, his footsteps make the train cars quake. Mourners swarm my car, drawing closer as they tumble through the windows and clamber up on the luggage rack. My gorge rises, fear threatening to seal my airway off. *They're going to find me,* I think, drawing my arms so tight to my chest, my muscles ache. *They're going to kill me.*

When the griefer roars for real, it's the sound of a lion in a barbed-wire collar remixed with a hawk's sharp cry, layered over a track of shattering glass. The rack on the other side of the train shifts, squeals, and snaps off the wall.

The roar seems to last forever, denting metal, ripping the seats apart. The air pressure spikes. I duck my head into my arms, pressing my knees into my torso, and shake.

Nothing moves in the silence that follows. All I hear are the clicking sounds of wheels on tracks, and a big, depressurizing sigh. Like a train coming into the station. I strain for another sound, but all that's left is a high whine, like I have flies trapped inside my head.

When I peek out from under my cloak, the inside of the tram is splattered with mourner gore.

"Laura!" Tuck's shout rips through the tunnel space. The

griefer growls, glass crackling underfoot. He sounds like he's at least one train car back still. "That bastard's shriek takes a minute to recharge! Get out!"

No-no-no-no, my gut says. *Don't reveal yourself. He might not find you—*

"Laura! Now or never!" Tuck shouts again. He sounds panicked, and must be, if he's dared to give away his position to help me.

He just risked himself for you.

You can do this, Laura.

Go!

Gritting my teeth, I throw back my cape and drop into the train's aisle, wincing at the pain in my foot. I look up. The griefer looms half a car down, its tentacles writhing. Huge claws extend from the creature's hands and wrists in a medieval, macelike weapon. Glass, twisted metal, fractured bone, and other nasty-looking detritus litters the car's floor. The dismembered limbs and viscera of dead mourners covers everything. A long strand of intestines decorates the tops of the seats. A broken leg hangs through one of the windows.

I see these things through the filter of panic. As a series of snapshots stretched out over high-pressure heartbeats.

It's a *nightmare.*

The griefer leaps toward me. I don't even think. I lunge across the aisle and vault through the window. A piece of sharp glass still embedded in the frames claws into my shoulder. Thanks to adrenaline, I hardly feel the pain. Tumbling down to the ground below, I land on my hip in a bed of glass.

The griefer slams through the window after me. Getting

stuck. The broken glass cuts large red canals in the monster's milky flesh, its tentacles bulging and bleeding, throat sac swelling, jaw dropping open, cheeks splitting. Bloody saliva drips off its jaws and onto my face and cape. Hunks of glass stick out of its shoulders and back like icy spikes.

I push off the side of the tram, sprinting for the armored tram on track four. It's nothing like the other trains on the tracks—the tram looks more like a midmodern tank than a train. Tuck's fighting up top by the cupola entrance, punching a mourner. I strip off my bow, take aim, and shoot an arrow through its skull. It tumbles off the tram, getting caught in the spikes. I dodge another mourner, yanking another arrow from my quiver and slamming it into the creature's jugular. Blood spurts over my hand.

"Laura!" Tuck shouts, hopping halfway down the tram's ladder and extending a hand to me. "C'mon!"

I charge forward, clapping my hand into Tuck's. He yanks me up the ladder, pushing me up to the roof. I drop through the tram's open topside cupola, collapsing to the floor. Breathing hard.

Through the tram's dingy windows, I watch the griefer fight free from the train car's window. He tumbles to the ground, stands, and makes eye contact with me while tugging a long, spear-shaped shard of glass from his arm.

Tuck leaps into the tram after me, swinging down with the cupola hatch. With a quick, midair twist of his body, he locks it in three places. Thick steel clamps reach up and chomp over the hatch to hold it closed.

Leaping past me, Tuck scrambles for the train's cockpit.

"Hang on!" he says, jamming his fingers into a button on the tram's control board.

The griefer leaps atop the tram, beating at the cupola with his fist. The metal rings like a gong.

"Not today, asshole," Tuck says as the tram lurches forward.

The pain from my broken toes hits me. *Hard*. The torment stabs up through my heel and bleeds through my thighs. Heat gurgles in my stomach and rockets through my chest. I vomit, half choking on the bile and a sob.

I drop my bow, which clatters to the floor. I inch away from the puddle made up of nothing more than a chalky energy bar and stomach acid. The smell burns my nose. The world spins and bucks, as if I'm drunk-dumping in deep-space flight training again. Through the haze of nausea and pain, I see a few pieces of glass wedged into my feet. Blood's pooling on the floor. I sling my quiver off my back but clutch it tight to my chest, hoping its precious cargo is still intact.

The train picks up speed, plunging into the blackness of a tunnel. Overhead, claws screech against the tram's roof. The sound hits me like a blunt shovel being jammed into the side of my head. Two heavy bumps hit the tram's roof, then nothing.

One last roar tears after us, fading as we pick up speed.

TUCK

Once the tram's rushing forward and the griefer's roar becomes a memory, I rush to Laura. She slouches against the tram's back wall, sobbing. Blood and vomit smear the floor around her. Tears collect in her lashes. Her shoulder's gashed, her big toe's got a compound fracture, and broken glass studs the soles of her feet.

But frag me, she's *alive*.

Breathing, too.

She wipes bile off the side of her mouth. Sweat sticks long pieces of her hair to her temples. A flashback of Holly grabs me by the throat. I shake it loose, shake it off, and sink to the floor beside Laura.

"Hey, you made it, you're going to be okay." I remove her cloak and balaclava, ball it up, and press it into her torn shoulder. I place her good hand over the makeshift compress. "Hold that there—that's good. 'Tis just a flesh wound, am I right?" I know she doesn't get the reference, but saying those words in a Python-esque voice still brings a shaky smile to her face.

"How long till we get to safety?" she asks.

"Fifteen minutes," I say. "The tram's operating on partial power."

"Ay, ay, ay," she says, gulping down a big breath. Closing her eyes, she rests the back of her head against the wall. Her fingertips curl against the hollow of her throat.

"If you want painkillers—"

"It's not the pain that's bothering me," she says.

Propping one of her feet in my lap, I pick slivers of glass out of her skin. "How do you say 'liar, liar' in Spanish?"

"It doesn't matter what language you say it in," she says through gritted teeth. "Trust me, I've had worse."

What could be worse than this? Her feet are wrecked. A fractured bone in her big toe juts out of her skin, a white shank coated in blood. Glass hunks glitter like rubies growing out of her skin. Small tufts of insulation cling to her wounds.

If I'd been injured this bad, I would've pussed out back on the train.

"Anybody ever tell you that you're a badass, Laura Cruz?" I ask, plucking a chunk of glass from her foot. I flick it under a nearby seat.

She shakes her head, lower lip trembling.

"Well, they should. I've never seen someone outrun a griefer. All I've got in this first aid kit is a mild painkiller. Do you want some?"

She nods. I drop the pills in her palm, then spend the next few minutes picking glass out of her skin, before bandaging the wounds as best I can with the first aid kit in the tram.

"You going to take those pills?" I ask her.

"Maybe with a little water."

"Oh, duh." I hand her my canteen.

The lights flicker overhead, glitching. Laura glances up at them as she swallows her pills, exposing her throat. In the hollow between her collarbones, something moves beneath her skin. I narrow my eyes.

That was too big to be a pill.

Gently, I place a finger on the nub in the hollow of her throat, smearing blood on her skin. A bone-hard mass rests inside the tissue. Her chin snaps down and her eyes widen. Before I can pinch the thing between my finger and thumb, it sinks deeper into her flesh. Laura gasps in pain. Air whooshes through her windpipe, but the thing's gone.

"What the hell is that?" I ask.

Laura takes her hand from mine, curling her fingers back into the hollow of her throat. Defensive, almost.

She parts her lips to speak. Pauses. Then purses her lips.

She tries to say, "It's what's really bothering me, a *s-s-s* . . . I-it's, I should say . . ." But she chokes on the words. Her throat convulses. I brace her good shoulder with one hand. When she coughs, tremors shake her whole body. Each breath sounds like someone's using sandpaper to scour the inside of her throat— hoarse and painful.

"Breathe," I say. Her eyes are bloodshot from the violence of her coughing fit. The big V-shaped tendons stick out in her throat. Her jugular veins throb under her skin.

What the hell's going on? I wonder.

"I still can't . . . can't talk about . . . ," she says, gasping. "It . . . it won't . . . ." Whatever she's trying to say gets interrupted by more coughing.

"Stop, stop, stop," I say. The sight of her like this—gasping for breath and injured—kindles the anger in my chest. Something tickles in the back of my mind, some old memory of Aren. In a past life, he worked for the CIA an as engineer. He left the agency when they asked him to build "parasitic tech," a sort of device that could be used to infiltrate and monitor a target with or without their knowledge. *Not a very democratic request, eh?* he'd asked me then.

I'm certain tech's gotten better in the last four hundred years. Smarter. Whatever's in Laura's throat doesn't allow her to talk about it; however, there's a second of lag before it's able to shut her dialogue down.

So I just have to game the shutdown.

"Let's play Twenty Questions," I say, once she's breathing normally again. "It'll take your mind off the pain for a while. I'm going to ask you a bunch of yes-or-no questions. Blink twice for yes, once for no, fast as you can. Don't think. Don't elaborate. Okay?"

Laura cocks her head and wrinkles her nose, but says, "O-*kaaay.*"

"Here we go—do you like pizza?"

She blinks twice. *Yes.*

"With pepperoni?"

One blink. *No.*

"You monster," I say.

She half laughs, wincing. "I'm a vegetarian!"

"Hey, no talking! Do you play soccer?"

One blink. *No.*

"Is history your favorite subject in school?"

Two blinks.

"Do you have a boyfriend?"

A scarlet flush burns across her cheeks. One blink.

Score.

"That was a rude question," she says.

"Was not, and you're breaking the rules again—" Though I'll admit the question had a personal motivation. "Do you have siblings?"

She blinks twice.

"Older?"

Twice.

"Younger?"

Twice.

"Ooh, a forgotten middle child," I say with a grin.

She makes a face, wrinkling up her nose and pursing her lips. "Nobody gets *forgotten* in my family."

"You're really bad at following game rules, huh?"

She bats her eyelashes at me.

"Yeah, that's what I thought. Do you have a good relationship with your parents?"

Two blinks.

"Lucky. I loved my mom, but she was a workaholic and I didn't see her much. Do you speak two languages?"

One blink. Which means she speaks *more* than two languages, since I'm guessing she's fluent in English and Spanish.

"Three?"

One blink.

"Four?"

Two blinks and a grin.

"Damn, that's impressive." Then casually, so coolly, I ask, "Is there a piece of parasitic tech in your throat?"

Laura blinks once. On the second blink, her eyelids freeze halfway down. Her face twitches as she tries to force her eyes closed, tears forming on the lower lids.

"Good hell," I say softly.

She seems stuck for a few seconds, and then looks up at me. Despondent. Afraid. Two emotions I've known every damn day of my life since the jettison. I've never been good with sympathy or empathy or any of the *pathies*, really. At least according to Mom.

It's not that I don't care. It's that I don't know how to *articulate* that I care.

Show, don't tell, Tuck, Mom snaps at me in my memories. *You don't have to say anything. Do something.*

Gently, I ease down beside Laura. I put an arm around her shoulders. Gathering her cloak up from the floor, she presses it to her chest, shivering. I tuck the edges around her. The tram's fragging cold, but I'm not sure that's why she's shaking.

She rests her head on my shoulder. My muscles lock up. Warning bells go off in my head—*if you don't want to care about her, don't touch her.*

But I'm not stupid enough to think I don't already care for this girl. Or stubborn enough to deny I *want* to touch her, either. Who wouldn't want to be close to someone like Laura Cruz? Smart, quick-thinking, and tougher than almost anyone else I know. So I relax, drawing her closer, but careful to keep my hand away from the injury on her shoulder.

My HUD blinks, notifying me that Aren's initiating a private chat. *"Tuck, you there?"* he asks.

"Yeah?" I respond.

"Just checking in—you've been quiet for a while now."

I lean the back of my head against the tram's wall. *"We're on our way to the park now. The tram system's been rebooted. Keep it to tracks four and five on the t-Two and t-Three levels, though. Everything else's busted."*

"Dejah didn't tell me the trams were back online," Aren says, confused. *"Hold on, let me change to a public channel to include her."*

My coglink beeps, the sound echoing through my skull, as Aren opens our chat channel to include the ship's AI.

"Dejah, are you listening?" Aren asks.

No answer.

I frown. *"Dejah? Hello?"*

"Dejah, can you hear us?" Aren asks. When Dejah fails to respond after a few seconds, Aren swears. *"Now what?"* he almost growls through the coglinks.

"When was your last communication with her?" I ask. I hadn't been paying attention to Dejah, too busy trying to keep from getting ganked by the griefer and his little mourner buddies.

"Ten minutes ago, right after I met with the captain and officers of the Conquistador,*"* he says. *"Could they possibly have done something to the ship's systems?"*

"You mean besides crash their fragging ship into us?" I reply. *"I don't know. Odds are we have an enemy in their ranks. Laura—the girl I'm with—claims the ships were crashed by a hacker."*

"Do you trust her?"

"Yeah," I say without hesitation. *"If she wanted to harm the* Muir, *she had a hundred chances in the deepdowns. She saved my life. Twice."*

"Okay," Aren says with an implied sigh. *"I'm going to see if I can figure out what happened to Dejah. In the meantime, get your ass back here."*

"We'll be at the park platform in ten. The girl needs a medic. Bad."

"Understood. See you there."

Once Aren signs off, I rub my face with my free hand. I'm frustrated. Dejah doesn't "disappear." She doesn't go offline. Dejah *is* the *Muir*'s heart and soul. She has access to 90 percent of the ship's functions. And for the last twenty-two months, she's been our only link to the bridge—the ship's foredecks have been overrun with mourners since stasis-break.

We curators haven't stepped foot on the bridge since.

Without Dejah's support, there's no saving the *John Muir*.

"Tuck, do you realize you're grinding your teeth?" Laura turns her face up. "I'm sorry, but it's annoying as hell."

"Sorry," I say. "But it sounds like the other curators located the rest of your crew and got them back to the park. We'll be there soon."

Laura presses her lips together, looking down at her busted toe. She tries to wiggle it, sucking in a tight, pained breath. "Promise me one thing?"

"Anything," I say.

"When my enemies come for me, remember how much I wanted to save this ship."

Her words wobble. A single tear escapes down her cheek. I reach down and wick it off with my thumb.

"At the risk of sounding *hella* retro," I say, "anyone who tries to hurt you will have to deal with me."

Laura snorts. "You're right, that did sound hokey. But"—she kisses me on the cheek—"thank you."

I don't know what I've just signed up for, but I do know for sure:

If this girl's got enemies on this ship, so do I.

L A U R A

I can't believe *Tuck*, of all people, noticed the enemy under my skin.

I wince. Every time the tram shifts, pain bursts through my shoulder and sparks in my foot. I breathe through it, like Mami would tell me to do. At least some of the adrenaline's draining out of my system, leaving my limbs, mind, and heart heavy. We're safe enough for the moment, but I don't know what I'll find when we get to the park.

At the very least, Tuck knows about my subjugator.

Nobody on the *Conquistador* ever realized what was wrong with me. Hosting a subjugator isn't like suffering from an illness or malady; there aren't widely publicized "warning signs" the population is told to look for in a victim. And the device's AI adapts too quickly for most people to realize it's present at all.

Speaking of my parents . . . I shift my left arm out from

between my body and Tuck's side, shaking my wrist to wake up my ioScreen. It shoots out of my bioware node, startling him.

"What the hell?" Tuck asks, sticking his fingers through the screen. Blue light gilds his skin. "What is that thing?"

"It's an ioScreen," I say, selecting Mami's ping message and typing out a reply: *Lo siento, Mami. I'm safe, and I think I'll see you soon.* Once I click send, I continue: "For privacy reasons, only the bioware user can interact with and see the information on their personal ioScreen. You can see my screen's light and shape"—I frame one side with my hand—"but you won't be able to see what's on the display, unless I decide you can."

"And the screen comes out of here?" Tuck asks, tapping the bioware node on the back of my wrist.

"Correct," I say.

"That's some serious Skynet shit you have going on."

"Says the boy with a chip in his head."

"Touché."

I turn my attention from him as Mami replies to my ping:

¡Dios mío, m'ija! I've never gotten a ping that's made me so happy! I read these words and smile to dam up my tears. *Are you okay?*

Somewhere aboard this ship, my mother lives and breathes. If Mami's okay, and my family's okay, I'm okay.

Yes and no, I reply. *I'm alive, but I've got broken toes and a few nasty cuts.*

Where are you?

I type: *On a tram with one of the ship's crew members.*

You're on your way to the park? she asks.

I think so, yes . . . who made it? Who's still alive?

My mother doesn't respond immediately, and something dark and nauseous gathers in my gut as minutes pass. When my bioware pings again, all Mami says is: *I think it's better to have that conversation in person, m'ija. I'll see you soon. Te quiero.*

Te quiero, Mami.

Mami's answer makes my heart ache worse than cracked bones or cuts that turn my flesh into slavering, gory mouths. I know, without question, that people I love are gone.

I rub the hollow of my throat with my thumb, anxious. My fingers itch. I want to ping everyone I know and ask them if they're okay. From the messages on my screen, I know Dad's alive. My brother Gael, too. Alex and Faye. A few of my tías. But I don't have pings from my little sister, my grandmother, or several of my cousins.

It doesn't mean they're dead, Laura. As I'm about to shut down my bioware, a new ping from the Noh Mask hacker pops up in the corner of the screen:

That was quite the performance, the ping reads. *I watched via the ship's old security cameras. You were the picture of grace, leaping out of that train car.*

I sit up straight, sucking in a breath as pain echoes through my body. *You turned my bioware back on when Tuck and I restored the ship's power, didn't you?*

Of course I did, the Noh Mask hacker responds. *Who else would be cunning enough to find a way to link the* Conquistador's *systems with the* John Muir's?

"Laura?" Tuck asks. "What's wrong?"

"The other hacker's alive," I say. Hitting a couple of keys, I remove my ioScreen's opacity so he can read the hacker's messages.

"*Other* hacker?" Tuck asks, suspicion creeping into his tone. His gaze shifts from the screen to me, brows drawing close across his forehead.

I wince. *Oops.* "So the night of the crash . . . I broke the law. I hacked my parents' ship to escape, well, you know." Tuck taps the hollow of his throat, and I nod. "Apparently, I wasn't the only hacker who decided to attack the ship that evening, and—"

Ping!

"I should have told you before," I say breathlessly. "I'm sorry."

"We were strangers."

"We are *still* strangers."

"Are we?" he asks, and suddenly, I realize how uncomfortably close we are. I scoot a centimeter or two away, under the pretense of getting comfortable. "How many strangers have picked glass out of your feet? I think I at least qualify as a friend, yeah?"

That makes me smile. I bob my head. "Friends, then."

"Friends."

I open up the Noh Mask hacker's next message.

Listen, the ship's AI was getting in my way, so I deleted her—

Tuck sucks in a breath. "Ah, crap. So that's where Dejah went."

"Who?"

"The ship's AI, Dejah," he says. "She stopped responding to the curators a few minutes ago."

It's a pity, really. She was an elegantly programmed artificial being, much smarter than the throttled AIs the Panamerican government allows these days.

"Screw you, asshole," Tuck mutters under his breath.

I type back, *You had no right to do anything to her—*

The hacker's next reply appears before I finish typing: *I know you have a hard time functioning outside your strict moral code, Laura. But unless you learn how to play dirty, this is a game you're going to lose.*

That sounds like a challenge, I say.

We're hackers, Laura, the Noh Mask hacker replies. *Challenges are what we live for.*

Before I can reply, the tram jerks to a halt.

"We're here," Tuck says.

With Tuck's assistance—as well as help from strangers—I manage to climb out of the tram. Once I'm topside, Tuck sweeps me into his arms, bow and all, and my face feels like it might catch fire. We're back in the tunnels, exposed and in danger, so I don't dare protest. Tuck *knows* I can't.

At least not till we're safe behind a big, sound-proofed door.

When the pain grows to be too overwhelming, I lean my head against Tuck's chest. It's odd to feel the heartbeat of an almost stranger, quasi-friend. More friend than stranger now, I suppose. Still, there's something comforting about knowing that despite the four hundred years between us, our hearts still beat the same. Our species evolves in terms of technology, philosophy, and culture, but the human heartbeat hasn't changed for a hundred thousand years.

Cloaked figures stand on the platform, motionless, silent, their faces hidden by their hoods. Their presence fills me with a thick sense of foreboding. Tuck carries me across a gangway and past the other curators, who turn to follow us through the large bulkhead. The door panels stand thicker than Tuck's shoulders are wide. Once the door's hydraulics engage, the panels slide closed, hissing as they go. A loud *boom!* echoes up the tunnel when the panels meet.

Despite the dimness, I take in the tunnel's smooth, rounded walls and the procrete bolsters placed at regular intervals. The air smells filtered, mostly odorless with a twinge of chemical disinfectant. I expected it to be warmer inside, but the cold still nibbles on my bare skin. The path ahead slopes upward, toward a well-lit tunnel.

Once we're inside, something prickles in my gut. I feel as though these shadowy strangers are looking at me. Discussing me. In their heads. I sink my fingers into Tuck's shirt, curling closer to him.

It's not the welcome I expected.

"It's okay, Laura," he whispers. The other curators slide their hoods off their heads, most of them as pale as eggshells. *They look like ghosts*, I think.

But it's not till Tuck reaches the top of the ramp that I see the specters from my own world:

Dr. Smithson and Sebastian stand at the top, beside a tall, broad-shouldered man in a stiflecloth cape. His thick, dark hair is frosted silver at the temples. He looks past me and straight at Tuck. A gurney waits beside them, one with thick nylon straps, plus armed Smithson bodyguards to spare.

I recoil, a gasp lodging itself in my throat. There isn't any need to ask who the gurney is intended for, or what those straps are meant to do. Tuck senses the shift in my body language and halts, eyeing the gurney.

Tuck asks the question anyway: "Who's the gurney for, Aren?" He looks pointedly at the tall man in the cape.

Aren lifts his chin. He clears his throat, stalling for the right thing to say. "You said the girl was injured—"

"I think I'll just carry her to the medbay," Tuck says. "It's not too far from here."

Aren sighs, pinching the bridge of his nose. "Kid, let's not do this now, okay?"

"Do what?" Tuck says, his barely suppressed growl roiling in his chest. "The right thing? That's not a gurney for an injured person, that's a gurney for a *criminal*."

Dr. Smithson shakes her head. "We need to stop pussyfooting around the issue, Aren." She looks straight at me. "Laura Cruz is to be arrested on charges of conspiracy, terrorism, and destruction of a national monument."

Tuck's laughter booms up the tunnel, so loud and derisive, it masks the rage I feel trembling through his entire frame.

"Where's my mother?" I ask, my voice so hoarse it scrapes against the back of my throat. "I demand to speak with Capitana Cruz, *now*."

"You can speak to her from a holding cell," Dr. Smithson says.

"She needs a *doctor*!" Tuck snaps, looking at Aren. "And maybe I should remind you, that while you assholes were safe here at the park, Laura and I were risking our lives to get the power back on in the deepdowns."

His voice rings through the hall, drawing silence down in its wake.

Aren presses his lips together till they're bloodless. "Do you trust this girl?" he asks Tuck.

"With my life," Tuck says through his teeth. He and Aren stare each other down for a few seconds, and I know, I *know* they're talking about me. It's strange, watching two people discuss one's fate without words, and not being given the right to defend oneself in the argument.

"Fine, carry her, then," Aren says gruffly. "But I will hold you responsible for her behavior."

"Oh yeah, there's a threat that will keep me up at night," Tuck says, rolling his eyes. Aren turns with a dramatic swirl of his cape and starts down the tunnel; Dr. Smithson follows him. The Smithson mercenaries take hold of the gurney, pushing it uptunnel. Sebastian remains behind, lip curling as he watches Tuck and me, his eyes growing sharp at the corners.

"Come here, Laura, cariño," he says, grinning when my muscles jerk so hard, I tumble out of Tuck's arms. Pain shoots up my legs. I bite down on my lip to keep from crying out, steading myself on Tuck's shoulder.

"Haven't you missed me?" Sebastian asks.

I hate you. My subjugator forces me to take an agonizing step forward. Waves of pain roll through my calves and knees and thighs, the heat so bright I draw a quick breath to keep myself from passing out.

"Laura, don't!" Tuck cries. My next step squelches as if I've stepped on a wet sponge, fresh scabs breaking, blood bubbling between my toes. My bandages stick to the ground as I lift my foot.

Greed makes monsters of all men. I had such high hopes for

Sebastian once; now, it seems as though he's no more capable of human empathy than the monsters in the deepdowns. And just like the mourners, Sebastian can tear me down with nothing more than his voice.

I hold Sebastian's gaze, letting him see all my fury, all my pain, and all my rebellion. "I. Am. Not. Your. *Cariño*," I say.

My words echo off the tunnel walls.

The grin falls off Sebastian's face when Tuck scoops me back into his arms. As we pass Sebastian on our way up the tunnel, Tuck inclines his head in Sebastian's direction and asks, "That them?"

I blink twice before the subjugator can recognize my betrayal.

Tuck swears hard. "So much for a hero's welcome."

TUCK

I escort Laura to the medbay from the Ingress bulkhead, shocked by the number of people waiting in the foyer.

Laura's family engulfs her, exchanging kisses. Hugs. Tears. Happy squeals of delight and relief. Spanish and English twine together. The room feels warm, but not in temperature. I don't have the words to describe this atmosphere—I don't understand family on this scale.

To me, *family* always meant a mother sequestered in her study. An endless parade of boyfriends, nannies, and Mom's work friends. Loved ones on loan.

I hang at the door, a pit in my gut.

I'm no good with people. Especially a crowd of them.

Ducking back into the hallway, I pull my hood over my head. My palms sweat. Even though I'm moving forward, it feels like the ground's crumbling under my feet. I need to get back into the deepdowns.

I need to run.

So I do.

LAURA

When the anesthesia curls into my brain, I dream.

Of a mountain with only half a face.

And a path that dives into a hole in a rock.

I dream of a round, bronze door in a dark place.

And a woman sitting behind a huge wooden desk.

She looks a little like Tuck, only older. Or maybe Tuck looks like her.

Tanned, and not pale as flour, like the others. Her forehead's lined like ancient paper. A single shock of gray hair falls on the left side of her face. There's white dust on the sleeves of her blouse.

"Hello, Laura Cruz," she says, looking me straight in the eye.

She pronounces my name correctly.

"Who are you?" I ask, but she doesn't seem to hear me.

"I can get you to the *John Muir*'s bridge," she says.

"What do you mean?"

"You're the only one who can save her now."

"She's waking. . . ."

I stir. *Let me sleep.* I want the comfort of oblivion, and to hold on to the vestiges of my dreams.

Another voice intrudes: "When she wakes, press this button on the pod. . . ."

Cállate . . . don't you bogus people realize we need to be quiet? I think, trying to block the voice out. The comfort of this bed draws me down into a dark, silent space. The sheets rustle over my bare legs. I settle deeper into a warm comforter, tugging it up around my face. But the harder I try to hold on to sleep, the more I scramble to catch ahold of the fraying end of the dream, the quicker it slips away.

Gone.

"Laura? It's Sofía, can you hear me?" one of the voices asks. The tone has a plasticky, odd quality. Other sounds burble in the space outside, inorganic beeps and the shuffle of feet. Voices.

"Get back, everyone," someone says. It sounds like Faye. "Give Sofí some room."

My eyes drift open, shadows blurring the soft blue lights overhead. They seem to stab small needles through my corneas and into my brain. I groan and throw my forearm over my eyes to block out the light. The sound has substance and weight, but it travels the space of centimeters.

Smashing my eyes closed against the light, I reach up and touch a concave surface overhead. I slide my palms along the inside until something clicks and there's a *whoosh* of escaping air. I try to open my eyes again, but the lights are brighter now, more insistent.

Cold air creeps over my skin, tearing the last wisps of sleep away.

I'm surrounded by blurry faces. I sit up. The blood rushes to my head, and I fold forward, cradling my forehead in my hands. Someone puts a hand on my bare shoulder, bracing me. My long hair falls forward, curtaining off the room's light. My throat's dry. The drugs in my system tug on my eyelids, trying to drag me back to sleep. Pain still needles the soles of my feet.

"Laura?" a small voice asks. I lift my head and see my little sister, Sofía, standing next to my bed. She reaches up and tucks my hair behind one ear, like Mami would do. Her smile's tentative, unsure. "Are you okay?"

"I think so," I say, croaking the words. Her eyes fill with tears, and she throws her arms around me. I hadn't gotten a chance to see my sister before they rushed me into surgery for the cuts on my feet.

That's right, I'm in a medpod.

I outran a griefer.

I met a boy who was born on Earth.

The room comes into focus around me. I'm sitting inside an open surgical pod. A smattering of vials filled with blue, green, and clear liquids stand on my right side, pumping medication into my veins. The walls are eggshell white, and checkered with panels and screens. My vitals are displayed nearby: my blood pressure, heart rate, and organ function all look normal. The pain lessens with each breath I take. The world sharpens, too.

Evidence of my family's presence abounds in the room: Mami's leather jacket is draped over one chair; Dad's favorite water bottle stands on a tray by my bed. Most of my personal belongings are here, too: the stiflecloth cloak from Tuck and my bow and quiver stand forgotten in a corner. I blow out a breath, relieved to see someone brought my quiver along from the tram.

Alex is sitting in a chair beside my bed, leaning forward, elbows resting on his knees. Though he looks at ease, he exhibits a preternatural sense of awareness, the muscles standing out in his shoulders and jaw, his locs spilling over one shoulder. A few cousins hold vigil here, too. The whites of Isha's eyes have turned pink from her tears, and her eyelids have swollen. Lena's sporting a black eye and a split lip. Everyone's injured. Sofía's right arm is cradled in a sling. Bandages hatch both Faye's and Alex's limbs.

I pull back from my sister, smiling as I wipe her tears away. "It's going to be okay, gordita," I tell her. "We're together now."

"I told Mami it wasn't true," Sofía sobs. "I told her you weren't a terrorist, but Dr. Smithson says I'm just a stupid little girl and don't know any better—"

"Shush," I say, pressing my sister's head to my chest. It's only then I realize two of the *Conquistador*'s armed mercenaries stand guard at my room's frosted glass doors. No, *four*. I frown. I hug my sister as I look to Faye, jerking my head in the mercenaries' direction. She presses her lips together and flips them off with both hands.

I take two seconds to calm the rage rising in me.

"It's not true, right?" Sofía asks.

"Don't listen to that gringa," I say fiercely. "You're an intelligent girl with a loyal heart."

"Laura, you shouldn't say something so terrible," Sofía says.

"I know, cari." I frame my sister's small, innocent face between my hands, then press a kiss into her forehead. My wrists are stiff with needles and tubes. The way the metal shifts under my skin makes me want to vomit. "None of their story is true, at least not in the way they tell it. The Smithsons"—my subjugator shifts in my throat, ready to catch any words I might say that its masters wouldn't like—"have misinterpreted a few things."

"If the Smithsons don't know the whole story, how come they just make it up?" she asks.

"I don't know," I say, wishing I could tell her the whole truth, wishing it all wasn't locked away in my head and heart, sealed behind a piece of tech in my throat. "But sometimes, people take one or two details from a story and let their biases fill in the rest."

"But that's not *fair*," Sofía insists, her tears peaking again.

"I know, I know, cari." I turn to our cousins, saying, "Lena, Isha, will you take her and find one of the tías? I need a minute."

I think they understand what I mean: *This is frightening Sofía. Will you take her and feed her?* With a family as large as ours, the aunts and uncles who enjoy cooking always have something on the back burner. Food is love, no matter what part of the universe we're in.

"Come on, Sofí." Lena pushes off the wall, a bright smile on her face, extending a hand to Sofía. "Let's go."

My little sister gives me another fierce hug.

"Te quiero, cariño," I say.

"Te quiero," Sofía whispers back.

"Be brave."

"You too," Sofía says, before leaving arm in arm with Lena

and Isha. Two of the mercenaries outside shift their big plasma rifles off their hips, pointing the muzzles at the ground. I gather my blankets up around my chest, uncomfortable with the men looking into the room. After all, I'm wearing a flimsy hospital gown.

They close the door behind my sister and cousins. The old-school lock hammers into the doorjamb, startling me.

"What the *hell* is going on with you?" Faye asks, putting her hands on her hips. Alex rises off his chair. They're both dressed in EVA flight suits from the *Conquistador*—the Cruz lion rears across their chests in red, white, and green—which means they must've changed before exiting the ship.

"Can I have some context for this conversation?" I ask, looking back and forth between Alex and Faye.

"The Smithsons are claiming you're responsible for the crash," Alex says.

"You know that's not true, Alex," I say.

"Of course I do, Laurita," he says. "But I can't prove it."

"You're under twenty-four-hour guard, with restricted bioware access," Faye says, hands on her hips. "And I swear, Laura Cruz, if you're lying to me about what you were doing on that bridge, I . . ."

But tears crest on her lashes. She turns away fast, tilting her head back and wiping her lower lids with her fingers. Each sniffle feels like a dart thrown straight at my heart.

"Faye?" I ask softly.

"Her father didn't make it," Alex says.

"Oh god, Faye, I'm—"

"No," she says, pointing a finger at me without turning

around. "I'm not grieving him until this is over. For now, we're pretending *everything is normal.*"

"I'm still sorry," I say.

"I feel worse for you," Faye says. She turns back to us. "Dr. Smithson wants you disconnected, Laura."

I shudder. The dregs of Panamerican society are sometimes referred to as *the disconnected*, people who've committed federal crimes great enough to have their bioware removed or disabled. Sometimes they're people who've done self-surgery to slip away from the law. Or those who are so poor, they sell their equipment on the black market to survive.

Without bioware, a citizen can't captain ships, or raid, or even work in the mecha bays. Everyone aboard *any* Panamerican starship must have registered and updated bioware. Our ships can't calibrate correctly without being able to read the bioweight aboard.

Basically, Dr. Smithson wants to ground me for life. No, she's asking to *end* my life, my career, my chances at becoming the person I'm meant to be. And for what crime? I had the audacity to date her son. I overheard the details of how she planned to use her own influence to gut my mother's reputation, thus allowing her to seize the Cruz family's collections.

And, perhaps, because Dr. Smithson thought I could be a pawn.

"I wish I could say I'm surprised," I say, not bothering to keep the bitterness out of my voice. I shake my arm to wake up my bioware, only to be greeted by a big red *Access Denied* on my ioScreen. They must have shut the system down while I was in the medpod. "Where's my mamá?"

"In a meeting," Alex says. "Along with the ship's surviving officers and the crew from the *John Muir.*"

"How'd she take the Smithsons' allegations?" I ask.

"Let's just say there was a reason the conversation couldn't stay in the medbay," Faye says with a smirk.

Sometimes I can't believe how quickly Faye can hide behind an emotional mask. She's like a chameleon, slipping in and out of emotional states, sometimes with no warning. Yet it's still so comforting to hear her voice, to be around people I've known my whole life.

"They don't call Dr. Cruz the Lioness of Baja for nothing," Alex says. "Your mamá's fierce."

"I need to talk to her," I say. Tuck will tell Mami about my subjugator, and I'll tell her about what the Smithsons said on Launch Day. Their plans to discredit our family in order to seize the Declaration of Independence will come to light. But the *John Muir*'s a much greater prize, one they will fight hard to steal from my family. "Actually, Tuck and I need to talk to her *together*."

"Who's Tuck?" Alex asks, bracing both his hands on my medpod.

"The guy who brought me into the medbay," I say. "Tallish, dark hair, looks grumpy all the time . . . he slipped out before I had a chance to introduce him."

"Oh, you mean the handsome one," Faye says, then cocks her head from side to side. "In a brooding sort of way."

Alex wrinkles his forehead. "You *would* think an attitude makes a guy more attractive."

"He's a little too pale for my taste," Faye says, making a popping sound with her lips on the word *pale*. "But Laura does have a thing for gringos—"

I smack her arm. "Hey, it's not like that, okay?"

Faye ignores me, leaning over the medpod to whisper to Alex. "I heard he carried her *in his arms* out of the tram and to safety." She presses the back of her hand against her forehead. "Just think! It's so *Romeo and Juliet*. Two people from different sides of time—it's so romantic I could *die*."

Alex chuckles, shaking his head. His locs swish against his back. "Gorda, you *do* know what happened to Romeo and Juliet, don't you?"

"Aren't they just like . . . the quintessential fairy-tale romantic couple?" She looks to me. "Were they real?"

Groaning, I flop back on my bed as my cheeks burn like furnaces. I yank the covers over my head. "Ay, ay, ay, Tuck only carried me because my toes were broken," I say through the fabric. I wiggle my toes to make sure I'm healthy again. "I could barely walk."

"So it's true!" Alex says, pinching my leg through the comforter. "The proud Laura Cruz let some guy carry her busted ass to safety."

I narrow my eyes under the covers, thinking of the few steps I *did* walk, and the way Sebastian grinned at me as I bled on the tunnel's procrete flooring.

"Our little girl's getting so big, Alex," Faye says dramatically. "Capturing ships and the hearts of boys lost on the other side of the universe—"

"It's not like that!" I moan through the comforter.

Faye pulls down my blanket. "You know he was like, *born on Earth*, right? But in a way that's kind of hot. How many girls have boyfriends *from another age of humanity*?"

"I gotta admit, it does fit our history girl," Alex says, grinning at me.

"¡Ay!" I say, laughing as I sit up. "I told you, it's *not* like that." I can't say I'm entirely *opposed* to the idea, though. Tuck's clever—and not just because he saw past my layers and straight to the subjugator at my throat. Under all the sweat and dirt and blood, there's a brave, intelligent boy with razor-sharp cheekbones and broad shoulders. He's courageous. I admit he's in excellent shape, too, with lots of toned muscle under that stiflecloth. Tunnel running's been good to him, if not mentally, at least physically.

But those hazel eyes of his always look so sad, even when he's laughing. I wonder what I'd do with such a lonely boy, one who carries a broken heart in his chest and pretends it beats the same as everyone else's.

"We need to find him," I say, kicking off my comforter. I rip the gauze off my hands, and then yank the needles out from under my skin. Gems of blood well from the backs of my wrists. "Find him, and get him to Mami."

"Great idea, chiquita"—Alex motions to the men outside my door with his head—"but those pendejos aren't letting you go anywhere."

I'd almost forgotten about the mercenaries outside my door. They're going to make saving the *John Muir* and extricating myself from this web of lies more difficult. Especially since I've got enemies in every arena. In front of the ships' crews, the Smithsons disparage my reputation. Online, I face a hacker who's bested me on several occasions. In the tunnels, there be monsters.

Even now, perhaps *especially* now, only saving the ship will prove my innocence. I know what the Smithsons' case against me must look like from the outside. Climbing the Narrows. Hacking Mami's chair. Being on the bridge when the ships crashed. I played right into their hands.

Now I'm going to have to outwit them—and a mysterious hacker—to save myself.

Which means I have to escape.

Faye sets her hands down on the medpod, her bioware flashing at me. Like a spark, it sets an idea on fire in my head. I'm looking at a loophole, and I think I know how to exploit it.

"Do you know what Tuck looks like?" I ask, turning to Alex. "Do you think you could find him for me?"

"Claro, there aren't too many people on this ship," Alex says, reaching out to take my hand. He sandwiches it between his own, his skin dry and warm. "You trust this guy? Is he going to follow me easy?"

I nod. "Tuck saved my life. I helped him restore power to the ship. He'll help."

"Right, then," Alex says, giving my hand a squeeze before standing up. "I'll find him. You staying with her, Faye? Someone should."

Yes, Faye, I think. *Someone should most definitely stay with me.*

"Sure," Faye says, plopping into the chair next to me. "Though I would so love to go with you and get a better look at Laura's new boy."

"He's not *my boy*," I say, rolling my eyes. "You can't own a person, Faye."

Alex flashes me a grin, knocks on the glass door, and slips out when the mercenaries open it for him.

When the door settles back into place, the privacy frost

coating the glass again, I drop back on the medpod with my legs crossed under me. "Bioware, please," I ask Faye, my hand out.

"What? Why?" she asks, twisting her lips into a neat little pout.

"Because I'm worried one of the Smithsons might be the black-hat hacker who crashed our ships," I say. "If that's the case, their guard will be down now that my bioware's out of commission."

"Well, in that case," she says, offering me her wrist. "But you'd better not be lying about the terrorism allegations, flaca. Otherwise, I'm going to get jail time for this, and I will *never* forgive you if I don't get into Frida Nacional because I spent time in an orange jumpsuit. There's no way I'm going to some subpar art school, just because you needed a fix. ¿Comprendes?"

I click my tongue at her. "You know me better than that, Faye." I bring up the command menus inside her bioware, tunneling into Mami's bioware in seconds. "All I want in the world is the freedom to live my life and raid ships."

"Laura, you *are* free. I mean, besides all this." She gestures to the men at the door.

I look Faye straight in the eye, swallowing hard, but have no answer to that.

Using her bioware, I locate the GPL tags for all four mercenaries outside, plus Faye's. *Sorry, cari.* I increase the users' serotonin levels to the highest threshold possible. Bioware secretes a whole range of biochemicals, ones it distributes via nanomechs in the bloodstream to keep the human body stable and healthy. *Usually.*

Switching to a different menu, I input Mami's passcodes and release the locks on my own bioware devices.

The nodes in my arms flash red, then turn their usual, pulsing sky blue. I rub my wrists, heaving a relieved sigh. Several ping messages appear when I shake open my ioScreen. Most messages are well wishes from friends and family; expressions of shock flow in, too. A few of them are accusatory, angry. I ignore them all, except for one in the middle. It contains an image.

I click the message. A map appears on my ioScreen, one so old it takes several seconds for my bioware to convert the file type.

At first, the data doesn't make sense to my drug-addled brain—but then I realize someone's drawn a path through what looks to be Yosemite National Park, one starting in an area marked *Medbay* and ending at *Spider Cave*.

I clap my hand over my bioware node. The words *I can get you to the bridge, Laura,* flow back from my dreams.

You're the only one who can save her now.

A small chill runs down my spine. *Is this another trap?* I wonder. *Who was that woman? And how did she get into my dreams?* Could my black-hat hacker have co-opted an old image from the *John Muir's* files and set a trap to condemn me once and for all? I try to find a record of the sender on the ping network, but there's nothing. No trace.

Not even a hacker could gain entrance to my dreams. But if not a hacker, then *who*?

If I stay here, I won't have a chance to save the *John Muir*. If I go, at least I'm not under surveillance, locked out of my own bioware and hopeless. As the old saying goes, it might be a chance I have to take.

"Does your mamá know you can override her system commands?" Faye asks as I slide on a pair of fitted khaki pants, part of an outfit Mami probably left for me. I find a reddish scar on my thigh, where the shrapnel hit me. The flesh is almost fully healed now, que bueno.

"Does your mamá know you engaged your bioware's birth control protocols?" I shoot back.

"Flaca, she showed me how," Faye says, rolling her eyes. "You are the only girl I know who's squicked out by sex. Ask Tuck, I'm sure he'd be happy to—"

"Faye!" I half shriek, throwing a pillow at her.

She laughs and catches it easily, then points an index finger at my face. "See? You're so uptight, Laura. It's like you're afraid to make a mistake, but how are you supposed to learn if you're not"—she pauses, yawning so big she flashes teeth—"making . . . mistakes . . . ?"

"I've made plenty of mistakes," I say. *The whole last year of my life with Sebastian was one long mistake.* "I'm going to end one now."

She yawns again. "What *are* you talking about?"

I wish I knew for certain. Leftover grapes lie on a plate near my medpod, and I shove a handful into my mouth. My nerves are jumping so much, I almost swallow them whole. I clip a bra behind my back, and then pull a clean tank top on.

Faye yawns again and stretches, languidly. "I'm so tired all of a sudden. . . . Laura, did you do something . . . ?"

Socks next. Then a newish pair of boots. Finally, I grab Mami's jacket and slide it on. For luck. She'll kill me when she realizes it's gone, but I don't know what I'm going to find out there in the park. I need some part of her to go with me.

One by one, the guards slump to the ground outside. Their plasma rifles clatter to the ground.

"Laura Cruz, you little . . ." Faye doesn't finish, resting her head on the gurney with a sigh.

"I'm sorry, Faye," I say as I take my bow and quiver from the room's corner. "I know you'll be pissed when you wake up, but this way nobody will think you're involved."

I take a moment to remove the Declaration of Independence from my quiver and leave it rolled up on a nearby table for my parents to find, partially hidden beneath my discarded hospital gown. It's the only way for me to say *trust me*, without pinging them to tell them I've escaped. I refuse to implicate my parents or family in any way.

If I'm going to do this, I'm going to do it alone. It's not the way my parents taught me to solve my problems, but if I don't move now, the Smithsons may try to use me as a tool against my family. I refuse to let that happen. I wish I had time to wait for Alex and Tuck, but I'm not certain how long the guards will be unconscious, or how much longer the *John Muir* will survive.

I need to go.

Lo siento, Mami, I think, shutting off the room's lights. *I know you'll be disappointed in me, at least for a little while. Dad, I hope you understand.*

Slipping from the room, I sneak past the nurses sitting at their desks, absorbed in their work.

Then I run.

TUCK

I run to the edge of my universe. To a place where the air gets cold and breathing becomes a blood sport. I gulp air, but still feel punch-drunk from the lack of oxygen. My fingers turn blue and my tongue feels clumsy.

The ship's so quiet here, the silence hums in my ears. Tuneless. Dejah's not around to check on me. The mourners don't venture into these rooms, so far from their colony in the bridge and sources of food and heat in other sectors.

It's just a dying ship and me.

From the observation deck in Sector Three, I get a good look at the crash site. The ship's deepdowns arc in a great curve around the terrarium. Laura's ship carved a canyon in the *Muir*'s flank near the aft decks. The nebula's light throws millions of pieces of debris into relief. Shattered parts of the ship spin like tops in zero gravity. An eerie fog engulfs the site, one made from the air and water expelled by the crash.

The wreckage tears me open, too. I knew saving the *Muir*

would be difficult. But this . . . we're not coming back from dev-astation on this scale. The pressure in the deepdowns drops by the hour. My HUD's readings and projections look dangerously low, our problems accelerated by Dejah's disappearance.

I'm not sure how long I stand on the observation deck, just watching the ship exhale irreplaceable air into space. Long enough for my feet to go numb and for the tips of my fingers to turn blue. The cold dulls more than the nerves in my skin. It puts my ragged heart on ice. Helps me not to think about it for a while, 'cause other things hurt more.

What's it like, having family so happy to see you? All I've ever been to the adults in my life is an inconvenience—first to the father who left, then to Mom. Aren's okay, but we're not family. Not in Laura's sense of the word, at least. More like partners in survival.

"Tuck, do you copy?" Aren asks, speak of the devil. *"Where are you?"*

"Yeah, Aren," I reply. *"I'm in Sector Three, observing the crash site."*

"You didn't have authorization to head back into the deepdowns," Aren says, not trying to hide his annoyance.

"Yeah, well, I don't get authorization for a lot of things," I say. He snorts. *"What's going on?"*

"She's gone, Tuck."

"What do you mean, she's gone?" I ask, my heart rate kicking up a notch.

"Laura Cruz. She's disappeared. I need you at the Ahwahnee, stat, for a ship-wide meeting and search."

"I'm on my way," I say, turning to run before I even finish the message to Aren.

It's only then that I realize:

I've come to care about a girl I barely know at all.

Thirty minutes later, I walk into the Ahwahnee Hotel's make-shift council chamber inside the old dining room. Late for the meeting, of course. I don't want to be caught up in the group's bureaucratic stupidity—I want to be out looking for Laura.

I stopped into the medbay on my way here, just to check for clues. A note. Anything. But all Laura left behind were four un-conscious guards, a woozy girl, and some mysterious artifact the adults are now bickering over. One of the nurses said Laura left the Declaration of Independence behind, but that's got to be a load of bullshit. Where would Laura have hidden the Declara-tion, if she had . . .

Oh.

Well, I suppose that's why Laura refused to leave her quiver behind.

Light shoots through the Ahwahnee's great hall windows. Ever since we lost the bridge, the old Ahwahnee Hotel's been the crew's de facto meeting area. Birds chitter in the rafters, bounc-ing atop the hall's big wooden beams. Even their small sounds make me twitch. I killed two mourners in the tunnels today. Ran from ten more. They're panicking out there. The tempera-ture's dropping fast. In an hour, maybe two, nobody will be able to run the deepdowns without an EVA.

And that's a problem, seeing that all the *Muir's* EVA suits have been missing since stasis-break.

I knock my hood off my head as I walk toward the assembled crews. Officers sit on one side of the big table, facing the room.

Everyone else sits in chairs gathered close, a jagged aisle running up the center. I pause at the top, hooking my thumbs in my belt.

Frag me, there are a lot of people in the room. Fifty? Sixty, maybe. My palms start to sweat at the sight of them.

"You're late." The woman at the center of the table stands, her shoulders thrown back, head high. It's the same pose Laura strikes when she's feeling defensive. This woman, however, wears her authority and confidence with ease. Nobody needs to introduce her to me. I've spent enough time memorizing her daughter's face to see the resemblance.

"Please, don't stand up," I say, sauntering closer. Anxiety scrambles through me, clawing at my insides. I'm conscious I wear my piss-off attitude like armor. I'm also aware it makes people not like me much, but I'll be damned if I care.

I don't get to run this time.

Laura's gone.

Someone's responsible.

As I get closer, I'm certain that woman's Laura's mom—I saw her in the medbay foyer. I'd bet the man on her right is her husband. The guy's huge, with silver-shot black hair and stubble on his chin. He leans back in his chair. Crosses his arms over his chest. Watching me with a stare so heavy, I could probably bench its weight.

A lot of people sit at the Ahwahnee's long council table. Some of the *Muir*'s, some of theirs. The crew of the *Conquistador* is like Laura, long-limbed and lithe. Future humanity must've eradicated acne and wrinkles. Everyone's got great skin. My people look pasty compared to the way Laura's people glow in rich shades of umber, tan, and brown. See also: My crew's spent four hundred years in stasis. We survived. In many cases, our melanin didn't.

Neither did the deodorant.

I'm conscious of this as I walk toward the council table.

The council table's lit up, holoscreens showing the ship's current status. Spectrograph schematics of the *Muir* float in front of me, the seven sectors lit up in greens, oranges, and reds. Our air levels have dropped to 40 percent in the deepdowns. Pressure's low. Water's looking worse, with the ship reporting massive losses in four tanks and freezing in the deepdown sea. The sea doesn't just provide water to the park, but coolant for the ship's systems, too.

"Explain yourself," the woman says.

"I don't answer to you," I say.

"That's exactly your problem. You don't answer to anyone, Tuck," Aren says to me, tossing his pen on the table.

"You want my help?" I ask. "Don't bust my balls over a meeting. I was checking on the goddamn ship. And you know what they say about messengers with bad news."

"What, that they get shot?" the woman says. Her tone tells me she has no problem shooting first.

Or a problem with shooting me, for that matter.

I chuckle. "I'd rather not get shot, Mrs.—"

"*Doctor*—"

"Dr. Cruz," I finish.

She lifts a brow. "How do you know who I am?"

"Your daughter glares just like you do," I reply, deciding to switch tactics and play it complimentary. "And she had zero tolerance for my bullshit, too."

"Interesting choice of dying words," Dr. Cruz says as she sinks back into her chair, exchanging a glance with Aren. "Do you know where Laura's gone? She disappeared from the ship's medbay almost forty-five minutes ago."

There it is—through her hard-ass veneer, a small crack in her voice as she says her daughter's name, one I'm sure few others recognize. They see the captain. The leader. Underneath, she's also a mother. And I see she's worried about her kid.

"I don't know where Laura's at," I tell her, raising my voice to make sure everyone hears me. "But I *do* think that anyone who accuses her of terrorism is either, one"—I hold up a finger—"an idiot. Two, hiding an ulterior motive. Or three, disloyal to their respective crews and countries, and trying to push the blame off onto someone else."

My words ring a little too loudly in the hall.

Several of the *Conquistador*'s crew members tense.

Chairs groan as people shift their weight.

Maybe that was a little too forward, but someone in this room deleted Dejah.

Someone tried to destroy my ship.

A blond woman leans back in her chair, smirking. I recognize her immediately—she met Laura and me at the neardowns bulkhead entrance. She sits a few seats down from the Cruzes. *Smithson*, I think her name was. I've seen her kind before. Mom's work brought a lot of them into my orbit—smirking, sniffing, holier-than-thou. They parcel out backhanded compliments like candy. In four hundred years, it doesn't look like humanity's learned how to handle its money or its ivory towers.

Big surprise. So much has changed, so much has stayed the same.

"You can wipe that grin off your face," I say, pointing at Dr. Smithson. "I don't know exactly what you've done to Laura, but I'm sure as hell going to find out."

Her grin loses a bit of its smugness. "I am certain I don't know what you mean."

"Yeah, I'm sure you don't," I snap, anger flaring.

"Laura Cruz is a dangerous girl," Dr. Smithson says. "She's a hacker and a terrorist sympathizer, one who attempted to destroy the *John Muir* and everyone aboard the *Conquistador*. Do you have any idea what losing this ship would've meant for the advancement of mankind, boy?"

Humanity, not mankind, I think. Dr. Cruz responds first: "*Alleged*, Dr. Smithson," she says. "My daughter's an *alleged* sympathizer. You have no proof aside from circumstantial evidence—"

"Your daughter is *gone*, Elena!" Dr. Smithson snaps. "Caught on secure-cam knocking out her guards and sneaking from the medbay, alone—"

"Damn, Laura," I say with a chuckle, but I'm not surprised, either. The girl moves like water. Try to put her in a container, and she'll shift form and evaporate. "Look, I don't know what your endgame is, lady, but I can tell you one thing for sure: Laura Cruz isn't an enemy of the *John Muir*. And if she's your enemy, well, that's on you."

"That's preposterous," Dr. Smithson says.

"Is it, though?" I ask.

"How can you be certain she poses no threat to the ship?" Aren asks me. "The girl had unauthorized access to the *Conquistador*'s bridge and captain's chair at the time of the crash."

Both Dr. Cruz and her husband look to me, breath bated, like I'm a lifeline.

"I don't know about any of that," I say. "But if Laura wanted to make sure the *Muir* was lost for good, all she needed to do was put an arrow in my back. Easy. Instead, she learned to tunnel run. She helped me get the auxiliary power hives online. And when we went code yellow against a griefer, she held her own and survived." I spin to face the room, like I'd seen Mom do when she was trying to convince people to listen to her. "Now, remind me—how many of you jerks were in the deepdowns when the ship's power grid went down?"

The other curators in the audience look away. At the floor. The walls. Nobody meets my gaze.

"Yeah, that's what I thought," I say, turning back to the officers' table. "If I know Laura Cruz—"

"But you don't," Dr. Smithson says. "Not like we do."

I ignore her and continue, "If she moved *alone*, it's because she doesn't or can't trust someone in this room."

Whispers slither over the floor.

"But who?" Dr. Cruz says, her gaze pinched. Pained.

"Give you three guesses," I say, looking at Dr. Smithson. "While we're throwing around wild accusations, Dr. Smithson, do you want to explain the piece of parasitic tech I found in Laura's throat?"

Dr. Smithson goes so still, she seems to turn to stone.

"Parasitic tech?" both Dr. Cruz and Aren ask in tandem.

Dr. Smithson recovers: "Don't you try to make me look like the antagonist here, boy—"

"No, Angela," Dr. Cruz says, holding up a hand. "Let him speak."

"Don't you see? She's charmed him," Dr. Smithson says, rising from her seat. "Laura has filled his head full of lies, ones that will rip this crew apart while *she* runs off and destroys the ship—"

"You know what I saw?" I say, gesturing at Aren. "*I* saw a girl with broken and bleeding feet walk five steps because this woman's asshole son told her to do it!"

Dr. Cruz slams her fists on the table and shoots out of her chair. The legs shriek against the floor. Everyone falls silent.

"Is this true?" she asks.

The birds leap from the rafters, chittering.

Aren presses his lips together, giving a small nod. "That's what it looked like."

"You're all fools," someone says behind me. I turn, seeing Dr. Smithson's son sitting in the front row, smirking at me. He rises, spreading his arms wide. "One of the greatest criminal masterminds is conducting a symphony of chaos around us, and you're all lining up to be in her orchestra."

I fragging hate this guy.

"What's your problem with Laura Cruz?" I ask, dusting off my right knuckles with the palm of my left hand.

"She's a criminal," he replies.

"Bullshit," I say, taking a step toward him. Then another. "Answer the question."

"She's a dangerous hacker with a predisposition toward upsetting the status quo—"

"Wrong answer." I punch him, just once, nice and clean. The cartilage in his nose crunches. His mother screams. Blood spatters down his face, across his lips and chin. Chairs shriek against the floor. People leap to their feet. I grab him by the shirtfront. "You know what? Laura doesn't have a criminal bone in her body. But me? I've got no problem being an asshole."

I shove him back into his chair.

"Tuck," Aren shouts. "Enough!"

"One and done," I say, shaking my hand out. The pain feels good. Wakes me up. Anger can be useful.

"You animal!" Dr. Smithson snarls at me. "If his nose is broken—"

"Lady, there's no *if* about it," I say. "Go ahead, sit here and bicker about who's fragging loyal to your cause. I've got a goddamn ship to save."

My cloak swirls around the floor as I pivot, heading toward the door.

I've got to find Laura.

She's in more danger than I realized.

LAURA

I head through the *John Muir*'s vacant halls. *Where is everyone?*
My stomach squelches with nerves, my insides slipping and slid-
ing against each other, wondering if there's some new danger
I'm unaware of, or if the halls of this ship are always this empty.

I walk past a large sign that reads NEARDOWN TUNNELS,
which I suppose just means these tunnels are nestled against
the park, rather than being located in the ship's orbital bands
like the deepdowns. Despite being well lit, the *John Muir*'s tunnels are still marked with rust and age. The tunnel walls are
made from unpainted, slate-gray metal. Fluorescent lighting
runs on tracks overhead, glaring at me. The temperature's chill
enough to make me grateful for my jacket and boots.

As I approach a bulkhead marked VALLEY FLOOR—LOWER
YOSEMITE FALLS, I pull up the park map on my bioware. It's my
stop.

The bulkhead's unguarded. The large door whooshes open
for me, probably on a sensor. I walk through an air shower that

blows the tips of my hair around my face, and step into the park proper.

None of the photos I've seen or VR trips I've taken have prepared me for the splendor of *real mountains*.

At first, the light's so bright, I hold a hand up to shield my eyes. It's brilliant everywhere, with augmented solarshine glittering off the stone underfoot and the granite mountains rising into the pseudo-sky. I blink hard and fast, hot tears streaming down my face, trying to see past the glow around me.

The sky darkens at the aerodome's apex, where the atmosphere's at its thinnest. Up there, the crescent-shaped gravity ring is visible, one that arcs around the ship every twenty-four hours. A thin, stretched-looking cloud drifts across the sky. The mountains tower almost as high, enormous, ancient sentinels that have guarded this valley for millions of years.

And everything, *everything* grows out of the ground, like magic. A spicy, sharp scent tickles my nose. I inhale deeply, taking in a smell I can only describe as *green*, and then sneeze. Tiny particles invade my lungs. Birdsong hops through the air, undercut by a long, low whistle. The air feels cool against my cheeks.

Beauty like this doesn't exist in the Colonies: our terrain's one-dimensional and only a meter higher than the engineered sea level. There aren't canyons, mountains, or sweeping vistas; we have low hills for drainage purposes, not aesthetics. Our atmosphere isn't thick enough to make the sky a deep, brilliant blue—not like this. The terrarium has the *sky blue* my bioware's coloring set promised me as a child, the color I've seen in paintings and pictures from all over the world. I don't understand how a pre-Exodus culture could possibly have created something so stunning with lesser tech.

No, humanity didn't create this beauty—this was our home, before the Exodus. This is a small piece of the glory we had on Earth.

Seeing this place, I can almost empathize with the people who started the Pitch Dark movement. Pictures of the park simply don't do it justice—one has to be dwarfed by these mountains, and to have the fingers of the wind in her hair, to *really* understand why the early ecoterrorists lashed out in vengeance against the whole human race.

But did they see the hypocrisy in their actions, I wonder? Or did they, like so many other villains in Earth's history, believe they held the moral high ground, despite the misery they bred? What might've happened if the *John Muir* and ships like her had made it safely to the Colonies, as they were supposed to?

I wish I could admire the park for hours, but neither the ship nor I have that kind of time. Shaking my bioware awake, I check my map a second time. Several trails shoot across my ioScreen, but only one takes me to the cave entrance half a kilometer away. The trail arcs through trees that spear the sky like arrowheads, ones that smell like nothing I've ever experienced before.

I have to save this place. No time to waste.

I slide into the forest, leaving the ship's metal tunnels behind.

I find the entrance to the Spider Cave ten minutes later, its mouth hidden in a thick tangle of foliage. The opening stands about as tall as me. The rocky ceiling's slanted, low, and rough to the touch. I step inside, ducking. A gritty coating of dirt clings to my soles and the toes of my boots. The air's chunky with dust—it clogs my nose and I sneeze again, and this time, my eyes water. *Was all of Earth this dirty? Ugh.*

I venture deeper. My jacket scrapes along the walls as the tunnel gets smaller, tighter, forcing me to my knees. I turn my bioware on for light. An ambient blue glow washes the walls in color, revealing a claustrophobic, rocky canal.

Cool air buffets my face, drying the sweat on my forehead. It's a promise, I hope, that the cave isn't a dead end.

Before long, the tunnel forces me into a crawl. This remnant of Earth is trying to swallow me whole. *Dios, I hope I haven't made a massive mistake in coming here.*

Everything within me shakes, most especially my nerve. In all my sixteen years, I've never felt the slightest twinge of claustrophobia, no matter how deep I've been buried in an excavation. But I've never been pressed between two palms of rock before, in the darkness, without anyone knowing where I am. I could die here. Nobody would ever find me.

The thought is both a terror and a thrill.

I drop to my stomach, crawling along the floor like a lizard. My clothes and quiver make a shushing noise as they scrape against the rock's throat. Bits of rubble stab into my forearms. My breath comes in forced, shuddering gasps. Something crawls over the tops of my fingers, a tiny creature with too many legs. Disgusted, I fling it away. My heart beats so hard on my bones, I worry the tightness of the space will squeeze it right out of me.

The deeper I go, the more my thoughts race: *The cave is going to collapse on me,* I think, shaking. *Is the space getting smaller? I'm going to get stuck. Can I back up? Should I?*

The ceiling pitches lower, pressing my bow and quiver into my back. I follow the slope, trying to make my rib cage as compact as possible.

I attempt to ease forward again, but I'm stuck. I can't move. Can't breathe. My chest won't expand. I'm going to die buried in the rubble, while crawling things chew my toes off and nibble my eyeballs like grapes.

Not today, I tell myself. *If you don't survive this, Laura, you'll never see your family again, and they will live the rest of their short lives thinking you betrayed them. Your friends, too, including Tuck.*

Not today. Not—I push myself harder, muscles straining—*today.*

I worm my way past the chokepoint, sliding out of my bow. In another few wriggles, the space around me expands. The darkness grows so large, my bioware's light can't reach the walls. Collapsing in the dirt, I close my eyes. I breathe it in. Sneeze.

When I catch my breath, I retrieve my bow and quiver from the passage, and then stagger to my feet. The cave's dark. Empty and cold. I turn my bioware up to full brilliance, holding one wrist up over my head. Toothy stalactites hang down from the ceiling, sharp as a wolf's canines. Something drips in the darkness, a lone *plop-plop-plop*.

As I move into the room, my light gildes across a round door set directly into the cave wall. It must stand two and a half meters in diameter, maybe built of brass. Large patches of greenish verdigris cover its surface, the metal dull with age. It looks like nothing else I've seen on this ship, not in style, color, or design.

I'm probably the first living person who's seen this place in hundreds of years, I think, turning slowly to see if there's anything else in the cave, any other evidence of human habitation. But there's nothing but rock, shadows, dripping water, and the door.

As I get closer, I notice an insignia inlaid in the metal, a dragon wrapped around the rim of planet Earth. It looks suspiciously like Pitch Dark's logo, with a few key changes—for one, the insignia depicts a dragon, not a snake. Two, the dragon's wings open around the Earth, as if shielding it from damage.

I reach out to wipe the dust off the design. When my fingers connect with the door, it pulses with white light, then decompresses and rolls into the wall. Startled, I step back as if burned.

Dappled light dances across the floor of a large room beyond the door. Warmth gushes out, as well as the rich, slightly musty smell of old libraries and even older books.

Cautiously, I step inside. Wooden floorboards squeak underfoot. *Wood? They used wood for flooring?* Kneeling, I run my hand over the boards, made from lacquered light and dark woods set in a checkerboard pattern.

The whole room is paneled in floor-to-ceiling bookshelves, with alcoves for curiosities along the tops. But the claw-foot desk commands my attention more than anything.

It's the desk from my dreams.

I walk into the room. Once upon a time, my father showed me images of the rain forests of Earth, hundreds and thousands of kilometers of trees extending in every direction. Millions of them. Earth had so many trees that by the time humanity was ready to abandon the planet, there were still enough to create this desk, this floor, and all these books.

It seems like such a waste to me, born in a time when bamboo is the closest thing we have to wood, where every city had a few parks with the few scraggly trees we were able to coax from hydroponic containers. I lift a glass paperweight off the desk, smearing the dust off with one hand. Geometric shapes glimmer inside, their colors prismatic. Vibrant. I'm puzzling over how it was created when a voice says:

"Hello, Laura Cruz."

Startled, I drop the paperweight. It hits the hardwood floor and shatters, pieces scattering. I whirl around, startled to find a woman standing behind me.

No, not a woman. She's the *projection* of a woman. I stand frozen in a sea of gleaming glass, looking at a woman who is both here and *not here at all*. She appears three-dimensional, but the room's light and shadows don't play across the planes of her face. She's transparent. A digital *ghost*. Something about her seems familiar, but I can't decide why. Her dark hair's threaded full of silver and twisted into a messy pile of curls atop her head.

"I certainly hope you didn't treat the Declaration of Independence with such carelessness," she says, lifting a brow.

"Who are you?" I whisper, my shoulders inching toward my ears.

"I'm Dr. Katherine Morgan, the designer of the USS *John Muir*," she says, spreading her hands wide. "Or rather, I *was* Dr. Katherine Morgan. Now I'm nothing more than a scrap of consciousness left in a machine. Pretty cool, eh?" She waggles both brows.

Cool? I squint at her, confused. "I-I'm sorry, I don't understand—"

"Do I look like Princess Leia on R2-D2's message in *A New Hope*, or what?" she continues, gesturing to her ghostly form with one hand. "I considered recording myself saying, 'Help me, Laura Cruz, you're my only hope,' but in the end I couldn't get the files to work properly with your bioware. Sending you a map had to suffice."

I stare at her, openmouthed, unsure how to respond, or counter, or rebut what she's telling me.

"Princess Leia?" Dr. Morgan asks after an awkward pause. "Darth Vader? The *Millennium Falcon*? You call yourself an Exodus-era scholar and archeologist, and yet you've never seen *Star Wars*?" The lilt of her voice hooks a thought out of my memory. Or maybe it's the mention of a midmodern movie, or my recollection of my first conversation with Tuck, when he said he was glad his mom wasn't around to learn about the other jettisoned ships. I'd assumed she'd been the captain of the *John Muir*, maybe, or its navigator; I hadn't imagined her relationship to the Exodus ships was far more personal.

"You're Tuck's mother," I whisper.

"Or rather the digital human connectome that's left of her," she retorts.

"I know you. I've *read* about you! You didn't design just the *John Muir*, but the entire Exodus fleet!"

"Well, most of them. Don't blame me for your defunct torus colonies—I told Dr. Beck his designs would eventually fail your capacity for food production, but did he listen to me? No. Did Beck ever listen to me? *No.* He insisted upon designing colonies to look like that *stupid* video game . . . what was it called? Tuck used to play it with friends—"

"Tuck thinks you're *dead*," I cry.

"He would be correct in that analysis," she says. "I *am* dead, and have been for many centuries. Rather than interring myself in hyperstasis, I remained awake in order to perform specific modifications to the ship, ones that would be necessary for her long-term survival with a maintenance crew in absentia."

"How long were you alone?" I ask, horrified by the thought.

"Ten years," she replies. "It took quite a long time to map my own mind. I didn't want to leave anything to chance—if I stood upon the thinnest possible edge of rescue, I needed to ensure my work would continue, regardless of the state of my corporeal body."

I take a step back from her, shaking my head. "Tuck should be here right now . . . he's your *son*, he's *family*."

"Not long ago, you encountered a holographic representation of your mother while under extreme duress," Dr. Morgan says, watching my reaction intently. "I take it the effect wasn't comforting?"

"No," I reply, wondering how she knows about what happened on the *Conquistador*'s bridge, post-crash.

"Exactly. Now, as much as I love digression, we don't have much time. One of your crew members hacked the *John Muir*'s servers and deleted our AI, Dejah," Dr. Morgan says, all the mirth gone from her voice. "I need you to take me to the bridge and upload *my* connectome as a replacement AI for the ship."

"Tuck told me the bridge had been overrun with mourners," I say. "Getting there would be impossible."

"That may be true, for anyone who doesn't have access to

one of these." Dr. Morgan snaps her fingers. The bookcases around us tremble and groan. Dust tumbles into the air in great swathes, swirling through Dr. Morgan's form. Her light makes the particles sparkle like micro gems. Two of the cases automagically descend into the floor, revealing a secret alcove behind the books. Frosted glass panels retract into the walls.

I gasp.

A custom EVA suit stands inside the alcove on its own, with no props or support. The helmet gleams in the alcove's light, opalescent blue as skybike shields and dragonfly wings, and shaped as elegantly as an egg. The rest of the suit's made from matte black fibers, sleek and ribbed like exposed muscle. The material doesn't hold still, shifting and twitching every few seconds, perhaps due to some sort of nanotech. Blue lines of illumination run from the knee to the hip, up the sides, across the waist, and under the breast. The shoulders are armored with sleek titanium guards sporting built-in, 360-degree lighting elements.

"Wow," I breathe.

"Not bad, eh?" Dr. Morgan winks at me.

I take a step forward. Honeycombed anion armor panels made of blue light appear over the suit's chest, arms, and upper thighs. The suit looks several sizes too big, better made for a person Tuck's size than for me.

"The EDDA suit is one of my unfinished masterpieces," Dr. Morgan says, her words wistful.

"Unfinished?" I half squeak, eyeing the suit.

She continues as if she didn't hear me at all: "When I set out to design a new spacesuit, I wanted something with a high armor quotient but zero bulk. The suit is intelligent enough to respond to the environment in real time, deflect attacks, heal damage to both itself and its user, and look good while doing all of it. Unfortunately, it won't be possible to train you to use each feature properly—"

Great wings of cerulean light extend off the EDDA's back. I gasp.

"—so I'll need to be loaded directly into the EDDA suit first, so that I might control your shields, flight paths, and such. Plus, you'll need my fingerprints to access many areas of the ship."

"How am I supposed to load you into this thing?" I ask, still bathed in the EDDA's light.

"You have two options, neither of them ideal," Dr. Morgan says. "One, you could take the time to build a custom user interface for the EDDA, a system to bridge the gap between the suit's heads-up display and its sensors. Without a UI, we won't be able to communicate once you're in the deepdowns, which means you won't have access to maps, thermostatistics, gravity and pressure readings, damage meters, *et cetera, et cetera, et cetera*."

"Bueno, I need those things to live. What's option two?"

"In option two, you integrate your own bioware system into the EDDA, the drawback being, of course . . ." She taps the hollow of her throat, indicating my subjugator. "With a custom UI, you could ignore commands given to you by someone with subjugator permissions, via the noise-canceling tech inside the EDDA's helmet. Integrating the EDDA's AI with your bioware will not afford you the protections of a custom build."

"It seems a custom build is my only option, doesn't it?"

Dr. Morgan holds up a finger. "It might be, if not for our lack of time. Dejah regulated several mission-critical processes within the ship's life support systems, ones our hacker has failed to maintain. At most, the ship has one hundred twenty minutes before total system failure, but perhaps as few as eighty. Whatever time you spend building a UI for the EDDA will be time taken away from the business of saving the *John Muir*."

I draw a sharp breath. "You're sure?"

"I did write the user manual," Dr. Morgan says. "I won't make the choice for you, Laura. I only ask that you try to save this ship, my life's work"—she glances to the side, heaving a sigh without drawing a breath—"and my son."

"What about the world?" I ask her softly.

"That's the folly of the human heart," she says, smiling. "We make macro decisions based on micro motivations."

Hours ago, I know which option I would have chosen—the safe route. The *smart* route, in which I would spend the time to program a quick and dirty UI for the EDDA suit. Never would I undertake such an important endeavor without a well-thought-out plan. But if I've learned anything in the last twenty-four hours, it's that my best-laid plans can't possibly account for every variable. *Especially* the human one.

Back then, I exchanged vast amounts of preparation for confidence. Now it lies in myself. *I can do this,* I tell myself. *I'm a Cruz.*

"Fortuna y gloria," I say, stepping up onto the platform with the EDDA suit. "Bioware it is."

Fifteen minutes later, I finish merging my bioware systems with the EDDA suit, and then load Dr. Morgan's consciousness in, too. Without her chatter, her office lies quiet as a tomb and just as eerie. I strip off Mami's jacket, taking it to Dr. Morgan's chair and draping it over the back. I remove my boots and pants next, everything, until all I have on is my white tank, bra, and underwear.

As I step into the alcove, the suit emits a low hiss and unzips itself down the middle, exposing the chest cavity. The EDDA's torso material spreads wide, like a pair of ashen black wings. The helmet lifts, suspended by the suit's titanium spine. The entire ensemble looks like a Rorschach test designed to analyze my mental state. *What do you see in this inkblot image, Laura?* I imagine Dr. Morgan asking me.

The EDDA looks like the shadow of opportunity, I think, reaching toward the feathery edge of the suit's material. It wraps itself around my finger, velvety-soft and thicker than I'd imagined it would be. *Its wings may carry me far, but also so high I might die from the fall.*

I take a deep breath, stepping one foot into the suit, then the other. As I settle my back against the EDDA's metal spine, the suit begins to shrink.

Here goes nothing.

The EDDA's tendrils close around me, sealing themselves along invisible seams. It clings to me like a second skin, applying pressure to compensate for no-or low-pressure environments. The suit's nanites hum against my body, constantly shifting, moving, aware of my environment and feeding information in real time to my bioware.

A trickle of sweat snakes down my spine, more from stress than from heat. The gravity of what I'm about to do rests on my shoulders, featherlight at first and growing in magnitude. My palms feel damp inside the suit. I don't know what horrors I'll face on the bridge, or on the trip there. And once I reach my destination, I'll have to hack into an ancient system using what little I know of pre-Exodus tech, while fending off a hacker who's bested me. *Twice.*

The helmet lowers itself over my head. After a few seconds of whirring, the suit's airflow kicks in. I take a deep breath of filtered air. A map appears in the lower left corner of my helmet's visual field, showing me a way out of Dr. Morgan's office I hadn't been led through earlier.

I grab my quiver and bow, then follow the map to a lift, which ascends into an aged wooden shed and clanks to a stop.

Light slants through the cracks between the wooden boards, dust motes dancing in the light streams. The floor looks like a Jackson Pollock painting, spattered in bird excrement, leaves, and small animal carcasses. Broken furniture, rusted tools, and flattened hoses are piled against the walls. It's a mess compared to the orderliness of Dr. Morgan's office.

There's a large, bulky object covered with a tattered cloth in the middle of the shack's dirt floor. On my helmet's screen, the EDDA draws a bright outline around the object. Dr. Morgan must mean for me to take whatever's underneath; she did say her interactive mapping would help me find my way to the bridge.

Curious, I throw off the drop cloth, revealing an Exodus-era skybike. It's bulkier than the sleek, free-energy-driven bikes we have today, and almost twice as long. It stands on four telescoping feet. Ancient, circular thrusters occupy the underside and aft of the bike. Despite the cracked leather and the rust along the edges, she's in decent shape.

My helmet beeps at me. The nanites on my right thumb buzz, creating tiny ridges to replace the suit's smooth surface, whorled like a fingerprint. I press my thumb into the ignition button.

Without a sound, the skybike lifts from the ground. Tiny, spiderlike maintenance bots leap off the bike and scatter, disappearing into the piles of refuse in the shed.

I open the shed's door and walk the skybike out into the park. The wind picks up, pushing me back a step. I've never felt wind so strong. Two deer lift their heads—at least I *think* they're deer—and flick their ears at me. They're fawn-colored, and the backs of their tails have a pure white patch of fur.

They leap away, frightened, their tails flashing in the park's solarshine. I've never seen live deer before. It occurs to me they've probably never seen a girl in an EDDA suit, either.

Here, the savagery of nature and the neat protocols of technology have existed together in harmony for centuries. If the *John Muir* could beat the odds over four hundred years, what's to say she won't do it again over the next two hours?

In the distance, a siren shrieks. Red light washes across the sky. I glance at Dr. Morgan's map in the corner of my helmet's heads-up display—it shows a route through the park, past the Big Valley bulkhead, out the Ingress bulkhead, and into the deepdowns. I'll head through the deepdowns for a few kilometers, then Dr. Morgan is rerouting me through the ship on foot. Should all go well, I'll be at the bridge in less than an hour.

Then I hear the screaming.

Mourners.

Swinging one leg over the skybike's seat, I crank the throttle. The back of the bike spits dirt at the shed, but it gains traction. My heart tries to grab ahold of my ribs as the bike shoots forward, tearing across an open meadow and hurtling toward a path.

Headed for the fray.

PART THREE

THE BRIDGE

As we look at the long history of our species, the question we must ask ourselves is this: Is humanity worth saving? If all our destructive traits are a combination of our nature, our nurture, and culture, can we reject the worst parts of ourselves and become worthy of redemption?

Until we find a way to answer that question, we will continue to wage war against an unknown and unnamed enemy. And perhaps that's the most frightening part about Pitch Dark—to this day, we have no idea who ignited the movement, or what would have turned that person against her or his own people, their families, and their own history.

FROM "HUMAN BEINGS, BEING HUMAN: COUNTERARGUMENTS
TO PITCH DARK"
LAURA MARÍA SALVATIERRA CRUZ
COVER ARTICLE IN *SMITHSONIAN MAGAZINE*, AGOSTO 2434

TUCK

I'm halfway through the Ahwahnee's foyer when someone calls out: "Hey, *vato*, wait up!"

Looking back, I spot a guy following me out of the dining hall. He's got skin the color of clay, a warm umber. A rubber band holds his thick black locs at the nape of his neck. He's dressed in one of the *Conquistador*'s flight suits, boots, and a grin.

I eye him, turning on my heel. Unsure of his loyalties. "What do you want?"

He lifts a hand parallel to his chest, palm down. It looks like a handshake—*it's got to be a handshake, right?* "I just wanted to shake the hand of the guy who broke Sebastian Smithson's face," he says.

A tick before things get awkward, I clap my hand into his. His grip's firm, warm.

If he's not a friend of Sebastian's, he's a friend of mine.

"Alex Mello," he says by way of introduction. "Can't tell you how long I've wanted to hit that *güero*."

"Not going to lie"—I chuckle, dropping his hand to look at the new cuts on my knuckles—"it felt pretty good."

"It's Tuck, right?" he asks. When I nod, he glances around, dropping his voice low. "Laura sent me looking for you—"

"She *what?*"

"*Cállate*, yeah?" he says, putting a hand on my back and guiding me away from the dining room. I flinch at the touch. "She said you could vouch for her in front of the crew and the *capitana*, but . . ."

"I covered it back there?" I ask, jerking my head in the direction of the dining room.

His laugh's short. "I'm sure that's exactly what she intended the *capitana* to hear."

"You on her side or theirs?" I ask.

"Hers," Alex says. "Laura's my *hermanita*, she's a little sister to me. As for the Smithsons? They can go screw themselves."

Shouts barrel out of the dining room after us, angry, loud. I pause, glancing back.

"We need to find her," I say, motioning to the front doors. Alex follows me outside. Dappled solarshine from the park's grav-rings falls through the dense trees. I take a deep breath of fresh air—never quite like Earth's, but close—and shake my fist out a second time. Hard to believe anyone would want to end this place. But like Mom used to say, *Radical isn't rational*.

"Any idea where she'd go?" he asks.

"None." I flex my fist. The fresh scabs on my knuckles tear and bleed. The pain's good. Real. Easy to understand, unlike people. "You?"

Alex chuckles. "If I know my Laurita, she'll try to save the day."

"Then we're going to need some EVA suits. It's cold enough to shrivel your balls in the deepdowns," I say. "Got any?"

"Balls, or EVA suits?" he asks.

"Both."

When he grins, I see the kindred spirit of mischief in his eyes.

I think we're going to get along just fine.

We lift a pair of EVA suits from the *Conquistador*'s crew quarters at Half Dome Village. Their EVAs are black tightsuits with a lion roaring across the left shoulder in green, white, and red. The suit's multilayered, with a compression core and light armor around the important bits of you. Slender cells along the back hold liquefied air. The patch on my left breast reads *Delgado*.

Hope the guy's still alive.

Sorry for stealing your suit, bruh.

The *Conquistador*'s registration number and Panamerican flag are stitched on my right arm. I run my fingers over the patch, which isn't made of thread but of tiny, light-sensitive particles that shift to the touch.

"Do you know how to shoot?" Alex asks, pulling his boots over his feet. They self-seal themselves to his legs as he pulls gloves over his hands.

"Guns?" I ask.

"Rifles."

"I know the basics." As in, point the barrel of said weapon at whatever you want to die. Pull trigger. You know, the *basics*.

Alex goes to a closet and pulls out a pair of sleek, long-barreled rifles. They're made of pearly white metal, with bright blue lines of light down their sides and black rubber on their grips and stocks. He extends one to me by the handguard. When I reach for it, he pulls it back. "Don't shoot me with it, *comprendes*?" he says.

"Yeah, I *comprendes*."

Alex chuckles, then hands me the gun. "You're going to have a lot to learn when we get back to the Colonies."

"What?" I ask as he turns and walks out the door. "What'd I say?"

"Let's go, *gringo*!" he calls over his shoulder. The cabin's screen door bangs closed in his wake.

"All right, all right!" I grab my helmet off the table. And under my breath, just because I can't help it, I say, *"All right."*

We're halfway to the Big Valley bulkhead when an alarm rips the air in two.

"Ah, crap," I mutter under my breath. The solarshine bleats red, bathing the park's terrain in nightmarish light. The evergreen trees turn black. Clouds gather like blood blisters against the terrarium's hard outer shell. Shadows stretch their limbs, reaching for us. The ground shakes as the smaller bulkhead doors close in unison, sealing the park off from the neardowns. Fear grabs me by the throat.

I told Dejah red emergency lighting would be traumatic, but did she listen to me? *No-o.*

Alex pauses in the road, turning, looking around. "What's going on?"

"Neardown breach," I say, trying to maintain my cool for his sake. "Mourners have gotten past the Ingress bulkhead and are in the neardowns, so most of the crew will flee to the park for safety."

"This happen often?" he asks.

"Only *never*."

He curses under his breath. "Laura."

We sprint down the road, headed for the Big Valley bulkhead. Of the fifteen bulkheads connecting the neardowns to the park, only the Big Valley will remain open for evacuation after the alarms sound. Upon the sounding of the siren, anyone in the neardowns has five minutes to drop what they're doing and run like *hell* for the park. Several areas—like the medbay—have reinforced blast doors to keep their occupants safe in the event of a breach.

A roar tears into the park as Alex and I round the final corner. The trees give way to a large clearing. Up ahead, the Big Valley bulkhead rears high, mouth open, throat dark.

I catch glimpses of the growing chaos as we run past:

People flee into the safety of the park. A girl drags her father off the road, the man's chest a mess of gore. Gunfire lights up the bulkhead interior. Alex steps off the road to avoid the nurses running by with a gurney. I dodge a mother hurrying past with her screaming toddler in her arms. Thirty meters away, near the bulkhead's mouth, a flash brand explosion rocks the ground.

I thought my time in the deepdowns was a horror story, but it was nothing compared to *this*.

"Faye!" Alex slides to a stop, calling out to a dark-haired girl in the crowd. When she doesn't hear him, he fumbles with something on his helmet, making the face pane on his helmet retract. He calls her name a second time: "Faye!"

She turns her head, face crumpling when she sees Alex. She runs to him, throwing her arms around his neck. Alex puts an arm around the new girl's shoulders. I follow them to the edge of the path, where we duck behind a large boulder.

"I—I didn't know what she was doing," Faye says, tears glittering on her lashes. Her hands tremble. "I swear, she promised me she wasn't doing anything wrong!"

"What are you talking about?" Alex says.

"L-Laura," Faye replies, rubbing her eyes with her knuckles. "She used my bioware to knock me and her guards out and escape. H-how was I supposed to know she could do something like that?"

"*Cálmate*," Alex says, pressing a kiss into her forehead. "It's going to be okay. Did Laura mention where she was going?"

Faye shakes her head. "She said something about 'finishing a job' and that she'd 'made a mistake' . . . what if it's all my fault and she blows up the ship and we all die because I trusted her with my bioware and—"

"That's not our Laurita," Alex says, taking her face in his hands. "Faye, you *know* that's not our girl."

"You weren't there!" Faye shouts, pushing him away. Alex stumbles back a step. Tears gush out of her eyes. "Not when she left, not when I woke up to one of those *lloronas* screaming in the medbay. You didn't see a man explode like a piñata, Alex!"

I shake my head, fiddling with my helmet until the face-guard releases. "Laura isn't going to harm the ship—"

"Don't try to defend her!" Faye snaps at me. "You don't know her the way I do."

"Laura saved my life out there." My voice rises as I point at the bulkhead. I don't like this girl. Something's off about the way she's acting. And that's when it occurs to me, *she's acting.* But why? "If you have to question where Laura's loyalties lie, you don't know her as well as you *think* you do."

"You listen to me, *chico*," she says, stepping forward and shaking a finger in my face. "I have known Laura Cruz since we were—"

A roar rocks the tunnel up the road. Faye claps her hands over her ears. My EVA helmet protects me from the worst of it, but screams abound in its wake:

"What the hell is that thing?"

"Oh god, oh god—"

"Shut the bulkhead! Shut it down!"

"Run!"

"Get to the park bunkers!"

Taking a knee, I peer around the boulder's edge. Near the bulkhead, people dive behind the big rocks or flee into the trees. The *Muir*'s own guards scramble from the tunnel into the park's red solarshine, carrying their injured and shouting at one another. The bulkhead door groans, its large, toothy panels starting to close like massive jaws.

Seconds later, a wave of mourners slams into the door panels. Hundreds of them froth over the bottom partition, making the bulkhead look like it foams at the mouth. The panels keep closing, and the monsters fight one another as they try to scramble into the park. Those that succeed get shot by the park guards.

Then, something big rams the bulkhead door, interrupting the panels' closure sequence. One massive hand grasps the door's upper partition, shoving it back into the wall and jamming the bulkhead open. The monster climbs over the lower partition and into the park.

I swear, I'd piss my EVA suit if I had any fluids in me.

The monster towers over the park guards. Rather than being built on a griefer's muscular frame, this creature's body wobbles like a rancid Jell-O mold. Putrid yellow cysts cover its skin. Two massive, flabby arms sprout from his shoulders—and it's definitely a *him*—while a smaller, malformed set of limbs hangs below. It almost looks like the big bastard has T. rex arms, but before I can laugh at the image, the creature's blistered chest begins to swell.

Ah, crap! I drop behind the boulder again, motioning to Alex and Faye to get low. "Duck!"

"What the hell is that, *vato*?" Alex shouts, hunching down and pulling Faye with him.

"How the hell am I supposed to know?!" I snap.

"You live here!" Alex shouts.

"I don't know if you noticed," I shout back, "but it's a glitching *giant ship*!"

A scream splits the air. The boulder at our backs shudders and cracks. Alex rolls to his feet, rifle barrel pointed down. Faye sits on the ground, rocking back and forth, hands clapped over her ears. A thin trail of blood traces the side of her neck.

"*Hijo de puta*, the guards are down," Alex says, peering

around the boulder's other side. I turn to look, just in time to see the *Muir*'s version of the Stay-Puft Marshmallow Man crush a guard's corpse underfoot. I'm real grateful for Dejah's red light all of a sudden, because it masks the carnage on the road.

Alex and I fire at the beast, driving bullet after bullet into its gut. The rifle kicks me in the shoulder. Black blood pumps out of twenty holes in the monster's torso and belly, but it keeps lunging forward. Closing the distance between us. As it comes down the road, people flee for the bunkers under the Ahwahnee, almost a klick away.

Let me tell you, killing monsters in video games is *way* easier than it is in real life.

The bastard's ten meters away now.

All my seconds begin to slow down, as if the film reel of my life hit a snag.

My heart pounds in every pressure point in my body.

This is how it ends—

That thought barely rolls through my brain when something big whizzes past me. It slams into the mourner, making the creature explode like a gory firework. What's left of the body— and the projectile—tumble over the ground, sliding to a stop near the half-open bulkhead.

It takes a minute for me to realize the object's a skybike.

Mom's skybike.

A woman lands in the middle of the road, crouching to absorb the impact. Wings of light retract into her shoulders. She's wearing a black EVA suit that gleams like a metal skin. It's got zero bulk, protected by a set of translucent blue neo-anion armored plates that glimmer down the wearer's spine, chest, arms, and legs. Light glows under her toes, feet barely striking the ground.

One shoulder's stamped with the letters EDDA-02.

My memory is jogged, catching on a moment, long ago, when I walked in on Mom playing with a handful of nanites. *I'm going to build an EVA out of these someday,* she said, dropping a bit of the dark material into my hand.

The nanites spread out, coating my hand in an impenetrable layer. I picked at them.

The EDDA suit will be an intelligent one, capable of mending itself while in use. Mom sat back in her chair, smiling at me. *These nanites apply pressure directly to the body, and will protect the wearer from extreme temperatures, radiation, microwaves, and more. The suit will revolutionize the way we move around in the vacuum of space.*

In an age of bulky, awkward space suits, Mom sounded like a dreamer.

I had no idea she'd built a working prototype.

If I'm not mistaken, there's only one person who could be wearing that suit. Only one person who would know how to operate it, one person who knew where it was located on the ship.

I lunge out from behind the boulder and shout, "Mom?"

The woman pauses.

Turns.

Her helmet's front panel dissipates. The other sections retract into a raised, armored ring around the back of her neck. A burst of breeze catches strands of her hair and tugs them loose from her ponytail.

Laura?

I remove my EVA's helmet.

"Tuck!" Grinning, she runs to me, hitting me like a sack of bricks. Her suit's angles crash into my bones. Hugging her hurts. But bruises be damned, I drop my helmet to the ground and crush her against me like she's the last human being on Earth, lifting her off her feet.

"Where did you get the EDDA suit?" I ask, releasing her back to the ground.

"From your mother," she says.

What? My stomach rattles around the rim of my ribs, making me feel like I'm falling. "My mom is *dead*."

"Yes, she is," Laura says. "Dead, but not gone."

I take a step back. Behind us, the skybike gutters and shuts off. A low whine echoes through the park as its engine dies. Alex crosses into the road, removing his helmet and sweeping Laura into a hug. Faye hovers by the boulder, glaring at us.

"How?" I ask Laura, gesturing to her suit.

Laura taps her wrists. "There's not much time to explain, I'm afraid. Your mother contacted me while I was in the medbay and has asked me to carry her connectome to the bridge, where she will function as an alternate AI—"

"Laura, you can't trust my mom," I say, gripping her shoulders. "She was brilliant, a genius . . . but she would do *anything* to keep her work from being compromised."

"That's where you're wrong," she says, clasping my face between her hands. The nanites in her suit shift against my skin. Warm. "Your mother loved you, Tuck. *You* were the only thing that ever mattered to her."

I turn my face away. My mother never loved me the way Dr. Cruz loves Laura.

"No, *escúchame*," Laura says. "Sometimes people make macro decisions for micro motivations." She holds me fast, forcing me to look straight into her eyes. She opens her mouth as if to add something. Pauses. "Screw it," she whispers, and kisses me. Full labial contact. No tongue. Still, I feel like she's lit something in my chest on fire.

Alex claps and laughs, but I don't hear what he says. For the three seconds her lips are pressed to mine, Laura is my entire world.

So dammit, I'm reeling as she steps back. Her cheeks turn the russet red of autumn apples.

"There's not much time," she says. "I'm sorry, I have to go." She pivots on the ball of her foot, moving toward the bulkhead. Which, you know, is now coated in mourner gore. I'm paralyzed for the space of two or three of her steps, confused by the emotions snarling in my chest: gut-checking anger blending with the rush of desire, the latter making my brain all sorts of promises that don't make any sense. Anxiety and fear seethe underneath.

Go after her, you idiot! they scream at me. *Don't let anything happen to that girl!*

I start after Laura, just as someone calls out, "Stop right there, Laura Cruz!"

Engines roar on the road behind me. I turn to look back. The park rangers' Jeeps skid to a stop, bringing the head honchos down to the Big Valley bulkhead, I'd guess. Armed park guards and mercenaries from the *Conquistador* pile out of the vehicles. Dr. Cruz leaps out from the back of a Jeep while it's still in motion. But when she tries to run to her daughter, one of the mercenaries cuts her off, catching her by the arm.

"What is the *meaning* of this?" Dr. Cruz snaps at him. "Let me go!"

"Dr. Cruz, I think this situation has spiraled beyond your control," Dr. Smithson says. "I'll take it from here."

"Like hell you will!" Dr. Cruz says. "Or have you forgotten that *I'm* the captain of this mission?"

"And *I'm* acting captain of this ship," Aren says. "Weapons down, everyone. Nobody else is going to get hurt today."

Thanks, old man, I think. *For once.*

"With all due respect, Aren," Dr. Smithson says. "This girl is a dangerous criminal who needs to be contained—"

"*I'm* the criminal?" The glare Laura throws Dr. Smithson has steel and edges and points. Laura rolls up onto tiptoe, engaging the thrusters in the EDDA's feet and hovering a few centimeters off the ground. Feathery, translucent wings extend off her shoulder blades, lifting her higher. When the red emergency light spills across her, she looks like an avenging Valkyrie. Badass. Dangerous. Jaws drop. Alex backs up a step from her, his eyes wide. Faye bites her lower lip, rubbing one hand up and down her arm while she watches Laura.

Now *that's* an EVA suit.

Damn, Mom. *Damn.*

"The conquerors write the histories, Dr. Smithson," Laura shouts. "I will not let you write mine. And after I have saved this ship, I will make sure *you* are forgotten. When the world discovers what you've done to me, what you've tried to do to my family, you will be forever ruined, shamed, and cast out of society."

Dr. Smithson steps forward. "Laura, st—"

"No, *you* stop!" Laura shouts, pointing at Dr. Smithson. "I will *never* take orders from you again. And if I have to shout to drown out your voice, so be it!"

With a mighty flap of her wings, Laura launches herself almost fifteen meters in the air, landing beside Mom's skybike. The EDDA suit cushions her landing, blue light pulsing under her feet. She dislodges the bike from the mourner's huge corpse, flinging some gore off the seat.

As she straddles the bike, I shout, "Laura!"

She looks back over her shoulder. "Yes?"

"Don't do this," I say. "Not alone. Let Alex and me come with you."

"What was it that you told me before?" Laura asks, a slow smile creeping over her face. "Oh, I remember now—*hasta la vista, baby.*" The EDDA's helmet cascades around her head. She cranks the skybike's throttle, spins it around, and races toward the sagging bulkhead door panels.

In seconds, she's gone.

LAURA

I shoot through the park's Ingress bulkhead, moving too fast to be caught by the mourners' shrieks. My muscles tremble, full of nervous energy. Fury races in my veins, right next to fear. Did I go loca? I *shouted* at Dr. Smithson, and almost expected her mercenaries to shoot me when I leaped away. Under normal circumstances, my actions would have brought swift repercussions down on my head.

But my current circumstances are anything but *normal*.

I slow down on the train tracks outside the Ingress bulkhead, pausing beside the armored tram Tuck and I rode in on. Ping messages rumble through my wrists. Out here, the bike's headlights spill over the forms of several white lumps on the tracks. *Mourners.* Their bodies quake, rib cages expanding and contracting with furious speed, fighting to get enough oxygen into their lungs. I almost feel bad for them—but if they can't breathe because of the low air pressure, they can't scream, either, and that's a relief.

The EDDA's nanites scroll back to reveal my bioware beads. I shake my ioScreen on, checking my messages. Mami begs me to come back to the park. Dad threatens to ground me for the next year, but who is he kidding? It will be a miracle if my parents ever let me fly again after this mission.

My bioware rumbles with another ping, this one from Alex. *Tuck and I are coming after you, flaca,* he says. *You may not need our help, but we're coming along anyway.* His message brings a smile to my face.

Faye's message wipes it right off again: **Thanks to you, I almost died in that medbay, you little malinchista.** The word *malinchista* hits me with physical force. It means *betrayer* on the surface, though the word's historical significance is far more complex. It's possible—given my history with Sebastian and the way Faye teased me about Tuck—that she knows *exactly* what she's saying, but I'm not sure. I try to shake it off, to tell myself she's reacting out of fear and grief; after all, she lost her father today. But for her to call me a traitor when I'm risking so much to save us, well . . .

It hurts.

The next message comes from Sebastian: **You're making very dangerous decisions, Laura. My mother is sending a team after you, one with orders to shoot on sight.**

I want to snap, *What, so your puta mother can cover her tracks?* but my subjugator won't let me type those words. Besides, the next time I see Sebastian, I'll have saved the *John Muir* from obliteration.

I don't answer him, or Faye, or Alex, or my parents. I have a ship to save.

After uploading Dr. Morgan's map into my heads-up helmet display, I punch the skybike's throttle and head downtunnel. Unlike our skybikes at home—speed-inhibited and protected by airflow shields—this one moves so quick, my insides spoon my spine. Adrenaline pounds in my ears as I shoot through the darkness.

A ping message from the Noh Mask hacker appears next, popping up on the helmet's display: **Headed somewhere, Laura?** I ignore the message, lip curling. Whoever the hacker is, I'm going to find them. Expose them, and make sure they're brought to justice.

The hacker's next ping sends a hot flash through my veins, followed by a slow, roiling chill. **I'll be watching you.** He can track my location via my subjugator, as can the Smithsons. My best hope now lies in speed.

On the skybike, it only takes a few minutes to reach my destination:

PLATFORM 4

B-CLASS QUARTERS

BIOSPHERE GREENHOUSES A, B, AND C

BIOWASTE RECYCLING

BACTERIAL CLEANSING PLANTS

The headlights wash over faded letters and numbers on the tunnel walls. I ease up on the bike's throttle as I approach the platform. The bike's free-energy engine is silent, displacing debris underfoot. Aged papers and bits of rubble roll away, whickering over the ground. Small tendrils of the ship's fester covers the tracks, recoiling when light touches them. The stuff coats the platform, hanging off the edge in thick, heavy sheets.

I swing myself off the bike and stash it out of sight under the train platform. No need to leave evidence for Dr. Smithson's people. I'll go the rest of the way on foot, according to Dr. Morgan's map. She hasn't given me a straight path; rather, it meanders through the rest of Sectors Two and Three, dumping me somewhere in the foredecks' middle tier.

Deep groans rumble through the ship. A few casual shrieks, too. I expect to see white shadows lope out of the darkness, but nothing stirs. A few wall-mounted signs flicker and spark as I cross the tracks and climb up onto the platform, procrete crumbling under my grip. The fester squelches underfoot.

It was one thing to go charging out of the park, riding a high wave of adrenaline. It's another to head into a dark hall, my fury evaporating, nerves startling at every small sound. One lone bulb flickers in the distance. Paper flyers and notices shudder on the walls like old flaps of skin. Odd piles of bones climb against the walls, stained with dried blood. Dust motes tumble on shifting air currents.

In the distance, a light flickers.

On.

Off.

On.

Off.

Each time the bulb dims, the two lights mounted on my shoulders flare bright.

On.

I step into the tunnel, glancing over my shoulder.

Off.

When the light flicks on again, a lone figure stands under the bulb, tentacles sliding up over its shoulders and curling around its waist. Two-legged. Shadows pool under its eyes, the erratic light throwing its shape into silhouette. It tries to draw a breath, its throat sac fluttering in the low air pressure.

I skip back a step, courage shattering, grabbing for my bow as the light goes out. My heart feels like it pounds on my lungs, making my breath come in fast jerks. I nock an arrow and fire at the darkest part of the shadows. Even if the monster can't scream at me, it still has its claws.

When the light blinks back on, the pendejo's gone.

Where did it go? I ease forward, keeping an arrow nocked. My footsteps fall silently, cushioned by the EDDA. Step by step, I ease into the tunnel's depths. Fear grips my heart so hard, I feel its nails bite into my flesh. On my helmet's HUD, a bright dot indicates my position on the map. I follow the path in my peripheral vision, hurrying toward an area of the ship called BIOWASTE RECYCLING.

Lovely, Dr. Morgan, I think, glancing back again. *Thanks for sending me through the ship's biofarm.*

Nothing moves as I cross the last twenty meters of tunnel. The intersections look clear. I find my arrow in shatters along the wall, still surprised the griefers move as fast as they do. . . . Or worse, that the monster's doing it in a no-air, low-pressure environment. Nothing *living* should be able to survive in this sort of a climate without an EVA.

I open the biofarm doors, air rushing from the room into

the tunnel. I push inside, using the EDDA's interface to bolt the doors behind me. Dim light shudders from the high ceiling. Huge cylindrical tanks hold bubbling liquid and gaseous materials in putrid shades of green, black, and brown, their colors not unlike the storms on gas giants like Jupiter and Saturn. The tanks march in neat lines across the processing field; some cracked or leaking, matter caked on the outside and inside. Big sluices run on either side of the floor—which is made of interlocking grates—which would have allowed the ship's former workers to push processed waste into the sluices to be flushed away.

In Tuck's era, it would have taken a ship almost five years to travel from Earth to Mars. The crews aboard Exodus ships wasted nothing, using biofarms like this one to break down biological waste and recycle it into its component materials.

In the *John Muir*'s heyday, this place could process thousands of pounds of biowaste per day. Old tools litter the plant's tables, rusted and dull: bone saws, scalpels, and other wicked-looking, nameless things. The fester spreads over everything here, hanging like gory medieval tapestries from the walls, or bubbling from broken cylinders. It forms mounds along the floors and shrouds the lights in the room.

The EDDA scans the air quality, a red light blinking three times in the upper right-hand corner of my vision. *High levels of methane present*, a notice says. The suit also reports stable air pressure levels. I'll have to be careful.

As I head into the plant, a splash echoes from under the floor's wide grate. I freeze, looking down. Large drops of mossy green liquid quiver on the toes of my boots. In the low light, a single thread-like tentacle surfaces, slipping through the grate and looping around a bit of metal. Heart pounding, I ease away from it, taking a knee between two large tanks. More tentacles rise from the murk and take hold of the grate, punching through a square of the flooring and tossing it away. One hand reaches up, sludge dripping off its fingers as it grips the edge of the floor.

My thoughts scatter like panicked birds. Blood pulses through my limbs, hot and energizing and mind-numbing. I back away, heading down a new row of tanks, listening as the griefer blows out a wet breath. I glance over my shoulder. Through the urine-yellow contents of one tank, I watch the monster rise, its tentacles writhing off its back. Before it turns, I duck low, slinking between the tanks, following Dr. Morgan's map as best I can.

A small ioScreen pops out of the node on my wrist, displaying a ping. A Noh Mask icon appears beside the message, *These ancient cameras have terrible definition, but I can see you cowering behind that tank.*

Mentally cursing, I scoot to the next row. Heavy footsteps clank across the floor. I hold my breath, straining to hear which direction they're headed.

Let me help you get out of a . . . sticky situation, the hacker writes.

An alarm sounds, startling me. The tanks around me begin to beep like heart monitors. An announcement rolls through the plant as the floor lurches, almost knocking me off balance: *"Plant purge initiated. All staff exit immediately. I repeat, plant purge initiated—"*

The floor whirs, clanks, and groans. Sludge pops through

the grate's holes like rising loaves of bread. The stuff sucks at my footsteps, slowing me down.

Oops, the next ping reads. ***Maybe that wasn't helpful?***

I slip in the rising muck, going down on my hip with a loud *bang!* The murk bubbles around my body. As I push myself back to my feet, the *bam-bam-bam* of quick footsteps resounds through the floor. Metal shrieks overhead. I look up and lock gazes with the griefer, who's perched atop one of the tanks, its tentacles fanning out from its back.

It grins.

TUCK

The bulkhead door yawns open in Laura's wake. I jam my EVA helmet back on my head.

Of all the idiot ideas I've had over the last twenty-six months, this ranks in the top ten.

Nah, top five.

What I'm about to do is *way* more stupid than zero-gravity windsurfing in the HVAC systems.

"Let's go!" I shove Alex's shoulder forward.

"What?" he shouts at me.

"Move! Now or never, hambre!"

"*Gringo*, it's *hombre*!" he snaps as we take off running.

"You say *hombre*, I say—"

"Just shut up and run!"

Fair enough. We sprint down the road, headed for the bulkhead door as the adults shout "Stop!" at our backs. But what are they going to do, *shoot* us?

The bulkhead door towers over us, its huge, interlocking

metal teeth still open. I swing left, jamming my palm into the closing mechanism. Alex leaps up, pulling himself atop the bottom partition's toothy lip. The top panel screeches inside its metal frame, moving slower than it should. Damaged, perhaps, by that big bastard. The door lowers toward its partner.

Alex vaults past the bulkhead door as it groans closed. I scramble after him, tumbling off the door's teeth and into a pile of trampled mourner corpses. Alex lands on his feet and drops into a crouch.

Meanwhile, I'm over here, flopping around arse-deep in corpses. Overhead, the bulkhead door rumbles as it slides shut. The great *boom* sends a shudder through my chest.

It's a glitching horror film on this side of the bulkhead, something straight out of either *The Shining* or one of Tarantino's wet dreams. The ground gleams crimson. Red waves of gore mark the walls, the line as high as my shoulder at one point. Corpses—both humans' and mourners'—lie in the frothy wake, some still twitching, either shot or killed by friendly fire. Eviscerated guts are splattered in blue-black piles everywhere.

The surviving mourners look up from the meals they've made of their mates. Blood glistens on their lips as they snarl at us.

Alex jams the butt of his rifle against his shoulder. "This godforsaken ship." He fires, hitting a mourner right in the forehead. He takes two more down before I manage to get back on my feet.

"Where'd you learn to shoot like that?" I ask as we jog down the corridor.

"Military flight school," Alex says.

I almost take a hard right at the intersection—then, realizing the hall's full of mourners, motion Alex forward. We'll go around. "Can you fly a mecha?"

"Like a biomorphic mecha? Yeah, probably."

"Good," I say as we duck through a set of meeting rooms. "If we're going to catch up to Laura on the bridge, we're going to need them."

L A U R A

I'm going to die.

The griefer leaps off the tank and lands in front of me. He seizes me by the throat, his hands so massive and powerful, they close off my airway despite the EDDA's protection. I sink my fingers into his hand as he lifts me, a twisted intelligence flaring in his eyes. The creature's chalk-white skin is riddled with patches of coral pores, each one so large it's a pit. Tiny gray tentacles writhe inside the holes. Some are blistered, tiny digits twitching inside vats of pus.

Air! my body screams, sight reddening around the edges. The world turns black from lack of oxygen. Pain makes it roar back again. My helmet beeps as my vitals plunge and my heart rate spikes.

The creature carries me a few steps forward, cocks his head at me, and then slams me down on a table. My head hits the back of my helmet, which makes my brain rattle in my skull. Something snaps under the EDDA's rigid spine, dry as a dead bone. Instruments tremble. I open my mouth to scream, but it's more of an agonized dry heave. I kick my feet, trying to find purchase. The monster's too strong.

The griefer picks up a hacksaw with his free hand, and then considers the blade's edge. I imagine those rusted teeth cutting into the soft parts of my body, the griefer grinning as it pops my lungs like balloons. My nerves shrivel. Sweat breaks out at the small of my back. I grasp around the table for something, *anything* I can use as a weapon.

My fingers wrap around a metal instrument. Blindly, I jab it into the bend of the creature's elbow. With a cry, the griefer stumbles back.

I don't wait. I roll off the table, landing on my toes. As the creature lunges for me again, I pull a pair of arrows from my quiver and thrust them at his face. Their tips strike the bone of his nose, slice sideways, and plunge into his eye socket.

He seizes up, but his momentum does not—he slams into me. We tumble through the muck, head over heels, until I strike the side of a holding tank.

"Ay . . . ," I say, pain resonating in every part of my body. As my vision clears, I push my torso off the floor, wishing I could cradle my head in my hands. The muck lies ten centimeters thick along the floor now, and rises quickly. Two meters away, the griefer twitches as the dark gunk deepens, starting to swallow him up. The dual shafts of my arrows stick out from one eye socket.

Trembling, I get to my feet. My head throbs. The world whirls around me for a few seconds, then settles back into its proper place. I'm in pain—I would be shocked if I didn't have a cracked rib or two—but wedge me, I'm alive. Breathing. Unlike the griefer, who stares at the ceiling, one-eyed, as the plant's murk crawls up around his shoulders like a macabre blanket. His black blood bubbles in his eye socket.

A ping reverberates from my wrist. *Well, well, Laura, that was very impressive, even for you.*

You'd better hope I never find out who you are, I reply.

The hacker replies with his signature smiley face.

Dr. Morgan's path leads to a door, and behind that lies a room full of pitch-black shadows and silence. The lights mounted on my shoulders flick on, their beams slicing through the darkness. They touch upon piles of body bags, some split open to show the grinning skulls of beasts; barrels of waste are stamped with fading marks that might've once read *For Immediate Disposal* on their sides. Under any other circumstances, I would've found this room fascinating . . . despite its macabre contents.

Now, I just want to get the hell out.

My flashlights glide over the torn edges of a large hole in the metal floor. Detaching from my shoulders, they float a few meters forward, illuminating whatever I turn my helmet toward. The hole's edges have snarls of metal teeth, loops of fibrous cords, and frayed bits that still spark. The ship's fester grows down one side like a long, slick tongue. I can see the ship's struts and bones, and the hole stretches some ten meters in diameter.

The map on my HUD turns three-dimensional. My route? Down.

Here goes nothing. I leap inside the hole, feeling the EDDA's wings stretch out behind me.

Letting me drop into the darkness.

TUCK

In the deepdowns, the mourners can't breathe.

The air pressure hovers above the Armstrong limit, aka the point where human beings can no longer survive without life support. One pound per square inch. For scale, the air psi at the top of Mount Everest was almost five. People used to black out at the summit. If Alex and I tried to run this without EVA protection, our saliva might've boiled in our mouths after the lack of air punched us out.

Not a pretty way to go.

But look, Ma: no mourners.

I step over a weeper as it spasms on the tram platform outside the Ingress bulkhead. Mourners—even the big ones—lie in cancerous lumps all over. They're hyperventilating from lack of oxygen, their chests struggling to rise and fall. They're freezing. Dying. Mourners, weepers, it doesn't matter. Nothing's surviving the gutting of the *Muir*.

To be honest, I'm not sure we will, either.

The armored tram still waits for us at the plat. I drop inside, scanning the space. *Clear.* I wave Alex down and lock the cupola hatch behind him. He frowns at the bloodstains on the corrugated metal floor. I head for the cockpit, grabbing a seat and programming the tram for Plat 10—the one closest to the offboard station's airlock. Since we can't follow Laura's trail, I figure our best bet will be to meet her at the bridge.

The only way to do that is to lift a few maintenance mecha from the offboard station and *fly* there.

Alex eases into the seat next to me. "There's a lot of blood back there."

"It was Laura's," I say, switching on the tram's engine. It rumbles at the back of the tram, warming up. "That's why we need to hurry—we've got to save her from whatever's lurking on the bridge."

He snorts. "*¡Qué pendejo!* Laura does not need your *gringo* ass to 'save' her."

"What's that supposed to mean?" I ask, turning to him. My EVA suit creaks every time I move. Good thing there's not much air left in the deepdowns—no way would we be able to move around out there without attracting attention.

"She doesn't need a white knight, or a savior," Alex says, propping one boot on the dashboard. "That *flaca* can take care of herself. If we go after her, it's because we're her friends, and because our survival's linked up to hers. Got it?"

I bite back a snarky reply, irritation prickling under my skin. Part of me wants to snap. Another part knows he's got a point—Laura *can* take care of herself. Who did Mom send to save the ship? *Laura.* Who outran a griefer over a floor full of shattered glass? *Laura.* Who inspired me to keep fighting? *Laura.*

"You're right, bruh," I say as the tram rumbles forward. "Laura's got this."

"If anyone can save this ship, it's her." Alex chuckles, shifting in his seat and resting his rifle against the wall. "You sure this is the fastest way to the bridge?"

"Unless you want to fight your way through one of the largest mourner pods on the ship?"

"Right, then," Alex says.

The tram ambles down the tracks, moving at quarter power. Every klick seems to crawl past. It's akin to torture, the waiting. The wondering. Especially when Alex says, "Damn, she's not responding to me," and shakes his wrist to shut down his bioware.

I won't deny Laura's capable. Tough. But I can't *not* worry about her, either. She's headed into territory I've not touched. I don't know what she'll face out there, but my imagination's happy to fill in the blanks.

The tram's LE-1 bulbs flicker out, plunging us into darkness. My HUD lens fritzes, then snaps off. The tram jolts, then lags, sliding to a stop in the middle of the tunnel on a screech. Outside, heavy clicks and groans resound through the ship.

"Ah crap," I say, getting out of my seat. Emergency lights flicker on the tracks outside.

"What?" Alex sits up, peering into the darkness ahead. "What's going on?"

"The ship's nonessential systems are shutting down," I say,

cleaning a circle in the window to check the tracks outside. Nothing moves. "She's going into hibernation mode, either because the AI's not around to handle certain maintenance functions, or because the power grid's busted again. The ship will only run mission-critical functions till someone can make repairs."

What I don't mention? If the *Muir*'s plunging into hibernation mode, we don't have much time left. Unless Laura can reach the bridge—and soon—the entire ship will shut down. We might have an hour. Maybe two.

"*Tu . . .*" Aren's voice scratches through my head. "*Can you . . . me?*"

"*Aren? Hello? . . . Aren, you're breaking up,*" I reply, but if he answers me, I can't hear him.

"We'll have to go the rest of the way on foot," I say aloud to Alex, making my way toward the back. Tossing my rifle's strap over one shoulder, I pop the cupola and climb out of the tram.

It's strange to not worry about my footsteps, or the sounds I make. To leap off the edge of the tram and land on the ground, near soundlessly. Alex follows me down.

My EVA suit's helmet switches over to night vision mode. It illuminates the space around me in a strange, grayish light. In one corner, the helmet's HUD shows me how much power and air the suit has stored: *Two hours, twenty minutes.* While it might not seem like much, it's probably more time than the ship's got.

It takes us seven and a half minutes to walk from the tram to Plat 10. Once the platform appears in the distance, I pick up the pace. The signs for the platform are so corroded and old, I can't read anything on them but:

The rest of the words are scratched or faded out.

Nobody's used Plat 10 in ages. Without EVA suits, we've had no use for the tunnels leading to the offboard station air locks.

I climb up the steps to the platform. The dust lies so thick, it pillows my steps. In low air pressure and normal gravity, the dust keeps perfect prints of my boots. It's quiet—*too quiet*, as that dead-horse trope goes. The ship's systems don't hum. No mourners howl in the tunnels. Only the hiss of air moving in and out of my helmet breaks the silence.

What freaks me out, though, are the hundreds of EVA boot prints stamped into the platform's dust. Someone's been using this place, and they sure as hell weren't curators from my crew.

"Did you hear that?" Alex asks quietly, looking around as we move into one of the tunnels.

My stomach bucks, sweat breaking out in my pits. I stop in my tracks, almost turning to look back at him, ready to slice a finger across my throat. Logic stops me. I know talking through the EVAs' comms isn't dangerous. Fears aren't logical, though. They live in your gut, not your head, just like the months and months and *months* of training and conditioning I've had out here.

"What?" I ask, once I've managed to get a grip.

"It sounded like an engine."

"How's that possible? The ship's dying, and there's barely any air in this tunnel."

"You tell me," Alex says emphatically. "You're supposed to be the professional here."

"Never thought I'd hear that word applied to me."

Alex snorts.

We stand on the edge of the platform. Watching the tracks. Straining to hear anything through our EVA suits.

"We should keep moving," I tell Alex, motioning for him to follow me away from the platform and into the tunnel. "But stay alert—my crew hasn't had functional EVAs in years, so we've had no use for the outboard mecha. I don't know what we're going to find out there."

"Someone's been here," Alex says, looking at the footprints in the dust on the floor.

"A lot of someones, probably."

"Not your crew?"

I shake my head. He swears under his breath.

My thoughts exactly.

It's a five-minute walk from the platform to the air locks, the ones that will lead to the outboard stations . . . and hopefully, to Laura. Here, everything's rusted all to hell. A few time-eaten EVA suits line the walls. Most of their parts lie rotting on the floor. Helmets hang on hooks, their skulls cracked, crushed, and covered in dust. Several rest on the ground. Round windows look out into space. The outboard stations aren't visible from here—I'll have to open the Air Lock B to see them.

"The place is a mess," Alex says, kicking a helmet with one foot. It bounces off a wall. I cringe, even when it doesn't gong quite as loud as it might have before. You know what they say about old habits.

"Sorry, I didn't exactly have the time to clean the place up for you," I say, checking for a viable hydrapack or two. Most of the packs look pretty busted, their telescoping arms broken off, parts lying in piles. *C'mon*, I think. *I just need one—*

"What are you two doing?" someone asks through the comms.

That wasn't Alex's voice.

A man in a dark EVA suit steps into the air lock, rifle pointed at my chest. His suit's design, though similar to the one I'm wearing, has a yellow sun burning over the left breast and shoulder.

That symbol itches at my memory. I've seen it before. A museum.

With Mom. In Washington, DC.

It was at the Air and Space Museum.

Run by the Smithsonian Institution.

Dammit. He must've followed the tram somehow—maybe he took one of the Jeeps from the park, or one of the skybikes from the rangers' station.

"Is this the part where you tell me to put my hands up?" I ask the suit. "While we exchange witty repartee underscored by mutual loathing?"

"Shut up and . . . *shit*, just put your hands up," the suit says. I'm not 100 percent sure, but it sounds like Sebastian in there.

"Do you want me to drop my weapon first?" I ask, goading him. Alex snickers behind me.

"Goddammit, *yes*." He turns on the interior lighting inside his helmet. The white butterfly bandages bridging Sebastian's nose glow blue-white. Beneath them, a purple bruise turns his entire face into a Rorschach test. I don't know about you, but I see a bastard in the inkblot.

I'd say I improved his overall look.

"Put your guns down," Sebastian says.

"Or what, you'll shoot us?" Alex scoffs. "We don't have time for this, *vato*." He taps the glass faceplate on his helmet. "Clock's ticking, and we've got to find Laura before our suits burn out."

"You're taking me with you," Sebastian says.

"You?" I laugh. "You'll just *die*."

"I caught up to you, didn't I?" he says. "I'll be fine."

"Do I need to say it again?" I ask. *"No."*

Sebastian fires once. The bright bullet glances off a pile of broken EVA helmets, leaving a black mark on the wall. Alex's shoulders rack up around his ears.

Sebastian's knuckle curls tighter around the trigger. My gaze zeros in on his micrometer movements of metal and flesh. "My mother took a group of men after Laura—"

"Bruh, your *mom* didn't even take you with her," I say.

"And if you think I'm letting you get within a hundred meters of Laura, you're wrong," Alex says, taking a step toward Sebastian.

"Stop right there," Sebastian growls.

"You don't have the *cojones* to shoot me," Alex says, taking another step.

Sebastian's finger tightens on the trigger.

I lunge for Alex. "Hold up—"

Sebastian fires.

For a full second, nobody moves.

I don't think anyone even *breathes*.

Then Alex stumbles back a step, catching himself against the wall. I can't see his face. He presses one hand to his side. When he pulls it away, blood slicks his gloved hand. In the shadows, it's nothing more than an oily gleam on his glove. He shakes and shudders, the pain visible as it breaks through his initial shock. His suit hisses as air escapes. He breathes a curse, doubling over.

I race forward, grabbing Alex under the arm and helping him ease to the ground. "Are you crazy?" I shout at Sebastian.

"No, just serious," Sebastian says, racking his rifle and pointing it at us.

"*Seriously* an asshole!" I snap. Shock's making Alex too shaky to provide adequate compression on the wound. I shuck my slimpack off my back. "Hey, man, just keep breathing. You're going to be okay. You hear me?"

"You're going to take me to Laura," Sebastian says. "*Now.*"

I apply pressure to Alex's wound with a gloved hand. "If he dies, you're a murderer."

"That depends on who's telling the story, doesn't it?" Sebastian says.

My anger rises like a welt, hot and red.

"Like Laura said, the conquerors write the stories," Sebastian says, "and I very much intend to be *finishing hers*. As far as the world will know, Alex got shot while valiantly trying to stop Laura from destroying the *John Muir*. Cooperate, and I'll at least let him go down in history as a hero. Don't, and you'll all go down as villains."

I glare at him. "By the time this is all over, your nose won't be the only part of you that's broken."

"I'm trembling, truly." He smirks. The flicker of fear doesn't show in his eyes. It's in the almost-imperceptible hitch in his breath, though. The flutter of his Adam's apple. Proof he's in over his head. He gestures to Alex's wound. "You'd better help him, Tuck. He's looking a little pale."

Alex tries to push up from the floor. I grab him by the shoulders and force him back down. He's strong, dammit, even injured. Maybe that'll give him a fighting chance. "Sit down, don't talk," I say.

"Play dead, dog," Sebastian says.

"Shut up," I spit at Sebastian. Taking a knee, I pull a compression-tourniquet pack out of my bag. The pack's a type of bandage that, once inserted in a wound, will expand until it clogs a hole. If any of Alex's major arteries or organs have been damaged, it will stopper the bleeding for a few hours. The pack's rocket-shaped and chock full of medicaine. I insert it into his wound. The bandage responds to blood absorption and begins to swell.

Alex gasps in pain. "The hell—"

Did I mention the compression-tourniquet burns like a glitcher?

"Don't move. That's going to make you feel better," I say, clapping Alex on the shoulder as I stand. My bloody handprint gleams on his black suit. He grunts. "Give that two minutes, then we'll tape your suit."

If Sebastian's got two brain cells to rub together—two chambers of a heart, even, since he sure doesn't have any balls—he won't keep Alex around. "Let Alex go back to the park," I tell

Sebastian. "He's only going to slow us down now. I'll take you to Laura."

"No, no," Sebastian says. "He's one of Laura's closest and dearest friends, and a bargaining chip. Laura would do anything to make sure her precious Alejandro Mello was safe."

Alex coughs, spattering blood on the inside of his helmet. "Screw you. Can't wait to see . . . your ass in jail . . ."

"That's cute, Mello." Sebastian laughs, full-bodied and mocking. "People like me don't go to prison for *self-defense*."

"No, but they sure as hell go to jail for being *cowards*," I snap. Four hundred years of development and progress, and humanity's still worshipping money, power, and fame? Good on ya, human race. Glad to see you've dealt with your baggage.

"Now, give me your rifles and get him on his feet," Sebastian says. "Or else I shoot him in the head and claim you did it later, Tuck. After all, who will the courts believe? The golden son of one of Panamerica's foremost scientific minds, or some filthy savage we found on the far side of the universe? *Rifles*. I won't ask again."

I disliked this guy before, but now I'm certain Sebastian's not coming back from this run. Hope he kissed his mommy good-bye. While I might not be cold-blooded enough to shoot someone at point-blank range, I've seen a hundred deaths in the deepdowns.

Time to put that knowledge to good use.

If Sebastian thinks I'm a savage now, he hasn't seen anything yet.

LAURA

After a few seconds of gentle descent, some of the tension leaks from between my shoulders. Only the sludge from the biofarm crawls into the hole after me, *tap-tap-tapping* as it drips. As the suit's wings carry me down, and thrusters engage under my feet. The EDDA's lights have already automagically detached from my shoulders, sensing the nearness of the walls. One hovers over my head. The other floats below me.

As my heart rate slows, I take a deeper breath. My throat feels bruised, and every breath burns like the inside of my windpipe's been reshaped by a laser. I take quick stock of my suit, brushing off bits of gore and grime.

If I plan to be at the bridge before the EDDA runs out of power, I need to move. The suit's powerpac currently sits at 65 percent and is draining rapidly. The flight function appears to burn through the suit's resources faster than almost anything else.

In the darkness, the descent seems endless. Mourner corpses

are wedged in the tunnel's walls, all in various states of decay. Some hang suspended, their limbs tangled in cords or torsos speared on sharp objects, as if they've somehow fallen into this place. Others slump over ducts.

When my feet finally sink into the fester on the floor, I sit down, curling my knees into my chest. Shaking. Something clatters to the floor beside me. Startled, I reel away, getting tangled up in my bowstring, before I realize what I'm looking at:

Half a bow.

Half. My. Bow.

My heart jags as the EDDA's lights settle back on my shoulders. I pick the bow's broken wooden shaft up—the break's not clean, the wood splintered like a broken bone. I wish I could tell the EDDA's nanites to spiral off my fingertip and knit the bow's pieces back together. If I'd only managed to stay out of the griefer's range . . . If I'd moved *faster*, this wouldn't have happened.

I twist the string away from my body. I try not to cry, since I can't wipe my tears away through the suit's helmet. Of the three artifacts I managed to save, I'd grown the most attached to the bow. I stick the pieces in my quiver, determined to still take them with me.

Static crackles in my helmet. I catch a snippet of Tuck's voice, echoing through the speakers inside.

"Tuck?" I ask, getting to my feet. I scroll through the menu options inside the EDDA's helmet, looking for a communication device. Anything to help me home in on the sound of Tuck's voice. "Tuck! Are you there?"

No one answers. For one desperate, wild moment, I wish I could hear Tuck's voice; I *need* to hear his voice. My knees shake, and my shoulders curl forward and sag under an imagined weight. I've been on my own in the deepdowns for less than an hour. No pasa nada, right? At least not compared to Tuck's *two years* out here. Walking in darkness and silence, with only the voices in his head for company. It makes a person weary of one's own thoughts and their fear echo louder than it should.

Now I understand why Tuck looked at me the way he did when we met—like he couldn't believe his eyes, like I was a mirage. Or perhaps some creature out of mythology, a girl with antlers growing out of her forehead, or like I had skin the color of emeralds.

Rather than spend another moment in that lonely headspace, I check Dr. Morgan's map. A blue line snakes across the *John Muir*'s foredecks and ends in the bridge, a small directional arrow bouncing atop my destination: the ship's server room, via the bridge.

I'm so close. A kilometer and a half away. Closer, I think, than anyone's been to the *John Muir*'s bridge in centuries, perhaps. Listening for the mourners' telltale chirps, I move forward. My eyes scan every shifting shadow. I step with care, sliding over the large, snakelike ducts that rise to hip height, sometimes crawling under them. Mountains of rubble tower around me. Large branches of webbed plastic create a strange canopy overhead. Spines stick out from the fester, curling like massive spiders' legs. The occasional light twinkles, sparking like the eyes of great beasts.

Despite the lack of organic material, this place feels primeval. Wild. Before long, the floor grows spongy underfoot. Glancing down, I pull my boot out of a puddle of rust-colored moss. Spores cling to the EDDA, dusting my ankles and calves, almost like the fester but more . . . *vegetable*. A few meters more, and strange mushrooms bloom, some standing two meters in height, their stalks as thick and wide as the park's tree trunks. They shrink away from the light, skins wrinkling.

In some places, the floor sags under my weight. In others, it's rotted away, leaving massive holes behind. I test my steps before I take them, and travel almost a kilometer before my bioware's OS pings me with a warning message:

Alejandro Mello is currently in critical condition.

"What?" I whisper. I shake my bioware awake and ping Alex and Faye a panicked, **What's going on?** Did the mourners manage to break into the park? Or were the *John Muir*'s systems failing faster than we'd anticipated? My thoughts whirl as I log in to Mami's FamiliaStar account, bringing up Alex's vitals on-screen:

Heart rate? 150 beats per minute.

Blood pressure and volume? Low.

Hemorrhaging in the lower abdomen.

Infection imminent.

Bioware response? Overloaded.

No, this can't be happening. Not to Alex, he cannot *be dying,* I think, trembling. *What's happened to you, cari?* I switch over to Mami's GPL locator, which shows a hazy version of the *John Muir*'s deepdowns, and ask the GPL to search for his bioware's location.

Alex isn't back at the park—he's seven kilometers away from me, in some strange corner of the ship. Away from medical aid, away from help.

For some reason, he's with Sebastian. In the middle of nowhere. *Dying.*

My gut twists. If my friends went into the deepdowns with Sebastian, something's gone horribly wrong. My mind whirls, presenting me with a myriad of scenarios, each one more awful to contemplate than the last. Alex and I have been friends all our lives. Our parents studied archeology together at the university. To me, he's family.

Answer me, I ping Faye. *What's going on? Why aren't Alex and Sebastian still in the park?*

I wait, begging Faye to reply, unable to look away from my ioScreen. When she doesn't respond, I glance over my shoulder at the footprints I've left in the moss. Every part of me yearns to run to Alex, to find out what's happened, to *help him.* He's been in my life for sixteen years, and I expected him to be in it till our faces wrinkled and our hair turned white. We dreamed of striking out on our own when we got old enough, and running our own outfit under my family's umbrella.

But if the *John Muir* fails, everyone dies. Mami. Dad. My family. The crew of the *John Muir.* Tuck. To abandon my mission now would be to forsake them all, because I have no guarantee I'd be able to retrace my steps safely in either direction. If I'm not moving forward, I gamble with the last chance we might have to save the ship.

Sniffling, I take one shaky step forward, toward the bridge. My heart needs to go back for Alex. My head knows I can't, not if I want to save the ship. The needs of the community, of *humanity*, come before my heart's.

Lo siento, my friend. I grit my teeth and hug myself. Every step I take feels like a betrayal. I'm turning my back on someone I love dearly; and the forces of what I *must* do and what I *want* to do each take a corner of my heart and pull. They seem to tear my heart in two, despair hemorrhaging in my chest and flooding my whole soul.

I'm sorry. I put another foot down.

I love you. Then another.

Please don't die on me.

One step after another, all the way to the bridge.

<u>TUCK</u>

The air lock panels shake open. Keeping one hand anchored on the lip of the *Muir*, I step outside. Gravity lets go. I tighten my grip on the air lock to keep my ass from floating away into space. The world drops out from under me. I forgot how much I hate looking down at stars twinkling under my feet. My equilibrium's always glitched for hours afterward.

Everywhere you look, stars stretch into forever. Endless. They run so thick out here, it's like being trapped inside a glittery snow globe, with some crazy perverse god who keeps shaking the damn thing. *Frag this place.* If I survive this, I'm never traveling to deep space again.

Never say never, my mom's voice echoes in the back of my head.

Shut up, Mom.

Outboard Station B lurks in the darkness, its lights blinking. A magnetic orbital system tethers the outboard ships to the *Muir.* I don't remember how long Mom made the tethers. With zero reference points between here and the station, I can't tell how far away it lies. Not exactly.

A knifelike cold slices down my spine.

What's powering the outboard stations? Did they reboot when we brought the ship back online?

I think of the footprints in the dust back at the platform.

None of those prints were made with a curator's bare feet.

Fan-fricking-tastic. Can't wait to see what's hiding out there.

"I've got a visual on the outboard station," I say to the others, floating back into the ship. "Let's move."

I help Alex to his feet. I've patched up his suit the best I can, but even with the compression-tourniquet, he still hunches over, holding his stomach. Sebastian keeps his rifle pointed at us, but stays out of reach, too. I admit Sebastian's not as stupid as I'd like him to be. He's thinking strategically, complicating an already thoroughly fragged situation.

I grab one of the old hydrapacks off the floor, one with blasters that will carry us between the ships. Out of the fifty left in Air Lock B, only two would fire up for us. So we're sharing. No matter what era it was built in, tech doesn't last. It breaks down, it dies, it changes, becomes obsolete, forgotten. Useless. Part of me thinks humanity might be just as frail. We weren't built to last ages—not without evolution. We're supposed to learn from our pasts. Rise up. Become better.

Turns out we're not so good at that, though.

"I might be happier dead," Alex says, groaning.

"No chance in hell." I use a makeshift harness I rigged out of a busted hydrapack to secure Alex to Sebastian. He's taking Alex with him, if only to keep me from sabotaging his hydra. "Do you know what Laura will do to me if anything happens to you, *vato*?" I throw the Spanish in to rib him.

Alex grins, but it's more half a wince than anything else. "Tell her I gave you a free pass."

"I'm not going to be your Dr. Kevorkian," I say, turning on my hydrapack and hoisting it onto my shoulders. The pack's four arms engage, whirring as they lift overhead. "No way am I going to let you die."

"Doctor who?" Sebastian keeps his rifle trained on me.

Oh, now that's an opportunity I can't pass up: "Doctor *Who*?" I say with an edge of mockery. "You call yourself archeologists and you don't know about *the* Doctor?"

"Which doctor?" Sebastian asks.

"The madman with a box?" I ask. "Bad Wolf? *We have a lot of running to do*?"

They both look at me as if *I'm* the one who's lost my damn mind.

"All righty, then," I say, stepping over the edge of the air lock. "*Allons-y*. Let's go."

I launch myself into space.

For a few seconds, I let my forward motion carry me. The weird thing about free flight in space? The stars don't move around you. Everything's so big and vast, the nebula stays locked in place. My stomach senses my forward motion, but my eyes can't make sense of it all. I engage the hydrapack's four thrusters. The pack's octopus-like arms engage, slowing my trajectory. Controlling it, too. I rotate to look back to check on the others.

"Move it, Mello," Sebastian snaps. They end up in a tangle of limbs and tethers, stumbling through the air lock. After a few minutes, they manage to catch up. Sebastian's wearing the pack and pushing Alex forward with his rifle's muzzle.

I wheel, flying forward. The outboard station looms, a boxy ship stretching some three klicks. Ships of the *Muir*'s size had anywhere from five to eight large outboard stations. Before the jettison, these stations functioned as escape pods. Mecha storage, too. If something happens to your big rig in deep space, you don't want your major repair tech going down with the ship.

Light blasts through the ship's large windows. As we get closer, I try to see what moves inside. All that's visible are boxes, old mecha parts, and a jumble of rusted tools.

After several minutes of flight, we reach the old docking station.

I alight as the outboard station's gravity tethers kick in, drawing me down to a small platform. The door bears the ship's name and ID marks—USS JOHN MUIR NPS-3500—as well as the ouroboros symbol underneath. I run my fingers over the snake's back as the others reach the platform. It leaves a fine white powder on my gloves. I rifle through my memory for the outboard door codes, but nothing comes to mind. I'll have to crank the door open. Goody.

Sebastian stiffens. "Why would there be a Pitch Dark logo out here?"

"Damned if I know." I jam my door crank between the panels. Exterior doors have a better sealing system. Plus, it's possible these doors haven't been opened in years. Centuries, maybe. I'm sweating before I've cracked the door even a centimeter.

"You'd better not be leading me into a trap," Sebastian says, unhooking himself from Alex.

"I told you not to come," I say with a shrug.

"Why would the terrorists be out here?" Sebastian asks.

"Probably because the *Muir*'s crew couldn't reach them out here. Not without EVAs." A bead of sweat rolls down my forehead. I try to wipe my brow with the back of my hand, but bang my fist into my helmet. *Dammit.* "We might be knocking on their front door. Or on their tombstones."

With an *oof,* Alex sinks down to the ground. None of us have a lot of time left. Not Alex. Not Laura. Not the *Muir.*

"I suppose we have advanced tech," Sebastian says.

"One of us does," I say, glancing at his pulse rifle. Guns in my time sure as hell didn't shoot laser beams, or whatever the bullets are made from.

He shifts his weight. "We can deal with whoever's in there."

You keep telling yourself that, man. I put my back into cranking the door open. Around, and around, and around. My mind reels, too, presenting me with a different death for Laura every few seconds. We need to hurry. She might have the EDDA suit, but not even Mom could make her invincible.

Once I jack the door, we step inside the air lock. As the door slides closed behind us, the lights flicker on. Only half of them work, but half's enough. To knock out my nerves, I whistle "Never Gonna Give You Up" while we wait for the air lock to pressurize. A horizontal gauge on the wall above the ship's door moves from red to orange.

"Will you shut up?" Sebastian asks me.

"Nervous much, newb?" I ask, lifting a brow at him. "I guess if I die, you're screwed 'cause you don't know the way to the bridge. If Alex dies, Laura won't tell you shit. You're the only one with a gun in here, and only God knows—"

The air-lock doors *ding!* bright.

"—what's in there," I say, inclining my head toward the doors as they slide open.

Sebastian blanches a little.

I move in first, the asshole in me grinning. It covers up the sheer terror that's turning my heart into bubble wrap. Each beat pop, pop, *pops,* fast and brutal.

We step into the station's mecha hangar. Tall metal ribs arch overhead. The space stretches so large, the crew could rest an entire mecha here flat on its back. I blink, telling my HUD to zoom in while I scan for movement. Metal crates of supplies and tools are stacked in haphazard piles, as if the world's drunkest Tetris player dropped them here. Massive cranes soar overhead. A few lights glow from the walls. One of them blows out as we walk in, sparks dancing down to the floor.

"This place is a shit heap," Sebastian says.

"Your mom's a shit heap," I mutter under my breath.

"What was that?"

"I didn't hear anything," I say with a grin. I glance at my EVA's metrics, which show real-time updates on the air quality and pressure. The oxygen levels seem a little low, but the pressure's around Earth's sea level. Temperatures here are in the upper teens. With no mourner presence, this area's the cleanest part of the ship, outside the neardowns.

Alex drops down next to a corrugated crate with a long sigh. He leans his head back against the metal. "Let me take five, *vatos,*" he says, closing his eyes.

"Stay with him," I say to Sebastian, motioning at Alex.

He turns his rifle on me. "Have you forgotten who's in charge, Tuck?"

"Fine," I say, turning around and putting my hands up. I inject boredom into my tone. "Then order me to go check the perimeter and find the mecha—"

A loud *clank-grrk-clank!* echoes through the station, alarm lights sounding. The floor shakes. A sign on the wall lights up: MECHA DOCKING IN PROGRESS, as the large station doors begin to open. Air whooshes until the oxygen barrier kicks in, and—

Ah, crap.

"What's that?" Sebastian asks.

"Our bad timing," I snap, backing up a few steps. "*Hide*, you idiots!"

I duck behind a large stack of corrugated metal crates, wedging myself between the boxes and the station's wall. Alex slips behind another set a few meters away. I don't see where Sebastian ends up.

Except hopefully *caught.*

Four loud bangs echo through the outboard station's port side. *They're parking now,* I think, poking my helmet to turn off all sources of illumination from within the suit. My heart pounds. *Just how many of these guys were hiding out on the* Muir? *Ship seems to be lousy with them.*

There's a rush of air, a whooshing and whirling. A heavy clank vibrates through the floor as the outboard station's doors seal shut.

Footsteps echo across the floor. Alex glances at me.

"How is that possible?" a woman asks. Her voice is unfamiliar, irregular, filtered through her EVA's audio system. The answer's not audible. "She *what*? Through the biofarm? And she killed one of the big ones?"

Laura.

That's my girl.

"Where is she now?" a man asks. I don't dare crane my head around to try to see them, and I don't recognize their voices.

"Howell says she's off the grid, but close to the destination," the woman replies. "They seem to think she's working in tandem with Dr. Morgan."

"Impossible. Morgan's dead," the man snaps.

Thanks for the reminder, asshole.

There's a pause. Even their footsteps halt.

"Send a team," the woman says. "Kill her. Take the other girl with you—she'll probably be able to get closer to the target than you. No, I don't particularly *care* how you kill her—go ahead and feed her to the Queen Mother, if you so desire."

Queen Mother? I wonder. *What the hell is that?*

"How are we getting out of this?" Sebastian asks through our comms. "There are probably ten of them out there, all armed."

"Maybe if *someone* hadn't taken our rifles away . . . ," I say.

"Shut up, Morgan," Sebastian snaps.

Craning my neck, I look for something, *anything* really, that I can use to distract the people on deck.

On the other side of the station, a large red button calls out to me—it looks like a cabin purge button. Hitting that button would evac the station's oxygen barrier and suck the air out into space, along with anything or any*one* not tied down. Including me, if I'm not careful.

It's a crazy-stupid idea.

But desperate times call for crazy-stupid measures.

The outboard station stretches about forty meters wide. I'll run that length in four or five seconds. Maybe less. *Basically, run,* I think with a grin. I'm always running. At least this time, I'm running *toward* someone, rather than away from them.

"Everyone holding on to something tied down?" I ask through the comms.

"Wait, wait, why?" Sebastian asks, suspicion creeping into his voice.

"You'll see." I roll into a crouch, eyeing the station's purge button. No more than five meters to the button's left, there's a rebar ladder welded to the wall. I'll grab onto that when all hell breaks loose. "Stay where you are. Hang on, or you'll die."

Every muscle in my body coils.

"What are you going to do, *vato*?" Alex wheezes at me.

"Something crazy," I reply, easing around the deck's bolted-down crates.

Here goes nothing.

I push off the wall, bursting past the crates. Breath fogging the inside of my EVA helmet. Legs pumping like pistons. Out of the corner of my eye, I spot an old *Muir* tech named Howell, who's so shocked, he doesn't even try to stop me. Like the woman on his right, he's not wearing an EVA suit.

Pity.

This won't be a pretty way for them to die.

Two guys rush me from my left. Sebastian snipes at them before I can even hit my brakes. Men stumble and jerk as bullets slam into their torsos and helmets. I dodge past, shouts erupting behind me. Someone's shouting at me inside my helmet, too. I can't hear anything that's said, not past the drumbeat of blood in my ears and the pounding of my feet in these massive boots.

I catch myself against the opposite wall, break the glass case around the button with my fist, then punch the purge button hard. Sirens scream across the deck, citrine-yellow hazard lights blaring in my eyes. A woman's voice comes over the station's PA system: *"Air purge initiated. Oxygen barrier will drop in five, four, three . . ."*

The station heaves, bucking underfoot. I stumble, almost losing my balance, and then leap forward to grab the rebar ladder on my left. I hook my arms through the rungs as the station's air lock cracks open. Outside, stars twinkle, peaceful and yet so very malevolent.

The air shrieks as it exits the station. Crates tumble end-over-end toward the void. Cranes swing overhead, their heads dragging across the ceiling and raining showers of sparks across the deck. They slam into the walls, breaking off entire metal panels and pylons. As the vacuum suction increases, everyone scrambles for a handhold. Some people fly loose, plunging headlong toward the void. Ten, maybe twelve bodies disappear through the ship's maw.

"What'd you do?" Sebastian shouts over the noise.

"Something real stupid, so hold on!" I shout back.

"You're making it awfully hard, Tuck!" Sebastian snaps.

I chuckle. "Oh my god, did you *think* about how that sounded before you said it?"

"Now isn't the time for dick jokes," he snaps.

"That's not a thing, asshole!" I say.

When the oxygen barrier snaps back into place, I sink to the ground and put my head against the wall. *Too close that time,* I think, wishing I could wipe the sweat off my face.

The station's air lock panels rumble closed. I don't hear their vibration, but I can feel it through the floor.

I look up when the light shifts in front of me. Alex limps over and sits down next to me. Sebastian emerges from inside one of the crane operating booths, keeping his rifle pointed at the ground.

Ah, crap. I'd hoped Sebastian would've at least lost the rifle, if not his life.

"You're right about one thing," Sebastian says. "That was stupid."

"But I made them disappear, right?" I ask, looking around the deck. I spread my hands wide. "Ta-da."

"Who's the murderer now?" Sebastian says, motioning to me with his rifle.

Touché.

Both Alex and Sebastian follow me into the mecha docks. Splashes of green, turquoise, and purple light coat the floor and ceilings. Turning a corner, I walk onto the wide dock. On either side of me, the heads of the mecha are positioned inside airtight loading stations—we can drop down into the cockpits from there.

I ignore the ouroboros symbols carved into the mecha's flanks.

Bastards.

Built from smooth black titanium, most of the mecha look shipshape. The cockpits glow with soft, colored light. Their colors tell me what the mecha's used for. The two purple mecha have two-meter-long ion saws built into their right forearms. They're for demolitions, and come equipped with a range of targeted explosives. Beyond them, there are four each of the green machines, and four of the blue. If I remember right—and I probably don't—the green mecha have welding tech, and the six-armed blue mecha are powerlifters. Several are missing from the dock, but we only need three.

Circular, hip-high screens display the mecha's status. Most of the circles glow in green "ready" states.

"So, who knows how to fly a mecha?" I ask with a grin.

LAURA

After running another half a kilometer, I emerge from the mourner tunnel onto the *John Muir*'s massive bridge.

Thin light falls through the bridge's tall, age-clouded windows. Darkness hangs like a fog over the entire space, but the *John Muir*'s bridge appears to be several times larger than the *Conquistador*'s. At first I think the ceiling's caved in toward the middle, but no. When I squint, the EDDA's helmet magnifies what I'm looking at . . . but to be honest, I'm not sure *what* I'm looking at.

From where I stand, it almost appears that the bridge suffered massive trauma. The floor and ceiling have been wrenched open and curled into strange, alien patterns. On my right, an entire section of computer terminals rises like an old-world tsunami over my head, their monitors dangling by cords from bent desks. Broken chairs and debris rest along the floor at the wave's foot.

Tuck told me the mourners had overrun the bridge, but

nothing moves. It's so quiet here, even my breath sounds like a scream. Old, shed skins rest in discarded piles on the floor, or hang from the equipment like gray ghosts. I flinch away as one wafts toward me, carried on a dying current of air.

Though humans built this place, it looks like the primitive home of some ancient, eldritch horror. There's no question the *John Muir* is a massive ship, but this is the first time I've wondered if it might swallow me alive.

As I venture onto the bridge, the map hovering at the edge of my sight changes. It displays my route across the devastation, up one flight of stairs, down a short hallway, and through the ship's control room to the server room. I'm close.

I clamber over a large pile of rubble, shocked to find the floor ends abruptly underfoot. I grab a handhold to keep from sliding into a large sinkhole in the bridge. It must be forty meters in diameter, much larger than the tunnel I used to reach this place. Small, black-branched plants grow off the sides of the walls, their white fruit glowing like small stars. By their light, I see the large, moist membrane plugging the entire space. It twitches, a shiver rippling from its center to its edge, a strange belly-button-shaped opening in its middle. Something trembles inside the mass, and I draw back from the edge of the hole.

What is that thing? I wonder. *What sort of monster bores holes in starships?*

Whatever it is, I hope it's not home.

Skirting the hole's edge, I head for the second-story bridge control room, passing beneath it as I head for the stairwell. I take the steps slowly, using the EDDA's lights to search every nook and cranny. I need to be careful with the lights, as the suit only has a quarter of its power left. Dr. Morgan did say the suit was very much a prototype, its powerpac still insufficient for its needs.

Just a little bit farther, I tell myself. *We're almost there.*

At the top of the stairs, I find myself in a utilitarian hallway with metal floors, rust-eaten walls, and broken lights. The fester spreads across most of the space, heat still rising from its spongy dankness. Spiny growths retract into the wall as I pass. Flat white worms wriggle through the fester, recoiling whenever my lights fall on them.

To my right, I find a hefty, blast-proof door marked MISSION CONTROL in chipped paint. To my left, the hallway wanders off into the darkness. The fester grows thick here, bubbling out of vents. A pus-filled blister explodes on the wall to my right, weeping a steamy, yellowish liquid. A few of the worms slip out, writhing on the floor. My skin crawls beneath the EDDA's protective layers.

The touchlock beside the door glows green. The blast doors are vacuum-sealed, so I need to be careful. If the room beyond is pressurized, it will be dangerous to open this door. The blast of escaping air from a higher-pressure environment to a lower-pressure one may blow me back several meters into the fester. I wince at the white tapeworms sliding into the shadows behind me. *Ugh.*

I search for a handhold. Something to cling to, in case of a massive pressure shift. I tug on a nearby set of spines, find them well-anchored to the wall, take a deep breath, and tap the touchlock.

As the control room doors slide apart, escaping air hisses

into the hall. I brace myself as the door panels widen and the airstream roars into gale-force winds. The air spirals past me and dissipates. As it slows, I wrench my hands off the fester's spines and step into the control room, shucking goo off the EDDA suit.

Once I close the door, the air pressure rises in the room, the HVAC still circulating massive amounts of air through the space.

Bueno, I'm here.

The control room sits a floor higher than the rest of the bridge, one architectural mainstay that persists in shipbuilding to this day. Most of the bridge is visible from these control room windows. Reaching out, I slide my hand along a computer monitor, knocking a waterfall of dust to the desk below. All the chairs and workstations in this room stand at attention, as orderly as the day the crew of the *John Muir* went to sleep.

What must it have been like to tidy one's desk before entering an indefinite stasis? To be Dr. Morgan, wandering the vast halls of the *John Muir*, alone and without hope of rescue? To wonder if you and your work had been forgotten by humanity as a whole? As an aspiring archeologist, I'm tasked with the mission to find those voices lost to time, to preserve them, and amplify their message. I promise myself the crew of the *John Muir* will not be consigned to this dark corner of the universe forever. It's my duty to see their stories returned to the Colonies, not just as an archeologist, but also as a member of the human race.

I weave my way through the desks, headed for the server room. I pass pictures of children, smiling families. An abandoned novel. A coffee cup stained with someone's lipstick. I wonder how many of these people made it, and how many were turned into monsters.

The EDDA's nanites whirl on my palm and fingertips as I approach the server room door. I press my hand into the touchpad. The panels slide back into the wall, revealing the ship's labyrinthine server room. Row upon row of black towers march into the darkness, their multicolored lights blinking across their surfaces like a myriad of stars. A few of the towers have collapsed, their guts made of wires and circuits spilling out onto the floor. I step inside, surprised by the room's warmth and the quiet hum rising up from the floor and through my feet.

This room reminds me of Lucita and Etel back on the *Conquistador*. The longer I'm in this nerve center of humming machines, the more my anxiety lessens.

Then someone says, "Stop, Laura," from behind me.

My body halts, the subjugator locking my muscles down. The voice sounded female. *Dr. Smithson?* I wonder. After a few seconds pass, I turn, coming face-to-face with a woman in a *Conquistador* EVA. The Cruz lion rears across her left shoulder in green, white, and red. Her mirrorlike helmet obscures her face.

She aims her plasma rifle at my chest.

"You were never any good at escondidas, Laurita," she says, her voice garbled by the EVA's external speakers. "I don't know why you'd think you could beat me now."

No manches. I take a step back, as if struck.

"Faye?" I whisper.

TUCK

"Hey, brainiac," Sebastian says over the comms. "What now?"

The three of us—Alex, Sebastian, and me—float inside maintenance mecha, positioned about fifty meters outside the *Muir*'s bridge windows. I took a purple mecha, and then instructed Alex to take the other one. Sebastian rides in a green mecha—no way do I need him running around outer space with demolitions equipment.

My original plan was to use the mecha to cut our way back into the ship. It relied on my HUD lens, which I thought I could use to identify a safe, non-mission-critical ingress point to bust into. You know, a place that wouldn't completely glitch the ship.

How was I supposed to know my HUD lens wouldn't work outside the *Muir*'s walls?

"*Órale*," Alex says. "Do you guys see those lights?"

"Where?" I ask.

"Inside the bridge, starboard side," Alex says. I can see him pointing from his mecha's cockpit. He's right. Two tiny, bright lights bob through the bridge. They wink in and out like fireflies as the user—or *users*—cross the area.

"I thought you said there wasn't an interior path to the bridge, Tuck," Sebastian says.

"Not any I know of," I reply. But the *Muir* is massive. While I've explored a lot of her over the last two years, she still harbors her secrets, even from me. Dejah only had eyes in so many places. And we closed down entire sectors of the ship to protect the park's resources and assets.

I float closer to the bridge. Inside, Laura steps into the control room and closes the door. She scans the area. As she moves left—toward the server room—she knocks some dust off a computer monitor, letting it swirl around her fingers.

Alex was right, I was stupid to think Laura needed me to save her. She's brilliant. Badass. Tough as nails, as the old saying goes. When we first met, she looked me straight in the eye and insisted we fight for a cause greater than ourselves. She made me feel less alone in ways the crew of the *Muir* never managed. Laura made me care about this universe again, and where I might belong in it.

When I met her, I promised myself I'd save her from this disaster.

In the end, *Laura* saved *me*.

"Where is she headed?" Sebastian asks as Laura examines the room. "What is she doing?"

"It's been about four hundred years since I've been on the bridge, bruh," I say. "My memory's not great. Can't say I know what she's doing there."

Lies. All lies.

"Well, it can't be anything good," Sebastian snaps. "Find a way to access the bridge. *Now.*"

I respond by making a fist with my mecha's hand. "Oops," I say, holding a middle finger up to him. "I think one finger got stuck. It's an old mecha, after all."

Alex laughs so hard, he starts coughing. Wetly. I can hear the damage the plasma bullet did to his body through the comms.

"Careful there, *vato*," I tell him.

He gives me a thumbs-up through his mecha's cockpit, letting me know he's okay.

I spend the next few minutes putzing around. I knock on the ship's metal flank as though "looking" for a place to cut into her sides. I muse aloud, pretending to worry about hitting the ship's "valence coordinators" or her "beta-blocking sensors," or whatever other imaginary parts of a ship I can dream up. The longer I keep Sebastian away from Laura, the better.

Using my mecha's thrusters, I float beneath the *Muir*, still pretending to search for a way inside. The ship settles over me like the shadow of death. Every twenty seconds, the underlights flare, throwing the clunky machinery into sharp relief. Unlike the rotten interiors of the *Muir*, the hull's metal looks fairly shipshape. With no air to degrade it, and no water to eat it away with rust, the only damage I can see is fine pitting from micrometeorites.

I sweep my mecha's high beams over the ship's belly. The shadows lie so deep here, they almost seem to solidify outside the cone of the mecha's highbeams.

Alex asks, "Who's that?"

"Who's what?" I ask, examining some strange scoring on the ship's belly. Bright silver welts gleam in the black metal. *What hit the ship?* I wonder, because it looks like some sort of massive space monster raked the ship with its claws. *Huh, weird. Cthulhu, eat your heart out.*

"Someone wearing a *Conquistador* EVA just entered the bridge," Sebastian says. "It's probably one of my mother's agents."

"One of your mom's agents," Alex says, taking a shaky breath, ". . . would be in a Smithsonian EVA."

"Then who's that?" Sebastian asks.

"I'm more worried about why they have a *gun*," Alex says.

Sebastian scoffs. "Laura's a dangerous criminal—"

"Who's the dangerous criminal?" I snap. "You *shot* someone!"

Sebastian tuts. "Only in self-defense—"

"Are you *kidding* me?" I laugh, derisive, angry. "You don't get to pretend it was *self-fragging-defense*—"

"Can you two *vatos* stop arguing and find a way into the goddamn ship?" Alex says, coughing again. "Whoever's in that EVA has a gun pointed at Laura. If something happens to her while you two flex your e-peen, I'll shoot *both* of you."

The pressure pounds through my veins. I don't remember the layout of the bridge. We might have to cut straight through the bridge's windows, which might be dangerous if the bridge is still pressurized. *Think, you idiot!* I tell myself. *There's gotta be a way—*

The ship's underlights flare again. Something shifts out of my peripheral vision. My adrenaline spikes. I wheel the mecha around, heartbeat drumming in my fingertips and banging through my temples. My mecha's headlights ripple over a translucent skin, its occupant long gone and its mouth open in an eternal shriek.

There's other detritus here, too—*Look, Mom, an SAT word!*— bits of the ship suspended in space, as if a large section of its hull had been blasted out with explosives.

I drive the mecha closer. The light from my high beams slides over the gunmetal-gray plates, then snags on a tangle of metal. The *Muir*'s been ripped open as if made of nothing more than aluminum foil.

Something's bored a hole straight through the bottom of the ship.

"Ah, crap," I say, shifting the angle of my high beams. Not only has something created a massive hole in the ship's hull, but it looks like there's something *hiding* in it, too.

Probably shouldn't have cracked that joke about Cthulhu.

"What?" Alex asks. "Did you find a way inside?"

"Sit tight, kids," I say, looking at the pulsating membrane overhead. I fire up the mecha's big, sparking ion saw. It casts a bright glow around the mecha's right fist.

"What are you doing, Tuck?" Sebastian hisses.

"If I don't come back, guys," I say with a grin, angling my ion saw, ready to rip the membrane open from edge to end, "make sure to avenge my death."

L A U R A

"You're the Noh Mask hacker." I step back into the control room, as if saying the words aloud will help me comprehend them. "You . . . you crashed our ships. You thrust us into this waking *nightmare—*"

A soft, sad smile spreads over Faye's face. "Not exactly, cari. Before I explain, take off your helmet, Laura."

She pronounces my name wrong, and the sound of those syllables so *mangled* in her mouth aches more than almost anything. Still, the nanomechs in my blood respond, forcing me to lift my hands and remove the EDDA's helmet.

"I don't want you to be able to engage your helmet's noise-cancelling features, now," she says.

"And you called *me* the malinchista." I slide a cold note into my voice, even as my heart cleaves itself in two. I have locked eyes with the monster of betrayal before; I am acquainted with the emotional carnage it leaves in its wake. Three months ago, it sank its teeth into my throat. Now it has come for my heart.

"You knew about what the Smithsons had done to me, but didn't try to help me escape them?"

She presses her lips together in a bloodless line, saying nothing.

"You let me suffer," I say. "You tried to *kill me*."

"To be fair, I tried to kill everyone," she says drily. "It wasn't personal, Laura."

"The hell it *wasn't*. You're supposed to be my best friend!"

"Am I?" she asks, keeping her gun pointed at my chest. I put my hands up and back toward the control room windows. "This is the first time you've seen past my mask. Am I really the person you thought you knew?"

I shake my head slowly, as the pain builds in my chest. "No," I say, backing up a step. "N-no, I've known you since we were children—"

"You were easier to play than some, cari," she says. "It's easy to dupe the girl who thinks she's smarter than everyone else in the room, the girl who will knock you out with your own bioware and set herself up to take the blame for you."

"I don't think about myself like that." Though I admit, I'm analyzing the situation and looking for loopholes, looking for a way to outplay Faye. There has to be some way out of this situation that *doesn't* involve a bullet in my head or chest. *Think, Laura!* But my brain keeps latching onto the variable of Faye's gun. Or it reminds me she could use the subjugator to order me to kill myself on the spot. That's not to mention my added complication—the EDDA's powerpac continues to dwindle, with little more than 15 percent of its battery life left. If the EDDA dies, I'll lose Dr. Morgan and there won't be a way to salvage her connectome before the ship expires. The ship will fail without Dr. Morgan, and everyone I love will die.

I've got to outwit Faye.

"Well, you're not the smartest person in *this* room," she says with a smirk. "After all, I did just follow you all the way across the ship. And my father and I did outsmart you back on the *Conquistador*—while I pretended to be at the party, he confronted you in the Narrows, and then distracted you while I placed a *very* long distance call back to the Colonies."

"To whom?"

She shrugs. "Someone had to warn the resistance."

"Is that what you call yourselves, a *resistance*?" I spit. "You're *terrorists*."

"You've written so many scholarly papers on Pitch Dark, but you still don't understand us, do you?" she says, her brows knitting together across her forehead. "To the resistance, you human apologists are the terrorists, making excuses for a species capable of destroying a living planet. *You* are the empire looking to colonize a new world, without having addressed the evils that drove you to destroy your last. Look at what the Smithsons did to you, Laurita! They used their technology to try and seize resources, selfishly attempting to rip apart a community and family in order to get what they want. . . ."

The words spill out of her so quickly, she pauses to take a steadying breath. I'm surprised to see tears glittering in her eyes. "You're the historian here," she says. "Don't you see that *this* has been humanity's story since the beginning of time? All we ever do is cycle through our misery."

"¿Y que? Misery, past and present, doesn't give you the right to sentence five hundred million people to death," I say, choosing my words with precision, while looking for an opening in her defenses. "I'm not going to give up on the future, just because there are moments of pain in our past."

"You should," she says. "We've had more than *moments*, cari."

"But I won't."

"I know." She shakes her head. "There you are, always insisting that people are good and deserving of empathy, even when they've burned down the world. You little fool."

"I think you are good, Faye," I say softly, and it's true. "You're still my best friend . . . even if you are a real bruja."

"Do they make those old 'best friends' necklaces for archnemeses—you know, best friends for *never*?"

I laugh, dislodging an ache in my chest. For a second, I forgot she was holding me at gunpoint, ready and willing to take my life. She sounded like Faye again—*my* Faye. The chambers of my heart constrict at the thought, because I realize the girl I loved was never more than a smoke screen. *My* Faye wasn't real.

"I suppose this is good-bye," Faye says. "Get on your knees, Laura."

My subjugator kicks into action, ratcheting my heart rate up several speeds. The EDDA's helmet slides back into the suit, and my legs almost crumple beneath me. I hit the ground so hard, my knees clack on the rusted floor. The pain reverberates up my body, even aching in the pits of my teeth.

"Stay, Laura," she says, as if I'm some sort of dog that can be commanded.

My mind races through my options, searching frantically for a way out while keeping track of my ten-second buffer. "You really are going to kill me, aren't you?" I ask, trying to keep her talking.

Faye crosses the room, coming to stand behind me. She places the rifle's muzzle against the back of my skull. "It was a very good game, wasn't it? You did better than I expected you to, pulling that last-minute stunt with the shipbuilder. In the end, I still held the trump card—your subjugator."

"Hija de puta." I chuckle, before my breath seizes in my chest.

The subjugator let me insult Faye. She told me to *stay,* not *stop.* I wriggle my fingers. Inch my right leg back a few centimeters. Faye stands close to me, within striking distance—so certain she's won, she hasn't realized her mistake.

"Sticks and stones, cari," Faye says, nudging my head with the gun. "Resistance leaders have tipped off the ISG about the *John Muir,* mostly as a stunt. By the time the authorities arrive, all that will be left of this place is a husk, plus a few survivors shivering in a dark corner of a ship. Are there any last words your tearful, heartbroken best friend can relay to the world for you, Laura Cruz?"

Before she can fire, a deep groan resounds through the ship. "What was that?" Faye whispers. I watch her boots pivot, just a little, as she turns to look over her shoulder.

She screams.

TUCK

Well, I found a way inside the bridge, which is awesome.

But there's a hitch.

A really, really *big* hitch.

A tentacle snakes around my mecha's waist. The metal squeals, denting inward. I suddenly empathize with every soda can I crushed back on Earth, especially as the creature grabs me and yanks me into the bridge. The world whirls, like I'm on the universe's most god-awful carnival ride. Confusing. My stomach bucks till the movement stops.

Ten seconds ago, I floated outside the ship, cutting into what I *thought* was just some membrane-like plug over a hole in the ship. Turns out it wasn't a membrane at all.

It was a monster. The biggest damned griefer I've ever seen, too.

"Tuck!" Alex shouts. As far as I can tell, both he and Sebastian are still outside the bridge, near the windows. "What the hell is that thing? How did you get"—*cough*—"into the bridge?!"

"No way," Sebastian says. "No *effing* way. You guys are on your own with that thing!"

My head clears. I find myself face-to-fester with the bridge ceiling. Which means I'm high. Several *stories* high. Dinner-plate-sized suckers sweep past the cockpit window, the flesh the color of rancid milk. The surface looks nubbly, finger and elbows and toes sticking past the skin, like it took a hundred mourners to build this one piece of monster. Some sort of goo coats the mecha's windshield—the wipers only manage to smear it across the glass.

The mecha's cabin lights shudder on and off as the tentacle squeezes me tight. My coglink picks up a high-pitched whine, one that grinds into the side of my skull like a buzz saw. Pain spikes in my right temple. I groan.

Stella. Great.

There's a giant space monster on the *Muir's* bridge.

Because *of course there's a giant space monster on the* Muir's *bridge*.

"Tuck!" Alex shouts. "Can you hear me? Dammit, I'll check under the ship—"

"Don't!" I shout, but the tentacle drops me.

Have I mentioned there's still gravity aboard the *Muir*?

I plummet three stories in seconds, the back of my mecha crashing into the bridge floor. The impact jams the breath from my lungs. The back of my helmet strikes my seat. I'm dazed as hell, for I don't know how long, before my gaze focuses on the pale shadow of a tentacle rising over me.

I jam the mecha controls left, rolling sideways as the monster slams its tentacle into the floor. I feel the vibration, the crack of the metal through the outer hull of my mecha, but it's weird for everything to happen so *silently*. To see the ground split open like a lightning bolt, to feel its tremors in my gut, but for it not to register in my ears; especially after having been so terrified of sound for so long.

Note to self—do *not* get hit by the tentacles.

I scramble to my mecha's feet as the rest of the tentacles rise through the hole in the bridge. Some tentacles are as thick as a California redwood at the base, tapering to a fine point at the end. The tentacles branch, too, which makes them look like a massive network of striped veins. Nothing's visible through the maelstrom, except a clutch of green-white eyes that burn like phosphor.

The terrorists in the outboard station called this beast the *Queen Mother.*

And I thought *I* had mommy issues.

I glance through the control room windows. Laura's gone. The server room door's shut. If I want to help her, I'll have to go through this thing first.

I start my mecha's ion blade. The teeth on its massive, two-meter-long blade glow so bright, they slice through shadows. I'll cut off every one of Queenie's damned tentacles if I have to—if she's going to stand between me and Laura, she's going to lose a few limbs.

Or all of them.

She swings the tip of one tentacle around. I saw it off, the ion blade running through her flesh. Her black blood sprays over my windshield as she retracts her tentacle, fast. Three more shoot out in its place.

"Ah crap, ah crap-crap-*crap!*" I shout, hitting the mecha's thrusters to leap over them. The mecha's head slams into a piece of metal that's been bent up from the deck, and I tumble straight into the tentacles' grips. One snatches me up, whips me around, tosses me straight into a wall. I nose-dive into the ground, my windshield cracking with the force of the blow.

This is going well.

"Where are you?" Alex shouts into the comms. "You okay, man?"

"No!" I roll over to avoid another tentacle, jabbing my ion saw straight up and into the flesh. When Queenie rips her tentacle back, she saws herself open. Hot blood splashes over the deck as she yanks her limb away. "I'm *not* okay, but thanks for asking!"

"Did you get into the bridge through this giant hole?" Alex asks.

"Do you *want* to die?" I ask him. "Don't come in here!"

"I'm not going to leave you alone in there, *vato*."

"Damn you and your honor." I shut my ion saw off, dart across the bridge, hit the floor, and slide under a bent metal ledge. Queenie slams a tentacle down, making the whole floor shake. Another tentacle tries to slip around my ankle. I kick it off, then scramble forward. Duck behind a large pile of junk. My heart's beating so hard, it's a fragging miracle it's not busting down my ribs like bowling pins.

"What do we do with it?" Alex asks.

"Let's start with *kill it!*" I say as something yanks me from my hiding place. A big tentacle pulls me over a mound of rubble, dangling me high in the air by my mecha's foot. Queenie roils below me. Down on the deck, Alex ducks, dodges, slices, and fights his way toward the control room. His mecha's coated in gore. I don't know how he's standing his ground—Queenie had me on the run. Despite his injuries, Alex makes piloting the mecha look easy.

I kind of hate him for that.

"Tuck, hey!" Alex shouts through the comms, turning his mecha toward me. "Need some help?"

"Oh, no," I say, sarcasm dripping through my tone. "I'm really enjoying being strung up by my ass!"

"Sarcasm is the lowest form of wit, *gringo*," he snaps back.

"That's punning!" I say, slicing off the tip of another tentacle that swings too close.

"*Pun*-derful, maybe!"

"You did not just make a pun—"

The tentacles unfurl, exposing Queenie's center. Wave upon wave of serrated teeth rise in her triangular mouth. Those devolve into an entire nest of spines down the monster's ribbed throat. I'm staring down into a whirlpool of death. Forty-eight hours ago, I might've looked into that abyss and felt nothing but relief.

Now, I want to survive. There's a life for me outside the walls of the *Muir*, and I want it. Bad.

The tentacle bucks, dropping me into the creature's maw. My mecha suit tumbles through the air. I slam into one of Queenie's big teeth. I'm stunned. The monster tilts, increasing the incline and sliding me toward the abyss. I jam my ion saw into the gummy flesh beside me, stopping my fall.

I don't think she likes my ion-saw-turned-giant-space-monster-toothpick. She grabs me bodily and flings me from her mouth. I bounce head over mecha feet across the bridge, coming to rest by the far wall. My ion saw shuts off.

One thing's for damn sure—I'm really, *really* tired of playing crash test dummy for the universe's biggest piece of sushi.

Alex charges toward me, using his mecha to help me off the floor. We duck behind a nearby pillar of junk. "You okay?" he asks.

I groan in reply. My mecha's beat to hell—the hull breached, my windshield cracked, the left arm now nonfunctional. I'm sure I don't look any better. I sure as hell don't *feel* any better. I peer around the pillar, keeping an eye on our resident space monster.

"Listen," he says, pointing to the glowing eyes on the top of Queenie's head. "We'll have a better chance if we take out the eyes. Without sound, she's relying on her vision to track our positions."

"You got a plan?" I ask as Queenie's tentacles surge forth, searching for us.

"That's it."

"That's not a plan!"

"It's an objective."

"An objective is not a plan!" I say, but the tentacles surge between us, forcing us to leap away from each other.

"Get her eyes," Alex says to me, lopping off another bit of Queenie. "I'll distract her."

"Okay, that's *almost* a plan—"

A tentacle swings from my left, colliding with my mecha. The cockpit shatters around me. The cabin lights shut down. Something sharp spears me in the gut. I'm thrown. My mecha plows through the bridge's big windows, which shatter under the pressure. The cockpit beeps uncontrollably.

Someone shouts, "Tuck!" through the comms.

Stars twinkle around me.

I'm outside the ship.

I am moving away from the ship.

Fast.

By the windows, the monster's tentacles retract into the bridge.

Get out, I tell myself. *Gotta get out, get out, get out.*

I unbuckle my harness to the mecha, groaning as a spike of pain hits me from abdomen to head.

Crawl from the cockpit.

And jump.

L A U R A

Faye scrambles away, almost tripping over me. Her eyes widen as she gazes at something outside the room's windows.

I turn my head. An enormous tentacle presses itself against the control room window-glass—only about a meter away from me—each one of its suckers larger than my head. They squeal as they scrape past, scratching the glass.

I recoil from the window. For the space of a whole second, all I can think is, *Oh god, those suckers have teeth.*

But they are also the perfect distraction.

Pushing to my feet, I charge at Faye and tackle her to the ground. We both grunt as we hit the floor, the breath going out of her. Faye drops her gun. It skitters under a desk and out of sight. Pulling an arrow from my quiver, I clutch it in my fist and jam its tip into her EVA's external speaker, right under her chin. Sparks erupt into her helmet. As they cascade over her cheeks, her mouth opens in a soundless scream.

The speaker is an exploit, the loophole Faye failed to secure.

Without her external speaker, she has no voice; without her voice, she can't command my subjugator. And Faye must have forgotten to extend the Smithsons' self-protections to herself, since I can attack her verbally and physically. It's not much, but it's something.

Shoving off Faye, I vault over a desk. Brittle old papers spill off the surface in my wake. I sprint for the server room. I can see the control room windows on the periphery of my sight—they're full of twisting, writhing shadows. I don't give them even a second thought. The EDDA's nanites have already shifted along my fingertips, mimicking Dr. Morgan's own.

And we don't have much time left.

I slap my hand against the server room's touchpad. The door opens again, its panels sliding back into the wall. I scramble inside as Faye gets to her feet, pulling my arrow out of her EVA suit.

If Faye wants to command my subjugator now, she'll need to remove her EVA helmet, which, of course, will make her more vulnerable to attack. In retrospect, I suppose I could have jammed the arrow into her throat—but I'm not certain I could hurt Faye. Not like that, no matter what she's tried to do to me. Even as we stand upon vastly different sides of a polarizing gulf, Faye could never be my enemy. She's my sister, my pachanguera; the artist who taught me about color, and brushstrokes, and beauty; the one who filled my childhood with laughter.

She isn't my enemy . . . but I also cannot let her *win*.

As the door slides closed, our gazes meet for a moment. Faye's eyes narrow, lips turning up in a twisted sort of snarl. I've bought myself minutes, but no more.

Turning to face the servers, I find myself in a labyrinth of towering computers. Their humming fills my head, and the tang of electricity dances across my tongue. Shadows fill the room like smoke. The temperature's warm here, almost balmy on my bare face. The servers' dark facades twinkle with lights. Every few seconds, the floor shakes and great, thundering booms roll through the ship.

Hands trembling, I locate Dr. Morgan's map in my bioware. As I pull it up, a ping from Faye resounds through my arm bones: *Don't think you can win this, Laura,* she says. *I can turn your bioware against you, as easy as you turned mine against me.* . . .

Ignoring her message, I hurry into the labyrinth, my heart pounding on my eardrums. My footsteps ring off the dusty linoleum floors. The farther I move into the server maze, the higher my shoulders hitch, inching toward my ears, as if I'm retracting into myself.

In so many stories, the heroine strides toward certain death without fear. But in reality, I am very much afraid to lose this battle of wits. I'm terrified I'll botch this chance to save my world; or that I'll never get to make tamales with my mother and tías again; or to tease Dad about his calligraphy projects. What if I never witness Alex fly his first starship, or watch one of those old movies with Tuck?

I don't find courage in the act of sacrificing myself on behalf of the people I love; rather, I find my strength in hoping I'll still have a life to share with them.

How are you feeling, cari? Faye writes, her ping glowing over my wrist.

The world reels a little.

She continues: *Remember how the ship's doctors uploaded antidepressant codes into your bioware after Launch Day? Apparently they don't mix well with the post-op painkillers you're currently on. The cocktail is actually quite toxic.*

Tremors roll through my body.

Game on, Lalita. Faye ends the message with a smiley face. In no scenario can we both win—she wants to destroy the *John Muir*, and I want to save it. We cannot compromise. Either I install Dr. Morgan's consciousness into the ship's systems, or Faye gets what she wants, and we all die.

I follow Dr. Morgan's map through every twist and turn, stepping over piles of exposed wires that spill from one of the servers like entrails. I pass under a cooling duct, which pushes wisps of hair into my face. I wipe them back, leaving trails of grit on my skin. My forehead burns.

As the EDDA's powerpac burns down to 2 percent, I round a corner and find myself on the server room's far edge. A long line of massive supercomputers marches along the wall. I press my palm into their facades as I pass. These machines are more than just the brains of the *John Muir*, they are the guardians of her secrets, too.

And there, some ten meters away, lies my final destination: an unmarked, unassuming machine, one among thousands. Were it not for Dr. Morgan's map, the system might have been nigh unto impossible to locate.

I stumble forward, bracing myself against the servers. My muscles ache as Faye's cocktail poisons me slowly, and my stomach feels like someone's drawing a rusty saw in and out of my gut. My breathing labors.

Just a few more meters. A few more steps. *No pasa nada,* I tell myself. *I can do this.*

When I reach the map's destination, I sink to my knees in front of the machine, so relieved I could cry. Colored lights wink across its surface. The EDDA shifts on my right forearm, opening up to reveal a midmodern computer chip, one plugged straight into the suit. It pulses with blue light, a tiny container for a whole human consciousness. My fingers quiver as I pluck at it, my movements unsteady.

In the distance, a door depressurizes.

Pausing, I listen for the sound of footsteps. My head feels like my brain's gray matter has been pumped full of air, all its substance evacuated.

The EDDA suit drops to 1 percent power. I'm running out of time.

"Laura, cari," Faye calls out, her voice difficult to hear over the roar of the HVAC systems. She must've removed her helmet. "Let's play one last game of escondidas, ay? I won't even use your subjugator to track you, to make the game more . . . *authentic.*"

I swear in my head, picking at the chip. On my fifth attempt, it pops free in my hand. The chip looks like it needs to be installed directly onto the computer's motherboard—at least I *think* that's what the devices were called. I run one palm along the server's outer casing, searching for a latch. The system's facade, however, appears smooth. I rifle through my memories, trying to find something about opening cases like these. I need to access the server's hardware without damaging the computer itself—

"Oh, and I hope you don't mind that I brought a few new friends," Faye adds. "And let me tell you, they're really *gunning* to meet you."

This is a game to you, Faye, I think, *but only because you believe you've won.*

My hand brushes across a slight rise on the server's case. Something clicks under my shaking fingertips. The machine whirs, a cross of blue light pulsing over its face. The server's facade cracks into four quadrants, which retract to reveal its motherboards.

Plural.

There are *twenty* motherboards, neatly stacked in roll-out trays. Some bear labels, others stand unmarked. Without the EDDA's helmet display to guide me, I slide the trays open, comparing Dr. Morgan's chip to various others installed inside. *Mierda.*

The echoes of someone's footsteps crawl up behind me. I freeze. A drop of sweat rolls off the tip of my nose and splashes on the server, which steams. I glance over my shoulder, but there's nobody behind me.

I don't move until the footsteps fade away.

Finally, on the eighth drawer down, I find a chip sized like Dr. Morgan's. The drawer is labeled *Dejah*, and while the name sounds familiar, I'm not certain that was the name of the *John Muir*'s former AI. *Here's hoping.*

I remove the old chip, and then install the new. Gently, I slide the tray back into the case, and then tap one of the facade's quadrants. The server closes back up, whisper-quiet.

Inside the maze, men call out to one another:

"Any sign of her?"

"Not here."

"Little *bitch*."

"Now, now," Faye says. "Where's your sense of sportsman-ship, boys?"

When I get to my feet, my world tilts sideways. I lean on one of the servers, pressing my forearm against my stomach to keep it from wrestling with my other organs. The EDDA shuts off, some of the nanites cascading off my forearms like sand. Reaching down, I peel the EDDA's thick boots off my feet, leaving my soles bare. The lights on my shoulders flicker off, leaving me hidden in the shadows.

A new ping message pops up via my bioware: **Good work, kiddo. I need five minutes to take control of the ship's main systems. Stay alive.-KM**

A clock appears over my left bioware node: **5:00**. And counting.

I need to keep Faye distracted and draw her away from Dr. Morgan's server location. But I'm outnumbered. With the EDDA deteriorating, I can't even flee into the deepdowns, hoping they give chase. I'm limited to the pressurized control and server rooms, unless I want to die swiftly, painfully, in a frigid, low-pressure environment. All I have left to me are three arrows, my wits, and the things Tuck taught me in the deepdowns.

Hurry, Dr. Morgan. Though, to be fair, I'm not certain how she plans to save me, either. She's a ghost in the machine, not one of Tuck's midmodern superheroes.

Taking my last few arrows, I enter the labyrinth. I walk like one of the *John Muir*'s curators, placing the outer edge of my foot down before the heel. Quietly. My heart throbs, and my breath comes in great, dizzy gasps. Every other step, the world rolls a little underfoot. I keep one hand on the servers, which feels more like an anchor than a brace.

My countdown clock now reads **4:13**.

Ten meters ahead, a man in an EVA suit passes between two stacks of servers, pale as a demon.

I backpedal before he can turn his flashlight on me, slipping behind the end of a row of servers. Even at this distance, I strain to hear his footsteps—the servers' humming and the HVAC's dull roar coat everything in sound. The men's flashlights, however, leave smudges of light on the ceilings over their heads. From where I stand, I count lights from five searchers, though there might be more.

Where are you, Laurita? Faye says in a ping. *Come out, come out.*

Someone moves close, stalking me on the other side of the server wall. Taking an arrow in hand, I toss it over the servers like a dart, as far as I can. It clatters against a procrete pillar several meters away, the sound ringing through the server room.

Several lights change direction, converging on my arrow.

3:27.

Despite the worsening anguish in my body—a pounding heart, dizzy vision, and convulsing lungs—I head left through the maze, pausing when I hear someone's shuffling footsteps. The longer I dodge Faye's men, drawing them farther and farther away from Dr. Morgan, the more my condition deteriorates. My body quivers and twitches. I trip over my own feet, ankles wobbling.

I won't be able to play this game much longer—I need to find a place to hide, just until Dr. Morgan manages to install herself in the ship's systems.

Just until we win.

2:45.

"Laura," Faye calls out, her voice far away. "Stop."

No.

My muscles lock up. I count backward from ten, my head swimming. My legs tremble, calves and knees ready to collapse. *So much for playing fair.*

Before I have the chance to break free of my subjugator, someone grabs me by my ponytail, and then shoves me into a set of servers. With a cry, I drop to the floor, scrambling backward on my hands and feet.

A man in a moth-eaten EVA stands over me, an ouroboros symbol on his shoulder and a gun in his hands. Fear turns my throat into a vise, making it difficult to breathe.

With my failing strength, I jam my last arrow into his leg, right under his kneecap, which dislocates under pressure. Hot blood spatters over my hand. The man screams, stumbling into the servers. His helmet strikes the metal cases like a gong, gun clattering to the floor. I snatch it up. It's heavier than I expected and clumsy to wield. My fingers barely know how to wrap themselves around the stock and trigger, and they still tremor with sickness.

Keeping the weapon aimed at the man in the EVA suit writhing on the floor, I back away until Faye says, "Stop, Laura," from behind me.

My body obeys, muscles turning still as stone. Faye's footsteps pound closer.

1:58.

Then, "Drop the gun, Laura."

My fingers relax, letting the weapon fall to the floor. Something cold and hard presses against my spine—the circular curve of its lip matches the barrel of the gun on the ground.

1:45.

"On your knees, Laura," Faye says.

I obey the order, exhausted. My personal history doesn't flash before my eyes, like the clichés promised; instead, through the haze of pain, I'm trying to figure out how to give Dr. Morgan the last minute and a half she needs, and to distract Faye long enough to keep her from pulling the trigger.

People in EVA suits surround me. Four, no, five. From my place on the floor, I'm only able to see their boots—some *Conquistador* issue, some *John Muir*. Traitors, all.

"Perhaps we shouldn't kill her?" Faye asks one man in an EVA suit, her voice lilting, teasing. "After all, she has skills we can use and a trusted family name. She would make an excellent operative."

I laugh, but the sound crackles with pain. "I would never betray my family."

"I know you wouldn't, Lalita," Faye says airily. "But that doesn't mean I couldn't *make* you. After all, you're still one of my favorite people, and I don't want to have to shoot you. So you can come with us by choice, or by force. Either way, welcome to the resistance."

1:08.

Somewhere in the multiverse, there may be a Laura Cruz who embraces this offer; one who treasures her own existence more than the lives of her family and friends. Whether she does it to infiltrate Pitch Dark to destroy the organization, or simply to save herself from a gruesome fate doesn't matter.

And I admit, it's a relief to think about the salvation Faye's offering. Or requiring, really. A numbness spreads through my fingers and toes. The edges of my sight darken. Death lurks nearby, wearing an ally's colors and a friend's face. But not all deaths are physical ones, and if I'm going to die here and now, I'll die on my own terms.

"No," I say, half gasping the word.

"What?" Faye says with a laugh. "You can't say *no*, loca, not when you're wearing a subjugator. I own you."

"I told you . . . back in the medbay," I say, breathing through a spike of pain. "You can't own a person, Faye."

Pushing my palms into the ground, I rise despite the agony echoing through every extremity. My right elbow gives out, spilling me back to the floor. I try again, then again, feeling like I might shake apart before I can stand again.

0:26.

"Laura," Faye says as I turn. The spark burns left red welts on the bottom half of her face. "*Kneel.*"

"No," I say, louder this time, my voice rasping. I hunch over, bracing myself with my hands on my knees. The subjugator wants me to kneel, the nanobots digging into my calves and thighs, but I fight to remain standing. The pain burns so bright through my veins, it blinds.

I refuse to let the last choice I make in this life be dictated by someone else.

"No," I repeat, shaking my head.

Ten . . .

Nine . . .

Eight . . .

Dr. Morgan's countdown clock ticks in tandem with my subjugator's release.

"Don't do this, Laura," Faye says. "Don't make me kill you, I don't *want* to kill you."

"Mentirosa . . . mentirosa," I say, still counting down in my head.

"You'd rather die, here and now?"

"I don't want to die today," I say, gasping through the pain. "But I would rather be dead than live someone else's lie."

0:00.

A ping appears on my screen: ***Done. Hold on, Laura, just stay still no matter how crazy things get. I'm not used to driving this old girl.–KM***

She's in. I sink to the ground, relief spreading through my body. It does nothing to assuage the pain. Faye calls my name, my subjugator twitching in response, but my exhaustion's so heavy, it smothers all instructions.

The server room door opens with a hiss. Air roars out. Several of the people in EVA suits turn, cocking their heads and looking at one another. I can't see their faces due to their helmets, but their body language speaks to their surprise.

Faye glances at the woman beside her. "Did Samuels send an additional team? And why does it sound as though the control room has been depressurized?"

The other woman shakes her head, motioning for two men to go check it out. They slip away from the group, disappearing back into the black maze of servers surrounding us.

Seconds later, gunshots ring through the room. Something flings a man, bodily, over the tops of the servers. He crashes into one of the machines and tumbles from sight. Huge white tentacles crest over the tops of the server towers, moving toward us, their festering skins leaving grimy trails on everything they touch. Their suckers rasp against the metal.

"How did that . . . that *thing* get in here?" Faye half shrieks, firing her rifle at the beast. The shots pound against my eardrums. One tentacle rears up overhead, so pale it almost glows in the darkness, and slams down into the floor, knocking everyone off balance. Another tentacle bashes one man into the servers with such force his helmet cracks like an egg. A third wraps someone up and squeezes till gore spills on the floor. A fourth takes a woman by the ankle and swings her around, breaking her body against a procrete pillar.

I hold my breath. *Don't move. Just. Don't. Move.*

The others scatter, fleeing into the labyrinth. One tentacle shoots over my head. A woman screams. I grit my teeth at the sloshy, suckling sounds behind me, especially as the tentacle retreats, grasping a girl by the waist. As it sweeps back, dragging her toward the door, blood runs downs her legs and drips off her toes. She looks down at me. Coughs.

Even through a haze of pain, I'd still recognize her anywhere: *Faye.*

She reaches for me, but there's nothing I can do for her or

anyone now. I don't reach back, or call her name, or so much as move.

The tentacle yanks her away. I expect something to lash out at me, to grab me with toothy suckers and eat me alive.

I'm not sure how long I sit in the aisle between servers, not daring to move, not daring to *breathe*. Unable to sit up any longer, I slide sideways till I can lean my head against the systems' panels. The metal sears to the touch but I'm a supernova anyway, blazing bright in the universe at the end of my life. The servers' lights twinkle like stars around me, and I am at their center. Floating. My pain fades, burned away by the fire raging in my veins, and a child's nursery rhyme plays through my head: *Estrellita, ¿dónde estás?*

A ping bounces through my bioware.

Me pregunto qué seras . . .

I see the ioScreen's light, but my vision's too blurry to read the words.

En el cielo y en el mar . . .

My bioware flickers. Shuts off.

Un diamante de verdad . . .

All the stars go out.

T U C K

An object in motion stays in motion, right?

It occurs to me slowly that I leaped off the mecha at a bad angle. My knee glitched out on the jump. As the ship looms, I realize I'm not going to collide with the ship at all. I'll skate past it by a few meters or so, and then spend the next few minutes tumbling through space till I either freeze to death or run out of air.

There's no stopping.

No changing direction.

No way to save my sorry ass.

Screw you, Newton.

"Alex!" I shout. "Hey, you there?"

No answer. Last I saw him, he was fighting off that monster on the bridge.

"Can anyone hear me?" I shout on the comms. My body heat drains out of my busted EVA suit. Oxygen, too. My EVA's display blinks wildly at me, flashing a very short sequence of numbers that comprise the rest of the conscious time I have in this life. Two minutes, nineteen seconds.

"Help!" I shout on the comms. But if either Alex or Sebastian can hear me, neither of them answer. Maybe they're dead. Maybe we're all dead, and trying to save this stupid, useless hunk of space garbage wasn't even worth the effort.

My teeth start to chatter. The cold drives long spikes of ice into my gut. I must be bleeding, but it's too dark to see anything but the ship and the stars. I'll be unconscious before I even pass the whole of the ship.

After all I've been through . . .

"*Tuck,*" Mom whispers.

After everything I've survived . . .

"*Can you hear me, kiddo?*"

Thanks for the big middle finger, karma.

Something warm and heavy wraps around my waist, dragging me back toward the *John Muir*.

"*Hang on,*" Mom's voice says. "*'Tis just a flesh wound, right?*"

The stars begin to darken.

Their lights blink out, one by one.

Then they're gone.

PART FOUR

THE COLONY

Quisieron enterrarnos, no sabían que éramos
   semillas.
They tried to bury us, but they didn't know we
   were seeds.

MEXICAN PROVERB

LAURA

My fingers wander back to my new bandage at the hollow of my throat, as if I need to reassure myself the subjugator's truly gone. I'm curled up in the medbay with a blanket, watching Tuck sleep off a surgery in which doctors reconstructed most of his abdomen. He's the only patient in here without any family to keep him company—since the incident in the bridge, Aren's been busy working with Dr. Morgan and my parents to salvage the *John Muir*, at least until help arrives.

Apparently the ISG will make an exception to their "no dead zone" rescue policy if you've found enough virgin Earth dirt to save the human race.

Mami enters the room, carrying a pair of steaming mugs. The bright hall light catches in her blond curls, and she lets the door swing closed behind her. "How's Tuck doing, m'ija?" she asks, crossing the room to hand me a mug of coffee.

I shift in my chair. "As well as anyone who had their intestines exposed to raw space would be, I guess."

She tucks the blanket tight around my body. "And you?"

"Tuck had his guts ripped out literally," I say with a defeated lift of my shoulders. "It was more . . . metaphorical for me."

Mami pulls up a plastic chair so that she can sit and face me. "Laura, I hope you know your family will never betray you."

"I do."

She puts a hand on my knee. "You should get some rest."

"If you wanted me to sleep, why did you bring me coffee?" I ask, looking at my reflection in the liquid's dark mirror.

"It's my job to pester you to sleep more, even if I know you won't." Her soft smile lights up her eyes, making the tawny flecks in her irises glow with warmth. "If you won't sleep, we should talk about what happened to you, and your subjugator."

I keep my gaze on Tuck, sipping the coffee Mami brought. The drink's black with no frills, and it tastes earthier than anything I've ever had back at the Colonies. "Do you think this is what coffee tasted like on Earth?" I ask her, sidestepping her question. "I'm assuming the beans were grown at the park. I wonder where this type was originally from—Colombia, perhaps? They were famous for their coffee, weren't they?"

"I would suppose so, sí," Mami says, hiding a smile behind the rim of her coffee mug.

"Even the texture seems different from what we have at home."

"Claro, I don't think it has anything to do with where the beans were grown," Mami says, setting her mug down. She leans forward, taking one of my hands in both of hers. "Listen, once we arrive home, Dr. Smithson and her son are going to go to jail for a very long time."

"Did Dad find any significant damage to the Declaration of Independence?" I ask her, not wanting to discuss the subjugator, or the Smithsons.

"No, but Laura—"

"I figured he'd probably kill me for rolling it up and shoving it into a medieval quiver. *It's an international treasure!*" I say, mimicking my father's voice as best I can.

"*Laura*," Mami says, reaching out, grasping my chin in her hand. She gently turns my face toward hers, forcing me to look at her. "We need to talk about what happened to *you*."

I look away, not sure I have the words to describe the void that's opened in my chest. Forty-eight hours ago, all I wanted was to be free. Now my body feels hollow, as if all my fueling fires have burned right through my core, leaving a husk of a girl in their wake. I can cope with the pain and exhaustion. The doctors are confident both Tuck and Alex will survive. The Smithsons are in custody—Dr. Smithson for implanting a subjugator in my throat, and Sebastian for shooting Alex.

My subjugator is gone.

But so is Faye.

When I asked Dr. Morgan what happened to Faye, she replied, "*The Queen Mother proved to be very difficult to control . . . she was made up of hundreds of the ship's crew members, which means she had all their coglink chips integrated into her systems. All I could do was save your life, and Tuck's.*"

It seems like an easy excuse, one I'm not sure I believe. Dr. Morgan had every reason to stand back while the Queen Mother killed Faye—after all, Faye and her father initiated the attack against the *John Muir*, nearly destroying Dr. Morgan's work and killing her son. But I had every reason to want Faye taken alive.

"I've won," I say quietly, timing my breaths with Tuck's digitally assisted ones for a few seconds. I don't look at Mami as my tears brim and a small sob expands in my lungs. "I've escaped; I've survived. Fortuna y gloria, and our family will deliver the most important archeological find to the Colonies in centuries. So why does it feel like I've lost?"

"Sometimes in life, we pay dearly for our victories." Mami wipes a stray tear off my cheek with her thumb. She smiles, radiant, so easily able to hide her sadness. "What do we always say in the hour of grief, m'ija? El camino de regreso al mundo de los vivos no debe ser hecho resbaladizo por las lágrimas."

"The path back to the world of the living must not be made slippery by tears," I repeat at her.

"People are complicated," Mami says softly, tucking my hair behind my ear. "We will mourn Faye and her father just as much as the others we have lost. We will remember their kindnesses, joy, and light, and not these last desperate moments of their lives."

"But how am I supposed to trust anyone again? First Sebastian, then Faye. Mami, I just . . . I don't know."

Mami smiles, but there's a touch of sadness in her expression, one I can't quite quantify. She squeezes my hand, and glancing over her shoulder at Tuck, says, "I think you do, corazón. I think you already do."

TUCK

I wake up centuries later.

A machine beeps near my head. I reach up and scrub my face with my hand—my face is rough with stubble. Needles are buried in my wrists. The skin aches. Hell, everything aches. Guess pain's a pretty good indicator that I'm alive.

Silver linings, right?

Shite.

"You're awake," someone says, their voice whisper-soft.

"Dunno if I'd call this *awake*," I say, slurring all my words together. I blink, turning my face toward the voice. A girl sits on the chair next to me. I can't see her face past the bright blue light, and wince.

"Sorry, I'll turn this off," she says. The light disappears. She rises and sits on my bed. Her weight depresses the mattress. My stomach heaves with the shift in my equilibrium.

I barely manage to say, "Gonna be sick," and turn to vomit over the side of the bed. Classy, I know. It tastes like stale acid and blood. When I blink again, there's a bucket floating under my face. "Frag me," I say, flopping back on the pillows. I've barely got enough strength to wipe my face with the side of my hand.

Flashbacks of waking from stasis pop across my mind.

I might vomit again.

"You survived a bad mecha crash, Tuck," she says, getting up. A few seconds later, something cool rests on my forehead. "Your guts are still knitting themselves back together, and you're suffering from radiation poisoning from exposure to space, too. Add the torus equilibrium adjustments, plus the inoculations against diseases you didn't have in the twenty-first century, and it's been a rough few weeks for you."

She sounds so much like . . .

The cold compress clears my head. My eyes focus on the girl standing over my bed, one with long hair and brown skin like burnished gold.

"Laura?" I ask. "You're alive."

She nods, smiling. "I think that's my line."

"Did I really just throw up in front of you?" I ask, scrubbing the bottom half of my face with my hand again. "Wait . . . it didn't splash on you, did it?"

Laura laughs. "No," she says, looking down and smoothing the front of her white shorts. She's dressed for summer, but some futuristic summer, wearing a loose-fitting tank top that shimmers around her body like she's wearing water. Wait, that didn't make sense. She's covered, but the fabric . . .

This is your brain on big drugs, kids. Any questions?

"Just kill me now," I say, pretending to roll my eyes up into my head. I stick my tongue out until she laughs again.

I'll never get tired of her laugh. Not as long as I live.

"Glad to see your sense of humor survived," she says, sitting in the chair beside my bed. She kicks off her shoes and draws her legs up, tucking them under her chin. Her skin's still bruised in places, but she wears those injuries like badges of honor.

There's a small white scar in the hollow of her throat.

Guess I know how that story ended, too.

"How long was I out?" I ask, rubbing my eyes with my fingers. If I keep looking at her legs, my thoughts will take an ungentlemanly tack. The thinness of the sheet's not doing me any favors. I've already embarrassed myself in front of her once; I don't need my body to make it two for two.

"Almost two weeks," Laura says. "You slept through the *very long distance* call we made to the ISG, the *entire* intergalactic wormport back to the Colonies"—she counts these things on her fingers—"decompression, desalination, deep space quarantine—"

"Okay, okay, I get it," I say, rubbing my face with my hands. "I was out a long time. And the *Muir*?"

Laura smiles. "Safe, or at least her contents are. Mami and Aren were able to repair the communications arrays and send an SOS back to the Colonies. When we told the ISG what they found, they wormported an entire deep-space construction team to the site, and built a special waygate just for the *Muir*." She plucks at my sheet with her fingertips.

"Damn, girl," I say. "You saved the day. I thought that was my job."

"It was a team effort," she says, chuckling.

Overhead, the light comes from a cloud of simulated stars, lit up in a gaseous blue like the Milky Way. The ceiling's one solid panel. White, not eggshell.

We're definitely not on the *Muir* anymore.

"Why didn't you tell me you were Katherine Morgan's son?" she asks after a quiet moment.

"Do you really need to psychoanalyze me three minutes after I wake up from a coma?" I swear, looking at the ceiling.

"Sorry."

"Are not."

She makes a face at me, scrunching up her nose and narrowing her eyes.

"If you've gotta know . . . it's because she left some big shoes to fill," I say. "When we woke up from stasis-break, Mom wasn't around, and I wasn't Mom. People didn't let me forget that, not for a second."

Laura scoots closer, chancing sitting on the bed again. This time, my guts don't buck. "Your mother uploaded her consciousness into the *John Muir* to protect the ship, and you." She smiles then, a sort of *I know something you don't know.* "When you're better, we'll go through your mother's logs. There are things you deserve to see."

"Sounds like a party," I say drily, trying to sit up a little more. "Where are we?"

"Home," she says. She snaps her fingers twice, and one of the wall panels turns transparent. Out there, lights twinkle like stars. They're concentrated strangely, collected in tall rectangles and in long streams of light . . .

It takes my brain a few seconds to recognize what I'm looking at:

A city.

Civilization.

People.

I swing my legs over the side of the bed and try to stand. Bad
idea. The world tilts. Laura catches me, steadying me until everything stands still. It's only then I think to check whether or not I
have pants on. Affirmative. They're scrubs or something.

We hobble to the window. My IV station floats behind us,
silent. The city's grand and stretches on for kilometers, the spi-
derweb of lights curving toward the sky.

I never thought I'd see anything like this again.

"This is the city of San Marino, in Nueva Baja," she says,
since I'm stunned into stupidity. She wraps her arms around
my waist and says, "There are fifty million people on this colony
alone, and every one of them knows you helped save the *John
Muir*. You never have to be alone again, not if you don't want
to be."

After a moment's hesitation, I put an arm around her shoulders. Press my lips into her hair. Figure I'm done running from
people, at least for now.

"I have a surprise for you," Laura says, reaching out and
touching the window. A screen ripples into view, one with an
interface that reminds me of the panels that shoot out of her
wrists. *Bioware*, I think she called it. She pushes a few buttons,
then squeezes my waist. "I shouldn't be here when you talk to
her, so press this button"—she points to a glowing blue square
in the middle—"once I'm out of the room, okay?"

"Talk to who?" I ask. Laura doesn't answer, just kisses me on the cheek.

"Do you want me to get you a chair?" she asks as she walks toward the door. "It might take her a few minutes to respond; she's been working with NASA on the park transfer."

"I'll be fine," I grumble as the door swings closed behind her. I'm not sure, but I think Laura laughs at me as the door swings closed. I reach out and tap the screen.

In that moment, I almost wish I'd listened to her about the chair.

"*Mom?*"

L A U R A

"What do you want to watch?" Tuck shouts as he rifles through Dad's film reels.

"Nothing with an alien in it!" I shout back, wandering down the adjacent aisle in my parents' underground vault. I pause to examine the intricate white flowers on the Blue Vase from Pompeii, which rotates in a floatglass case. Calling this place a *vault* might be generous—it looks more like a rabbit's warren, its twisting tunnels packed full of archeological finds. Shelves are heaped with artifacts from every era. On my left, an archway made of bookcases reaches over the door to a workroom, where my parents are working with other archeologists to restore the Winged Victory. A pair of Bastet statues from Egypt guard either side of the door . . . and probably keep the bookcases from collapsing, too. Ancient lamps stick off bookshelves, their wires unused, with newer, better bulbs stuck in their brackets. They cast cozy yellow light over the faux-wood floors. The furniture's mismatched, wooden armoires clogging up corners, a chandelier from Versailles' Hall of Mirrors hanging over a table made to look like Frida Kahlo's *Wounded Table*. Pillars painted in vibrant teals, reds, lime greens, and oranges hold up the roof. Faye painted them, in better days, and created the mosaics that snake across the ceilings. Looking at them makes an ache swell up in my chest.

I still miss Faye every day.

Every time my family's grounded, my parents consider tidying this place. Cataloging it. Throwing out the old, sagging heirloom armchairs and turning the family vault into a galleria. But I love this whimsical, loco space; it's home to thousands of stories and so many good memories.

"C'mon," Tuck says as I come around the corner. "The mourners weren't aliens."

"They weren't *human*, either," I say, joining him at the shelves. He nudges me with his elbow. I nudge him back, harder. The film reels are organized by year, more or less, on shelves. Dad's collected hundreds of them over the years, trading reels with other shipraiders. He and Tuck set up a projector in an unused workroom down here, then carried a bunch of old couches and chairs inside.

"Hell yes," Tuck says, pulling a reel marked DIE HARD in faded letters. "You're going to love this one."

"That's what you said about *They Live*," I say, lifting a brow.

Grinning, he takes my hand, pulling me away from the shelves. It's been almost three months since the disaster on the *John Muir*, but in the last few weeks or so, I've caught him smiling often. Laughing more. He's been playing soccer with Alex and my brother Gael in the park on weeknights, which helps him pick up more Spanish and some color in his skin. Don't get me wrong, Tuck's still the palest person in any room he walks into—but at least I can't trace the blue veins in his arms with my fingertips anymore.

As for me? The Panamerican Heritage Organization gave me a primary discoverer credit for my work in salvaging the *John Muir*, making me the youngest shipraider in Panamerican history to hold that honor. Fortuna y gloria, indeed.

To be honest, *glory*'s turned out to not be as fulfilling as I'd imagined.

The *fortune*'s not too shabby, though.

No, not just the fortune, I think, touching the scar where my subjugator used to be.

The freedom.

I flop on the couch as Tuck loads the film reel onto the projector. "When was this made?" I ask.

"The eighties," Tuck replies. I groan. He chuckles, threading the thin analog film into the machine. The flesh around his new bioware nodes still looks pink and tender.

"I will never understand the midmodern obsession with the 1980s," I say. "The hair was big, the special effects were bad—"

"Your taste is bad—hey!" He ducks as I toss a pillow off the couch at his head, before switching the projector on. It throws light up on a bare wall. The audio crackles as the film begins rolling. My bioware rumbles as Tuck settles down next to me, putting an arm around my shoulders. I lean into him, lifting my wrist and clicking on the floating notification from Alex.

Did you see this? he writes, attaching an article about Dr. Smithson's trial, which starts tomorrow. I already know about that, of course—I provided testimony during her preliminary hearings. My parents asked me if I wanted to attend the criminal trial as well, but I have no desire to see Dr. Smithson or her son ever again.

And hey, Alex continues, *I need to borrow your boyfriend around nine for a game. That okay?*

Tuck doesn't need my permission to go places with you, I type back as the movie's credits begin to roll. *He's not my boyfriend.* I've found it hard to use the *boyfriend* word, ever since my last one decided to shove a subjugator down my throat. The label seems tainted now, like it's not good enough or not clear enough for what Tuck means to me. He knows this, and Alex too, but the boys have formed an alliance and they love to tease.

With the way you two orbit each other? Alex writes back. *Mentirosa.*

"That means *liar*, Laurita," Tuck says, grinning.

"Snoop much?"

"Someone doesn't have their ioScreen's privacy filter on," he retorts.

"Because I should be able to trust my boy—" I grin at him, pretending to catch myself before the *boyfriend* word pops past my lips. "Ooh, sorry, I meant random guy I sometimes kiss?"

"Random guy, huh?" Tuck presses a kiss into the back of my hand, grinning. "Nice save . . . mentirosa."

The movie isn't as bad as I expected it to be—but I'm not sure it's as *good* as Tuck thinks it is, either.

About halfway through the film, Tuck starts getting twitchy. Antsy, almost, shifting his weight, tapping his fingers on his knee. I glance up at him, surprised to see a deep furrow in his brow.

"You okay?" I ask.

"Yeah," he replies.

I rub my index finger between his brows, as if I could erase his worries with a touch. "Then what's this?"

He faux-scowls, deepening the lines in his face and puckering his lips. "It's nothing."

"Órale pues," I tell him. *Yeah, right.* Tuck smirks—he hears it all the time from Alex, so he knows *exactly* what it means.

Five minutes pass. Tuck jounces his left leg, probably unconsciously.

Getting up from the couch, I pause the movie projector. I cross my arms over my chest, content to wait until he's ready to talk. I've only had a few conversations with Dr. Morgan since we arrived back in the Colonies—now that she's a digital force, she works twenty-four hours a day with Panamerican scientists to help with the Martian transition—but ay, ay, ay, she was right about how much her son hates to open up.

Tuck spreads his arms along the back of the couch, holding my gaze intently. "This a staring contest?" he asks, cocking his head to the left.

"Unless you want to talk to me about what's bothering you, sure."

"There's nothing *bothering* me," he says, lifting his palms, faceup, off the couch.

If I raised my brows any higher, they would disappear into my hairline.

"What more could I want?" he asks me. "I'm off that damned ship. I spend my days helping my mom prepare the park for the transition, and my nights watching retro movies with a girl who's pretty damn great. I'm playing soccer again. Doctors fixed my bum knee. Panamerica has *incredible* tacos. I'm a simple guy, Laura. I don't need much to be happy."

"But?" I ask, because it sounds like he's burying something important beneath all those words.

He *tsks*, turning his head to look at the wall.

"*But?*"

He grinds his teeth, making the tendons in his jaw pop, and drums his fingers along the top of the couch.

"You know you can tell me anything, right?" I ask.

He pushes to his feet in a burst of kinetic motion. "*But* I can't do this anymore," he says, pressing his palms against his eyes. He drops his hands, letting them smack against his thighs. "All the *meetings* and the *people* who want to come up and thank me, and the endless *interviews* and the biographers and the photographers who *just want a moment of my time*." He looks away, shoulders heaving, the muscles bunched and tight. "It's like the deepdowns all over again—I can't escape, I can't breathe. All I want to do is run, but there's nowhere to run *to*."

I step close to him, taking his face between my hands and running my thumbs over his cheekbones. He leans his forehead on mine. When I take a deep breath, he follows suit until our inhalations and exhalations synchronize. We started doing this a week after he woke up in the hospital, when we'd spend long nights talking about what happened to him on the *John Muir*. It probably doesn't sound very romantic to most, but I've never felt more connected to another human being than I do in these moments. Standing with Tuck. Just breathing.

"All I can think about is *what if?*" he says softly, reaching up to take hold of my wrists, grounding himself.

"What do you mean?" I whisper.

He straightens. I slide my hands down to his muscular shoulders, bracing him. "*What if* someone else survived?" he asks. "*What if* there's another jettisoned ship out there, with a crew who's given up on it all? *What if* I'm wasting precious minutes in interviews, when I could be searching for them?"

"You're starting to sound like a shipraider," I say, standing on my toes to kiss him. Tuck gathers me close, gripping my hips with his fingers. He's gentle with me, so naturally generous with his affection I often wonder how he ever starved himself of human touch for so long. When he runs a hand through my hair, he leaves the best kind of goose bumps in his wake.

When we break apart, I take his hand, threading my fingers through his. I walk backward for a few steps, tugging him along. "Come on, then."

"Where are we going?"

"The IGP's incident report referenced 'dark sites' in Faye's files and her father's computer systems, areas they think may potentially harbor additional Exodus ships. I doubt it would be hard to obtain those locations, and *accidentally*"—I tap the end of his nose with my index finger—"leave them somewhere 'convenient' for my parents to find."

"You serious?" he asks, a bit of light rekindling in his eyes.

"Ping Alex and let him know you're going to miss your fútbol game, querido," I say, turning with a little laugh. "We've got a database to hack."

AUTHOR'S NOTE

I started this book four years ago, in the middle of the night.

Had I known back then how difficult this novel would be to write, I wonder if I would have abandoned the effort to write something easier. In its earliest form, this novel wasn't supposed to be so personally meaningful, so infused with my own frustrations and fears. But in the midst of the second draft, I heard a candidate for the office of president of the United States call Mexican immigrants "rapists" and "murderers," and something inside me broke.

Now, I've had a tumultuous relationship with my mixed European and Mexican heritage since I was a child. My white mother didn't know what to do with the dark curls I'd inherited from my father's mother—my hair has *always* been a personal metaphor for my struggle with my identity. My father told me to check the "Hispanic—Not White" boxes on standardized state exams, while my mother insisted I check the "White" ones instead. (To my teachers' chagrin, I checked both.) Strangers called me "exotic" looking, or insisted I explain, point by point, my ethnic background because I looked "off" to them. *Where are you from?* they would ask, especially once I moved away from my Bay Area home. When I responded *California*, they would often respond, *No, where are you from from?* as if they knew the actual question they were asking was too intensely personal to be polite. And I never wore the "exotic" label comfortably—it always made me feel like I was some breed of spotted cat—beautiful, perhaps, but less than human. It took a long time for me to realize why these frequent exchanges made me uncomfortable, and to find the language to express that discomfort.

I will be the first to point out the privilege of my white-passing skin. I have not experienced the same oppression and vitriol some of my friends of color or family members have—and my road through life has been made smoother because I am so pale. However, when I hear my friends speak about their experiences with racism and oppression in this county, I hear notes of my own history in the echoes of their words. I empathize with them. To oppress one is to oppress all, so I stand at their backs in this modern struggle for equality. They belong at the forefront of this movement, but I am proud to stand in its ranks.

And so, when that man called Mexican immigrants horrid things in such a loud voice, this book took a turn I never expected it to take. I kept working on it through a very dark night of the soul, one that impacted me in profound and indisputable ways. The novel's mourners took on a specific metaphorical meaning. The ships' names changed. The subjugator surfaced. The Eurocentric globe flipped. Laura took the Declaration of Independence with her when she fled the *Conquistador*. The worse things became on the national stage, the more my frustrations appeared on the page. It is difficult to separate a writer's heart from her work. Every artistic choice started to become an act of protest, a way to look at my own attitudes and dissect them, and to think deeply about the lessons my parents taught me. Because when I started to list the things my mother and father taught me growing up, a subtle cultural divide between them became apparent. What they valued, at their cores, was different—but the lesson to be learned here is that it did not also make them incompatible.

More than anything else, we must understand that our voices have great power. We can use words to build bridges and ships and crews and families, or we can use them to oppress one another, or to rip each other to shreds. Whoever said, "Sticks and stones can break my bones, but words can never hurt me," obviously never had a drink with the person who said, "The pen is mightier than the sword." I side with the latter sentiment. Civilizations rise and fall by the written word. The United States certainly rose by these ones: "We hold these truths to be self-evident, that all men are created equal," and if we truly believe the spirit of those words, we as Americans will work together until we have achieved them in their fullness.

Use your words to liberate, not subjugate.

Do what is right, even when they tell you to "stop."

Build a better history for tomorrow, today.

Quisieron enterrarnos, no sabían que éramos semillas.
They tried to bury us, but they didn't know we were seeds.

Courtney Alameda

P.S. In the original concept for the Tomb Raider video games, Lara Croft was *Laura Cruz*, a Latina archeologist.

ACKNOWLEDGMENTS

If it takes a village to raise a child, it takes a small army of brave souls to write a book. My gratitude, first and foremost, always belongs to my masterful agent, John M. Cusick. It's been five great years, John. Thanks for being the Iron Man to my Ms. Marvel. I don't know what sorts of adventures are ahead of us, but I have a feeling they're going to be *awesome*.

To Liz Szabla and the entire team at Feiwel & Friends and Macmillan—thank you, thank you, *thank you*, not only for your support of this work, but your fathomless patience, guidance, and great passion for books. I made the words, but you gave them a home. For that, my gratitude is deep and eternal. Thank you for your excellent work, on all fronts, on this book.

To Yamile Saied Méndez, warrior woman and friend—you are a great light to this world. I cannot wait to see how brilliantly you will shine in the future. Thank you for your guidance and translations for this work.

To Chersti Stapley Nieveen—nobody critiques me and pushes me harder than you do, and for that, you have my deep gratitude. I am a better writer for it, and am proud to call myself your friend. Thank you for always being brave enough to be honest with me.

To my long-suffering, kickass, and wonderful husband, Bo—I heard you singing, "Ding Dong, the Witch is Dead," the day I turned this novel in for the final time. No book of mine has been more difficult to write than this; thank you for your unwavering support through every step of the process. Every writer should be so lucky to have a spouse like you in their corner. Love you.

And finally, to my great-grandparents who crossed borders and continents and seas to come to the United States . . . thank you. I cannot fathom the bravery the act of leaving your home countries must have taken, but I am grateful for your sacrifices, for your courage, and for the stories that you have left to me.